WILD WOLF

CAROLINE PECKHAM · SUSANNE VALENTI

DARKMORE PENITENTIARY

- GUARD TOWER
- GUARD TOWER
- ORDER YARD
- OUTER PERIMETER
- GUARD BARRACKS

L1	ELEVATORS — WARDEN'S QUARTERS
L2	KITCHEN — MESS HALL — VISITATION
L3	MAGIC COMPOUND
L4	CELL BLOCK A — CELL BLOCK B — CELL BLOCK C — CELL BLOCK D
L5	GYMANSIUM
L6	LIBRARY — CORRECTIONAL CENTRE
L7	BELORIAN HOLDING CELL
L8	FATE ROOM — MEDICAL
L9	ISOLATION — INTERROGATION
L10	MAINTENANCE

MAIN ENTRANCE ELEVATOR

PSYCHE WARD

Wild Wolf
Darkmore Penitentiary #4
Copyright © 2024 Caroline Peckham & Susanne Valenti

The moral right of the authors have been asserted.

Without in any way limiting the authors', Caroline Peckham and Susanne Valenti's, and the publisher's exclusive rights under copyright, any use of this publication to "train" generative artificial intelligence (AI) technologies to generate any works/images/text/videos is expressly prohibited. The authors reserve all rights to license uses of this work for generative AI training and development of machine learning language models.

Interior Formatting & Design by Wild Elegance Formatting
Cover Artwork by Caroline Peckham

All rights reserved.
No part of this publication may be reproduced or transmitted by any means, electronic, mechanical, photocopying or otherwise, without the prior permission of the copyright owner.

ISBN: 978-1-916926-33-2

Wild Wolf/Caroline Peckham & Susanne Valenti – 1st ed

This book is dedicated to all those who have been dangling off of the cliff for three years since the last book released. This one is for you, may you get a leg up onto that mountain and climb a littler high before inevitably falling to your doom once again. Or not. Who can say? Only the pages to come will tell…

WELCOME TO
DARKMORE PENITENTIARY

Your rights have been revoked, your punishment has been decided, your sentence is about to begin. Fight for your place like Fae, or die and be forgotten. This is your one chance for redemption. May the stars be with you.

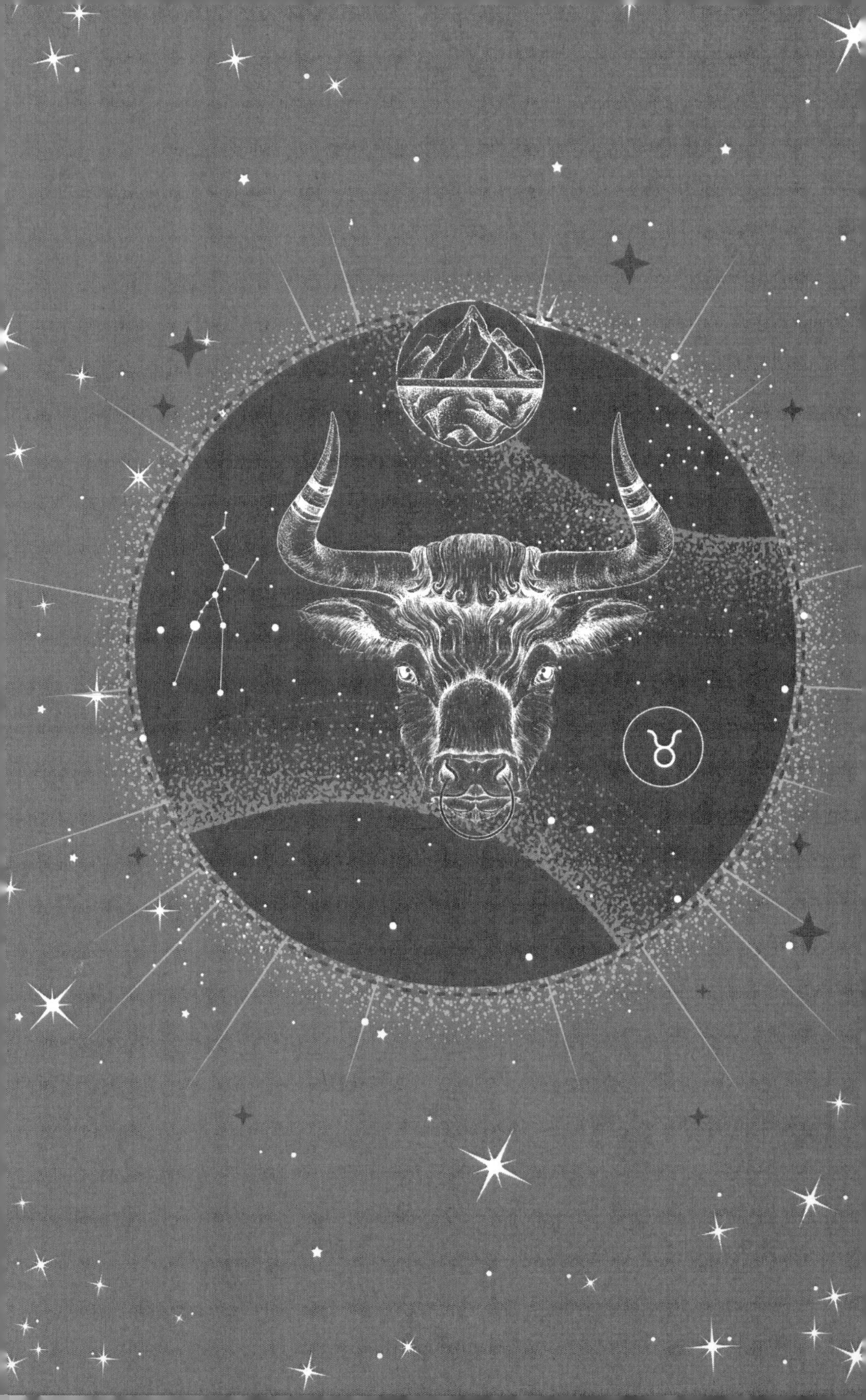

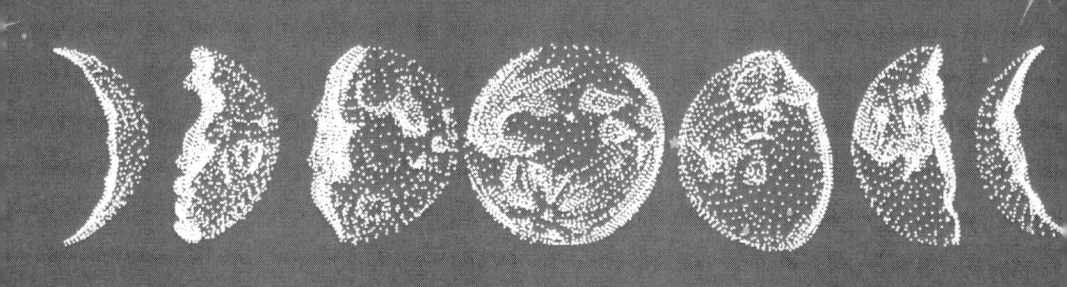

ROSALIE

PRISONER #12

CHAPTER ONE

The wind hissed through my hair, fat drops of rain driving against my cheeks and carving lines of ice across my skin, but I could barely feel it as we flew over a dark and unfamiliar terrain.

Mountains pierced the ground below in a jagged, broken formation which punctured the swathes of flat, open jungle between them, and fog hung in deep pockets over the valleys, hiding the secrets of the land.

This pain in my heart was a ruinous thing, set to devour me from the inside out, gnawing through me relentlessly until I found it hard to draw breath.

Dante banked hard, plunging from the sky and I braced on instinct, my body knowing how to move with him as he flew even while my heart broke apart within my chest and threatened to fall out of me piece by piece.

A flash of dark, feathered wings drew my attention to the Harpy who flew with us, my eyes tracing over a myriad of tattoos which were visible on his bare chest and back as he passed us. Gabriel had come all this way to help us but even with him on our side – the greatest Seer in Solaria – we had failed so horribly. Had he known? Had he *seen* it and not stopped it?

As the thought occurred to me, I dismissed it. He'd made it clear our odds of success were low in his predictions about the escape and yet I'd chosen to stack our fate in the hands of them anyway. I was certain he wouldn't have allowed this fate to play out if he had *seen* any way to avoid it, or realised that it was coming at all. But like all things, fate was never set, the future could change on the toss of a coin and even the greatest of Seers couldn't predict every outcome.

Esme was sobbing quietly behind me, but the others were all deathly quiet.

I didn't look to any of them. I couldn't. Not while I held so many of them accountable for us losing Roary. The men at my back had claimed such devastating feelings for me but had still ripped me away from the man I had sacrificed so much to rescue. They'd forced me to leave him behind. They'd taken that choice from me, and no matter what justification they might claim for doing so, my anger at them was second only to the raw pain tearing through my heart.

Leon still held me close, though the kids' arms had grown slack around my waist, their little bodies becoming soft with sleep during the long flight. I'd stolen strength from the love in their embraces, but I hadn't been able to look at any of them either, the weight of my failure ripping through me, the guilt grinding away my core. They'd never seen their uncle Roary in the flesh and had come all this way because they'd believed in me and my foolhardy plans. They'd been as eager to finally meet him as he had been to hold them in his arms at long last, but that sweet and beautiful moment had been snatched away in the wicked claws of fate.

They'd come to unite with him and had been forced to swallow the bitterness of my failure instead. I closed my eyes tightly against a fresh surge of tears as I tried to swallow the reality of that failure.

Dante tucked his wings and Hastings shrieked as we plummeted towards the ground with a low, rumbling snarl, electricity crackling from his scales and setting the clouds sparking with light.

"Oh my Jolly Rodger!" Plunger cried and Cain cursed darkly.

Thick beads of heavy moisture swept across my skin as we dove into a cloud, the world becoming swathed in thick grey all around us, the fine hairs lining my arms standing on end as the Storm Dragon's electricity infected the air itself, the static clinging to me and zapping against my chilled flesh.

The cloud cleared as suddenly as it had engulfed us, the rainforest filling the view beneath us in a rush.

We hit the ground with a violent thump, Plunger screaming as he fell from his spot behind me while Dante chose a perch on the side of one of the mountains, landing in a clearing between the towering trees that was big enough for his immense body.

The others began to dismount, but I remained where I was, staring out into the trees where animals squawked and bellowed, chirped and hooted. The air was muggy and thick with moisture, my filthy skin growing slick with it as I stared out at nothing and tried to come up with any kind of plan which might fix this.

Leon gave my shoulder a squeeze then lifted the kids into his arms and leapt down to the jungle floor, neither of them waking as he cradled them against him. I found myself watching them as he moved to speak to Gabriel in a low tone, the black-winged Harpy having landed several paces away from the escapees. My eyes fixed on them, their murmured words of loss and pain, of horror over the way this had gone washing over me as if they were hurling accusations at me with vitriol. I wished they really would offer me their anger. Instead, there was this air of bleak acceptance to Leon and Gabriel, their disbelief and sadness not bleeding into the rage I deserved for failing them.

"Rosalie, love?" Ethan murmured, his hand landing on my shoulder.

I jerked away from him, snarling darkly as I pushed to my feet and glared at him.

"Don't," I warned before turning my back and leaping to the ground. I couldn't bear to look at him after what he'd done to help drag me from that place without Roary in my arms.

The impact with the dirt jarred through my legs but I ignored the twinge of pain, stalking around Dante's large, dark blue body and moving to stand before his face.

He was utterly enormous in this form and I raised my chin as he looked me over, his bright Dragon eyes sizing me up in a way which might have made another Fae shit their pants.

"You left without him," I hissed, my body tight with tension, rage eating me alive and fury making me toss blame out in every direction I could.

Dante shifted suddenly, causing Ethan to curse loudly as he was dropped to the jungle floor in the process. I was forced to tilt my head back to glare up at my cousin who towered over me in his Fae form.

"We'll fix it, Rosa," he swore. "You know we will."

A lump formed in my throat, a thousand furious accusations tightening my gut. Those same words had been tossed around for the last ten years and they hadn't meant shit. This had been our shot to get him back. Our one chance. The backs of my eyes burned as my fingers curled into fists which threatened to crack bone, my agony desperate for an outlet that I couldn't offer it.

"Despair won't get you anywhere," Dante growled, catching my chin in his grasp and forcing my eyes onto his. I blinked and two tears spilled down my cheeks, racing one another towards their demise, their easy escape from the agony within me making me jealous of their brief existence. "Take that pain and forge it into something fierce, something powerful, something *real*, Rosa. Make it drive you or it will break you."

I flexed the fist curled at my side and he caught the motion, raising his chin to offer me a target if I wanted it. But punching him wouldn't make me feel better. I couldn't truly lay any blame at his feet anyway. This had been my plan. My responsibility. My failure.

"I need to return these convicts to custody," Cain snarled from my left and I whirled on him, happy to have a real target for my rage as I bared my teeth and advanced on him.

"Try it, stronzo," I said in a vicious tone. "See how far you get."

Cain looked from me to Plunger, Esme, Pudding, Ethan and Sin before finally finding Hastings who was skulking at the edge of the trees. Cain jerked his chin, glancing to Sin once more in a clear command, but Hastings shook his head, backing up a step.

"I'm done, Mason," he said in a shaky voice. "I'm fucking done trying to control those animals. You don't know what I saw in that place. They…ate Officer Kato's brain. They bound me and tortured me and I witnessed so many fucked up things. I saw potatoes endure a fate worse than death…"

"What the fuck are you talking about, potatoes?" Cain demanded while Hastings' eyes flicked to Plunger then away again as he cringed back into the foliage looking haunted.

"Oh, is it time for them to be used, Ma'am?" Plunger asked me, drawing my eyes to him where he stood butt naked, covered in smooth, grey hair, fists on his hips as he dropped into a squat.

"That's savage," Sin muttered, fascination lacing his words as his gaze remained on Plunger.

I wrinkled my nose and looked back to Cain, not needing to see any more of that fucked up nonsense.

"Looks like you're fresh out of friends," I hissed, taking a step closer to him and peering into his grey eyes with nothing but threat in my expression. "And you also seem to be in need of a dose of reality, so I'm going to lay it out for you. You're not *Officer* anything anymore, Mason. You aided in our escape, ran with us across that fucking minefield and leapt onto the back of the Storm Dragon just like the convicts you so despise. You killed to get us out of there. You plucked me up into your arms and used your speed to ensure I escaped. You and Hastings aren't going to be able to just swan back to Darkmore and say 'oh hey guys, sorry about that – we got caught up in the idea of running for our lives and forgot that, in doing so, we were aiding and abetting.' What do you think they'll do, stronzo? Give you a pat on the back and a medal of valour for trying so hard to stop us that you accidentally ended up helping us instead?"

"That's not how it was. You're twisting it from the truth," Cain growled, stepping up to me, fury burning in his expression. "I would never help this band of miscreants gain access to the outside world. I can prove it. I'll offer myself up for Cyclops interrogation and-"

"And let them watch you hunt me, lie for me, kill for me and fuck me before finally hurling me on to the back of my cousin and ensuring I escaped? Good luck explaining that to the FIB," I taunted and Cain's face paled.

Dante chuckled darkly while Leon spluttered in surprise, pointing between me and the asshole guard like he couldn't see it. But my poor, sweet choir boy stole the show by stumbling towards us and pointing his finger straight in Cain's face.

"You?" he gasped, any lingering remnants of his belief in good and bad fading away before my eyes as I watched his hero topple from his pedestal in a crushing blow that shattered his little choir boy heart with a dose of brutal reality. "You and her?"

My gut twisted guiltily at the pain I found in his eyes as he took in the truth of what had been going on right under his nose this entire time, perhaps seeing me clearly for the first time since we'd met. And seeing Cain for what he was too.

"It...I..." he spluttered.

I moved to him and took his hand in mine, squeezing softly as I looked up into his horror-struck eyes. The innocence which had been so present in them before had dimmed, a hardness blazing in those rings of blue which spoke of all he'd witnessed and survived. I'd done that to him. I'd dragged him into this.

"I'm not good enough for you, ragazzo del coro," I told him softly. "I'm all sharp thorns stained in blood beneath these pretty petals. You deserve a far sweeter flower than me."

He frowned, swallowing thickly, words building between us, but Sin got there first.

"And she fucks like a demon too, bro," he said seriously. "*All* the holes. Over and over. She likes to dominate, be dominated, get rough, get violent, choke on one cock while taking another in the ass, and you, my friend, daydream about pretty little good girls gasping your name between soft thrusts in dim lighting. Don't get me wrong – I ain't yucking your yum, but you never could have handled our wild girl."

He patted Hastings on the shoulder consolingly while looping his other arm over my shoulders. Hastings had turned beetroot and my cousin was shaking his head and making a show of covering his ears while Leon loudly announced that it clearly ran in the family.

"Enough," I snapped, shoving Sin's arm off of me.

"You were in on this," Hastings accused Cain and my hard-hearted guard seemed to soften a touch.

"It wasn't meant to happen. I just…" Cain looked at me and my throat thickened from the raw anguish in his eyes, then he tore his gaze from mine and shook his head at Hastings. "I'm sorry I'm not what you thought I was, kid."

"I don't think anything is what I thought it was anymore," Hastings whispered, anxiously pushing a hand into his soft blonde hair. "I think the stars are telling me something about myself too. Something deep and dark and ominous."

"Hastings…Jack," I said, moving towards him again and taking his arm so he was forced to look at me. "You could go back. You didn't do anything to help us. You were just trying to survive. I'm pretty sure that if you return to Darkmore you could-"

"No," he rasped. "I'm not going back there. Not now. Not ever."

I glanced at Dante who shrugged at me. He'd pulled on a pair of sweatpants so at least he wasn't naked now and he'd taken Luca from Leon's arms.

I sighed, looking between the rest of our group. The plan from here had been to dole out stardust then let everyone go on their way and try to keep hold of this chance at freedom. But we'd lost so many of our group. And I needed Sin to appease Jerome who would be waiting to see that his efforts in getting the Incubus released had paid off. Ethan had made it clear he planned on sticking with us anyway. Esme was looking at me like a wounded puppy, still wearing the leaf bra I'd forged for her while we ran and nothing else. That left Pudding, Plunger and the guards.

I didn't know what to do with all of them and my head was too full of everything that had happened to Roary to be able to come up with a plan at the moment.

"We're sticking together a little longer," I said decisively, not looking to anyone else for their opinion on this. "Let's head back home."

Dante glanced at the assembled convicts and guards, arching a brow at me which said 'seriously?' but he made no further complaint as Leon took a pouch of stardust from his back pocket.

We closed in around him and Gabriel looked up at the sky, frowning darkly.

"What is it?" I asked the Seer as he rustled the feathers of his obsidian wings.

"The FIB will raid the Oscura stronghold and surrounding vineyards in two days. The family lawyers have already been at work providing alibies for us – they even have eighty eyewitnesses who spent the night in Dante's company to prove it couldn't have been him who rescued you."

"You let Carson take on your appearance?" I asked my cousin, knowing already that it had to have been him.

"Yes. Though I will admit that I'm concerned about what he will have done to my reputation while I was supposedly at that party," Dante said.

The look of amusement on Gabriel's face confirmed that 'Dante' had gotten up to all sorts of reputation-altering nonsense, but I couldn't summon the interest in that to ask about it further.

"Time to go then," I said firmly.

We all moved close enough to be transported by the stardust, but Cain held his ground, folding his arms across his broad chest.

"I'm not going to a den of heathens in the heart of the criminal underground," he snarled.

I shrugged, past the point of caring about his wavering moral compass.

"It's that or hang out here in the middle of the Baruvian Jungle, stronzo. Take your pick."

Gabriel lifted a fistful of stardust above us, and I growled in a low tone as Ethan and Sin pressed in close either side of me before he tossed it over our heads.

A blur of motion announced Cain darting into the group a heartbeat before the stars snatched us into their grasp and we were whipped away into the embrace of the glimmering celestial bodies.

The whispers of the stars themselves hissed sharply in my ears as we were hurled through their embrace, the world whipping by around us in a vortex of sparkling light before they spat us out violently.

My feet hit the ground with a solid thump as we were released from the hold of the universe and deposited at the top of a steep hill where the Oscura vineyards stretched out away from us and the scent of home wrapped me in its embrace.

It was beautiful here, like an island set away from all the bad in the world where the sun shone down brighter on everyone who could lay claim to any piece of this stunning slice of land. In the distance, orange light was just beginning to crest the horizon, the sweeping landscape of hills and vineyards rolling away from us in every direction. It felt as though no other place existed in the world but this.

A sob clutched my chest as I inhaled deeply, the lack of my mate driving into me even deeper as I found myself back here without him. Everything about this was wrong.

The Wolves descended, a tide of Oscuras racing from the house, the vineyards, the woodland beyond and I was swept up onto the wide porch which ran along the front of the beautiful white villa where I had spent the best years of my childhood.

Cries went up, raised voices calling my name, then their excitement turned to confusion as they hunted for Roary. Dante's deep voice rang out to silence the questions, a dark promise of explanation falling from his lips as he beckoned the swarm of Wolves to follow him into the house.

My pack dragged the convicts inside too, my Aunt Bianca cooing about the state of them, promising hot baths, fresh clothes and a hearty meal. I felt her eyes on me but I didn't turn to look at her as Dante guided her away too, unable to face her penetrating gaze which always saw so much and understood so clearly.

Even Cain and Hastings were hustled into the house, all of them heading into the depths of the one place in this world where I had ever truly belonged.

I didn't follow them.

I moved to the edge of the porch and took hold of a metal flagpole which had been driven into a huge flowerpot there, a crudely painted Wolf fluttering on the white flag above my head as I looked out towards the horizon which had just brightened with the blazing orange of dawn.

Minutes crawled by as I watched the dawn rise and let myself feel the jagged truth of what had happened, my heart reaching out in a desperate cry for my Lion, my soul wanting to tear itself in two just so that some part of it could find its way back to him.

I clenched my jaw, my fingers biting into the metal pole which I was fairly certain had become the only thing holding me upright anymore.

This failure ran deep within me, this pain a river that washed through my blood and left nothing but a burning, pointless longing in its wake.

I had failed. In all of this, there had only ever been one goal which truly mattered to me. One thing I had dedicated myself to for ten years, one utterly uncompromising reality which I had to achieve and yet... *I had failed.*

It paralysed me this pain. It tore at everything good that I clung to in myself and ripped away at the tattered soul remaining beneath the bravado and bullshit I dressed myself in so easily. I couldn't live with this reality. I couldn't sleep or eat or fucking breathe until I had rewritten this fate, but I had nowhere to turn this frantic energy, no way of doing what I knew had to be done. There were no clues to my salvation and I knew that he was suffering with every moment I delayed. I had failed him. And nothing I did now or could do in the future would ever be able to rectify the terrible truth of that.

But as I stood there staring at the dawn which should have been such a beautiful sight with him right there watching it beside me, I swore that I would get him back. By the power of the moon, I would go to the ends of the world and beyond to return Roary Night to my side.

My skin began to glimmer with the power of the moon as it bound my fate to that promise, an echo of the one I had made ten long years ago, and I tipped my head back as it imbued me, releasing a long, sorrowful howl to the sky and swearing on all that I was that I would fix this, or give my life trying.

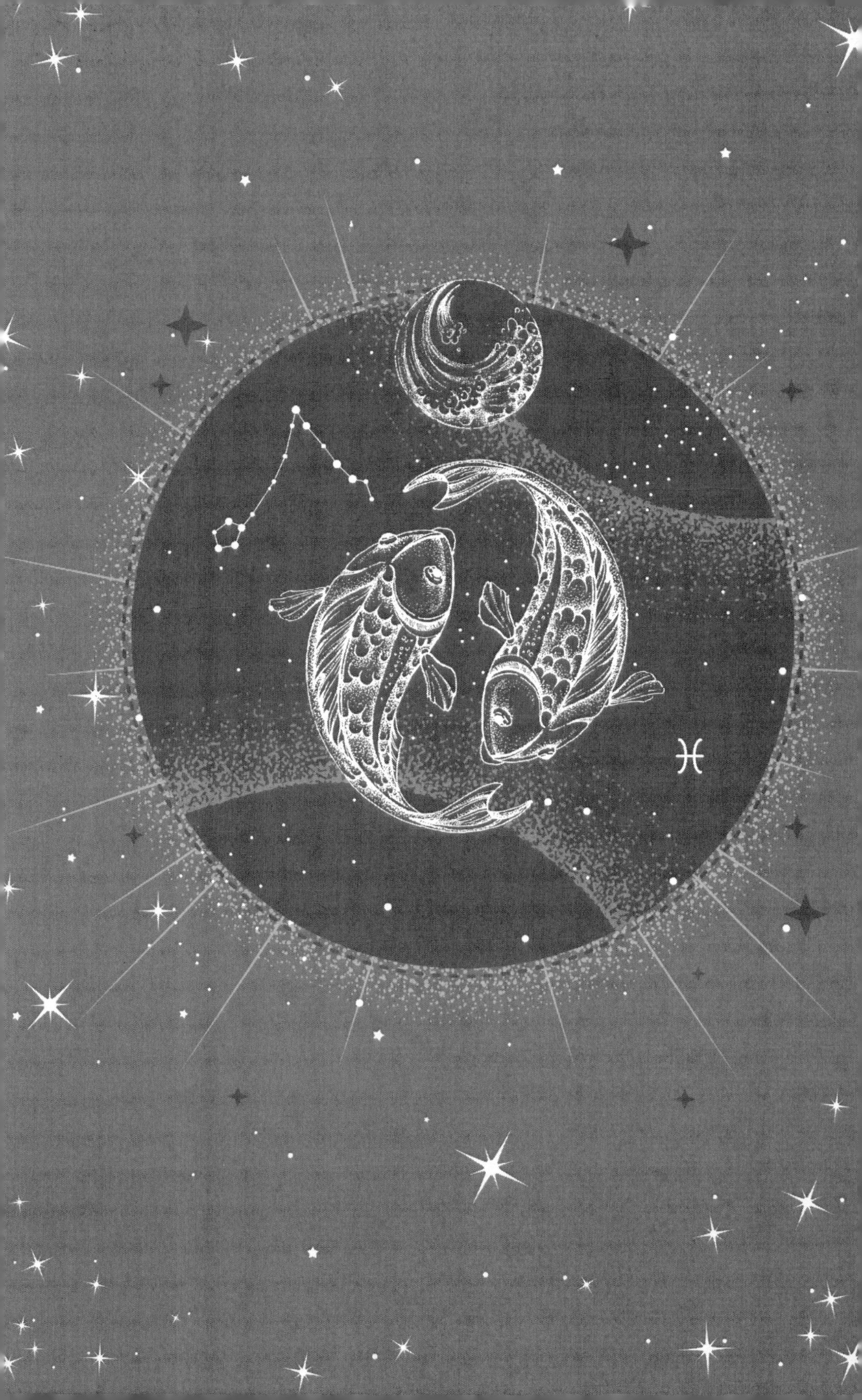

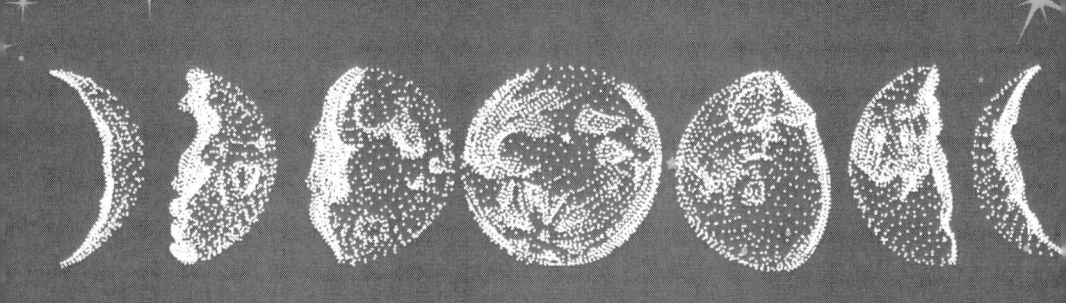

Roary

PRISONER #69

CHAPTER TWO

"Long ago, in a time where the world tasted of change, I dreamed of the miracles my gifts could weave," the male voice fell over me like a fog; it was soft, touched with reverence and laced with power. I could feel the penetrating gaze of this man right down to my bones.

I knew who he was. His face had followed me into the depths of the darkness when I had lost consciousness on that stars-forsaken operating table. Somewhere among the thick, impenetrable shadows of my mind, I had remembered him. The man with the scar through his left eye, an eye which was as black as death itself.

Reality came pouring in on me like the stars were tipping an urn of wakefulness over my head, not letting me escape the terrible truth that awaited me beyond this measure of darkness.

I fought it, preferring to hide in the recesses of sleep, but there was one reason to wake that I couldn't turn from. My mate. My Rosa. I could almost feel her shaking me now, refusing to let me shy from fate. "*Get up, stronzo! Fight!*"

I blinked, finding myself laying prone on a cold stone floor, the walls around me metal and dull as if the misery of this place had seeped into the making of it. The only thing in the room with me was the man with the scarred eye, his gaze fixed upon me, his features haggard, weathered by time, those lines around his mouth painted there by a thousand wicked smiles. One of which, he aimed at me now.

He wore all black, his hands clasped at the base of his spine and pride glinted in those malevolent eyes. Ownership too. As if he believed that I was his creature, his twisted little pet.

I shoved to my feet, taking in the magic-blocking cuffs on my wrists though that wouldn't be enough to stop me from destroying him.

A low growl rolled through my throat as I ran at Roland, the need for his death spilling through my flesh, clad in iron. A rush hissed through my limbs at the motion, some strange and unknown sensation tearing along my bloodstream and filling me with nameless power. The room around me blurred, my feet moving altogether too fast and I crashed into a clear pane of glass that I hadn't seen, my nose close to breaking as I fell back onto my ass with a bellow of shocked agony.

The world was still spinning as I glared up at him, his smile only growing.

"You are fast becoming my favourite miracle, Nightroary," Roland purred, his voice carrying through a speaker so I could hear it loud and clear in this room, though it sounded too loud, ringing in my head for far too long. Something wasn't right inside me, my own body didn't feel like my own.

Roland cocked his head as he admired me. "You probably don't remember the rise of the Dragon King," he said, lifting a brow. "You were locked away in Darkmore through that time. A forgotten creature. Powerful in your own right - but all that power was going to waste down there. Was it a crime to make use of it for the greater good? I think not. Do you realise what you are yet? You are so very special." His voice echoed inside my skull, too loud, then too quiet and I winced as my head spun from the unnerving sensation.

"What have you done to me?" I rasped, my body feeling so unlike my own. My movements were too fluid, and as I focused on this monster of a man before me, I felt like I could pick out every line and wrinkle on his face, seeing him all too sharply.

"If you survive the alteration, you will be my greatest achievement. You will change the world. No longer will the lesser Orders have to remain in the pitiful forms they were born with. A curse of the stars finally broken. You see, I saw what the Dragon King never did. To eradicate and exterminate is a trying cause. But to rebirth, to recreate? Ah, yes. There is so much more beauty in it, don't you think?"

I pushed myself to my feet, moving too fast again and stumbling as I adjusted to the strangeness in my limbs. Despite my size, it was as if I was walking on air, able to float along with barely any effort at all. A burning sensation was growing in my throat and as I lifted my head to take in the cut of my enemy, my gaze homed in on the throbbing pulse in his neck.

I could practically see the blood pounding through his veins, the flush of it in his cheeks and, if I really focused, I could hear it too. The pounding of his wretched heart was music to me, a lure I couldn't ignore the pull of. My tongue weighed heavily in my mouth and the burn in my throat grew deeper as wicked, hungry thoughts flitted through my head.

"What have you done to me?!" I bellowed the words this time, lunging at the glass and throwing my fist at it. The pane shuddered but didn't crack and I sensed there was magic imbued in it, because no normal glass could have withstood that strike.

Roland looked to a camera up on the wall beside me and gave it a small nod. At his signal, a hidden door opened in the wall and a woman was forced into the chamber with me. She was dressed in white scrubs and she let out a pitchy scream as a taller woman behind her fisted her golden hair and slashed her throat wide open. I recognised the bitch holding her as Angie, the one who had reached into my chest and taken my Lion from me.

I ran at her with a snarl of hatred tearing from my lips, promising her death, but she threw the blonde at me and quickly retreated, slamming the door closed. I caught the falling woman as she spluttered and choked, but as I looked down in a bid to help her, something switched in me. The burn in my throat grew to a roaring command and I felt my canines lengthen in my mouth. All at once, the blood spilling from her became such an irresistible desire that it stole every ounce of my focus. The need to help her subsided and instead, a far more terrible urge took over.

I wrenched her head sideways and dropped my mouth to her neck, acting on instinct alone while a voice in the back of my head cried out for me to stop. The metallic tang of blood against my lips sent sparks of light exploding through my mind. Without another thought, I drove my newly grown fangs into the exposed vein of her neck and before I could even try to stop myself, I drank. It was akin to ecstasy in a way nothing I had ever experienced before had been, the pure, sinful rush of it consuming every piece of me.

I swallowed one mouthful of her blood then another, and another. All I could focus on was how good it tasted, how much I needed this. But as the well of magic swelled inside me, and the woman's thrashing grew weak and finally fell still, a horrifying truth found me amidst my frenzy.

Roland's voice fell over me, naming my new Order. Though I was certain I could have guessed without his declaration.

"Vampire," he laughed, then he crowed it, celebrating his victory in me. "Vampire! You are a Lion Shifter no more."

As the burn in my throat finally eased, I dropped the lifeless body of the woman who had been murdered for the single purpose of exposing my new Order, scrambling away from her and feeling her blood drip from my chin. Horror coated me from the inside out and a tremor ran through my hands as I looked down at my red-stained palms. This wasn't me. This Order was foreign and wrong. It didn't belong in my body. I wasn't made for this, I was made for shifting, running in my Lion form. I was made for Charisma and pride. I was no Vampire.

"This isn't me," I denied Roland's words. "Take it back – fix it," I rounded on him, panic seizing me in its grip. "You can undo it!"

Roland shook his head. "You are what I made you to be. You have been born anew. You are my glorious proof of what is possible. The process has been perfected, and you will be my crowning example. The stars have bestowed me their powers of creation and I, like them, will be a maker of fate from this day forward." He turned his back on me, striding out of a door and leaving me alone in that chamber to shout after him in purest rage.

But between my despair and the chilling truth of my reality, I found something worse to fear than this fate. My mate, my beautiful, courageous mate who had never learned the meaning of fear, never knew when to back down, would be out there now looking for me. And I never wanted her to get close to this place. To that monster who knew how to do the unspeakable to Fae-kind.

"Rosa," I whispered thickly into the icy air. "Don't come for me," I ordered, repeating the words I had said to her in our parting moment, hoping the stars would guide her away from me now. "Don't search for me anymore, little pup."

I was Roland's mutation, my identity stripped in every way possible and reforged into something I refused to claim. My mate loved me as I was before, not as I was now. Like this, I was not her Lion anymore. And I was never going to be the Fae she had sworn her heart to again.

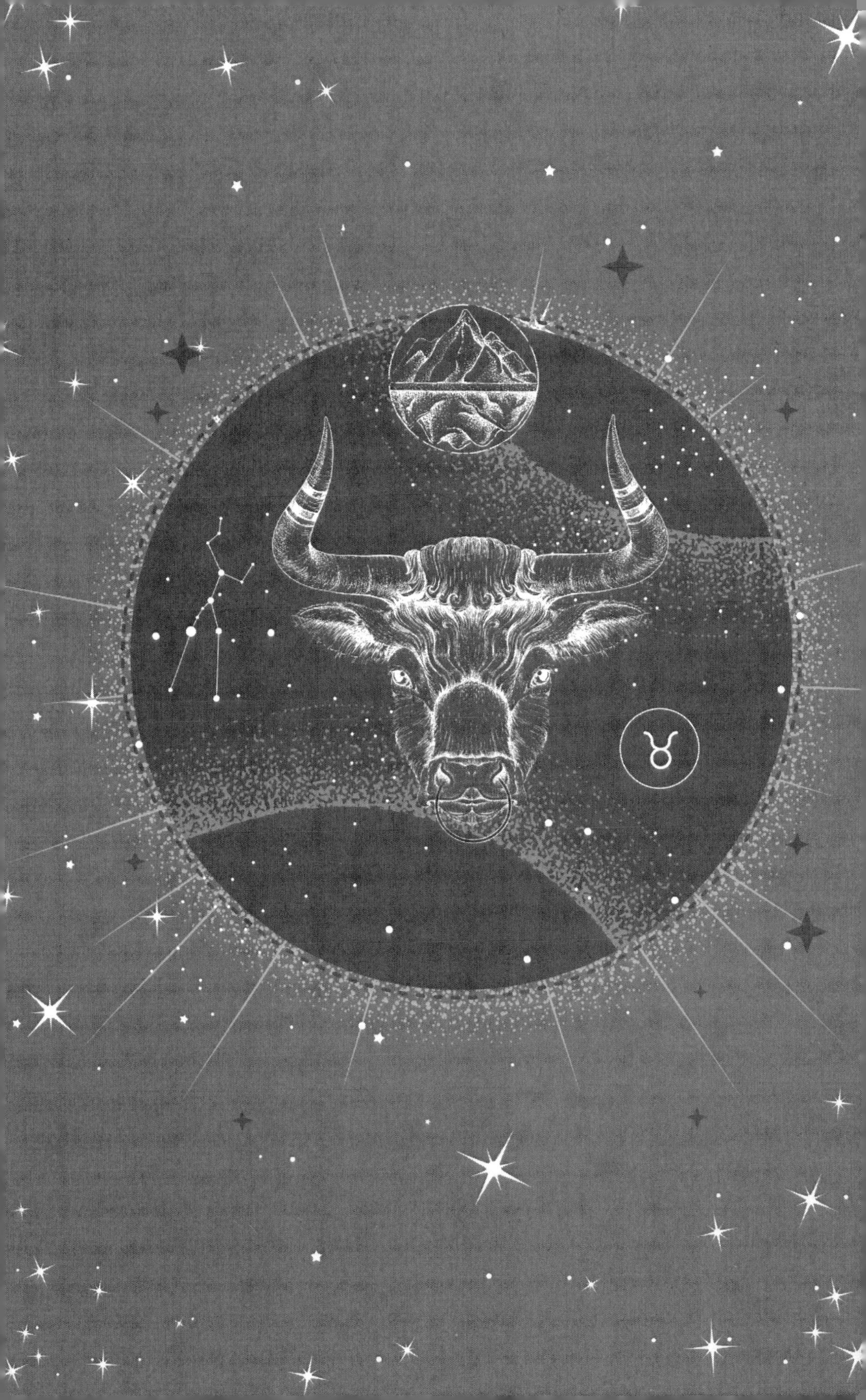

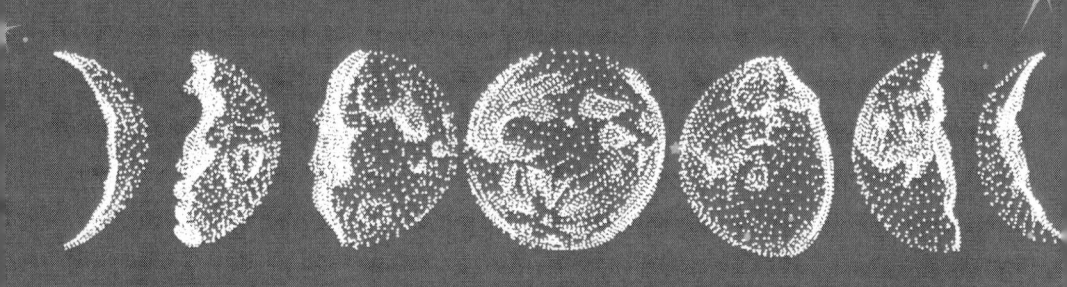

Rosalie

PRISONER #12

CHAPTER THREE

I took no pleasure in the steaming shower or the feeling of proper clothes hugging my body again for the first time in months. I didn't feel like the girl who had owned these jeans or claimed that blue shirt as her favourite. My room felt too big and too small all at once, tucked away in the top of the house.

When I'd first come to live with my Aunt Bianca and her huge famiglia, she'd spent ten minutes in my company before patting the back of my hand and bustling off to clear out this old loft space for me. It was a long room with exposed rafters which ended in a triangular wall set with a single, circular window above the white iron bed. The window was in a white frame which was scuffed from the hundreds of times I'd swung it open and climbed out onto the roof beyond to sit beneath the moon.

There was no dust in here – Aunt Bianca kept the place spotless and the scent of lemons lingered in the air. She used them to make her own cleaning potion from the tree in the courtyard at the centre of the property and that sweet citrus mixture along with the view across the endless rolling vineyards sung a lullaby of home just for me. But it wasn't home without Roary. Not anymore.

I ran my fingers over the mate mark on my arm that linked me to him, closing my eyes and praying to the moon for guidance. It wasn't like my bond with Ethan – I couldn't feel Roary's pain, but I feared that if I could then I would have been screaming by now.

Roary needed me. I'd gone to Darkmore to save him and I had the terrible feeling that I'd only made his situation worse when I'd failed.

A single knock at the door made me look up, tension lining my body as I expected Ethan or Sin or maybe even Cain to have come looking for me, but I released a heavy breath as I found my aunt pushing the door wide instead.

"Rosa," she said softly, the door snapping closed behind her before she approached me.

I swallowed thickly as she assessed me, this little woman with a heart bigger than the moon itself. She was short, her dark hair streaked in grey and coiled into her usual bun as she pierced me with eyes so like those of her son that I felt as though Dante were the one appraising me with that look. Bianca had stood at the head of this household for a long time since losing my uncle back in the gang wars which used to rule this part of the kingdom. She wasn't our Alpha but she was our mama. Me, Dante, the rest of her blood born children and a hundred other Oscura waifs and strays besides. We weren't all blood but we were all famiglia.

Bianca sighed as she took me in, carefully tucking a lock of ebony hair behind my ear, her fingers brushing against the rose vine tattoo that peeked out from the top of my shirt before she drew me into her arms.

I stiffened. I wasn't like the other Wolves in this way – I didn't need the constant tactile behaviour, endless hugs, or to sleep in a pack huddle. I liked my own space - which was precisely why she'd given me this room. Close enough to everyone here to know I belonged, but at enough of a distance to buy me the space I so often craved.

She murmured soft words to me in Faetalian and I slowly unravelled in her arms.

"Let it out, lupa," she encouraged, her fingers stroking through my hair, and I cracked apart just like that.

A sob shook my chest and tears spilled once more. She didn't ask anything of me. Didn't need to. In this house news spread like wildfire and I was certain that by now every detail of our escape and our failure to rescue Roary would have circulated three times already, the facts mixing with fiction, embellishments at every turn but the truth of it immovable all the same.

"Who are you, Rosa?" Bianca asked me after the world had shattered around us and grown anew again, more twisted and darker than before, the void where Roary should have been taking up so much space that it was hard to breathe around it.

"I'm a failure," I breathed.

"None of that," Bianca barked, still holding me like a babe but no give in her tone.

"I am…" My mind whirled with all the answers I could offer to such a question.

I was a creature made of malicious design raised in a house of hatred then given a home bursting with love. I was brutal and powerful, fragile and fickle. I was a thousand unheard wishes and one potent demand. This world hadn't offered me a place when I was born but I had carved out one for myself regardless. I was my scars and my pain, my honour and my love. I was a Wolf and a loner. I was a mate twice over, a lover more times still, a prisoner and yet freer than most Fae I'd ever met because in my heart I knew who I was and what I demanded from this life which was so prone to wickedness. I was Rosalie Oscura. And nobody told me no.

"I am Rosalie Oscura," I growled aloud.

Aunt Bianca nodded firmly as she stepped back and looked me up and down. She didn't wipe the tears from my face and neither did I. They were no sign of weakness but of the potency of my love for Roary Night and a mark of what I would do to get him back.

"A morte e ritorno, lupa," Bianca said firmly. "You have work to do yet."

"A morte e ritorno," I echoed and strode from the room with my chin high and heart pounding because I knew what I had to do.

I moved through the twisting house, enduring the embraces and soft touches of my many family members as they slipped from rooms and made way for me to pass. Their eyes trailed me as I walked, each of them moving aside for me as their Alpha, a tension rolling through the household which had everything to do with my pain. They were my pack so they felt it too.

The kitchen was a grand room at the heart of the villa, a table big enough to seat forty - and yet still often not big enough for all of us - dominating the central space while work surfaces, the sink and ovens surrounded it. As usual, a meal was being prepped across the longest counter, vegetables chopped and diced, sauce simmering on the stove.

I found Ethan sitting at the table, his hands clasped around a mug of coffee while four pups – my cousins' kids between the ages of six and nine - were huddled in close either side of him. They were petting his hair and prodding at the tattoos that were visible on his arms, asking for stories about each in turn. His eyes moved to me the moment I entered the room and I paused, the sight of him there among my famiglia so natural that for a moment I had forgotten that he had been so afraid to come to this place, to mix with the terrifying Oscura Clan.

I arched a brow at him as if to say 'I told you so' and he nodded, though the movement was a little uncertain and only grew more so as Dante strode into the kitchen behind me.

"What is this one for?" little Andre asked, poking the serrated crescent moon symbol of the Lunar Brotherhood where it was inked proudly across Ethan's chest – which had only been revealed because Roberto had grabbed the collar of Ethan's t-shirt and half ripped it in his eagerness to find more tattoos.

"You know that one, Andre," Maria drawled, all seven-year-old sass. "It's the same as Zio Carson's – the one Zio Leon calls 'his great shame' when he has his short hair face on."

"Maybe that one is a story for another time, eh kids?" Ethan suggested, trying and failing to yank his collar back up while giving Dante a wary glance.

I looked to my big Storm Dragon cousin, taking in the sadistic gleam in his eyes then I grabbed an apple from the bowl which was overflowing with them at the heart of the table and dropped into the seat opposite Ethan to watch the show.

"I hear you decided to mate yourself to my little Rosa while you were in that hellhole, Lunar," Dante said, spreading his fingers against the table as he leaned down to get a good look at Ethan. "Tell me, did fate whisper her name in your ear the moment you laid eyes on her?"

Ethan glanced at me, but I gave him nothing. If he couldn't face off against the big bad Storm Dragon then he wasn't worthy of a place in this family, moon mate or not.

"Something like that," Ethan hedged.

The silence dragged on, punctuated by the kids giggling and tugging at Ethan's shirt to seek out more ink.

Dante whistled sharply and they scattered, shrieking and howling as they ran, calling out to the other kids who were no doubt lurking in the closest rooms waiting to learn all they'd discovered about the new arrival.

"Look, I dunno what Rosalie has told you about the way this all happened," Ethan said, once again shooting me a look but I only stared back blandly. My mind was on more important issues than him figuring out the power balance with Dante anyway.

"Assume nothing. But I'd suggest against lying all the same," Dante purred like a bastardo and my lips almost twitched with a smile but my heart hurt too much for that.

"Where are the others?" I asked, having expected them all to have been ushered into this room – the heart of the house and all that, but there was no sign of them.

"Let's focus on the Lunar first, hm?" Dante suggested and I rolled my eyes but waved a hand, indicating he should get this over with.

I bit into my apple again, the juice rolling over my tongue but I tasted nothing.

Ethan blew out a breath. "Alright, I'll tell you straight – I fucked up. When me and Rosalie first met I knew I wanted her, shoulda seen then and there that it was more than simple want, in fact. She was my destiny staring me in the face pure and simple. She was beautiful - obviously – but it isn't that I fell in love with. Her soul is like a blazing mirror to my own. I've never met anyone as strong as her, in spirit and mind. She drew me in like a fish on a line and once she'd got that hook in me, there was no denying that I was utterly hers. But…"

"But?" Dante asked darkly and yeah, maybe I'd relayed a bit of the but to him and maybe he was looking all kinds of pissed off already. Ethan was gonna have to get used to that if he was going to become an Oscura though.

"Like I said, I fucked up," Ethan said on a long breath. "I…well I can fill you in on all of it if I must but what it comes down to is that I failed her. I didn't step up. Tried to hide what we were…*are*. It was fucking cowardice if I'm honest. I knew claiming her would equal the end of my pack, my rule and though I should have understood faster that she would be worth anything I lost in the claiming of her tenfold, I took far too long to come to terms with that truth. In doing so, I guess I lost my chance to claim her as mine alone but when Rosa was mated to Roary too I realised I hadn't ruined everything. He…I…*we* aren't a thing like that, but he's my pack now. The three of us are in this for the long haul and I'll spend every day I am fortunate enough to be able to call that stunning creature across the table from me mine making up for the ways I failed her in the beginning. I'll be worthy of her. I swear it. And if you harbour hatred for me because of the shit that went down back at Aurora Academy between us then-"

"Wait," Dante said, frowning at Ethan, electricity crackling in the air around him. "What shit at Aurora? I didn't go to school with you, stronzo."

Ethan narrowed his eyes on Dante then gave me an accusatory look. "Did you tell him to say that to fuck with me?"

I snorted. "No. You clearly didn't make much of an impression. Told you he wouldn't remember some jumped-up Lunar stronzo from ten years ago."

"I wasn't just some random Lunar – I was Ryder Draconis's second," Ethan said firmly, raising his chin and looking at Dante like that should be all it took to jog his memory. "I didn't have so much ink back then," he added when Dante looked just as non-plussed by him.

"Ryder's second was Scarlett Tide. You're not her."

"No," Ethan said. "Well…yeah, but also no. I was his second at the academy after all that Bryce shit went down. You gotta remember me. We had all those run-ins. I kinda assumed you'd wanna beat my ass for even looking at your cousin – not that you could, but-"

A booming laugh made me flinch so violently I almost dropped my apple and my head snapped up as I looked to one of the beams which spanned the roof of the kitchen where Sin now hung upside down, grinning at us.

"It's alright, kitten. Nobody minds that you were a nobody at school," he purred, tossing Ethan a wink.

"I wasn't a fucking no-"

"Lemon?" Sin offered, pulling a bright yellow fruit from his pocket and holding it out to me in offering.

"What the hell are you doing up there?" I asked him, accepting the lemon because I'd learned that if Sin Wilder offered you lemons, you just took them and didn't ask questions.

"Hiding." Sin pressed a finger to his lips but a shriek of delight came from the doorway where a hoard of pups had just come flying into the room.

Sin shrank so fast it was as if he'd disappeared altogether, a slight weight landing on my shoulder, followed by a tiny giggle letting me know where he was. His tiny feet pattered across my shoulder before he used a strand of my hair as a swinging rope and launched himself onto the table.

I watched as he sprinted towards the window, taking a running jump for it and shifting again as he did so, becoming a woman coated in ginger hair like a cat, long tail swishing wildly as he disappeared through the open glass.

The pups all whooped and howled in delight, most of them turning and bolting for various doors to get outside and chase after him, though a couple dove headfirst out of the window, almost sending a huge vase of wildflowers toppling after them.

Gabriel stepped into view outside it, catching the vase before it could fall and offering me a knowing smile which said he'd *seen* that coming.

"You've brought chaos into the future of this family by bringing that one to our door," he said, gazing after Sin who was now racing along the edge of the pool laughing maniacally as the pack of pups chased him.

"Oh I know," I agreed.

"Point is," Ethan said firmly, drawing the attention of the room back to him. "Rosalie is my mate and I'm not going anywhere. So if that's going to be a problem then we need to sort it out now."

He pushed to his feet, muscles bulging, jaw locking, staring down a Storm Dragon as if he did so every other Tuesday. I had to admit, Alpha asshole looked good on him even if I was still pissed at him for helping to drag me here and leave Roary behind.

Tension filled the air, Dante's lightning crackling against everything, making me curse him as I bit into my apple again and got a jolt to the tongue.

"Good," Dante said finally, dropping into his seat at the head of the table and taking an apple from the bowl for himself. "Welcome to the pack then, Lunar. I look forward to seeing if you can keep up with me the next time we run beneath the moon."

Ethan blinked, glancing to me as if wondering whether this was some kind of trap and I sighed loudly, waving a hand towards his chair.

"Sit down, stronzo," I told him. "You're in now. I told you it wouldn't hurt."

"Yeah," Ethan agreed, lowering himself back into his seat slowly, still seeming uncertain, though a smile was hinting at the edge of his lips. "I guess you did."

His gaze moved to me and fixed there, but I leaned back in my seat when he leaned forward in his, ignoring the hand he held out to me across the table.

"We'll get him back, love," Ethan said in a low growl. "I swear it on all that I am. We won't lose him."

"Maybe you should have considered that when you were running away instead of going after him back at the prison," I said acidly.

"You know we had no choice. They already had him. If we hadn't run then they'd have caught the rest of us too. And don't go pretending I went against him somehow by helping ensure you ran with us because that's bullshit and you know it. Roary wanted you to get out more than anything, love. He wouldn't have thanked any of us for getting ourselves caught with him. From here we can actually help."

I clucked my tongue, muttering some wholly insulting things about his idea of what was best for me in Faetalian and Dante sighed.

"He's right, lupa," Dante said to me. "You're hurting and you're angry but aiming it at the people in this house won't do shit to help get Roary out and you know it."

I shot a glare at my cousin then huffed out a breath. "I know," I ground out. "I just…we were so fucking close…"

Tears burned the backs of my eyes but I blinked them away. Crying wasn't going to help Roary but I was fresh out of other ideas too. Escaping from Darkmore once had been a miracle – trying to break him out twice was surely impossible.

"Rosa?" Aunt Bianca's voice called to me from the TV room and I got to my feet.

"What is it Zia?" I called back, heading through the house with Ethan stalking my steps.

"You're on the news," she replied and I stepped into the room with the huge TV hanging from the wall, enough couches lining the big space that it was like attending the movies coming in here.

I opened my mouth to tell her that I didn't have time to waste on watching news coverage of the escape but I fell quiet as my eyes fell on the screen where two rows of mug shots sat. Each image had been taken when we'd entered Darkmore, my own scowling face looking out at the camera from above the board denoting my name and number assignation.

My gaze skimmed the row of images from Ethan to Pudding to Sin, Plunger, Esme, and finally to Roary and Gustard whose faces sat right alongside ours.

"The convicts who managed to escape the so-called impenetrable penitentiary include notorious gangsters, a sexual deviant, a skilled thief and most alarmingly of all mass-murderer Gustard La Ghast who was convicted of the abduction, torture and eventual murder of more than-"

"Why are they claiming Roary and Gustard escaped with us?" I demanded, striding into the room and staring at the huge screen, my eyes on the image of Roary taken ten years ago, his hair long and eyes empty with despair. I swallowed thickly. I'd already failed the man in that picture by taking so long to come for him and now I'd done worse than that – I'd given him hope and seen it dashed before his eyes.

"They claim you kidnapped those two guards too," Bianca said, her chin bobbing in the vague direction of the room upstairs that she had given to Cain and Hastings.

I scoffed. "Those two are more trouble than they're worth."

"Is that so?" Cain's voice came from the doorway and I looked around to find him there, leaning against the doorframe, arms folded across his broad chest.

"I thought the door was locked to keep you out of the way?" I asked him in a bored tone but we both knew a little lock wouldn't stop a Vampire from escaping and that he'd never really been locked up anywhere.

"There was me assuming the lock was to keep your pups away from *me*," he drawled.

"The pups are far harder to contain than any Vampire," Bianca said with a dismissive snort. "But this is a problem," she added, waving a hand at the screen. "Escaped convicts they'll give up on eventually – kidnapped guards on the other hand…"

"Once they review the evidence, they'll figure out that Cain ran with us quite willingly," I replied. "My main concern is why they would lie about Roary and Gustard."

"Isn't it obvious?" Cain asked, going on when I gave him a blank look. "They don't want anyone asking about the bodies."

A snarl broke from my lips and I lunged at him for even suggesting that. Ethan grabbed my shoulder to stop me.

"Easy, love," he said. "That's not true anyway. They don't care about bodies in Darkmore and they aren't hiding the deaths of those other bastards who were trying to escape with us. Look."

He directed my attention back to the screen and my heart lurched painfully as I found Sonny and Brett's faces looking back at me alongside several of Gustard's cronies, the news anchor now naming those who had died in their attempt to escape before moving on to a list of guards who were killed during the riots.

I swallowed thickly. I hadn't wanted any of them to get hurt. I'd only ever wanted to get Roary out.

"Okay," I breathed, trying to focus on what mattered now. "So they're not covering up deaths but they are claiming Roary and Gustard got out with us. Which means…"

"They don't want anyone asking where they've gone," Cain finished for me.

I met his gaze, a flicker of fear running through me as I thought of the Fae who had been taken to Psych and of whatever fucked-up machinations had been taking place down there. Could this have anything to do with that?

"We need to figure out where they are," I said firmly, my brain turning it all over, each piece slotting into another. The escape, the FIB, the guards, the lies on the news.

"Is this a private party or are we all invited?" Sin's deep voice drew my attention back to the present as he strode into the room and threw himself down on one of the couches.

"Sin…" I said slowly. "Jerome was able to hack into the prison cameras while we were escaping. That means he might have still been watching when we got away, right? He might have seen where they took Roary. He can help us get back in."

Sin's eyebrows rose in understanding as he thought about that and a wicked smile crept across his seductive mouth.

"You know, kitten, I think you might just be onto something there," he purred.

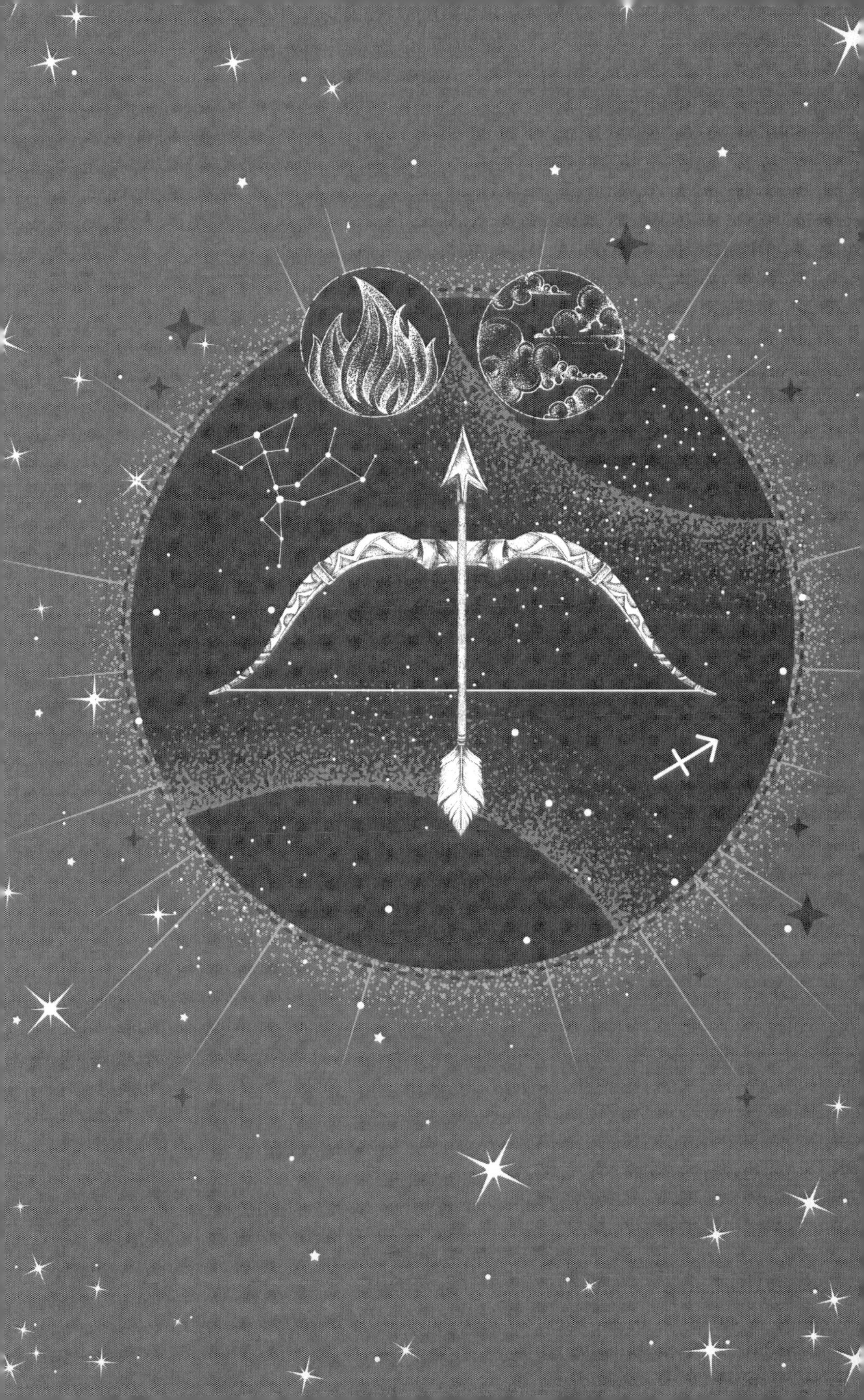

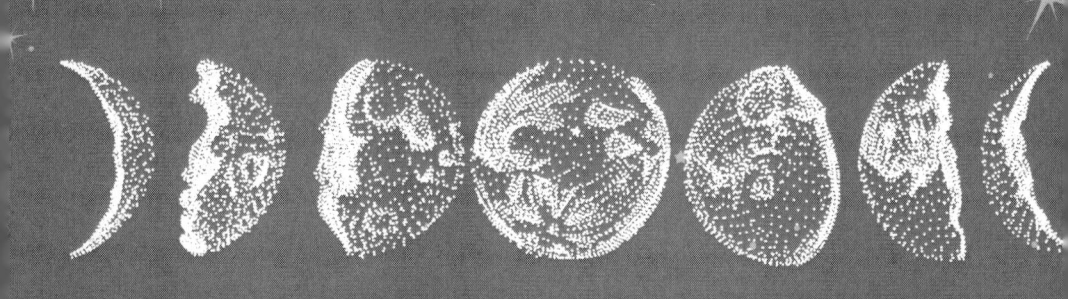

Sin

PRISONER #88

CHAPTER FOUR

"What are you doing?" Rosalie demanded.

It was pretty obvious though. I was on my knees, hunched over like an alley cat with my nose to the dirt, sniff-sniffing.

"*Sin.*" Rosalie gave me a kick in the ass, but there was no time for foreplay.

"I'm sniffing for FIB boots, sex pot. I can smell the nectar of beeswax in 'em. If they've been anywhere around here recently, I'll know it."

"Why would the FIB have been anywhere near here, stronzo? It's a dusty woodland surrounding an abandoned railway station that hasn't seen a customer in thirty years."

I did a forward roll and leapt to my feet in front of her. "Fair point, honey pie. But you can never be too careful when it comes to nosey lawmen."

"You and careful don't belong in the same sentence." She cocked a brow at me and I wiggled mine back at hers in a little silent eyebrow strip show.

"I got caught and fried once, baby cakes, I don't plan on being caught twice. Especially now I have you to dance the dingo with." I caught her chin. "Kiss me like the world's about to end." I leaned in, but she smacked my hand away like a little savage and my smile grew. "Are we about to play slapsy-fucksy?"

"No," she said, capturing my chin and taking control of me instead, angling my head towards the rusted train tracks that headed out of the trees up to the old railway station. "Jerome might have answers about Roary's location. Focus. For me, okay?"

"I can do that, sugar," I promised, taking her hand from my throat and nipping each of her fingers in turn. "Jeromeo will know-eo." I took off out of the trees, excited to reunite with my foster brother. Damn, it had been a long time since I'd seen him with these eyes. I was going to hug him so tight I might just puncture a lung.

I cupped my hands around my mouth and howled like a fully-fledged Oscura – which I was now, thank you very much. I'd run with the Wolves, cuddled the pups and played merry mischief in their backyard. Yup, that made me one of them now. I'd be getting my Oscura tattoo when I got back there later, I just couldn't decide if I wanted it on my ass cheek or right there in the middle of my forehead, blazing like a beacon of Oscura glory.

I'd surprise Rosalie with it one way or the other.

"What happened to careful?" Rosalie drawled as my howl turned to a song about a sea frog and a hesitant owl.

"I've secured the perimeter," I said with a shrug, my song falling dead in the middle. I couldn't remember most of the lyrics anyway – which was weird considering I'd been making them up on the spot.

Rosalie almost cracked a smile and I stepped closer to her as we approached the train station. Ever since we'd escaped Darkmore, her smiles were playing hide and seek with me and we were in a feisty little game that I was struggling to win. She was damn good, but I was the better player. Crafty, cunning and cool – I was great at cunnilingus too, which wasn't all that relevant to the game, but was always worth noting when the C words came to dance inside my mind.

"Tag - you're it!" I slapped Rosalie's arm and sprinted full pelt the last few steps to the station, shoving a rickety wooden door wide and releasing a wild laugh as I raced through the dusty space. Man, it was good to be free. It was like having wings, only the wings couldn't flap or make me fly, but they still took me places. Places I'd been unable to go for so many years. They let me use my magic whenever I wanted, allowed my Order to be unshackled and my smiles were bigger out here too. They were the stretchy kind, reaching for my ears and trying to tickle them.

"Sin?"

I whirled at the male voice, so familiar, like the squawk of a baby eaglet I'd shared a nest with.

"Jeromeo?" I gasped, my gaze falling on him as he stood from an old iron bench by a crusty window. I half-lunged half-sprang at him like a gazelle, slamming into him and wrapping my arms around his big body, clutching him tight and waiting for his lung to pop. I loved this man and love was a fickle fairy that liked to come and go, pulling up her skirt to lay tiny shits on my head, but when it came to Jerome, she'd laid an egg instead, and inside that egg had been a rainbow.

I kissed the side of his face then finally released him, still clutching the back of his neck.

"There you are," I sighed, my eyes scraping over his features just as Rosalie walked in. He wasn't quite as tall as me, his eyes all brown and leafy, his jaw as square as a box balancing on a totem pole, and his curling, dark hair was tidy, pushed back but quaffed a little like a cresting wave.

"Hell, it's good to see you," Jerome sighed then looked to Rosalie. "You did the impossible."

Rosalie shrugged, my girl buzzing like a humblebee. "Have you got my money?"

I knew she didn't really give a fig about the money, but my honey pie knew how to dance the dance, and it was time to tango I supposed.

Jerome released a laugh then moved to the bench he'd been sitting on, picking up a duffle bag and tossing it to her. She caught it, laying it on a table and cracking it open just enough to glimpse the stacks of auras inside.

"You look good for a guy who's been locked up in hell for years." Jerome looked me up and down.

"What can I say?" I purred. "I thrive in the dark."

My brother smiled again, and I pinched his cheek hard, shaking my head at him as I took in one of my favourite people in the world.

"Life was pretty boring without you around," he said as I dropped my hand. "I've been waiting a long time to get you back."

"We've got a lot of time to catch up on." I nodded. "Do you still see much of Mrs Piggles?"

Jerome snorted. "That's what you wanna know about first?"

"Who's Mrs Piggles?" Rosalie asked, glancing between us curiously.

"Only the best pig in the pageant," I said, aghast that she hadn't heard of her.

"What pageant?" Jerome scoffed, amusement colouring his face as he looked to my girl. "She lived wild in the woods out the back of our old foster home. And no, I don't see much of her, she's probably dead by now."

I gasped. "Don't go saying things like that. She's out there somewhere living her best piggy life."

"Sure." Jerome shrugged, moving to scruff my hair.

"As heart-warming as this little catch up is, I need some information," Rosalie said, all businesslike and as hot as a candy stick that had been shoved between a Dragon's lips – the mouth kind, not the pussy kind. She was a classy kind of hot, rough, edgy, the best tits in town and – oh shit I should have been concentrating.

"-help finding Roary Night. You had access to the camera feeds the night we escaped, so surely you saw something that could give us a clue as to where he's been taken and what kind of security they've got around him now."

Jerome scored a hand over his chin in thought, slipping his boring business hat on and I sighed at the turn this conversation had taken. Not that I didn't want old Roars back in the boat, but it was getting as serious as cereal in here and that wasn't my go-to vibe.

"Not that I recall," Jerome said.

I tried to get a read on him, wondering if he knew more than he was letting on. He was good at those kinds of games, the sneaky, big money kinds. But I'd always been more suited to dancing than dicing.

"Well think harder," Rosalie snarled. "They took him away then lied, claiming he'd escaped Darkmore with us. So wherever he is, they don't want him being found."

"So it's some kind of cover up," Jerome exhaled, a crease forming on his brow.

"Like a napkin over a small willy," I agreed seriously. "Hidden in plain sight."

"Well, I'll take a look for you, but I can't promise-" Jerome started but my lady love lunged, grabbing him by the throat and snarling in his face.

"You *will* promise," she hissed. "And you will fulfil on this. Name your price. Get me a location and I will pay whatever you want for it. You're clearly good for cash, so what is it you desire, Jerome?"

His eyes slid from her to me then back again, but I didn't step in. It was unFaely anyway, but regardless of that, I was overjoyed that they were bonding so quickly. Look at her gripping his neck like that. My sex pot and my bro, it was the sweetest friendship in the making, blooming right before me.

"Take your hand off of me," Jerome warned, the gravelly pit of danger in his voice making Rosalie pause. Yeah, my brother was a badass. The kind you didn't cross or you ended up dead in a ditch somewhere. Or at least, some of you did. The rest might find its way into a sewer, burned in Faesine, or maybe fed to a few stray dogs.

Slowly, Rosalie lowered her hand, a beast in her own right, but a clever one at that. "A price. Name it," she repeated.

"I'll think on the price," he said at last. "In the meantime, let me see what I can find out for you. I'll stardust home and be back here in an hour."

"We'll come with you." I stepped toward him.

"No," he said quickly. "The FIB are crawling all over the streets looking for you. You're safer here. I'll be an hour, maybe less if I can work fast."

"I'll be counting," Rosalie warned as Jerome took a small pouch of stardust from his pocket. The stuff may have been rare as shit, but my foster-brother knew ways of getting things that most Fae didn't know how to even get a whiff of in their daily bore-fest of a life.

I wiggled my fingers at him in goodbye as he disappeared into a glittering mist and I was left with my honey pie. I smiled big at her, but her smile hid again and she headed out of a door onto the old platform beside the tracks. I trailed after her, sensing something was off. But I didn't really know what. I mean, sure, Roary was lost and she had a thing for that Lion boy, but it was also sunny outside and the grass was so green. I'd never seen grass like that, I kinda wished I was a cow so I could enjoy the juicy lucys of it, but they had four stomachs – lucky mothercluckers – and I held just the one, dull stomach that only did the basics. Digesting grass wasn't for me. Of course, I could always give it a whirl and see what happened, but getting the plops wasn't on my agenda today.

Rosalie dropped onto the edge of the platform, her legs hanging down over the rusted tracks. I paced behind her, frowning then smiling as my thoughts flitted from one idea to the next while I tried to figure out what mood was ailing her. Always a challenge, these things. Moods and the like. Mine moved like the wind, this way, that way, but no weatherman could forecast me. Rosalie was different, but not how most people were different to me. She was a unique sprig of a dandelion. Blue or pink or any colour dandelions weren't supposed to be. And when her petals turned to seeds, she deserved the right person to come and scatter them to the wind, setting her free. She had her moon mates, but she had me too. I was good for blowing seeds at least, so if that was what she needed now, I'd fill my lungs and give her all I had to give.

"Sad, that's the one, ain't it? I think I've landed on it, petal," I murmured, moving closer. "I'll help you turn into a seed and fly away on the breeze."

She glanced back at me and I saw it at last, the raw pain in her eyes that she had done so well at veiling. Or maybe I was just a blind, blind man sometimes. It was difficult to see things through a clear lens when your mind was full of hopping rabbits and escaped crickets, but I had a view now and I was holding onto it while I could.

"That pain in you won't do," I said in anger, a storm riled in me by it. "I can't have it. Won't abide by it, in fact."

She released a breath then turned her gaze back to the tracks that no longer led to anywhere. No more trains were coming to this station, and maybe that was how my honey pie felt. Like there was no way forward without her Roary.

"You see, I'm a man of many boxes. All of them stored inside me, some full of clowns and others stuffed with knives. But this one here that you've broken open just now, that one's my darkest dealing, wild girl. I only open that one when I'm about to kill, you understand? I will bleed them out for you, cut down each enemy that stands along the path to your Lion. Because I will wage wars and raze hell to see you smile again."

I moved to sit beside her, my legs swinging as I took her hand in mine, and she blinked up at me, gazing into my eyes and seeking something there I didn't dare to hide. Let her see me, why not? Let her peel my skin from my bones and pick through each box until she finds out that I'm a monster made of many malevolent things. Let her find my wasted heart among them all too, discarded like the trash I'd often thought it to be and take it into her palm, caress it, stoke life back into its rotten core. She did it there and then, that look alone enough to heal something shattered in me, though I was the one who was supposed to be healing her.

I lifted her hand, kissing the back of it like I was some prince asking her to be my princess, but we were the opposite of that. A devil and his rogue beauty. Yes, we shared a dark kind of romance, she and me. We were cracked in all the hurty places, but together we filled each other's wounds and laced each other's scars in bliss.

"Kiss me now, pretty one," I urged. "Let me scatter them seeds to the breeze. At least for a moment."

"I think sometimes you see me like no one else quite does," she whispered. "You see the lesions on my heart, Sin Wilder."

"That's where I love you deepest, Rosa," I growled and she leaned into me at last.

I inhaled her scent before capturing her lips with mine, tasting her agony and letting it bind me to her deeper. My vows were unbreakable when it came to her. I would break bones and slit throats upon her word alone. Did she know how she quietened the demons in my head? How the world was so perfectly still when her mouth was upon mine?

I kissed her until the bitterness of her sadness sweetened just enough to know I had done right by her. Then we parted and I stared at my world, my reason for reaching for sanity, and I knew no face would ever compare to this one. I would stitch it into the backs of my eyelids so I could see it when I was away from her too.

She laid her head on my shoulder. "Tell me something good. Something that takes my mind off of everything."

So I did. I told her about the first time I'd seen Mrs Piggles, and the second time, then the third. I told her of the scarf I'd tied around her neck – stolen from an uppity woman who had called me an uncouth ballsack, or something along those lines, then I told her about the string of pearls I'd gotten for Mrs Piggles too from an old lady who I'd helped across the street. Then I told her of the times Jerome and I had gone on adventures together; our first thefts, our first kills. I told her all I knew until Jerome finally reappeared and came striding over to us with a piece of paper clutched in his hand.

We both jumped up and I eyed the note excitedly. "Is that a recipe for a Victoria Sponge, I could reaaaaalllly go for one right about now."

"No luck, Sin." He smirked, then handed Rosalie the note. "It's an address. Warden Pike's home address to be exact. I didn't see much on the camera feed, except the obvious fact that the Fae who captured Roary weren't FIB. They were marked with a symbol for a company I tracked down called Drav Enterprises. A quick and very illegal hack of their accounts showed an account number that flagged in my database. It seems Warden Pike has been receiving money from them for a long time. She'll have answers, I'm sure."

"This isn't close to done," Rosalie warned. "Once I find Roary, you'll help us get to him."

"For a price," Jerome reminded her. I'd seen a man or two promise my brother an untold price for help before then come up short on the pay-out. Not the best of moves on all accounts, but I knew my wild girl was good for it. Whatever it was.

"I'll pay in pickles and pears," I jibed, but neither of them smiled. They were staring at each other, a staring contest perhaps, and my girl won the trophy as Jerome blinked and stepped back.

"Contact me when you have more information." He clapped me on the shoulder. "Come on, Sin, I have a job I need your help with and I've got a safehouse ready for you to-"

I shrugged out of his hold, taking a step away and shaking my head.

"I'm not going with you Jeromeo," I said, frowning in confusion because surely he could see that – surely my love for this beauty beside me shone all around, lighting the space and screaming like a claxon that sang her name in a squawking tone that was impossible to ignore. "This wild girl stole my heart when she stole me from that prison. I'm her monster now. All hers."

Jerome snorted like I was joking, reaching for me again but when I ducked aside once more, bobbing and weaving like a whale in a jet stream, he fell so very still.

Scary still.

Psycho killer on the prowl still.

I side-stepped to put me in front of my babycakes and raised my chin. "Say it,' I growled, the badness in me roughening my voice because I could feel the challenge in the air as it ran down my spine.

"You can't be serious?" Jerome sneered. "You think you...love her?"

"Thinking is for top hats and cats with monocles," I reminded him. "It isn't my thinker that fell for her – it's my thumper." I put my hand over my heart in demonstration, its violent pounding a testament to that truth.

"More like your cock," Jerome replied dismissively, and I didn't like the way his lip was curling just a little, a sneer in my direction which he'd never offered me before. "Come on, Sin, you know how this goes. How many Fae have claimed to love you just because they're obsessed with fucking you? It's always the same though, isn't it? No one actually wants you. They just want the fantasy you paint for them and the feeling of your co-"

Pain and rage and blinding screams were filling up my skull to bursting point, but it wasn't them who lunged for him first – it was my wild wolf girl who shoved me aside and rounded on Jerome with a feral snarl.

"You say one more vile word about my man and I'll rip that festering tongue from your mouth before choking you with it, bastardo," Rosalie hissed with a venom that made my heart stall then race then do a triple flip, tuck, curl, whirly-loo-ha and flamble. Did she just call me hers??

Jerome straightened, fire flaring in his eyes because no one ever spoke to him in a tone even close to that and lived. No one ever threatened him and made it out the room - but she would. Somehow, as I met his rough and ruinous stare, I knew he knew it too.

"Tell me then," he said, that sneer still in place as he looked from her to me where I lingered at her back, the damsel for her to protect. "What form does he take to suit your desires, oh great queen of the Oscura Clan? What does he have to become for your love to burn so fiercely?"

Rosalie smiled darkly, offering him a sight of all those pearly whites as she offered me her hand.

"Show him, Sin," she purred, and I purred too, inside and out as I took her hand and looked straight at Jerome as I shifted into her perfect desire – and nothing happened.

The seconds ticked by and Jerome stared from her to me, confusion turning to a calculating comprehension. That fire burned hotter, fiercer, more furiously for a few moments and then he blinked and *poof*, it was gone.

Jerome straightened, a smile breaking across his dark features at long last as he saw it. "She wants you as…you."

"Only me," I agreed. "And she has me."

"And there was me thinking you don't have a heart," Jerome said, a little sting in his tail because he was obviously upset that I'd found new places to be.

"So he stays with me," Rosalie reiterated, and I shrugged, a pawn to her dominion.

Jerome nodded slowly. "I suppose I'll see you soon then, brother."

I nodded. "As soon as a spoon in a lagoon."

He tossed stardust over his head and was gone just like that, leaving me and Rosalie with an address which I snatched from her hand to double check there wasn't a cake recipe on the back. No joy. But I was soon going to find out if Warden Pike knew how to bake.

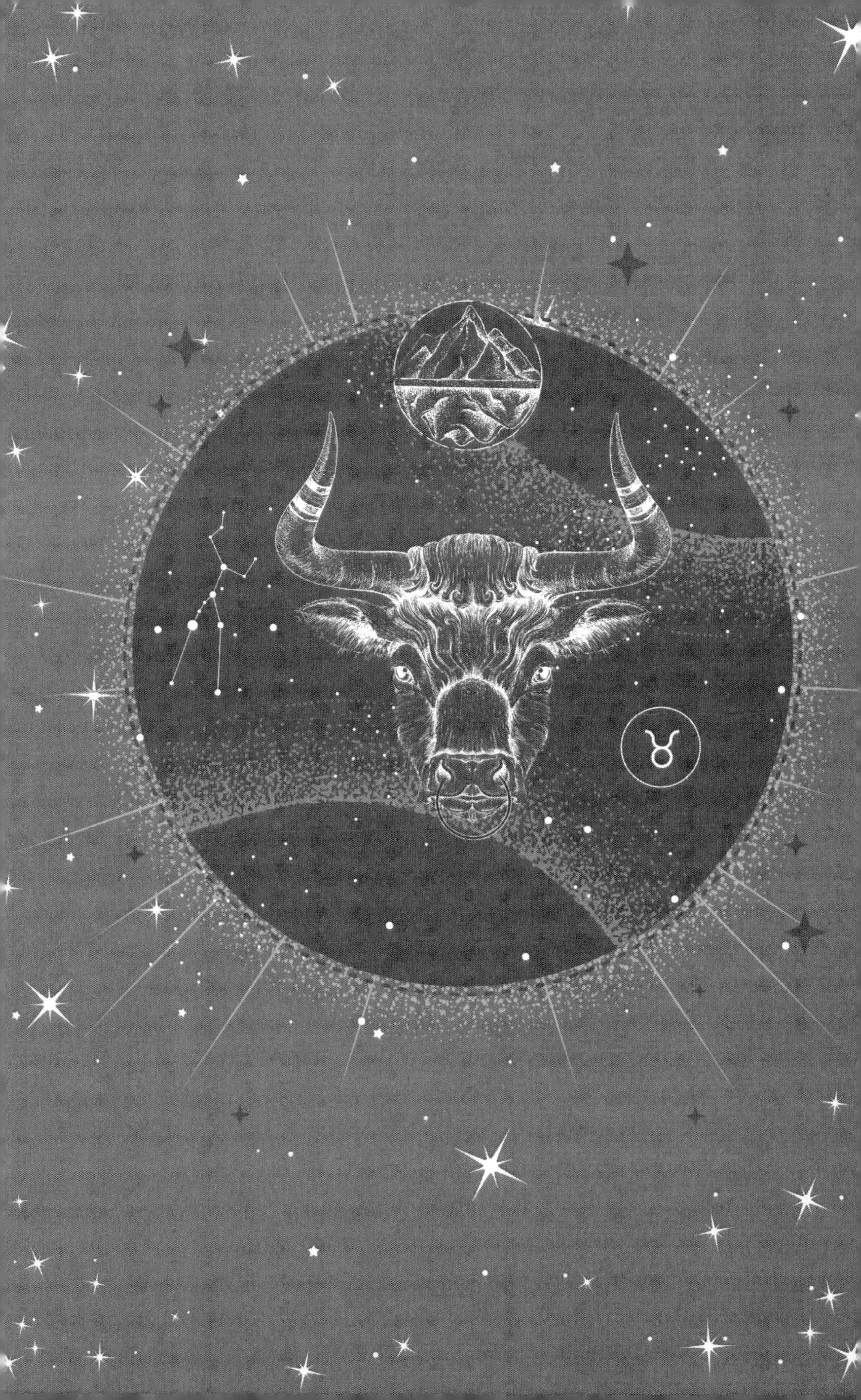

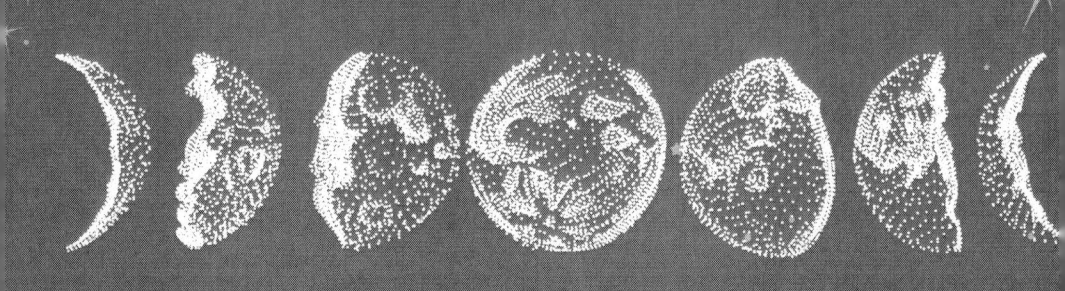

ROSALIE

PRISONER #12

CHAPTER FIVE

The raucous laughter and rampant howling of the Wolf pups greeted me as I stepped through the wide front door to Aunt Bianca's house again, the scent of something delicious calling out to me from the kitchen.

Sin draped his arm around my shoulders, his large body enveloping mine and making me feel secure in a way that had nothing to do with him protecting me and everything to do with the way his heart thumped in time with my own.

I looked up at him, meeting his dark eyes. "Welcome home," I murmured a beat before chaos descended and cousins, aunts, uncles and every vaguely related member of my famiglia appeared to greet us.

"Is it always this loud here?" Sin asked, smiling big.

"Usually a little less than this," I admitted. "But often louder too."

His smile only widened at that, his arm staying firmly locked around me as we moved deeper into the house. Gabriel had foreseen the FIB raiding the estate tomorrow in their hunt for us so we were going to have to leave tonight. Of course, in my famiglia that was the perfect excuse for a party so we would be joined by every Oscura from here to Mount Lupa and beyond.

Members of my pack reached out to brush their fingers over my arms and hands as we passed them, everyone beaming at me, clearly pleased to have me home at last. But the more wide grins I passed, the harder it became to draw a full breath, the heavier the weight in my chest felt. Until I wasn't able to stand it any longer and I strode through the house so fast that people barely recognised me before I was gone again.

"Are we having a race?" Sin asked, keeping pace with my fast steps and letting me steer us.

"No. We're getting out of here," I said.

I found Cain sitting in the corner of the huge TV room watching a documentary on sharks. Hastings sat beside him, cringing as a shark lunged at the camera while stuffing his face with popcorn from the huge bowl I suspected Aunt Bianca had provided for him. A small wooden bowl sat beside Cain – only half full and mostly made up of un-popped cornels. Amusement made my lips twitch momentarily – my aunt always had made it clear when she was displeased with someone, and I got the feeling she'd been making judgements on the new house guests. Whatever Cain had done to offend her wasn't clear – but no doubt she'd talk about it loudly from the adjacent room soon enough to fill me in. Subtle wasn't something the Oscura women were known for.

"We need to plan our next move," I said to the two of them. "Where are Ethan and the others?"

"Why should I know?" Cain asked, his narrowed eyes moving over the tattooed arm Sin still had draped around me. The Incubus smiled provocatively as he noticed Cain's attention falling to him and leaned close to speak in my ear.

"Biter boy doesn't know whether he wants to kick my ass for touching you or ask to watch while we fuck again. He's all kinds of torn up over it," he whispered loud enough for the pups in the yard to hear.

Hastings started choking on his popcorn, turning beetroot and doubling over while Cain irritably patted him on the back. He didn't deny Sin's claims though.

"Wait here, Sin," I said, taking his arm from my shoulders and propelling him onto the seat on Hastings's other side.

"But-" He tried to get up again but I pressed my hand to his chest and pushed him back down with a low growl.

"Stay," I warned.

Sin submitted with a raised brow, glancing over at Cain. "I think we should all play sub for our girl once we have Roary back," he said. "She could tie us up and use us for her pleasure however she likes. Make us into her harem of sex toys. I think she'd enjoy that."

"I wouldn't hate it," I admitted, giving him a warning look before I straightened and strode from the room.

Plunger had been given a room in the cellar – though Aunt Bianca had been concerned about him touching the wine collection so he'd been given a place with the food stores instead – I hadn't had the heart to tell her that she should probably be more concerned about what he might be doing with the root vegetables.

He'd agreed to stay put based on the idea that it was a good place for him to hide from the FIB, but in reality I just hadn't wanted him near the pups.

I headed outside via the kitchen, skirting through the sun-soaked courtyard where my aunt's famous lemon tree stood proudly. I took the well-worn stone stairs down to the cellar, knocking on the old wooden door and it swung wide, revealing the cool space beneath the house where shelves full of tinned goods, cleaning products and toilet paper lay stacked in neat rows. I'd once joked that Aunt Bianca kept this place ready for the apocalypse, but she'd replied that it was barely enough to keep the Oscuras fed and clean for a month. She was probably right, even if this place did feel like entering an honest to the stars store.

"Plunger?" I called, wondering if I should use his real name now or not.

There was no reply and I moved further into the dimly lit room, the cool air enveloping me. I walked down the long space and came to a halt by a wide hole which had been burrowed into it, a flagstone set aside next to a pile of dirt.

"Seriously?" I muttered.

"I do believe he thought it was time to head off alone." Pudding's voice had me leaping out of my skin and I whirled on the huge Bear Shifter, finding him sitting in a small alcove between jars of pickles and stacks of toilet paper.

"What the fuck, Pudding?" I gasped. "How do you even do that?"

"You are always in such a hurry, hound," he replied, taking a bite from a whole cherry pie which he had balanced on one knee. "You do not look around you for the whos and the whats and the whys. You miss the finer details."

"I've never missed a scary motherfucker lurking in the shadows aside from you."

"I know how to be one with the world as it is. That is all. You cannot stay still long enough to understand. Neither could the mole – he left you a gift by the way."

Pudding pointed his pie-coated fork to the other side of the hole that Plunger had made in the floor where a small pile of potatoes and a rather sorry looking carrot sat with a piece of paper.

I wrinkled my nose at the 'gift' and eyed the note. It wasn't long.

I decided it was time to skedaddle. Thanking you kindly for the freedom Ma'am and wishing you well in your future endeavours. You shall remain eternally in the depths of my plunge hole – Plunger.

"Ew," I grunted, straightening up again and glancing back at the door. "I still don't get why he dug a hole out of here – the door wasn't even locked."

"That is a conundrum. Yes," Pudding agreed, taking another bite of pie.

"Right. Well, that was why I was coming to look for him and you too – it's time for us to get moving. The FIB will be raiding this place tomorrow and we need to be gone."

"Gone," Pudding agreed, taking another bite of pie.

"Yeah…Did you have a plan for somewhere to go?" I shifted a little uncomfortably.

Plunger could do what he liked and I didn't really give a shit, but Pudding was good people. I wouldn't have been able to orchestrate anything about the change in plans for our escape once the riot had begun if it hadn't been for him and I didn't want to see him getting captured and locked away again, but I also couldn't keep him with us.

"I have family who live in the Wasted Mountains. We like to spend weeks or even months there roaming the wilds in our Order forms. There are good caves there. Good rivers too."

I smiled, not in the least bit surprised that Pudding enjoyed spending extended periods of time in his Order form. And I seriously doubted the FIB would stand much chance of locating a Bear in the woods.

"That sounds like a great idea," I told him, offering him a hand to shake and realising this would be goodbye.

Pudding gave me a slow smile, setting aside his demolished plate of pie and getting to his feet so he towered over me.

He ignored my hand and drew me into an embrace instead, enveloping me in his huge body and patting me roughly on the head.

"You're a good hound," he said, drawing a smile to my lips. "I will not forget this boon you have granted me. And I will be your loyal friend if ever you are in need of one."

"Dante can give you some stardust so you can leave once you pass through the wards," I told him. They'd been dropped on the night of the escape so that we could arrive here quickly but Dante had put them all back in place now, making sure that no one could arrive here unannounced as usual.

"Yes," he agreed. "Goodbye, hound."

"Goodbye, Pud." I gave him a final squeeze and we broke apart, heading back out of the cellar and exchanging one last look before he lumbered away towards the vineyards where Dante was partying with the pack, and I turned back to the house.

I found Esme lurking in the kitchen, her eyes wide as I approached, a low whine sounding in the back of her throat.

"You're sending me away?" she asked, looking like a kicked puppy and making me feel like shit. I was her Alpha and I was abandoning her. But keeping her with me would only bring her closer to danger.

"Just for a little while," I promised her. "We have a pack house in Tucana, up in the northeast of the kingdom – ever heard of it?"

"Isn't it that fancy town near <u>Zodiac Academy</u> where all the preppy assholes go to drink on the weekends?" she asked, looking utterly unenthusiastic about the place.

"It is. We have some business going down there – where there are preppy assholes there's plenty of money, after all. And the pack there are pretty cool too – they have moon runs on the beach and party like it's their last night on earth every damn night. There's mountains and forests and the sky is so dark up there away from the big cities that I swear the moon shines brighter than in any other part of Solaria. I think you'd like it."

Her expression lightened at my description and she nodded slowly. "If that's what will make you happy, Alpha," she said.

"Knowing you're safe and free will make me happy," I agreed. "And Louie said he will go with you, show you the ropes and stay up there for a few months too." It hadn't escaped my notice that Esme had been giving my cousin Louie the big eyes since we'd arrived back here and I figured the promise of his company would sweeten the deal for her.

As I'd guessed, her eyes brightened considerably at that announcement and she threw herself at me, a low howl escaping her as she hugged me tightly in farewell.

I found Ethan in the heart of the party taking place out by the vineyards, many of my cousins, second cousins, third cousins and assorted family friends all batting their eyelashes at him and working to gain the attention of this new and interesting Alpha.

He was drinking a beer with Dante, not seeming to notice any of his admirers but shoved to his feet at the sight of me approaching.

"Did you find what we need, love? Do you know where he is?" he asked me, striding over to close the distance between us, and some of the tension in me spilled away as he cupped my jaw in his rough palm.

"I'm working on it," I replied, taking his hand in mine. "I've got the others in the TV room so we can figure out where to go from here."

"You don't want to stay and party with us, lupa?" Dante asked me, his knowing gaze straying over my expression. Of course the pack had turned out in full to see me off again, but I couldn't stomach a night of partying while Roary was still locked up somewhere, and we both knew it.

"I think it's better if we leave now," I told him, though I could admit that my heart hurt to be parted from this place and my famiglia again so soon. But it wasn't home without Roary and I didn't deserve to enjoy it until I had him here with us.

Dante nodded. "Leon wants to help but the FIB are tailing him while they search for Roary themselves. I think he would be better off causing a distraction and keeping their eyes away from whatever it is you're doing than coming with you and potentially drawing more heat your way."

"Yeah," I agreed. "He should keep the FIB looking in another direction while we hunt. I'll get Roary back and then we can all be together again, the way we should be," I swore powerfully and Dante nodded his agreement, handing me a pouch of stardust.

"I know you will. A morte e ritorno, Rosa."

"A morte e ritorno," I replied.

Dante clapped a hand on Ethan's shoulder. "Do better, stronzo. Or you might end up wishing I still had no idea who you are."

Ethan raised his chin to that challenge but didn't disagree with it. "I will," he said. "You'll see."

I kept hold of Ethan's hand, leading him away from the music and the party, heading back to the TV room where Cain, Hastings and Sin waited for us.

"Jack," I said as I moved to stand before them again and Hastings raised his head to look at me, all lost lamb and still a touch besotted. I sighed. "You should go back to the FIB. You don't have to return to Darkmore – I'm sure they'll accept your resignation. We could wipe your memories of this place so they won't be able to tell that you ever came here-"

"No," Hastings said, more firmly than I had ever heard him address me. "I'm not who I was before. I'm…I think I'm a criminal now. My soul has been darkened and it won't ever turn pure again."

I glanced at Cain who rolled his eyes unhelpfully.

"You haven't broken any laws," I said slowly. "You aren't a criminal-"

"It's in my soul," Hastings replied, running his hands through his blonde hair and tugging on his fringe so that it fell forward to shadow his eyes. "Look at me. I'm a completely different man now."

I did look at him. I looked and I saw my choir boy with messy hair and a shit heap of trauma which would hopefully lessen once he got over the shock of all he'd witnessed. But a hardened criminal I did not see.

"Right…"

"Aww, can we keep him?" Sin cooed, slinging an arm around Hastings and squishing him to his side. "Look at how cute he is. And he wants to play dress up with us. I bet we could train him up to be our sub too – he already has the moon eyes for you, kitten, and he is pretty nice to look at."

"Stop appraising him like he's a cow come to market," Ethan snorted and Jack's cheeks reddened.

"I really think you should go home, Jack," I pushed.

"Let him be," Cain grumbled. "He's had his eyes opened to that place and the truth of it. If the shit that was going on down in Psych is anything to judge by, then maybe this is the better side of the law to be on."

I arched a brow at the Vampiro bastardo then gave in. "Fine. We need to move and this conversation is wasting time. There's a safe house in Kalia, which just so happens to be where Pike's penthouse is too, so we can head to that before making our next move. You can stick with us, Jack, and see if you really do like it on this side of the law – just let me know when you've had enough though and I can ship you right back home in the blink of an eye."

Hastings straightened as if accepting a challenge and I shook my head at the sweet fool before leading the way out of the house.

Of course I couldn't just slip out quietly; countless Oscuras including my aunt waylaid us and embraced me or slipped us supplies, lucky charms and offered out well wishes.

Mournful howls followed us down the long drive when we finally made it beyond the house and I led our band of miscreants to the edge of the magical wards which guarded this place from outside influence. Tomorrow, the FIB would show up with their shiny warrant and Dante and Aunt Bianca would graciously allow them through the wards to search to their hearts' content. We'd be long gone by then.

My magic buzzed in my veins as the wards recognised me and I parted them for the five of us, stepping into the dark lane beyond the vineyard and taking the stardust from my pocket.

I tossed it over us, letting the world whip away as the stars claimed us for their own. I tried not to dwell on how many hours had now passed since Roary had been ripped from my arms. I was on my way to reclaim him. And nothing in this kingdom or beyond it would stop me.

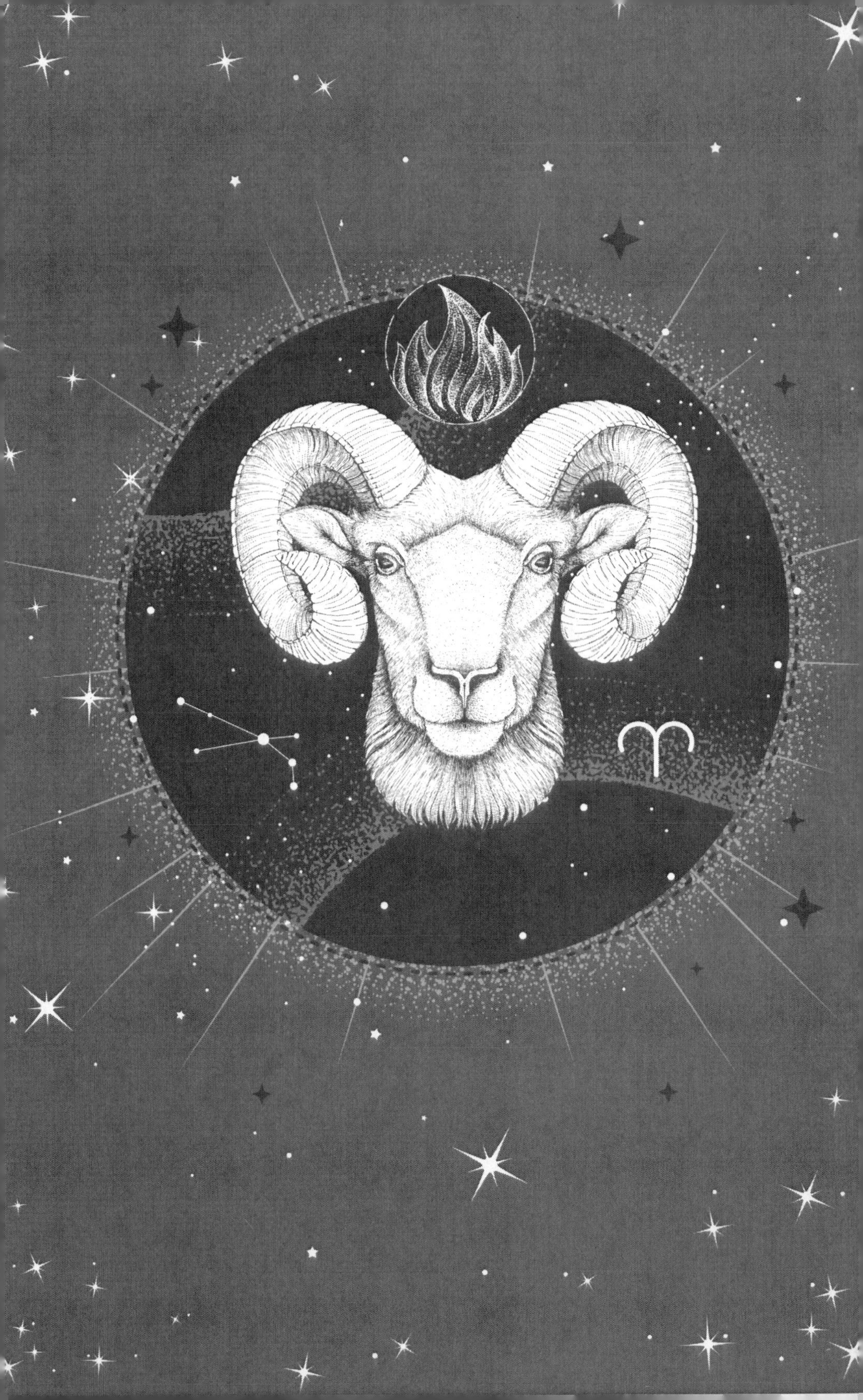

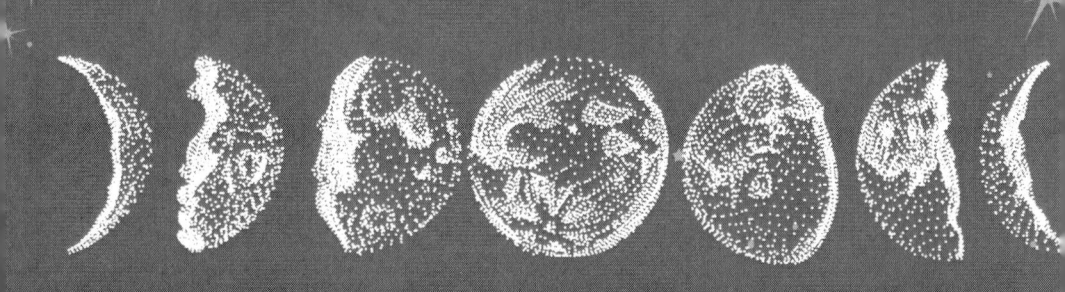

CAIN
COMMANDING OFFICER

CHAPTER SIX

The back streets of Kalia reminded me far too sharply of those I'd lived in while growing up in Benjamin Acrux's care. The memories of my friend Merrick were closer than ever, haunting me and reminding me why I had found a twisted kind of solace in dedicating myself to my job at Darkmore Penitentiary. There, I had found a purpose, and in that place, I had found nothing familiar to ring the bells of the past. When I'd been awake at least. Sleep was a different matter. The dead of night was where demons thrived and regrets evolved into beasts with sharp claws. Perhaps they were why I had been so doggedly determined to see Rosalie escape the clutches of that hell.

My heart hadn't attached itself to anyone since Merrick, and yet now she held it in a way no one ever had. But where had following that insanity-draped path gotten me? Cursed and hunted for by the FIB. Though it seemed they currently believed Jack and I had been kidnapped, a simple Cyclops interrogation would set the record straight if we were caught. So it seemed my life was on track for self-destruction with one potential option of redemption left to me.

I looked to Sin Wilder who was walking a few steps ahead of me, swaggering along at Rosalie's side, a silencing bubble around us all keeping our approach quiet. On her left flank, Ethan Shadowbrook stalked along, muscles primed for any attack that came our way, the mate mark behind his ear glinting faintly silver as the moonlight touched it. He was off limits because of his bond to Rosalie. But Sin…he was fair game. If I managed to chain him and return him to the FIB, I might just be pardoned and escape Cyclops interrogation for the act of clear loyalty.

Hastings had remained back in the safe house, given instruction by Rosalie to guard it for us, though as we crept through the dark like a stalking shadow, I had to think she'd really left him behind so that he wouldn't be implicated in whatever happened once we found Pike. She'd offered to leave me with him too but I hadn't graced that with a response and she'd only smirked at my silence, taken my hand and drawn me out the door. I hated the jolt my heart had given at the touch of her hand, hated the way my eyes remained pinned on her even though she'd long since released me, hated the truth of what she'd become to me because I couldn't stand the thought of losing her while knowing she wasn't mine to lose.

"Old long Johnson had a farm," Sin whisper-sung under this breath. "E-I-E-I-O. And on that farm he had a Cain." He tossed a glance over his shoulder at me, a wicked glint in his eyes. "E-I-E-I-O. With a bitch-bitch here, and a bitch-bitch there. Here a bitch, there a bitch, everywhere a little bitch."

"Shut it," I snarled, and he sniggered. Yeah, handing him back to the authorities wouldn't cause me any remorse. But as Rosalie turned an amused smile his way, the curse itched under my skin, warning me that she might not feel so forgiving if I took her crazy boyfriend away.

I was caught between a rock and a hard place, but still my feet kept following Rosalie wherever she went. Tonight was testing the limits of my loyalty to her. If Warden Pike saw me among her group, then tomorrow, the news would report it and out me as the true traitor I was.

Somehow, despite that knowledge clawing at me, I didn't slow my pace, didn't even think about turning back. I was a damn fool, following a woman I knew would never choose me, but my devotion to her ran deeper than I'd ever let myself acknowledge aloud.

"Here," Rosalie announced, turning down a narrow alley between two high rise buildings that stretched away towards the glittering night sky.

The three of us followed her into the shadows and Sin hung back a little to rub shoulders with me.

"She'll know your face, that Pikey Pike," he whispered, offering me a twisted kind of grin. "Or will she know your ass better from all the whipping she did on it to keep you in line? Bet she got you to pull down your knickers and bend over like a naughty school girl every time you fucked up. Tut tut, what will she do when she sees her little school girl playing with the local bad boys?"

"Shut your mouth," I hissed.

"You're a two-trick pony, all you can do is say shut up and growl like a grunty bear. Don't you do anything else? You're pretty, but I'm thinking my sex pot needs more than pretty to let you join the main gang. So maybe she just took your D to buy your loyalty to help her fly free from her cage. Guess it worked if that was the case." He smacked me on the bicep and I lunged, my fangs aimed for his throat as I shoved him against the brick wall.

Before I could bite him, his fist connected with my jaw, but I was fully feral, throwing my weight against him and shoving my forearm to his chest to pin him there. He leaned forward, his might forcing my arm to give before he placed a firm kiss to my lips. I reared back in anger and he skipped off down the alley with a bark of manic laughter. I was left with Rosalie cocking an eyebrow at me while Ethan continued on down the alley after Sin.

"Problem?" she questioned.

"He goaded me," I muttered, feeling like a fool under her scrutiny.

"He goads everyone," she said, stepping closer to me.

We hadn't spent a moment alone since the escape and I felt the tension between us shivering through the atmosphere. All I wanted to do was grab her and pull her against me, tell her I wanted her in any way I could have her. But my pride wouldn't let the words out, and they were a fool's hope anyway. She had two moon mates and a feral Incubus to keep her satisfied. I hardly brought anything more to that situation and I didn't exactly see how I could ever accept that three other men had a claim on her. We weren't destined for each other, and what Sin had said was a truth that left me raw. I was Rosalie's key to escape, nothing more. But here I was, still trailing along in her wake like a stray dog hoping for scraps. It was pathetic.

"Mason…" Her voice softened, her brow furrowing as she moved closer, her hand extending towards me. "Why are you still following me into chaos? You know what this will mean for you tonight."

Her thoughts were clearly aligned with mine. She saw my stupidity for what it was and there was no hiding from it now.

"I can't leave your side until you break this curse." Stupid fucking answer. The coward's one. I touched my wrist where the rose vine curled around it, the mark of the moon curse promising my death. I didn't know when or how, but I doubted I had much longer left. Somehow that didn't seem like the most pressing matter of my soul anymore. Her needs and desires were instead and treading this path to help her fulfil them was the only one I wanted to walk.

Her eyes darkened and she was suddenly cold, shutting me out. "Mm." She turned her back on me, heading after the others and I swore beneath my breath.

I stood there for two long seconds before following on, my decision already made. I wasn't backing out on this.

Ethan was waiting at the bottom of a fire escape ladder, but Sin had started up it, singing his farm song again and swaying his ass side to side as he climbed. The silencing bubble was keeping his insane bullshit from being heard by anyone outside our group, but I was unfortunate enough to be inside it.

"- and on that farm he had an Ethan, E-I-E-I-O. With an ass stash here and an ass stash there. Here's a grape, there's a grape, everywhere a bum grape."

"Will you be quiet and focus?" Ethan called up to him, pursing his lips.

Rosalie stepped onto the ladder, brushing past Ethan and giving him a seductive look as she went. He placed his hands on her hips as if helping her onto the ladder even though she clearly didn't need any assistance and his fingers roamed down to her ass, cupping before he let go and smirked as she climbed away from him. He went next and I followed, scaling the building all the way until we made it to the penthouse at the summit.

Sin already had a window popped open and was disappearing inside with Rosalie close behind him. When Ethan made it in, I swung myself after him off the ladder, landing in a dark hallway, the only sound between us the distant hum of a refrigerator.

Sin was silent at last, a violent look about him as he cocked his head and prowled down the hallway. "Come out, come out little warden."

This was the moment when I should have been concealing my face, working on spells to mask myself from being recognised. But as Rosalie met my gaze, a dark kind of protectiveness wrapped around my soul and I found I wanted to be seen here with her. Insane as that thought was, it stayed my hand from concealing myself and I stepped close to her instead in a show of unity.

Her eyes trailed over me curiously before she headed after Sin, and Ethan's shoulder touched mine as we followed as one.

I glanced at him and a silent understanding passed between us. She was our priority. Whatever happened here tonight, no wicked fate would befall her.

Sin pushed doors open, peeking into rooms and I couldn't help but notice the luxury home Pike had claimed for herself. The Darkmore Warden's salary had to be good, but this good? Doubtful. Rosalie had told me about the paper trail of money that Jerome had found coming straight from Drav Enterprises to Pike's bank account and I had to admit that being a ruthless bitch who mercilessly sacrificed Fae to a fate worse than death clearly paid well. The more I thought about it, the further it riled an aggression in me which begged to be let out.

People like her were leeches, just like the man who had raised me. They thrived when they were in control and only managed to taste greatness in life through the achievements of others. They had no integrity, no real talent of their own, yet here Pike was, standing on the backs of those who got in her path to build her pretty little empire. My hand curled into a fist at my side and Ethan noted the change, strangely attuned to me in that moment.

"What did she do to you?" he murmured.

"Not me," I said quietly. "But others."

"You've got an actual heart under that iron exterior, haven't you Cain?" he said, a slight taunt to his voice, but it seemed to be in friendly jest instead of a nasty jibe.

"Not much of one."

"I think it's the kind layered in scars. That's what makes you fit in with us. We're all broken on the inside." He moved on at a quicker pace, giving me no time to respond to that and a frown creased my brow as I hurried after him. Did he really think I fit with them? I was one of the officers who had kept them all in line, that kind of shit didn't just get forgotten. And hell, why was I even thinking about the hope that he might want to?

I ground my teeth, pushing out the errant idea and focusing on the reason we were here.

Sin sprang into another room with an 'ah-ha!' and Rosalie darted after him. A commotion broke out and I started running, chasing Ethan into the room and finding Sin standing over Pike in her bed, holding her down with his air magic while he set her pillows on fire and made them beat her round the head.

"Enough," Rosalie said calmly and Sin extinguished the flames, though he let the pillows whack Pike a couple more times before they fell still beside her. Her usually perfect ice-blonde hair was singed from the attack and she had lost half an eyebrow to the blaze, but she was pretty much unharmed apart from that. I noticed her mouth was open in a scream, but Sin had cast a silencing bubble around her to keep it quiet.

Rosalie took charge, stepping to the side of the bed and gazing down at my old boss. I didn't think she could see me from this shadowy corner of her room, but there was time for her to notice yet. The Incubus extended our silencing bubble over her, releasing the one that had contained her scream.

"Hello, Warden," Rosalie purred. "Remember us? The creatures you kept in cages, believing they would never find a way out and come creeping into your room at night like a living nightmare. But that's the thing about arrogant stronzos in their ivory towers, they never expect the dogs they kick to bite back." She nodded to Sin as Pike started answering her.

"Y-you have no idea what's going to happen to you if you kill me," Pike stammered, looking ruffled for the first time since I'd met her. This was not the control freak woman who had taken pleasure in keeping both guards and prisoners alike under her thumb. This was a frightened wretch in her bed who had finally realised she couldn't outrun karma forever.

"You can keep breathing if you tell me where Roary Night is being held," Rosalie offered. "I know he's not in Darkmore. The news is reporting that he escaped. But I saw him being dragged into a helicopter marked with the emblem of Drav Enterprises. So where has he been taken?"

Pike's throat bobbed at her words, like the name of that company was her undoing in so many ways. If the press got their hands on that information, she would likely end up in Darkmore herself with the hellions who she had ruled over for so many years. Their welcome would not be warm.

"How do you know about Drav Enterprises?" Pike asked in terror.

Sin pillow whipped her again using his air magic. "You don't ask the questions here, fish bitch!"

She cowered from him with a whimper. "A-alright. I'll tell you what I know. I think he's been taken to Grimolda Isle. I got an invite to the smugglers ball – it's like a black market where off record deals are made between the types of organisations which don't exactly conform to the law. Drav Enterprises are going to be showcasing their latest projects. It's in my nightstand."

"And why did they take him at all?" Rosalie snarled, making Pike cower.

"I don't know what they do with the prisoners they take to Psych. I just get paid to turn a blind eye, or to do the necessary cover ups."

"She's singing like a baby blue tit," Sin said excitedly.

"Yeah, this was damn easy actually," Rosalie commented as she reached into her nightstand drawer and took out a glittering silver invitation, glancing back at us.

"Ready to leave then, love?" Ethan asked.

She nodded and led the way out of the room. I moved for the door, but a gasp sounded from Pike and my name spilled from her lips. "Mason?" she balked, making my pulse thump erratically. "What…what are you doing with them?"

I turned to her as Ethan stilled, glancing from me to Pike with his eyebrows raised. Sin jumped off the bed, thumbing through some jewellery on Pike's dressing table and pocketing pieces of it while starting to hum his farm song again.

I raised my chin, accepting the fate being delivered to me by the stars and staring Pike in the eyes. I knew what this would mean. Knew the weight of what would happen if she went to the FIB with the news of my whereabouts.

"What do you want to do about this?" Ethan murmured, giving me a look that said he would back me if I decided on her death, but I didn't know why this asshole was so keen to make me his little buddy all of a sudden.

I didn't know if it was insanity or mercy that made my decision, but I strode from the room, leaving Pike to do as she would about seeing me here. Ethan kept glancing at me, but I said nothing on the subject, my choice perhaps earning some sort of feelings from him. Trust? Doubtful. Maybe he was just curious why I continued to make foolish choices.

As we made it to the window where Rosalie was climbing onto the sill, Sin came skipping down the hall, covered in blood with his song tumbling from his lips. "With a stab-stab here and a stab-stab there, here a stab, there a stab, everywhere a stab-stab." He clapped me on the cheek, marking me with his bloody palm print, and I stepped back from him in shock. "She's a goner."

"Sin," Rosalie gasped. "You killed her?"

"Was I not supposed to?" He looked to her innocently. "She'd tell everyone we got out of Darkmore."

"But everyone knows we escaped Darkmore," Ethan said in confusion.

"Riiight." Sin looked at me, his gaze intense and unwavering. "Well either way, dead little fishes don't whisper to the sharks." He turned abruptly away from me but left me with the baffling sense that he had killed Pike to cover for me. "Anyway, I put her head in a plant pot. She'll grow back. Given time and water and the right amount of sunshine. She'll be as good as new!" He threw himself at Rosalie and a cry left her as he knocked her out the window.

"Rosa!" Ethan bellowed, lunging to the edge and I did the same, my pulse climbing into my ears as I gazed out, finding Sin wrapped around her, guiding them down to the ground with his air magic.

"Fucking psycho," I exhaled, relieved she was fine, but by the stars, did he have to be so unpredictable?

"He kind of grows on you after a while," Ethan said, offering me a smile but I only frowned in return, confused by his behaviour.

As he swung his leg over the sill and started climbing down the ladder, I found my feet tracking back towards the bedroom where Sin had murdered Warden Pike. I glimpsed in at the carnage, her body torn to pieces and her head sitting snuggly in a plant pot, the fern dug out to make room for it. He had done this in less than a minute, and the thought made adrenaline puncture my veins. But as I stared at the horrified look in Pike's lifeless eyes, I felt something toward the rogue Incubus that I never thought I'd feel. Gratitude.

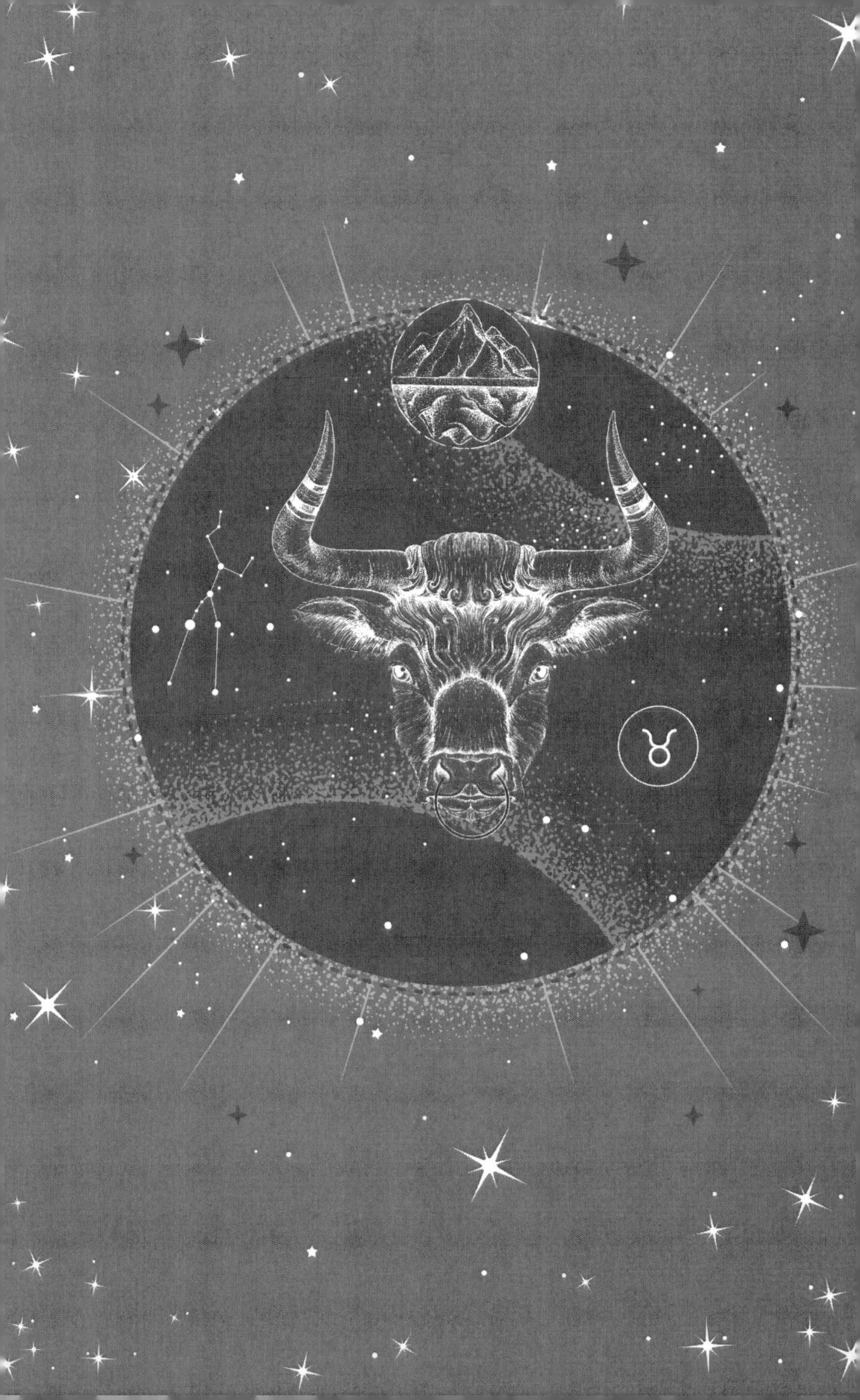

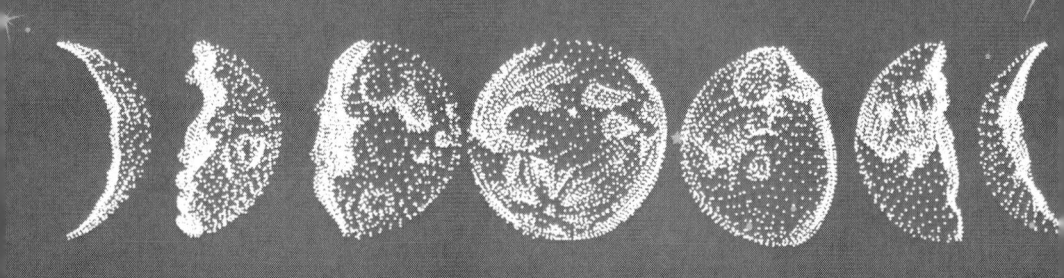

Rosalie

PRISONER #12

CHAPTER SEVEN

We didn't hang around in Kalia after Sin had murdered Pike, instead following the lead she'd given us and heading to the strip of land closest to the distant island of Grimolda. The lodge we'd claimed as our hideaway from the world was nestled on a cliffside on the western coast of Solaria overlooking a bay with the glorious blue sea cresting upon the golden sand in lazy, sultry waves.

The Oscuras owned plenty of safe houses like this one, each used in times of need by various members of the pack or just as a quiet vacation spot for some members of our inner circle. They were off the record locations, their ownership bought for in cash without any kind of paper trail to lead the FIB to their doors and, like this one, most were set away from other houses. It meant that we could come and go around the house without having to worry about being spotted despite our spreading notoriety.

Instead of news of our escape from Solaria's deadliest and supposedly most impenetrable prison dying down in the days that had passed since we'd achieved the previously assumed impossible, the story was only gaining momentum. Each day that passed drew more scathing criticism of the FIB, the rulers of our kingdom and even the members of the public who had failed to spot so much as a hair on any one of the escaped convicts' heads. I had hoped the interest in us would fade faster than this, but there was little I could do to combat it. Perhaps in a few weeks they'd get bored of us but for now we had to remain vigilant at all times.

The news of Warden Pike's death had been widely publicised too, the newscasters speculating that both Cain and Hastings were likely dead at the hands of the 'unhinged and psychotic escapees.'

Which probably made the plan we had concocted utterly idiotic. But I couldn't find it in me to care.

Grimolda Isle was a supposedly unoccupied island way off the western coast of our kingdom, surrounded by nothing but ocean for miles around and apparently home to an endangered colony of sea urchins, meaning that no Fae was permitted to approach it.

The invitation Pike had given us claimed different.

"Do you think the sea urchins were relocated?" Hastings asked, concern lining his brow.

"I doubt there were ever any sea urchins to begin with," Cain grunted in answer, leaning against the doorframe and looking out at the ocean just as I had been from my position standing on the wooden deck which surrounded the squat, white lodge.

I glanced at the two of them then back towards the sea.

"The moon is whispering to me," I told them because here by the ocean, where the power of my most adored celestial being called the movement of the sea itself into action, I could always hear her murmuring more clearly.

"Oh yeah?" Cain asked, perking up. Of course the stronzo would be interested in what the moon had to say – the rose vine mark on his arm stood out clearly against his bare skin as he stood there in a grey tank. As ever, he was hoping I might be focusing my efforts on providing him with a cure to it. "What's it saying?"

"*She*," I corrected because an entity as powerful as the moon was obviously female. "Is warning me about what awaits us in that place." I bobbed my chin in the direction of the island even though none of us could see it from here.

"And what's that?" Hastings asked, tugging his fringe down over his eyes and peering out through it.

"Death," I replied with a shrug. "A foul wind blows from that island, tainting all who breathe it in."

"Well isn't that just reassuring as shit," Cain grumbled, folding his arms so his biceps bulged.

"At least we've been warned," I purred while Hastings paled so much that he blended in with the paintwork.

I brushed past Cain and moved back into the little house. It smelled of the wood it had been built from, carved decorations hanging from the walls, beams exposed overhead. There was a large bed in the one room which led off of this one, and a kitchenette and a bathroom that required water magic to be fully functional. Luckily for us, we had Ethan and Hastings to help with that.

"That's a scheming face if ever I saw one," Sin commented as I moved to the kitchen counter and pulled a pen and notepad towards me.

"When isn't she scheming?" Ethan retorted and the corner of my lips hitched up a touch.

"She's baking a cake in her mind and I want a slice of it, a juicy, cream-filled slice." He licked his lips. The guy was obsessed with cake sometimes, I swear.

"Has Jerome pulled through on any intel?" I asked Sin who shook his head.

"Nothing. All he said was that he has the full layout of the compound, the entrance points to the island and the movements of around sixty boats which have recently docked at the island – along with a count of how many Fae departed them. It's as if he didn't even try."

I arched a brow, exchanging a look with Ethan who rolled his eyes.

"Any chance you have those figures written down?" I asked.

Sin sighed. "Your little Wolfy was listening and scribbled a thing or two down," he said, reaching across the counter and flipping my notebook open to reveal six full pages of notes and a damn good sketch Ethan had done based off of Jerome's information.

"And this is…disappointing to you?" I asked in confusion, scanning the detailed information which included notes on guard rotations that Jerome had managed to track using a satellite he'd hacked, as well as four different proposed points of exit he'd noticed that weren't watched well enough.

"Do you see any kill notices on there, kitten?" Sin asked. "Is there a single green flag beside any of those names with an asterisk stating 'this-dude-is-a-piece-of-shit-whose-head-would-look-better-off-in-a-cabbage-patch'?"

"There…is not," I agreed.

"And do you know precisely how long it's been since I killed a deserving motherfucker, wild girl?" Sin pressed.

"Like…eighteen hours. I'm pretty sure you still have Pike's blood under your fingernails."

Ethan snorted and Sin sighed dramatically.

"That barely counted – it was a pity kill for old rod-up-the-ass Vamp out there. I haven't been let loose in a long time and I have all this pent up murder in me which needs fulfilling."

I looked into Sin's desperate eyes and shook my head.

"Fine. Seeing as every asshole in this place is clearly a piece of shit willing to deal in the dirtiest of contracts and must at the very least be compliant with whatever the fuck is happening to Roary there – I will give you a green light on killing whoever the fuck you want-"

Sin opened his mouth wide, joy lighting his features and I held up a single finger to stop him before he could explode in celebration.

"But," I said firmly, cutting that shit off before it could begin. "You wait for me to tell you when it's time. If you murder so much as a flea before I tell you I'm ready for your brand of carnage, then I swear to the stars, Sin, I will dump you back on Jerome's doorstep and you won't ever see me again. Nothing is going to fuck this up. We will get Roary out or die trying."

"We'll get him back, love," Ethan swore, moving around the counter to stand behind me, his hands falling to my shoulders and rubbing firmly. "One more night and we can go to him. I swear we won't fail you or him."

I nodded but despite his efforts at massaging the tension from my shoulders, I couldn't even pretend I was relaxing.

"Stop," I growled, batting him off but he gripped the edge of my stool and spun me to face him, his growl matching my own as he dipped his face to mine.

"Roary wouldn't want you dwelling in pain, love," he snarled. "And don't go giving me the little girl lost bullshit because I know you well enough to know that despair just isn't your style."

"Oh yeah?" I challenged. "So what is my style, stronzo?"

I shoved to my feet, knocking the stool over behind me and smacking my chest into Ethan's in an attempt to force him back a step. Of course the bastardo didn't move, didn't cave, just stared me down with his blue eyes sparking like this reaction was precisely what he'd wanted from me.

"Anger," he said simply. "Red hot, volcanic, burn the fucking world down rage. So hit me if it will help. Punch me, kick me, bite me, I can take it."

"This tension in me won't be relieved like that, stronzo," I growled, shoving him aside and making to stride away but he caught my wrist and yanked me back to him, moving so close that his mouth was a breath from my lips, his forehead pressing to mine.

"We'll get him back," he growled again, glaring into my eyes, daring me to deny it.

"That pain you feel over losing him is nothing," I hissed my reply. "I spent ten years drowning in that agony, searching for a way to undo his fate. I planned and plotted and schemed and sold my fucking soul to any and all bidders in my desperation to free him from that place. It was my fault he got put there in the first place and whatever is happening to him now is my fault too – he was taken trying to leave with me, following me, *trusting* me." My voice cracked on those words, but Ethan didn't shy from them, gripping my waist and pulling me closer.

"This isn't on you, Rosalie," he swore so vehemently that I might have even believed him if my guilt hadn't already permeated every piece of me. "I want you to hear that, to know it and feel it. But most of all, I need you to believe that we will get him back. This fear, this pain and suffering you're experiencing isn't helping him and he would hate to think of you feeling this way."

"Half of my life has been drenched in pain and suffering," I replied bleakly. "I'm more than used to weathering it by now."

"But you deserve more than that, wild girl," Sin said, his eyes on us from across the room. "We want you to have more."

Ethan kissed me before I could protest any further and my anger rose sharply at the heat of his lips on mine.

I pushed my tongue into his mouth, shoving him back against the counter, my fists tight in his shirt.

Ethan groaned into our kiss, his hands finding the hem of my shirt and yanking it up.

I let him pull it from me, baring my body to him in the warm light of the setting sun which was shining brightly through the open windows. His hand roamed down the tattoos and scars lining the left side of my body as he kissed me again and I sank my teeth into his bottom lip.

His fingers moved to the button of my jeans, flicking it open before he shoved them down.

I grasped his shoulders and pushed him to his knees with them, letting him take my shoes and socks from my feet before stepping out of the jeans.

I knotted my hand in his blonde hair as he looked up at me from his knees, my heart pounding heavily in my chest, my lungs expanding on ragged, painful breaths.

Ethan parted his lips to say something to me, but I didn't want to hear it. I only wanted to feel something other than this pain.

Sin's eyes were fixed on us as I dragged Ethan forward, guiding his mouth to my core over the lace of my black panties and releasing a rough moan as he ran his teeth over my clit.

Ethan grasped the backs of my thighs, tilting my body so that he could worship me better. I rolled my hips against his mouth, the bite of his stubble grazing my inner thighs and making my skin prickle with the heavenly sensation.

He tugged my panties aside with his fingers, his mouth colliding with my core as I yanked him to me by his hair.

Ethan growled against my clit, licking and kissing me, making my heart thrash with want as pleasure began to build within me.

Sin made no move to join us, simply watching with a heated expression, his jaw ticking as I turned my head and met his dark eyes.

"Easy there, kitten," he murmured, taking a step closer and reaching out for me across the counter.

I let him take my hand, steadying myself with his strength while Ethan's tongue sank into me before riding up and over my clit.

My body was alight with tension, this coiled ball of anxiety demanding release but even with Ethan working miracles between my thighs, his mouth hot and demanding against me, I couldn't break through that wall.

My breaths came harder, my throat thickening and my grip on Sin's hand tightening so much that it had to hurt.

"That's enough," Sin growled. "Let go, wild girl."

My body hummed in anticipation, bliss lingering just out of reach but as I looked into Sin's dark gaze, I found my own eyes burning, tears blurring my vision.

"Fuck," I cursed, shoving Ethan back and stumbling away from him. "I can't do this," I panted, my chest rising and falling heavily, panic racing through my veins as I stumbled back again. "I can't. I just…I need…"

"Roary," Ethan finished for me, pushing to his feet and I burst into tears which felt so powerful that I was certain I'd be consumed by them entirely.

I tried to bolt but the two of them were there before I could take so much as a step, strong arms wrapping around me, holding me close and murmuring low agreements in my ears.

"A few more hours, love," Ethan said. "Just few little hours and we can head after him. I don't care what's standing between us and him because whatever it is won't be enough to keep us away. We're a pack. And tonight we'll be reunited come hell or high water."

"Fuck yes to that," Sin agreed.

And as my sobs fell still and my tears ran dry in their arms, I found myself believing in those words at last. We were a pack and we were one member down, but tonight that was all going to change.

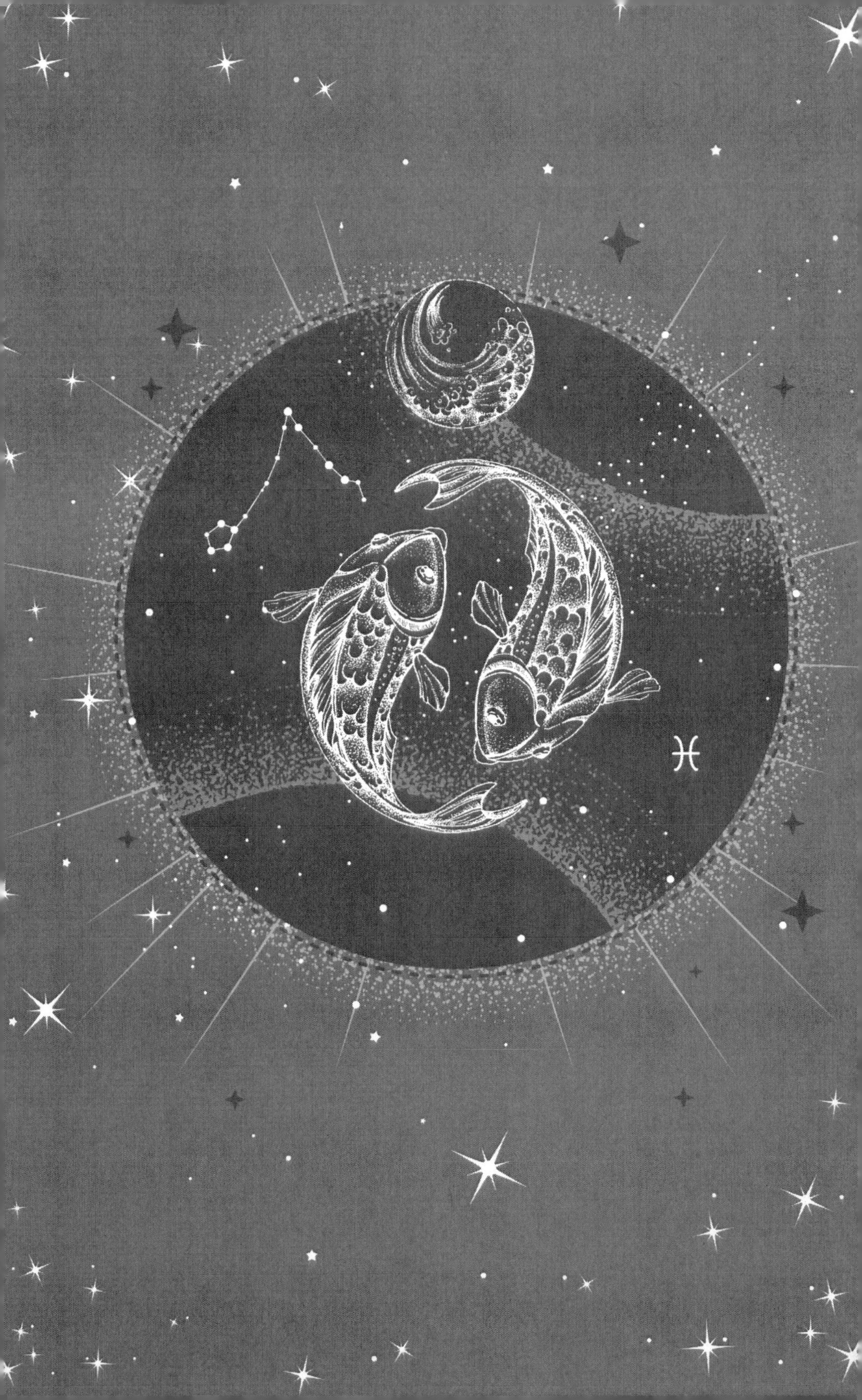

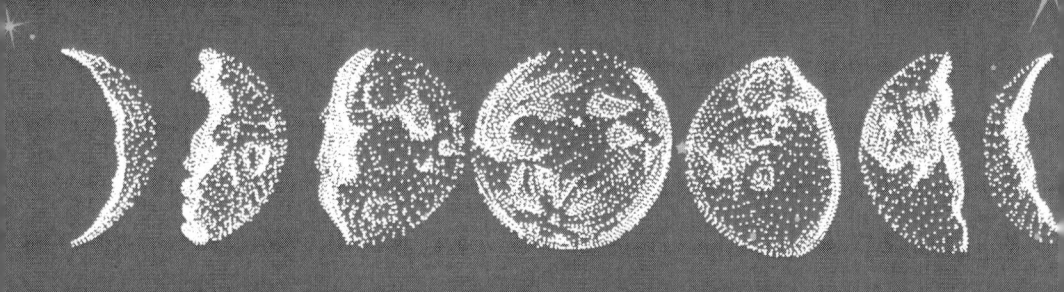

ROARY

PRISONER #69

CHAPTER EIGHT

I dragged my thumb over my right fang, then my left, a chill sweeping through me at the sensation. It didn't feel like my body anymore. I had no problem with Vampires, but their Order didn't belong with me. I ached for my Lion, longed for it in a way that fractured my soul. This wasn't me. My body had been taken hostage, forced to bear the wants and needs of another being. It was unnatural, and I refrained from flexing the gifts of this new form as I sat in my cell, my back to the wall where I sat, head bowed and breaths uneven.

My mind always found Rosa when I fell into the darkest pits of despair, her keen brown eyes and sharp tongue urging me to hold on. But for what? Even if I could escape this place and return to her, I would do so altered and with a vital part of myself missing. She wouldn't judge me, I knew that, but I was living in a false layer of flesh that sat upon my bones like an ugly lie. I didn't want to return to her like this.

I scored a hand over my hair, missing the thickness of my mane between my fingers since it had been cut off. Nothing about me looked like the Lion I had once been, and my chest tightened as I pictured my brother's face, Leon's fear, his horror at what had been stripped from me.

My mothers would weep, my father would…well, he had disowned me already. If he discovered what I'd become now, he would likely refuse to acknowledge my existence at all. But that was assuming I ever got out of here and managed to return to the people I loved to face their anguish over what I was now. That was the best case scenario. Or perhaps it wasn't. Perhaps it would be better if I rotted away in here so that none of my loved ones ever had to endure the knowledge of what had been done to me.

A hissing noise captured my attention and I glanced up at the narrow vents at the top of the walls. With a surge of energy, I shoved to my feet, moving too fast again and finding it disorienting. I didn't even bother to pull my shirt up over my nose as some gas was pumped into my cell. There was no escaping it. At first, I suspected Order Suppressant, but my eyelids began to lower and the heavy call of sleep rushed over me. My knees hit the floor and as my eyes shuttered, I saw a fine set of boots walking toward me from the open door.

"Sleep, precious one," Roland's voice followed me into the dark. "Fate is calling."

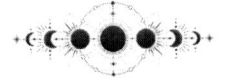

˖‹‹●●●››˖

The first thing I felt was motion. The floor was swaying from side to side and my stomach churned as the sleeping gas wore off at last. I had no idea how long it had been. Hours? Days? The only clue was the small measure of moonlight filtering through my eyelashes. Night had fallen, that was all I could be certain of.

I blinked and took in the cage I was contained in, the bars stretching overhead and pressing into my back where I lay. Just beyond them, a small, circular window let in the silver light of the moon, reminding me of my Rosa. She had such a connection with that celestial being, her power one of mystery and beauty. I'd always admired it, but now that I thought about it, maybe I'd never told her that. There were so many things I hadn't said. Too many words trapped in my heart, never to find their way to her. I hoped upon that moon and every star surrounding it that she wasn't dwelling on the loss of me. But it was a foolish thought. She had come for me in the depths of hell and had come so close to freeing me from the grasp of my chains, but she'd failed. And to her, that would be unacceptable. She would beat herself up and seek me out to the edges of the world to try to reclaim me, and of course I fucking loved her for that. Her strength was deeper than magic, it was a pure power of the soul. She would fight for me just as I would fight for her-

I frowned as that thought stalled me, my gaze falling to the full moon mate mark on my left wrist. She wasn't giving up, so why the fuck was I? I may not have been her Lion any longer, but I was still marked as her mate. She still deserved to have me do everything in my power to return to her.

A growl spilled from my lips as my new Order awakened, my fangs lengthening and that strange hunger stirring in my throat. I needed blood, and I'd gladly take it from any sorry asshole I found.

I pushed to my feet, that incessant rocking finally making sense as I got a better look out of the window. I was in a boat on the sea and from the feel of it, we had either recently docked or hadn't yet set off to wherever we were headed.

With the magic-blocking cuffs on my wrists, I still had no access to my power, but I did have this foreign Order to work with. I took hold of two bars of my cage, gripping firmly and trying to yank them apart. The Vampire in me awakened further, my strength increasing and the bars groaned then bent, wrenching wide enough for me to force my way through. I squeezed out and a burst of unexpected speed sent me crashing into the far wall. I cursed as I knocked over a stack of empty wooden crates, the sound sure to alert anyone close by.

"What was that?" a male voice barked up on deck.

"Check the cargo," a woman clipped and I was pretty sure I recognised Angie's voice.

I moved to the door, pressing myself to the wall beside it in the shadows

and waiting for someone to open it.

Several locks clicked along with the sense of a magical barrier fizzling out of existence, then the fool pushed the door wide and stepped into the room with his death.

I was upon him before he could do so much as scream, snapping his neck with my newfound strength and tossing his body to the floor. The urge to feed raced through me, but I had to get the fuck out of here first. With another burst of chaotic speed, I ran through the door and up the steps, racing onto the top deck and crashing into the main sail. The beam snapped from the collision, a wrenching of wood filling the air and drawing Angie's eyes my way from across the deck.

She gasped in fear, her hands raising and fire blooming in her palms.

"Stop!" she yelled as I ran at her, having no intention of following a single command she aimed at me.

The fireballs she sent flying my way were easy to avoid, my eyesight so sharp I could see them coming as if in slow motion. My legs responded even faster, weaving me left and right, even though I stumbled as I made it to Angie. We impacted hard, her body slamming to the deck beneath mine and I fisted my hand in her hair, threatening to rip her head clean off.

"Where is my Lion!?" I boomed in her face.

She flinched in terror, her hands clawing at my arms, her fire burning me, but I would never let her go.

"Roland has it!" she yelped. "It's already in the facility on the island. That way!"

She gestured and I looked, taking in the sandy beach and the rising hill that led up to a large walled compound at its summit.

I dug my fangs into her throat roughly, ripping into her skin and making it hurt until her screams quieted beneath my lips, finally taking a measure of vengeance in her death. I spat her blood from my lips, nothing about this bitch appealing to me despite my thirst, then I shoved upright from her limp body and leapt over the edge of the boat. I ran up the hill so fast it felt like I was flying, the palm trees a blur in my periphery, the moonlight blurring with the dark green foliage.

The moment I made it to the hill's peak, I realised I should have been more subtle. There were Fae everywhere, carrying cages filled with strange animals through a wide set of open wooden doors and down a series of steps into the building.

Roland was among them, standing beside a large cage where a beastly creature was hunched over inside it. My eyes locked on him and I ran faster, needing to claim his death this day and make him suffer for what he'd done to me. But not before he returned my Lion.

His dark left eye wheeled my way and he stumbled back in fright, his hand flying to the cage beside him and unlocking it with a flash of magic. The door sprung open and the beastly thing inside stepped out, placing itself between me and Roland while cries of fright punctured the air around us.

I came to a stumbling halt as the creature snarled at me, preparing to take it on and fight my way to the Fae I despised more than any other in this world. The beast was tall, layered with hair over thick muscles, almost ape-like in its gait, but its face…I knew that face, though his tattoos were now missing and his eyes were like two vacant strips of earth.

"Gustard?" I rasped, the horror of seeing him like this freezing me for too long. Whatever Roland had done to him had transformed him into a monster.

Gustard's fist swung at me, colliding with my skull and I staggered sideways, my ear ringing from the impact.

"Capture him!" Roland directed. "Do not kill him!"

For some reason, Gustard complied, swinging at me again, but I was ready this time, ducking it and throwing a punch of my own. It cracked against his ribs, but the impact was like striking iron, my knuckles screaming in pain.

"Use your psychic abilities to disarm him," Roland called to Gustard.

He opened his mouth, revealing sharp teeth and a horrid screeching noise ripped from his throat.

Everyone around me cried out as that noise pitched through the air and burrowed through my skull. But it wasn't aimed at them, it was aimed at me, driving through my head like an anvil and forcing me to submit to it.

I hit the dusty ground, clawing at the dirt while trying to get back up, but the power in that sound bound my limbs. It shuddered through me and weakened me until I was just a useless wreck at Gustard's feet.

Roland stepped over me, his hand slapping to my forehead and his two eyes merging together into one. *Cyclops.*

His power slipped into my head and I was helpless to fight it off as he forced my mind to shut down, making me sleep once more.

"You're mine," Roland purred as I fell away into oblivion once more. "Sleep now, Nightroary. When you wake again, we will have work to do."

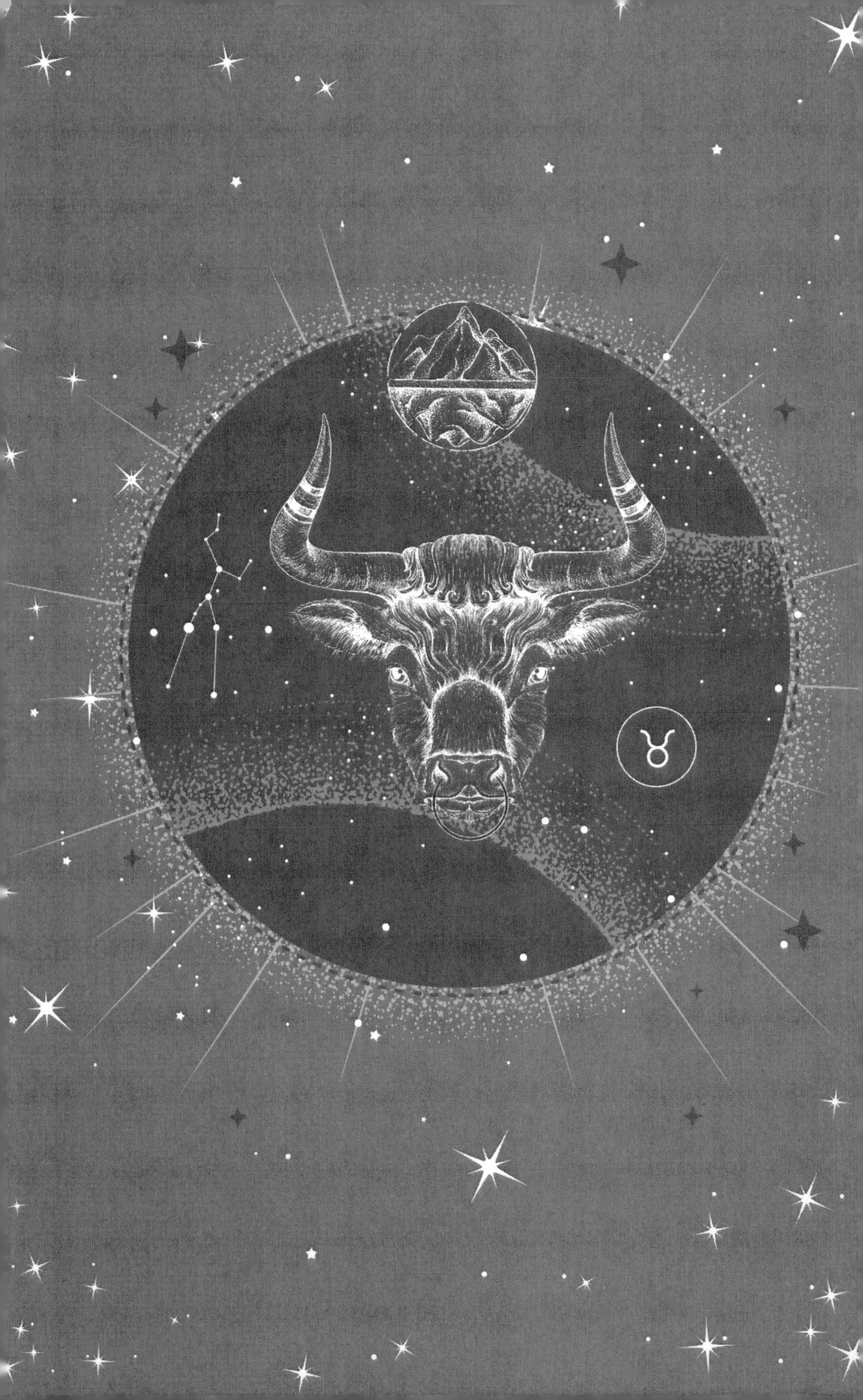

ROSALIE

PRISONER #12

CHAPTER NINE

The moon hung in a deep crescent close to the horizon in the distance far out across the sea, almost as if she were beckoning us closer.

I checked the small backpack I'd filled in preparation of our departure, counting the contents for the third time as if they might have somehow changed. We didn't know what we were heading into exactly and that left far too many unanswered questions for my liking. It was the kind of job I wouldn't have taken on if offered it. Too many variables, too many unknowns. I liked a challenge and the thrill of the odd surprise but this was all risk and high stakes beyond the point of any form of prediction. I was used to changing tactics and going up against bad odds but the island we were headed towards was almost entirely unpredictable.

We couldn't stardust there – none of us had been there before to be able to guide us to the place but even if we had known it, we couldn't learn enough about the location to attempt it as the ticket clearly warned that there were wards in place against such arrival. It was also why we hadn't been able to disguise ourselves magically. Jerome had been certain that there would be wards against all forms of illusion too so we'd had to go the old fashioned route of hair dye and bravado.

No doubt the entire island was going to be full of security measures, all aimed to keep the authorities firmly out of the nefarious business which was conducted in the criminals' secluded pit of sins, but they would work just as certainly against us too.

I wasn't afraid of what it might take to do this, but I was determined to succeed, so we had to be prepared.

In the attic of this little Oscura cabin, I'd located the arms cache and retrieved a handful of fire canisters from their depths. The small metal bombs had been created with a violent mixture of Faesine and fire magic – an everflame trapped behind a small, glass window within the metal contraption just waiting to be let loose on the incredibly flammable liquid. They smashed easily on impact with any hard surface and exploded instantly, but they were temperamental little bastardos and carrying them came with a fairly high possibility of going boom by accident.

Obviously, I wasn't going to be letting Sin anywhere near them.

Alongside my nasty little friends I'd packed some food, a bottle of water and a shot of a potion my great uncle Marco called 'jazzy eyes'. It was most definitely illegal as shit but he swore by it for any and all jobs he went on. I'd seen jazzy eyes in action and, in fairness to Marco, his shot of crazy potion worked a treat on anyone who happened to be in need of it. It was what Dante referred to as a later-than-last-resort tactic – basically a concoction of fuck knew what which would kick start even a Fae on their death bed. It would give them enough energy to run for their damn lives should they find themselves in a situation where their magic was tapped out and they needed to heal and escape. It didn't do shit to heal anything magically, but it blocked out pain and gave a jolt of adrenaline which could rival a shock from a Storm Dragon, though the side effects included hallucinations, hysteria and the potential for a serious case of the shits - to name a few. My cousin Luigi had once run three miles on a broken ankle to escape the FIB while riding high on jazzy eyes so I knew it worked – but I hadn't wanted to listen to the stories about the side effects all the same. Safe to say, I was hoping we wouldn't be needing it, but I'd gathered a shot for each of us anyway.

"Are you ready, love?" Ethan asked, shouldering his own pack of supplies as he walked into the room.

I looked him over, inspecting the new, dark colour to his hair just as he took in the deep red of mine. He was still easy to recognise if you asked me, but it did make me look twice and I guessed someone who wasn't so familiar with the curve of his lips, the sharp line of his jaw or the depth of his blue eyes might not realise who he was.

I said nothing. My heart was beating so fast that it was all I could do to concentrate on quieting it. Everything was riding on this. It *had* to work. Ethan moved closer to me, lifting a lock of my dyed hair between his fingers and inspecting it.

"It suits you," he said as I lifted my eyes to his.

He ran his fingertips along my jaw, looking at the makeup I wore, the edges of his mouth lifting. I'd gone heavy on the eyeliner and painted my lips a deep red while pencilling a scattering of freckles over my nose and cheeks. Again, it wasn't perfect but it was damn far from my usual style and the bare faced, dark-haired wild girl in all the mugshots.

"You look so…sophisticated," Ethan teased and I snorted. "The others are waiting outside."

I blew out a breath and took a well-worn deck of tarot cards from the coffee table, shuffling them slowly and letting my eyes fall closed as I began to deal them onto the table before me. My fingers tingled with each selection I made until I'd laid ten cards out before me.

My gaze roamed over the cards as I read them, Ethan's shadow engulfing me as he moved to lean over my shoulder and take in their meaning too.

The first card I'd drawn was The Hermit reversed, representing isolation and a loss of direction. The following few seemed to whisper of Roary's incarceration, the Nine of Swords, Justice reversed, the Wheel of Fortune reversed – basically a whole shit heap. But then I moved my eyes over the following cards, the ones indicating what the plan I'd made might lead towards; the Five of Wands whispering of struggle, The Hanged Man indicating sacrifice, The Tower hissing warnings of disaster, the Five of Swords which I took to indicate an escalation of violence but last of all, offering me the hope I so desperately needed, my gaze locked on The Devil who was blessedly, beautifully reversed. Freedom. Release.

Hope was a dangerous thing, but I'd been living for the flickering flame of it for too long to back out now and that little fire blazed brighter as I took solace in the message I'd gleaned from the cards.

"The cards hold good omens," Ethan said gruffly, squeezing my shoulder in reassurance.

I nodded in silence, not wanting to jinx anything by breaking it and fastening my pack carefully before lifting it onto my back. Adrenaline spiked through my veins at the thought of the combustibles I was now carrying, but I lifted my chin and strode from the door like there was nothing at all to worry about.

Cain watched me as I passed him, and I searched his eyes, expecting to find a reluctant kind of acceptance there but instead I found blazing concern. He hadn't said anything to me about the way I had clearly lost my shit over this, but the way he was looking at me made me think there was something he was holding back on.

"You don't have to come," I said, glancing at Hastings and including him in that statement too.

My little choir boy had dyed his hair black and styled his fringe to hang down over his eyes. He wore a backwards baseball cap and a leather jacket with a pair of jeans which looked like they might just fall off his ass. I wasn't quite sure what he looked like, but I guessed it wasn't the prim and proper guard with his finely pressed uniform anyway. Unsurprisingly, Cain had refused to alter his appearance at all.

I frowned. "I know you think the curse requires you to stick with me and help me or whatever, but I don't think that has anything to do with how it's broken. And I don't want anyone following me into this mess if they aren't all in. We might die out there. I'm *willing* to die if that's what it takes to rescue Roary. And I can't bring you with me if I'm going to have to worry about you grabbing hold of me and trying to whisk me away from there if things start going south."

"You expect me to stay back here like some cowardice piece of shit?" Cain grunted.

"No. I think you're a lot of things, Mason Cain, but I don't think you've been afraid of a fight a day in your life. That doesn't mean you won't pull the same shit you did back at Darkmore and try to rescue me again though. So I want your word that you won't and I'll take a star vow on it too – from all of you," I added, glancing at Ethan and Sin to make sure they understood this. I wasn't going to be leaving that island without Roary. "I can't leave him behind for a third time. If that means I have to go alone to get this done, I will. I entered Darkmore on my own, so it's not like I haven't done it before."

I held out my hand, waiting to see which of them would take it.

Sin didn't surprise me when he was the first to clasp my palm. "I'll follow you into death before I steal you away from your Lion, wild girl," he swore. "We leave with Roary in tow or we step through The Veil at his side – no more running away."

I smiled darkly at that promise and magic flared between our palms, binding us to it. Sin's eyes brightened with the thought of death. It didn't surprise me in the least that he wasn't afraid of it.

I turned to Ethan next, waiting as he looked me over, his jaw locked with tension. He met my eyes, the blue of his appearing brighter out here beneath the sky as if freedom from that underground hell had awakened a new spark of life in him. I knew it went against everything in his instincts to make me this vow. A Wolf protected their mate above all else, but that was also why he *had* to make it. Roary was my mate too. And Ethan had to know that I couldn't go on without him any longer.

"Whatever it takes, love," he swore, clapping his hand into mine, magic ringing between us. "He's coming home."

I nodded firmly, that oath lashing itself to my heart and giving me the strength I needed to face whatever it was we were about to go up against. Roary needed me at my best if I was going to pull this off and that's what he would get.

I turned to Cain last, Sin and Ethan backing me on either side and the man who had been my guard, tormentor, enemy and saviour surveyed me with a look so powerful that I could feel the weight of it running over me.

"This is madness," he said roughly. "You understand that, don't you?"

"No more insane than getting myself locked up in Darkmore with the intention of breaking out," I replied with a shrug of a shoulder.

He grunted his agreement, not seeming to know what to say to that.

"You're a force of fucking nature, Rosalie Oscura. I think back on every moment with you and wonder at which point I might have saved myself from the madness of you. But I can't find one. From the second I brought you into the prison, snarling and smiling with equal finesse, I think you held me captive. So I might as well admit that I'm lost to you at this point. My fate is in your hands. And if that fate requires this oath from me then fine. You can have it. I won't make you run from him a second time. I'll be by your side to see this through, come death or dawn."

He took my hand, sealing the promise with a clap of magic and I offered him a smile utterly free of bullshit for once.

"A morte e ritorno," I purred and his lips lifted a little, telling me he had picked up on the meaning of my famiglia's motto.

"A morte e ritorno," Cain echoed then Sin yelled it and Ethan barked a laugh before repeating it too.

I turned towards the path which led down to the ocean. Jerome had given us intel on a harbour in a town a few miles south of here where we'd be able to secure a boat before heading out to sea to track down this cursed island.

My boots skidded in the gravel as Hastings stepped in front of me, raising his chin and expelling a harsh breath.

"I will do what it takes to live up to your goals, Rosalie," he said, offering me his hand and I blinked at him in surprise.

I hadn't really expected any kind of promise from him – he was a beta at best, really more delta – mid level pack kinda dude, points for physical strength but deductions for not having the bite to go with that brawn. I didn't need promises from him because I had just assumed he'd follow our lead, and even if he didn't, I had no concerns over him being able to stop me from doing what I needed to if it came down to it.

"I knew I could rely on you anyway, ragazzo del coro," I told him, patting him on the arm and refusing to take his hand. I wouldn't prise a star vow from Hastings. If he needed to run to survive this mess then he was free to do so.

I started walking down the hill, leading the way but whirling back around as a shout of alarm cut through the air. Magic built in my fingertips, adrenaline spiking through me but I only found Cain and Sin wrestling in the dirt.

"Hold still and take it, baby. You'll like it once I'm done," Sin panted while Cain punched him so hard in the ribs that I heard bone crack.

I strode back over to them, barking an order for Sin to get off of Cain while he knelt over him, using air to pin him down.

I grabbed Sin's shoulder as I made it to them, but he leapt up without making me haul him off of Cain.

"There," Sin announced triumphantly, and I backed up as Cain shoved to his feet, swiping a hand over his mouth.

"Did you kiss him?" Ethan accused and Sin roared a laugh.

"Nah – Cainy boy only wants our Rosa's tongue in his mouth. I just got him on board with the incognito plan seeing as he wasn't playing ball. Can't have him exposing all of us with his recognisable face," Sin said.

"What the fuck have you done to me?" Cain demanded and a bark of surprised laughter escaped me as he dropped his hand, revealing the pencil-thin douchebag moustache Sin had scrawled over his upper lip with a pen. It had little flicks at the end and everything. Fuck knew how he'd drawn it so neatly while Cain had been thrashing about.

"You look…debonair," Sin announced, chuckling to himself as he casually healed his cracked ribs.

Cain bared his fangs and the effect was so comical with the little moustache curling up over them that I laughed louder.

"It's fool-proof," I agreed, taking the baseball cap from Hastings's head and placing it on Cain's instead, pulling the peak down to shadow his murderous eyes.

"Show me," Cain snarled.

"There." Ethan pointed towards the window of the little cabin which was casting a decent reflection in the moonlight.

Cain strode over to it to inspect his new look, a feral snarl spilling from him as he tried to wipe the moustache off.

"I wouldn't bother with that, kitten. This here is a perma-pen. No wishy washy is gonna get that sucker off for at least a week," Sin said.

"You fucking hypocrite," Cain growled at him. "You haven't made any attempt to disguise yourself either."

"That's because I can do this," Sin replied, shifting before us and becoming an extremely pale, bulky dude with long white hair that trailed down to his ass and a scar through his eyebrow. "I shrank my cock too – because that's the most recognisable part of me after all," Sin added in a sultry voice which was nothing like his usual rough tone.

"What possible reason might you have to get your cock out during this?" Cain hissed, taking the lead down the path and I let him because I wasn't sure I could stop myself from laughing if I had to keep looking at that moustache the whole way into town.

"That, my dear, dastardly, deprived dandelion, is precisely why you're so uptight. I can think of eighty-six different scenarios in which the exposure of my dick would be integral to this little mission of ours without even trying. What if there is a cock-sized hole in the bottom of our boat that needs plugging? What if I have to slap a dog but both of my hands are otherwise occupied? What if I'm tapped out and need a quick power fuck with my wild girl in the bushes – which, incidentally, I think I will need to do seven times before we make it to this boaty village place. What if-"

Cain threw a punch which Sin dodged before slapping him in return then taking off down the path at a sprint with a wild giggle.

Cain shot after him furiously and I watched them go while Ethan took my hand and kept pace at my side, Hastings trailing along behind us like a dutiful puppy.

"It's nice when the kids entertain themselves for a bit, isn't it?" Ethan purred and the smile which had found me since seeing that douchey little moustache on Cain's upper lip remained in place while we walked on.

The moon glimmered overhead and for some reason, I felt more sure than ever that we were on the path which would bring us back to Roary and guide our pack home together at last.

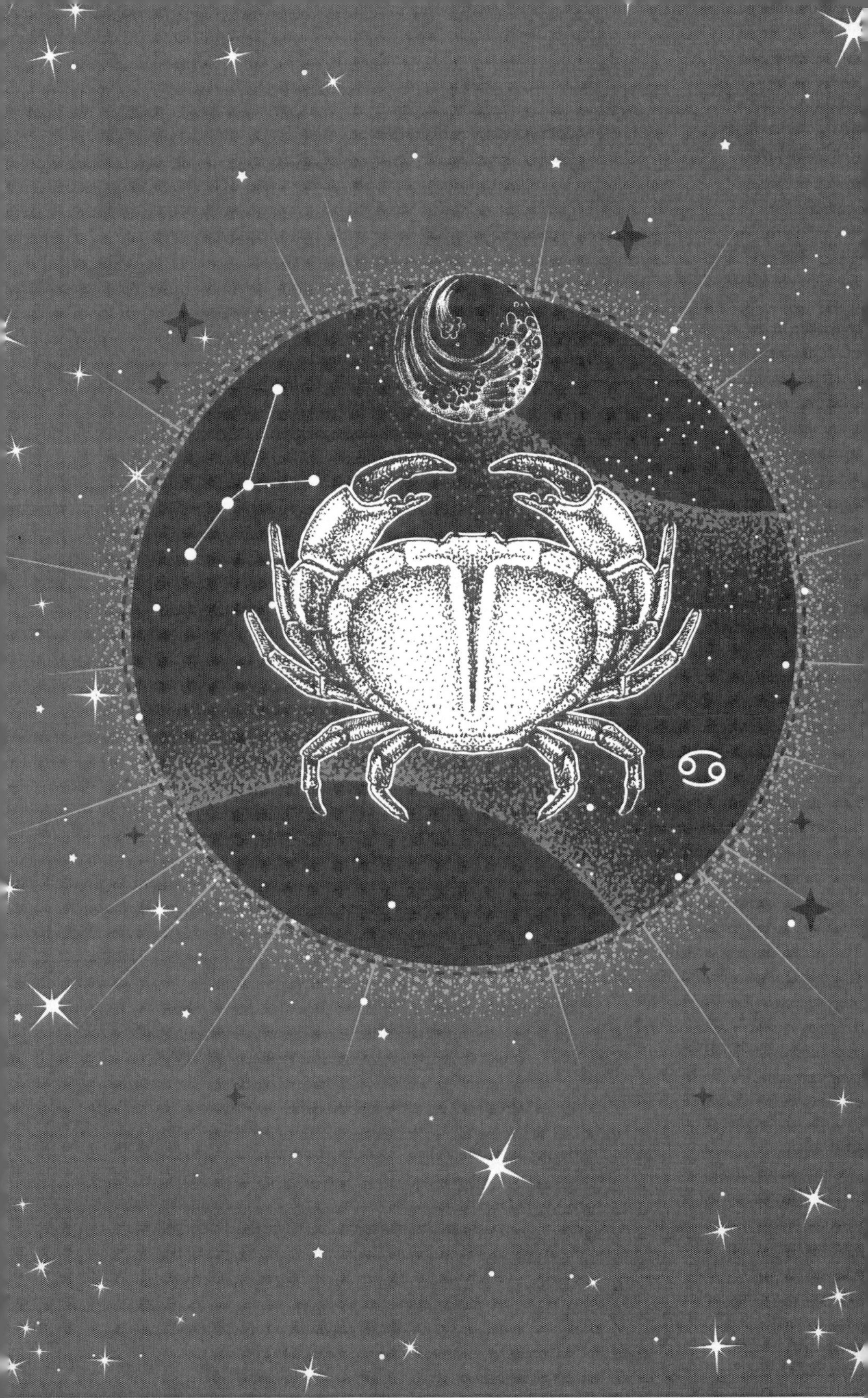

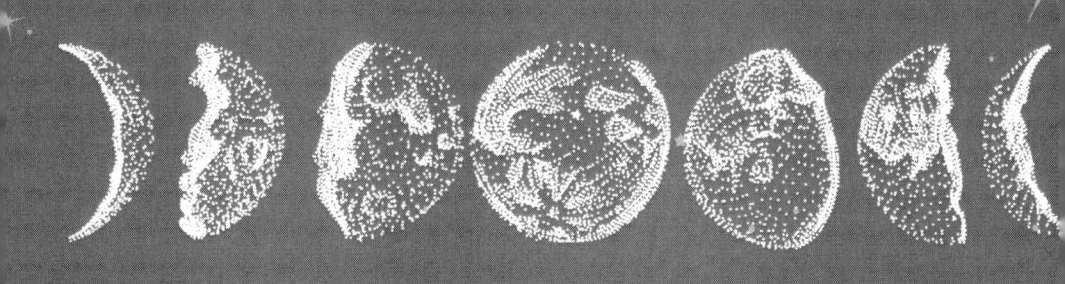

ETHAN

PRISONER #1

CHAPTER TEN

"This is bad," I hissed.

"As bad as a sinning lemon in a church full of pious melons? Lemons are the anti-melons by the way," Sin whispered back as he shuffled closer beside me in the long grass.

We were up on a hill, looking down into the town that swept away towards the sea in a narrow cove, a dock full of boats sitting there and waiting to be claimed. But unlike the quiet village we'd been expecting according to Jerome, this place was hosting some kind of wild party. A party that had gotten so out of hand that the FIB had shown up and were handcuffing a bunch of teenagers who had set a bakery alight.

"Any thoughts, love?" I asked, turning from Sin to Rosalie on my other side. The deep red of her hair caught my attention, the change making her look older somehow, or perhaps that was just the pain in her eyes. I liked the red but I preferred the black of her natural colour, the darkness suiting her best, dressing her up in swathes of night sky even on the brightest of days so that she could always appear close to the moonlight.

"Maybe we have no choice but to kill them all," Hastings said darkly just beyond her, flicking his head so his fringe swept to the right then fell back over his eyes.

Rosalie clucked her tongue at him. "Don't be an idiota," she hissed. "The FIB aren't here for us. We can sneak through the town."

"I say we head for the cliff and travel via the water," Cain suggested from beyond Hastings.

"The moustached fruit loop has a point," Sin agreed in a rough voice, still wearing the face of the long-haired man with the apparently small cock. "But the thing is…"

"What?" I turned to him, finding him springing to his feet.

"Distractions are more fun!" He raced off down the hill, shooting blasts of fire towards the sky and yodelling at the top of his lungs.

"Holy fuck," I cursed.

"A plan's a plan, even if it is one dipped in insanity." Rosalie shoved to her feet, directing us after her down the right of the hillside while Sin skipped away to the left, causing more and more of a ruckus as he went.

"Can't catch me!" he yelled, dropping his disguised form to reveal his true face and hurling something from his pocket at the group of FIB which looked suspiciously like a lemon. It whacked one of them in the head and they turned form the teenagers they were apprehending, finding Sin cartwheeling their way, his hands and feet on fire, setting light to the grass as he went.

"He'll get himself caught," Cain said gruffly, and I was surprised that he didn't sound entirely hopeful about that prospect. More concerned if anything.

"He's got this," Rosalie tossed back at us. "Now keep close."

"I'm ready to die," Hastings gritted out, flicking his fringe again with a toss of his head. "Chaos calls my name."

"Sure it does, bud." I slapped him on the shoulder, shoving him ahead of us because his legs weren't moving fast enough for my liking.

We made it to a busy street of partying Fae where banners with an image of a black sun hung around them on the walls. Rosalie slowed her pace, snatching a cup of wine from a woman's hand.

"Hail to the moon!" she howled.

"Awooo!" a few random Wolves howled in agreement, looking her way and recognising an Alpha in their midst.

I snatched a cup too, blending in as we moved through the crowd and chancing a look over my shoulder to try and catch sight of Sin. The hillside was going up in a blaze and I could just hear the shouts of FIB as they tried to capture him. It was a risky plan, but of course Sin had chosen this route instead of the subtle one. It was his ass on the line so I wasn't complaining, but the thought of him being caught did tug on something in my chest.

He had become a friend, unlikely as that prospect had once been. But his brand of madness was growing on me, and a wild creature like that didn't belong in the depths of Darkmore. Sure, his victims might say differently, but from what he'd told me of his ethos, they tended to be of the nasty variety, so all the better that he was out here killing Fae like that anyway.

"What are they celebrating?" I muttered to Cain and as he shrugged, a woman with her tits out and the planets painted around her nipples leapt towards me.

"You must know! It's Earth's Aphelion! We've been partying since dawn!"

"Oh, that's tonight?" I said, though I'd had no idea it was even coming up.

I'd spent too long in Darkmore and tracking astrological events had been kinda lost to me. It wasn't like the guards bothered to let us know when they happened anyway, but Earth's Aphelion had once been a big cause for partying in Alestria. It was the annual day of the year when Earth's orbit was farthest from the sun. It was often called the day of the Black Sun and was a day of possibilities, potential and vitality, but it could also summon chaos, and that could go two ways for us. Good or bad.

"Keep it moving," Cain urged, nudging me along and Rosalie nodded, guiding us forward, weaving through the crowd and hurrying down the winding streets.

We passed one road where people were taking it in turns attempting to ride a giant replica of the sun down a hill, the ground altered by earth magic to create a sort of pinball machine while air elementals blasted the ball in all directions. It was the kind of thing I would have enjoyed once, and I longed for a time where we could bask in peace again.

If we got Roary back, I didn't know where we would go next. We would always be on the run from the law now, hiding in the shadows, moving from place to place. How could we ever settle anywhere for long?

I thought of my family, longing to return to them too, but I couldn't risk being caught at their door. I needed the heat to die down before I made my approach, but in all the adrenaline building up to the breakout of Darkmore, I'd never considered that the dangers would be far from over once we made it out. I'd been so caught up in the dream of freedom that I'd forgotten the price it would come at. I would be an outlaw from now until I died.

I made to turn away from the street where the sun ball was being rolled back to the top of the hill ready for the next participant, but stalled as Sin came into view, racing along tossing fireballs and lemons over his shoulders at the FIB officers chasing him.

He leapt onto the sun ball, landing on his feet before hurtling down the hill towards us, the thing bouncing off of the obstacles while he used air magic to keep himself upright.

"Dalle stelle," Rosalie swore as Sin waved at us and the FIB officers came hurtling down into the obstacle course, slipping on some slick substance on the flagstones and stumbling all over the place.

Sin leapt off of the sun ball and landed in front of us, twisting around and using air to send the ball flying back at the officers. It crashed into them, knocking them to the ground as they scrambled to avoid it.

"Take that you ball-chafed sunfuckers!" he bayed, then he shifted as he darted into the crowd and the FIB officers cried out in confusion as they lost sight of him.

"Go!" Sin cried, wheeling around and shoving me on. He currently appeared as a busty blonde with legs longer than mine and pink glitter staining her skin, indicating a Pegasus shifter. But that chaos in his eyes was easily recognisable so I had no doubts that it was him.

Rosalie howled as she took off ahead of us and Sin powered along beside me with a feral look in his eyes and a twisted smile on his lips. The dock came into view as we turned down another street and Rosalie led us up a jetty, leaping onto a decent sized yacht called The Wave Wanderer.

"Untether her!" Rosalie called and Cain and I split apart to release the ropes holding the boat while Sin jumped onboard and started hoisting sails with Rosalie.

When I had the rope released, I looked around for Hastings, finding a couple of the FIB officers tearing down the street toward us. The ex prison guard stood at the end of the dock, his black hair blowing in the wind and his hands raised.

"Stay back!" Hastings cried. "I am the dark in the dead of the night!"

Water magic exploded from his hands and slammed into the officers, sending them skidding into a wall where he froze them in place.

I gaped at what he'd done, his stand against the authorities shocking me. He might have made declarations about being one of us now, but I hadn't truly believed the dude until that moment.

More FIB agents appeared, racing down the street, looking all around in confusion and calling out to each other in search of Sin. Rosalie flicked a hand out, casting an illusion of him further up the hill and sending it racing away along the cliff path with a raucous giggle. The FIB spotted the illusion and took chase with yells pouring from their lips and magic spilling from their hands.

"Come on," I barked at Sin and he wheeled around, smiling gleefully before slapping on a more serious look and nodding to me as he ran by.

He leapt onto the boat and I followed with Cain and Hastings close behind me just as Sin blasted air magic at the sails and we went flying out into the cove.

I hurried to the back of the vessel, wielding the water and forcing it to drive us to sea even faster, the FIB none the wiser about the rest of us being present and now fully occupied with chasing the false Sin along the cliff path.

The land was shrinking away and my heart rate settled at last as the town became nothing but a glittering slit between two long cliffs.

I turned, finding Rosalie leaping at me, her lips pressing to mine as I caught her.

"How's that for a night of chaos on the day of the Black Sun, love?" I murmured against her soft lips. She lingered against me a moment longer, pulling back and leaning into Sin who had closed in behind her, once again returned to his true form, his eyes blazing with victory.

He nuzzled her neck and nipped at her, making her smile gleam. She thrived here in the wildness, and I guessed that was why she wasn't angry at him for the plan he had concocted back there. I could see how the pieces of her fit us all in different ways. Even Cain brought out a side to her that was different to the one she aimed at me. But there was a part missing now and we were finally on our way to returning it to her, making our girl whole once again.

"How far to the island?" Cain asked, slinking out of the shadow the sail was casting.

Rosalie moved to him, her fingers winding between his and he pulled her close as if instinctively. I didn't know when I'd accepted Cain as one of us, but perhaps I'd known it for a long time now. It was that look in her eye when she turned her gaze on him. Even when she had been furious with him, there had always been something underpinning it. Like she had claimed him long before she'd realised she'd done it.

"At this pace, we should make it in no time," she said.

"The moon will keep my magic recharged, I can run laps of the boat when my power starts to wane," I said. "I can keep us moving like this if you want to stop casting air, Sin."

The Incubus inclined his head. "I can keep casting too so long as someone's sucking my cock. We can make a disco of it. Cain can hum a tune." He looked from me to Rosalie as if one of us was about to volunteer to go down on him then even tossed a sideways glance at Hastings.

"No cock sucking," Rosalie decided firmly.

"A ball rub?" he asked.

"No," she said.

"A finger up the butt?" he suggested, glancing my way. "You can do it to Ethan while I watch, you might find a trinket or two up there. It's how he carries his coin purse around."

"I do not," I snipped.

"*Sure* you don't," Sin said, tossing me a wink and I scowled.

I moved to lean against the back railing, guiding the ocean beneath our boat and pushing us onward while Sin headed off to swing on the boom of the main sail.

Rosalie stayed with me as the others peeled off too and I noticed Cain pressing a hand to Hastings' shoulder. I caught a snippet of the praise he handed his guard buddy for dealing with the FIB and Hastings' neck turned red, his chin lifting as he smiled at Cain.

Rosalie climbed up to sit on the rail, her legs swinging beneath her as she tipped her head back to look at the stars. "Do you think they're on our side tonight?"

"I think any creature that is watching you would be compelled to assist you in any way it could. The stars included."

"You're a sweet talker, Ethan Shadowbrook," she said with a dry look. "Full of the best kind of bullshit."

"No, love. I say it how it is. I call the sky blue and the grass green. You're the reason this plan has any hope of working. Because I believe the stars can't help but play favourites sometimes, and right now, you're their most prized treasure."

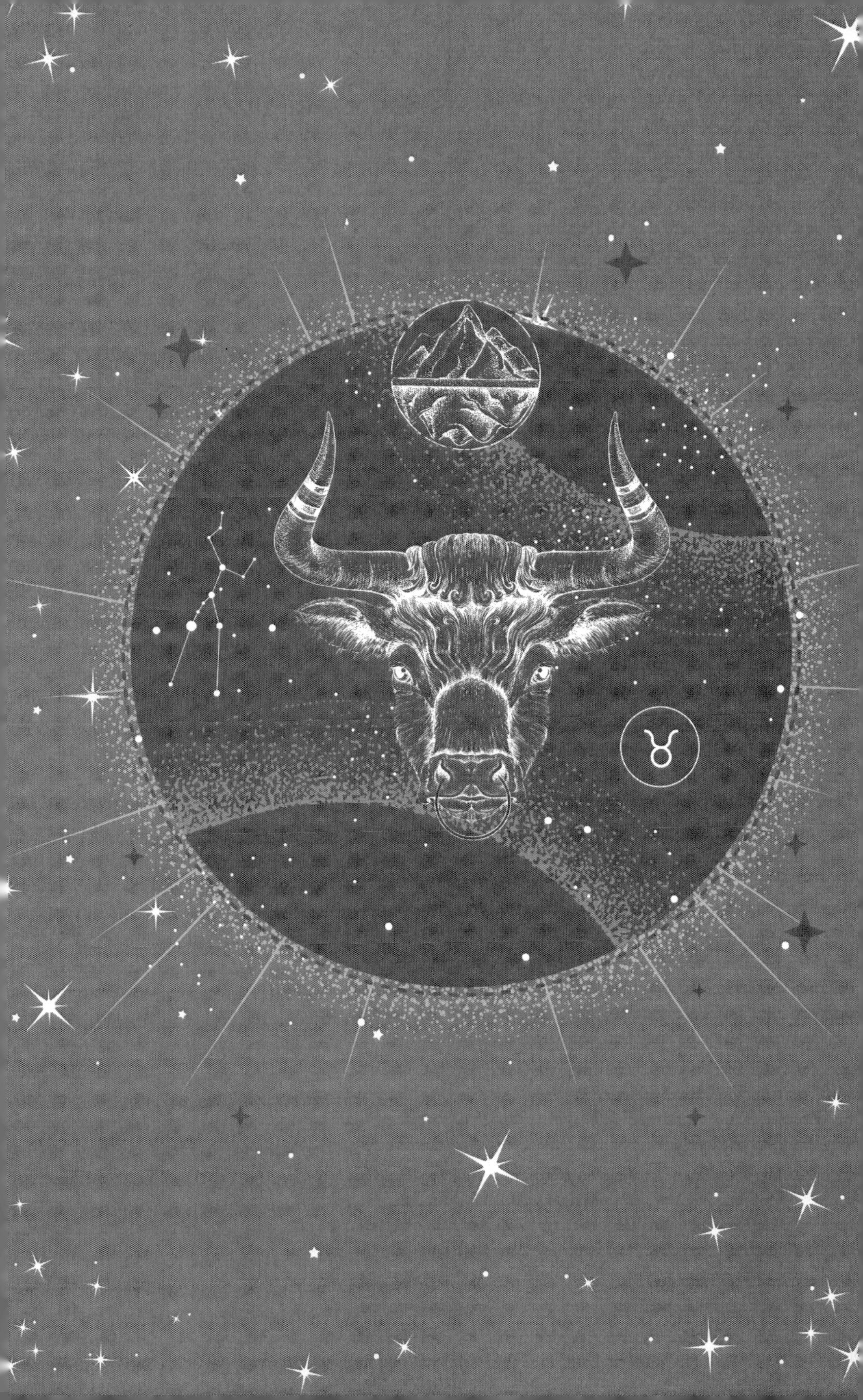

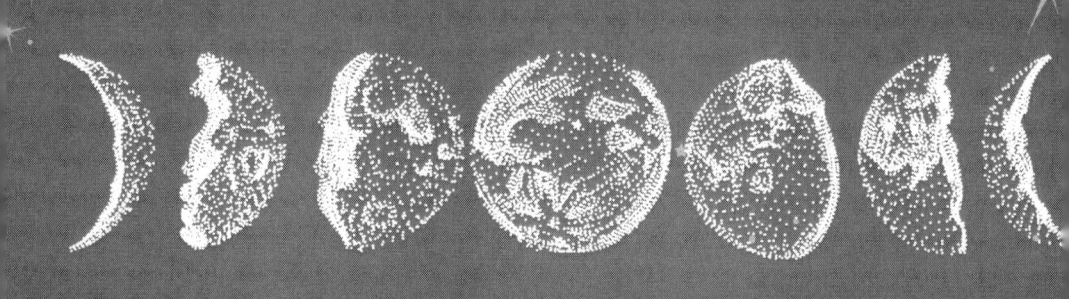

ROSALIE

PRISONER #12

CHAPTER ELEVEN

The night was balmy, the moon hanging low over the ocean and the repetitive lapping of the waves against the boat sounding like the hands of a clock ticking down. Ahead of us, where we expected Grimolda Isle to be, there was nothing but darkness, and yet we remained on course.

My skin prickled as we moved across the ocean, the night full of whispers and secrets. Ahead of us, the world grew even darker, the waves themselves fading into a black so impenetrable that it seemed unnatural.

"That's one hell of a concealment spell," Cain muttered at my side, my red hair blowing over my face in response to the wind caused by his sudden arrival.

"I guess they don't want to be found," I agreed, my eyes sweeping from one edge of that impenetrable darkness to the other as I tried to figure out the scale of the hidden island ahead of us.

"This thing isn't going to be pretty," Cain said, his hand curling around the wooden rail that lined the deck of the boat. His black shirt was unbuttoned at his throat and I moved closer to him, hooking my fingers through another button and pulling that free too, revealing more of his muscled chest.

"Pretty never suited me anyway," I purred, my finger roaming down to his next button before I withdrew it, leaving him swallowing thickly and forcing his eyes back out over the water.

All of the fear I'd been filled with, the angst, pain and pure terror was slipping away at last. I was a creature born for the fight and now that we were drawing closer to it, I finally found my pulse settling, that deadly calm which I knew so well falling over me.

This wouldn't work if we lost our heads. So mine was going to stay screwed on tight.

"When we dock you'll come with me," I told Cain. "We're going to slip right into the heart of that place and figure out where Roary is. As soon as we have a lock on him, Sin and Ethan will cause a distraction. Between my moon gifts and your speed, we should be able to get Roary out before they even realise what's happening."

"You're assuming we'll be able to find him easily," Cain replied. "What if he's locked up tight somewhere – what if he isn't here at all?"

"He's here," I replied firmly. "I can feel it."

Cain arched a brow but didn't seem inclined to disagree with me. Perhaps he was finally done underestimating me and what I was capable of. Besides, I was confident in my assessment of what we were about to face because the moon was urging me on and she was the one who had given me Roary in the first place, so I trusted her help in our reunion.

The darkness grew before us until I couldn't see beyond it without turning to face the rear of our small vessel.

"Into the dark we go," Ethan murmured, moving to stand on my other side, his fingers twining with mine.

"Oh how I thrive in the unseen places," Sin purred.

A dark smile captured my lips, the invisible wind tangling with my hair as our little boat sailed into the pitch black and enveloped us entirely.

"By the stars," Hastings gasped from somewhere behind me. "Oh sweet starlight please deliver us from this hellish nothing."

Whether the stars had granted his wish or fate simply chose that moment to deliver us from the dark, I wasn't sure, but the boat slipped through that void of nothingness and blinding light burned it away.

I lifted a hand to shield my eyes, squinting against the flare of two huge bonfires that were blazing on the beach ahead of us. I blinked while my sight adjusted, taking in the packed harbour and the wooden walkway beyond it which led to the beach and the gated citadel beyond.

A wall of wooden posts topped with sharp points spanned the beach in both directions, punctured only by the huge gate in its centre where a group of savage-looking Fae stood guard.

The scent of smoke filled the air, mixing with the salt of the sea and an underlying scent of decay.

"Here," I said, taking the vials of jazzy eyes from my pocket and handing one to each of our group. I'd explained the use of it to all of them already and I hoped we wouldn't end up in need of it, but I figured it never hurt to have a solid backup plan.

"How long until I can start killing things?" Sin asked me sweetly as our boat moved closer to the doc. He had changed his appearance again, now looking like a ripped Harpy with bronze wings and chin length auburn hair. It was a little unsettling to be addressing the face of a stranger but when I looked into his eyes, I could still see the man I knew so well peering back out at me.

"I'll give you a signal once we've located Roary. Until then, behave yourself, monster of mine," I warned him.

"Just call me good boy until further notice," Sin replied with a wicked grin and Cain snorted irritably.

I picked up my pack, carefully positioning it on my back and steeling myself for what would come next.

The boat jolted beneath us and I gripped the rail, looking down into the water as we were jerked forward and spotting a pair of Shark Shifters hauling us along at speed.

Ethan moved to look down into the water with me, but we remained silent now that we were so close to prying ears.

The Sharks dragged our boat into a position along the dock and I led the group as I disembarked onto the boardwalk.

Several leering goons watched us as we passed but I ignored them, striding straight towards the gates without so much as glancing in their direction.

Three sets of heavy footsteps echoed mine, a fourth stumbling along at a hurried pace at the back of the group. My jaw ticked. Hastings might have been a bad call for this job. He was eager and determined to find himself a new place now that he had abandoned Darkmore for good, but I was doubtful that he was cut out for a life of crime. Ethan had promised to keep an eye on him though, and I doubted he could cause too much trouble for us. So long as he didn't blow our cover before we made it inside.

We approached the gates together, the leering guards all turning their focus on our group as we passed between them.

I kept my gaze fixed on the big bastardo blocking the way on and ignored the rest. He was a Minotaur, not in his fully shifted form but his horns were on show, one of them cracked and broken at the tip, the other stained in what appeared to be blood. He had a large nose ring and a face tattoo of a charging bull beneath his right eye. Very intimidating, I was sure. For any other stronzo that was.

I held out my invite with an irritable sigh, casting a glance at Cain as he moved to stand at my side.

The Minotaur inspected the thick card, turning it in the light and casting some spell over it which I assumed was to assess it for authenticity.

I wondered whether there was anything about it which marked it as Pike's. News of her death was widespread after all and if they could tell this had been hers then we might have to fight our way in from the offset.

Luckily for the Minotaur and his buddies, that wasn't the case.

"Bidding is about to start if you're here for the auction," he grunted at me, waving us past him. "You're cutting it damn fine."

"Thanks for the tip, udders," I replied, sweeping past him, climbing a hill through the jungle and leading our group into the compound at its peak.

A dirt pathway opened up ahead of us, a crowd milling around a marketplace which took up the space, selling illegal wares and trading in dark curses. I could hear an auctioneer calling out in the distance, already taking bids on something but I had no interest in whatever that might be.

I eyed a stall filled with shrieking slifian horn crabs and took in the goat-like creature standing stoically behind them. It watched me with a knowing glint in its eyes, fire kindling around its pale lips.

Wordlessly, I cut a path between the stalls, ignoring the yells from traders offering all manner of ill-conceived and outlawed merchandise. Ethan hissed a command at Hastings to stop gawping like a virgin bride and I glanced over my shoulder at them with a firm look.

"Time to split up," I murmured as we approached a stone archway carved with vicious effigies of the star signs, the ferocious looking Leo symbol part way through ripping the head from a poor Fae who had crossed its path.

"And then I can-" Sin began excitedly but I caught the front of his shirt in my fist, yanking him to me and speaking so close to his lips that we were almost kissing.

"You will wait," I reminded him, staring into green eyes which weren't his at all.

He stretched his Harpy wings in protest then sighed, nodding once. "I'll wait, wild girl," he swore, tilting his chin to kiss me but I stepped back before he could.

"I'll taste your lips when they're your own again, Wilder," I told him. "Until then, behave."

He painted a cross over his heart and I looked to Ethan who nodded his own understanding. I was leaving him in charge and though I doubted he would be able to do much to rein Sin in, I was hoping he would at least stand a chance of keeping him in check until the time to act had come.

I clapped Hastings on the arm bracingly then turned to Cain and gave him a wicked smile.

"Come on, amore mio," I purred. "Make sure these stronzos know who owns me."

He blinked at me, taking in my command, the corner of his mouth twitching before he drew me under his arm and walked us through the stone archway ahead of the others.

I didn't look back to see when they peeled away from us into the depths of the crowd.

Cain kept me close and led me into the heart of this place of sin and seduction, the scent of death and pain coiling around us like a drug. It was loud in here, cries of excitement and terror mingling as one while Fae danced the line of debauchery and devilry so finely that it laced the air with its toxicity.

We passed fighting pits where blood stained the walls and brothels promising every kind of fucked up fantasy known to Fae, but we didn't pause at any of them.

The moon was calling me onwards, right into the heart of this place of broken lies and I was going to keep moving to the song of its call until my feet led me right to the man I loved.

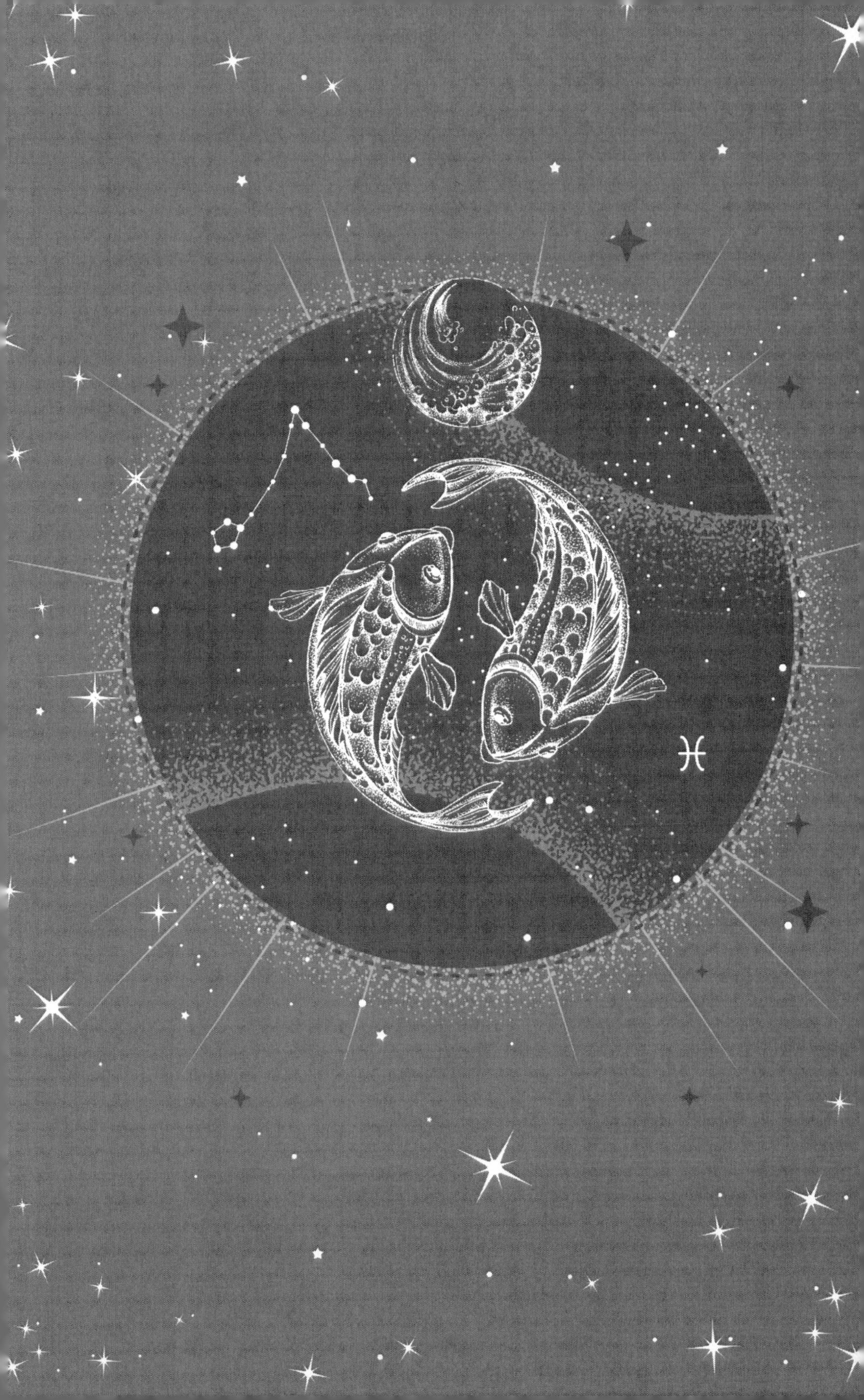

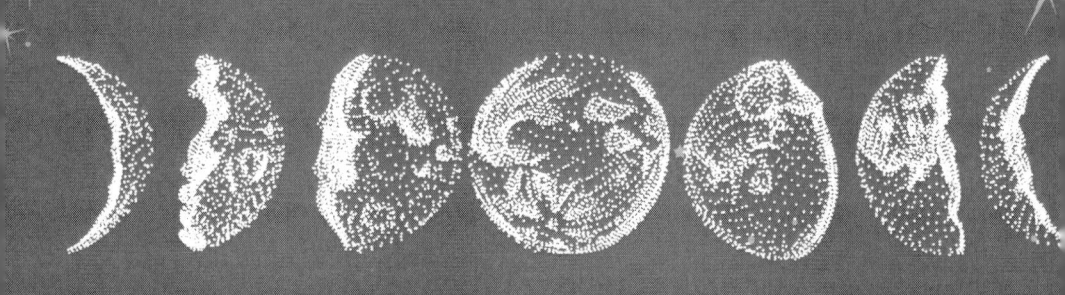

ROARY

PRISONER #69

CHAPTER TWELVE

The need to cast magic was turning from an itch to a burn. Even in Darkmore, I'd been able to cast to stop the madness setting in. But the possibility of going day after day like this was twisting my mind into a mess of jagged thoughts. The cuffs on my wrists were now accompanied by a thick metal collar around my throat that Roland had told me was designed to force me to return to him if I moved more than fifty feet away from him.

I paced the cell I'd been placed in in the basement of the building, the sound of screeching animals and the hollow moans and grunts of some unknown beasts calling to me from every direction. It was dark down here, but my keener eyesight picked out the wild horror in the magical animals' eyes around me.

There were caged kalini birds opposite me that were brightest pink and blue, their feathers shimmering with magic. They were rare creatures thanks to poachers capturing and selling them on for their ability to cause a trance-like high with their bird song. But they weren't singing now, they were shrieking, their talons scratching at the bars and wings flapping in desperation to take to the sky.

My chest tightened at the sight of their struggle, a murderous rage pooling in my chest at the assholes who were responsible for caging these creatures around me. Our freedom taken and our new purpose decided for us.

My gaze trailed to a cage of ghost hounds beside the kalini birds, their cage electrified to stop them passing through the bars and escaping like their kind were capable of. Each of their many tails swished angrily and they let out mournful yips and howls as they stalked the walls of their prison. There were so many more creatures contained down here, from feathered jaka monkeys to horned whisper mares. All were baying for freedom and a snarl left my lips as I joined them in their yearning, my fist thumping against the cage bars and making the whole structure rattle.

There was no bending these; I'd been placed in a cage of sun steel, the stuff as indestructible as it was rare, and regardless of that, the collar I wore was Roland's promise of my recapture anyway.

So I was forced to wait for my fate to come for me. As my thoughts turned to the stars, I wondered if they had any mercy left to offer or if they had turned their eyes from me, no longer caring what became of me.

At last, someone came, but the Fae in question only brought a sneer to my lips. Roland walked towards me with a purposeful stride, followed by a muscular blonde man who towered over him.

"Here he is, Benjamin. Take a look," Roland encouraged as a growl built in my throat. "My prized creature."

The well built, middle aged asshole scrutinised me closely, stepping into the light and glaring at me in a way that reminded me all too much of the Dragon Shifter who had ensured my imprisonment in Darkmore. The name Benjamin confirmed it. This man was an Acrux. The cousin of my very own villain Lionel Acrux. I'd learned of what this Fae had put Cain through and though I hadn't wanted to empathise with a prison guard, it had been impossible not to. You didn't survive an Acrux's touch without scars.

"So after all the strong Fae I sent you over the years for your experiments, not even one of them made it through the Order replacement?" Benjamin muttered at Roland in irritation.

"Not the Order replacement, no. But you provided me Ian Belor, don't you recall? My most wonderful monster in the making," Roland gushed.

"And yet, I hear the Belorian is now dead," Benjamin questioned and Roland's scarred eye twitched.

He cleared his throat, seeming emotional as he hurried on. "Yes, well. All greatness faces adversity. This one will be a target too." He caressed the bars and I lunged, trying to break his fingers, but he yanked them back fast before I could catch them, releasing a nervous chuckle.

"He was really a Lion Shifter?" Benjamin asked, looking me over. "Doesn't look much like one. Where's his mane?"

"He isn't a Lion Shifter anymore," Roland sniped and my fangs ached to dig into his throat, but I refused to speak to these cretins and give them the satisfaction of my rage. "He is my Nightroary. My Vampire. Made by my hand. No star in the sky chose this. I am akin to them now. A weaver of fate itself."

"Whatever you wanna believe," Benjamin shrugged. "I'm just curious about the price he'll fetch." He cocked his head to one side.

"You hardly earned your cut with this one," Roland said tightly and smoke spewed from Benjamin's nostrils, his eyes turning to reptilian slits and revealing the Dragon within.

"I've backed you for years. Kept your secrets hidden from society, broken plenty of necks to ensure nothing got leaked. And without all the Fae I sent to you, you wouldn't have achieved what you have with this one," Benjamin spat and my upper lip peeled back. "If you even think about not delivering me my twenty percent then I'll-"

"Alright, alright," Roland said quickly, backing away from Benjamin a step and revealing his fear of him. "Not to worry, I will deliver your cut."

"Both of you are dead," I whispered, drawing their attention back to me.

"What's that, pretty boy?" Benjamin goaded, sneering at me.

"You heard me well and good. Your death is written. You've given me fangs and I swear to the stars, I will rip out both of your throats with them."

Benjamin scoffed. "The problem with that little plan is that you're in a cage, clad in irons, all dressed up and ready to sell at the market."

"One chance is all I'll need. One moment of hesitation, one lapse in concentration and I will have you," I swore.

"Good luck with that," Benjamin said, turning his back on me.

Roland smiled creepily at me then swept after his Dragon friend. "The show is about to begin!" he called. "Bring him to the stage." He snapped his fingers at a man who stepped from the shadows, his shifted form showing that he was a Minotaur. His horns were covered in metal studs and a thick bar was wedged through his bull nose. He made swift work of unlocking the cage then mooed at me to get moving.

I stepped cautiously out of the cage, desperate to run, but knowing I wouldn't get far while he had magic and I didn't. The Minotaur attached a chain to my collar then tugged me after him with a sharp pull.

I growled as he guided me down the winding passages between hundreds of stacked cages, the din of distressed animals growing in pitch as they noted my passing. Like they knew I was destined for some terrible fate. Roland and Benjamin had gone ahead, no sight of them now as I was led towards an unknown fate.

My fingers balled into fists as adrenaline pitched through me, my fangs extending in my mouth as the call of bloodlust took over. My head was foggy with it, the need to hunt building and building within me. It was primal, a part of this new Order I couldn't fight as it coiled through me like a viper. I had to bite and kill and *drink*.

I lunged at the Minotaur from behind, my gaze homing in on a meaty vein in his neck, calling me to it and demanding I feed. He whirled around, his hand flying out, revealing a stun gun in his grip.

He jabbed it into my side and I roared as agony burst through me, my knees hitting the ground and pain flaring through every nerve ending in my body. He kept jabbing it at me with bruising blows, letting that electricity ignite in me time and again until I was ragged beneath him, gasping for breath. Then he yanked on the chain, forcing me to my feet and continued on like nothing had happened, leaving me nauseous and with an unwavering certainty in my soul that there was no escape.

He guided me through a heavy wooden door and the sound of a crowd filled my ears as we passed down a corridor towards a red curtain ahead. The din of the crowd grew louder and a voice echoed out above them all.

"I have worked for many years on mastering the ways of our kind, learning the intricacies of each Order and their inner composition. My work has made great advancements over the years, but not one of my subjects survived an Order replacement surgery…until now."

The Minotaur dragged me through the curtain, the chain going taut and making me stumble as I hit a step and staggered up onto a large stage.

Roland stood at the centre of it, his voice amplified by magic as he continued on, declaring me his greatest achievement. I blinked at the too-bright lights aimed my way, finding a leering crowd beyond, taking me in with scrutiny. I spotted Benjamin at the front of the crowd, his chin raised high and a greedy look on his face that said he was here for the payout and nothing else.

"Behold," Roland gestured at me, the tail of his long coat whipping out behind him as he turned my way. "A Nemean Lion shifter turned into a Vampire."

He nodded to the Minotaur who immediately unclipped me from the chain. And that was it, the need to hunt took over and I sped towards Roland in a blur of movement, my fangs exposed as I aimed to kill him. I hit an air shield someone had cast around him, crashing back onto the stage with a bang, my head spinning from the impact.

Mutters broke out in the crowd.

"How do we know he wasn't always a Vampire?" someone hollered.

"Yeah! Prove it!" a woman yelled then a series of boos rang out.

"You can't change Orders," someone laughed. "He's full of shit."

The Minotaur gripped my arm, dragging me to my feet and snapping his chain back onto my collar, leaving me snarling at him but knowing there was no point in fighting this. I would only end up on my back again.

"Of course you are sceptical," Roland mused. "It is only natural. Which is why I brought proof with me." He twisted around, gesturing to a large screen behind the stage and I scowled as footage from the Darkmore security cameras played on the screen. It showed me walking among the convicts, then changed to a view of me stepping into the Order Yard, stripping off and shifting into my Lion form. A noise of pain left me as I stared at the beast I'd once been, a hollow place inside me echoing with the loss of it.

"Give it back," I rasped and the Minotaur glanced my way, a frown furrowing his brow. "He took it from me."

The crowd gasped, looking from me to the screen as the footage replayed, proving what I had once been.

"How?!" someone cried.

"It's not right," someone else said in horror then retched, backing away from the stage and turning from me in disgust.

I shuddered, wanting to flee from my own skin, hating this altered form I was trapped in. I wanted my Lion. I wanted to be me again.

Not everyone in the crowd seemed horrified, a mix of gleeful and hungry looks falling my way too, but none looked so hungry as Benjamin, the scent of money on the air making his smile widen. The excited murmurs grew louder, my heightened hearing picking out too many conversations.

"This could change everything," a woman whispered eagerly.

"No more lesser Orders," a man beside her added keenly.

The crowd were chattering louder and louder until Roland finally called out for them to hush. "Drav Enterprises will be sharing this technology with the highest bidder here today. And not only that, but you will get to work personally with me! The Fae behind the genius. A man you once knew as the greatest Seer in Solaria and I have been hiding in plain sight all this time." He turned to the screen and the word Drav rearranged itself to spell out Vard instead. "Roland Vard!" He declared and the crowd fell quiet, confused looks passing between people. "*The* Vard," Roland pressed, but people only shrugged. Someone started clapping in the back of the room, but the applause quickly petered off. "As in the Dragon King's Royal Seer!" he bayed and it suddenly clicked who he was. Leon had told me about him during the war several years ago. He had been Lionel Acrux's right-hand man, but it was thought that he had died in battle. He was responsible for heinous war crimes and seeing him here now made fury rise in me that he had escaped all along. He deserved worse than death for all he'd done, and I ached to be the one to deliver it to him.

"Vard?" the Minotaur beside me breathed, a tremor to his voice.

"You know him?" I grunted.

"Know him?" he hissed. "He was part of the Order segregation. Him and Lionel Acrux, they were responsible for declaring certain Orders as lesser. The Minotaurs were forced to go into hiding. We were accused of thievery, made out to be enemies of the kingdom, but it was all lies." He stamped his foot in anger and I stepped closer to him as Vard kept crying out to the crowd to explain who he was, and it appeared people were starting to catch on now. They might not remember his name, but they remembered the rise of the Dragon King alright. Likely plenty of these motherfuckers supported Lionel Acrux.

"How much for access to this science?!" a man hollered and Vard gestured to an auctioneer at the side of the stage.

A bidding process started up and a clamour of noise filled the air as Fae desperately tried to secure the technology from Roland.

"He truly changed your Order?" the Minotaur whispered, horror dawning on his face.

I glanced up at him and nodded. "He's a monster."

"Everyone in this place is," he said darkly. "But Roland Vard has already done the unspeakable, and now he seeks to do even worse." He shuddered. "What if he targets my kind? My Order? My family?"

"Maybe you should do something about it before it's too late," I urged.

He fell silent for a beat then spoke to me in an even lower voice. "I think I know where they're keeping your Order." He leaned in closer, slipping a set of keys from his pocket and subtly sliding it into mine. "That'll deal with the collar and cuffs."

"Where's my Lion?" I rasped, my heart thundering with need as he leaned in even closer and breathed the location in my ear.

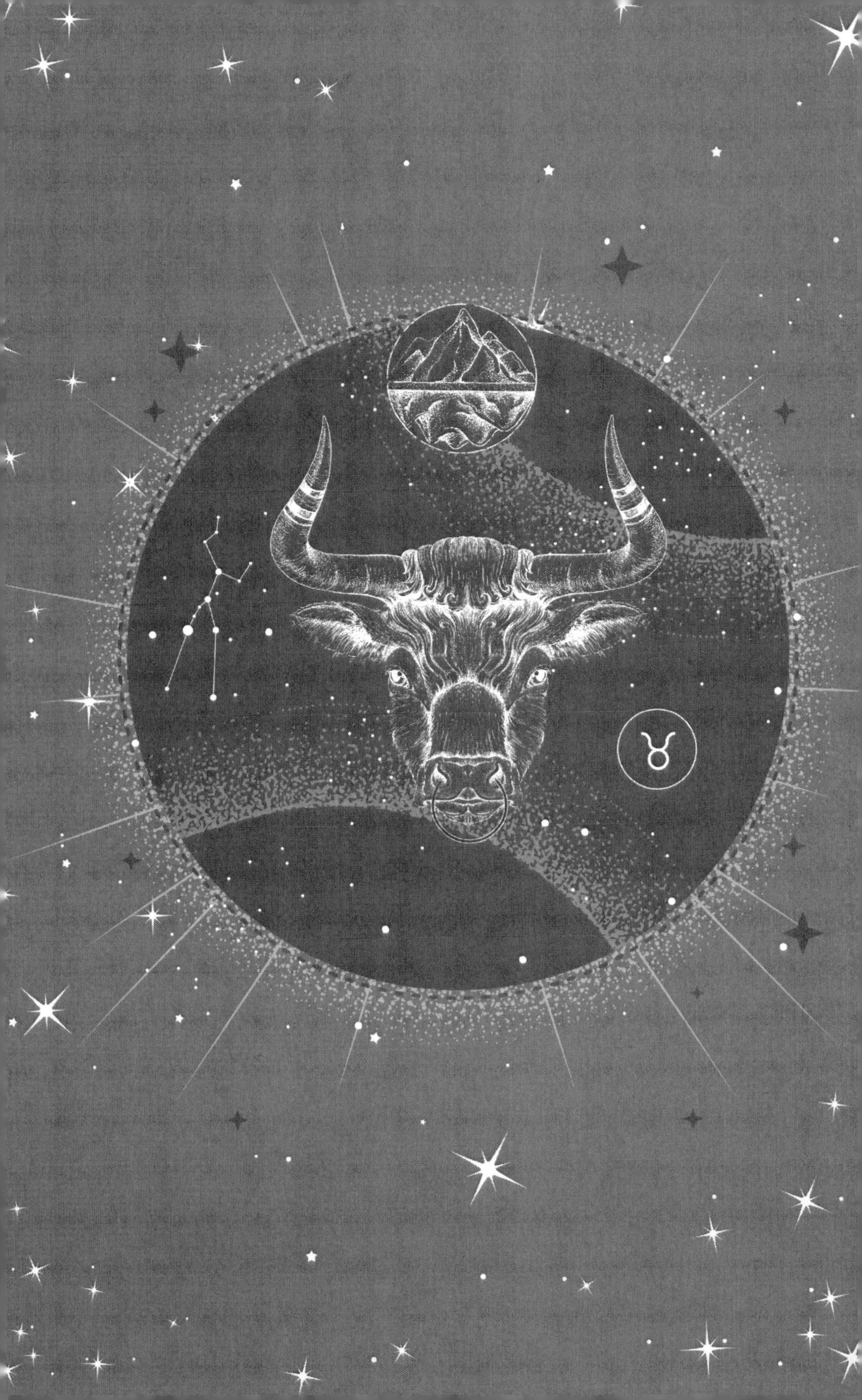

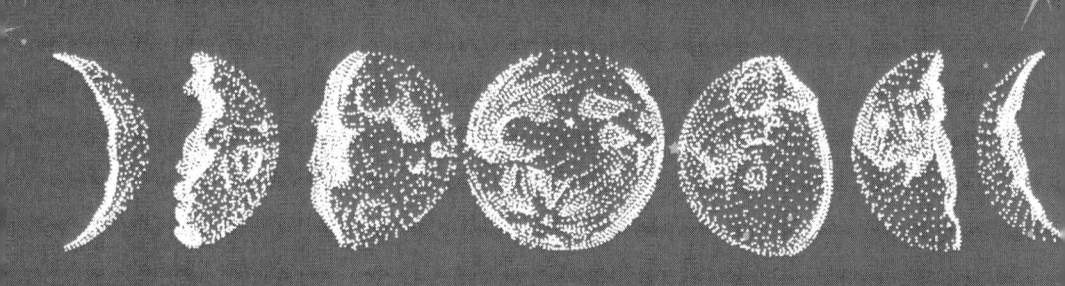

Rosalie

PRISONER #12

CHAPTER THIRTEEN

We stepped into a room where a man stood on a stage, talking loudly to a crowd of onlookers raised up on seats that formed a half circle looking down on him. From my vantage point it was hard to see precisely what they were all looking at but as I moved along the narrow walkway between the raised seats, my presence concealed within the shadows, the man's face was revealed. More importantly, so was the man chained behind him, a collar leashed around his neck, a thick chain held in the fists of a Minotaur who loomed over him threateningly.

I lurched forward a step but Cain snatched my arm, hissing a low warning to me as a silencing bubble fell over us.

"That's Roary," I hissed, trying to tug my arm free, my eyes fixed on the wretched form of the man I loved where he stared at the ground by his feet, looking utterly broken and alone. "We have to get to him. We have to-"

"There are guards standing in every corner," Cain snarled. "Our moment will come. We know he's here now. We just have to keep our-"

"Nightroary is a marvel of scientific and magical ingenuity!" Vard boomed and I tore my gaze from the man I loved to look at the vile bastardo who had stolen him away from me. "He is the first in a new and vibrant generation of Fae who will get to choose their fate. Why allow the stars to condemn you to an Order you did not wish for? Why follow a path laid out by another when you can claim your own fate and grasp destiny for yourself? For a price of course…"

The crowd yelled out, jeers and scathing declarations meeting with enthusiastic questions and excited exclamations.

"What has he done to him?" I breathed, my eyes back on Roary who looked so shattered, so broken, so haunted. It was as though something was missing, some vital piece of who he was now absent, and my hands began to tremble as the fucked up shit I'd witnessed back in Psych flooded through my mind.

"I don't know," Cain muttered, his eyes darting around the crowd, towards the exit, the sides of the stage, his mind clearly racing to form a plan while I simply fell into an abyss of despair as I stared at my mate and felt the sky caving in around him.

Some stronzo hurled a beer bottle towards the stage and it shattered against an air shield which had been cast before Roary, making him look up and snarl in fury.

I sucked in a sharp breath, stumbling back a step and smacking into Cain as my eyes fell on the fangs which Roary now bared at the crowd, the impossibility of them making my gut churn with terror.

"That's impossible," Cain breathed while I simply stared, tears burning the backs of my eyes as I took in the horror of what fate had befallen upon my strong, beautiful Lion.

"We have to help him," I gasped, trying to go to him, not caring if there were a hundred bastardos waiting to leap from the shadows to try and keep me from him. My mate needed me and I couldn't fail him any longer than I already had.

Cain's grip on my forearm was bruising as he held me back in the shadows while Vard strode from the stage, a group of simpering sycophants closing in around him, keenly asking questions about what he had achieved.

Bile thickened my throat, a strange ringing filling my ears. I couldn't speak, couldn't move. I'd felt Roary's anguish while we'd been separated, I'd known in my soul that he was in desperate need of me, but this…

Cain yanked me away from the stage, tugging me into the shadows beneath the stacked seating, pushing me back against the wall there.

"There isn't time for you to lose your head, Rosalie," he growled, taking my face in his hand and forcing my gaze up to meet his. "You came here to get him out. You knew he might not be in the best state when we found him. This is worse than we'd expected but he needs you more than we even knew. You can't fail him now."

I jerked back, my spine hitting the dusty wall. "I'm not going to fail him," I hissed.

"There she is," Cain replied darkly as he took in the furious rage in my tone. "Now let's go get your boy."

Shock still held me in its grasp, my lips parting on some command, some plan which wouldn't form.

"That motherfucker is supposed to be dead," I growled in a low tone, my eyes on the door where Vard had now disappeared. Roary was being yanked along by the collar on his neck, drawn through a door to the other side of the stage and panic gripped me as I lost sight of him. "I fought in the war. They found his body. He – Drav – *Vard*. He tortured Tory Vega, he-"

"I don't care if he orchestrated the entire fucking war and was the reason behind every death that took place in it," Cain said firmly. "The only thing that matters is that he is standing between us and Roary and I can't bear to keep seeing that heartbreak in your eyes. So if he's blocking our path then we'll pass right through him."

"He'll *see* us coming. He has The Sight. If we plan anything directly against him then the stars will warn him and-"

"Who needs the stars when we have the moon on our side?" Cain demanded, his gaze iron, tone unflinching.

I wasn't sure why he was so determined to help me now when his assistance had seemed reluctant before, but his words were a light to a fuse inside me.

I could feel the heavy weight of the moon's power surrounding me, her energy suffusing me and helping drive away my fear. He was right. It didn't matter what stood between me and Roary because there wasn't anything in this world that would keep me from him. And I did have the moon on my side.

"Give Shadowbrook and Wilder the signal," Cain commanded, and a surge of excitement ran through my veins at the rough tone he took with me.

I tipped my head back and howled, long and low and pure. The sound carried from my lips like a broken lament, but just in case my dark souls weren't close enough to hear me, I threw my fist into the wall hard enough to break bone. Ethan sure as shit would have felt that thanks to our mate bond.

I cursed, pushing healing magic into my fingers before shaking my hand out and striding from our hiding place, my shoulder brushing against Cain's arm as I moved.

My skin prickled as I reached out to the moon, asking her to hide me from the world as she had done before and adrenaline pounded through me as my body faded from sight.

A new presentation was beginning on the stage, a man with an assortment of dark objects still in the process of laying them out while the crowd murmured among themselves.

I didn't turn as Cain moved closer beside me, I only reached out and took his hand in mine so that he knew where I was.

"Tell me when," he said in a low tone.

We were jostled by people who were heading to the seating around the stage or abandoning it, several Fae cursing loudly as they met with the sharp edge of my elbows when they moved close enough to walk into me.

I remained quiet for a few moments, plotting, strategizing. If we settled on a plan to go straight at Vard, he would *see* it coming but he might just *see* us coming for Roary too if the avid obsession I had witnessed in him was as potent as I feared. Roary was his prize possession, the culmination of his abhorrent tests and experiments. He wouldn't give him up easily. Hell, he might already know we were on our way. We needed to draw his attention away from us and what we were doing.

"The door to the right of the stage," I whispered.

Cain whipped me off of my feet without another word, shooting me towards it so fast that the world blurred around us.

I had to blink to orient myself as he set me back on my feet in the shadows by the door. Roary had been taken out through here just minutes ago, but I could feel the wards in place on it, could hear the guards murmuring on the other side of it. This wasn't going to be the best way to get to Roary – but it would do for one hell of a distraction.

I released my moon gifts, reappearing in the shadows at Cain's side and taking my bag from my back. I unbuckled it, flipping the top open and reaching inside to take one of the incendiary devices from their place within it, but I became utterly still as my eyes fell on the contents of my pack. Where there had been six carefully packaged fire bombs now sat six bright yellow lemons.

"That fucking Incubus," Cain snarled as he caught sight of the fruit.

I straightened, a lemon in hand and the useless pack abandoned at my feet.

"I'm going to kill him," I hissed but before any real ideas about all the ways I would make Sin Wilder pay for going against my clear instructions and acting as though we were in on some special little secret plan together *again*, an explosion rang out in the direction of the marketplace and the entire world went to hell.

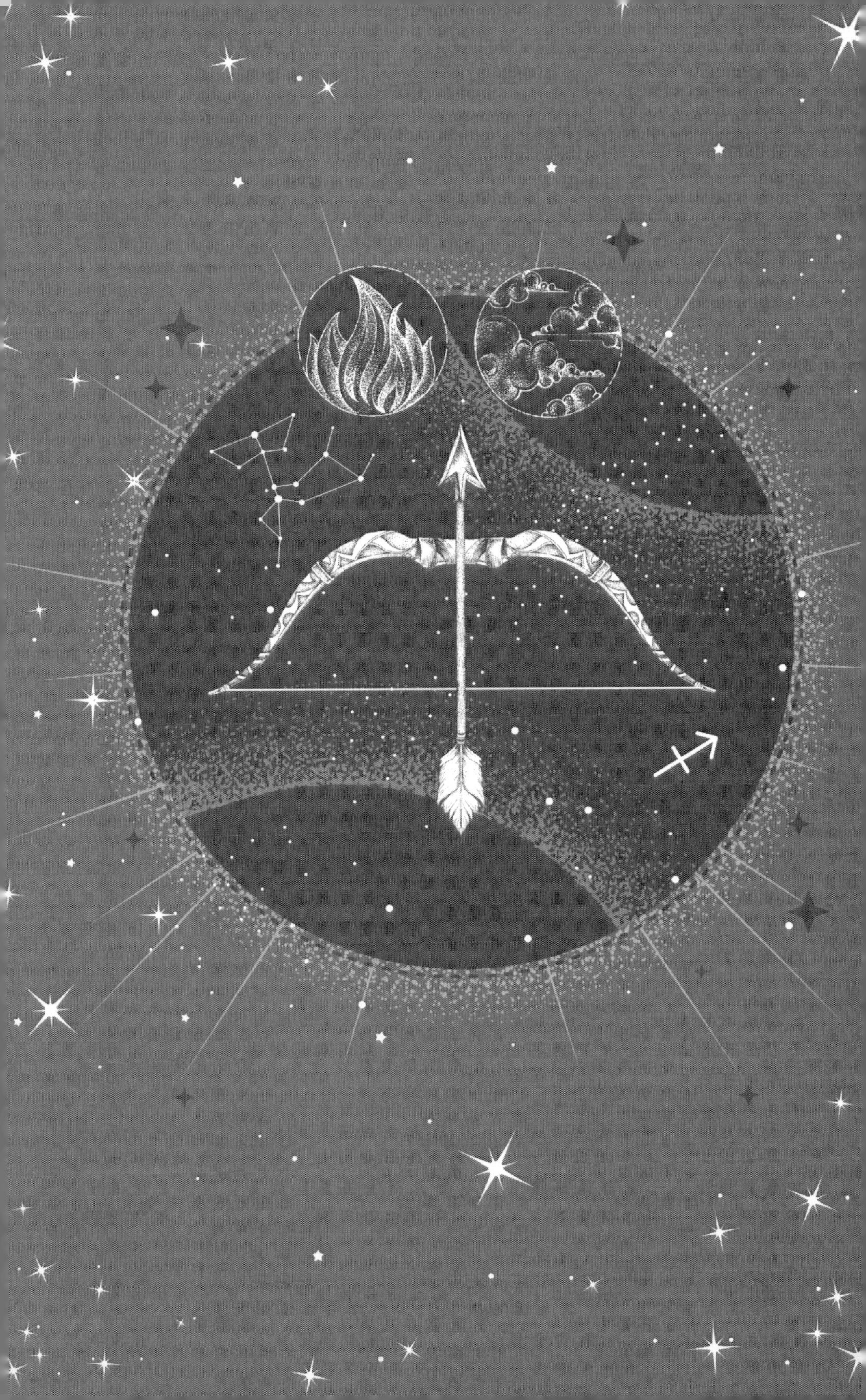

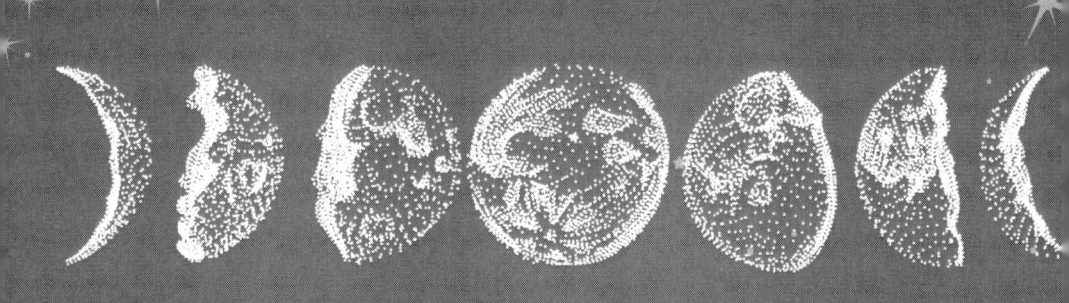

SIN

PRISONER #88

CHAPTER FOURTEEN

Mayhem was the prettiest word I knew, and I embodied it now, my little friends giggling in the bag that was swinging from my fist as I selected one of the feisty fire bombs and preparing to toss it at a nasty-looking man who had just slapped a duck and was frantically gathering things into his briefcase. What had that duck ever done to him? It flapped away with a quack of outrage and I saluted it.

"Catch!" I yelled and the man's hands flew out automatically to snatch the pretty little fire bomb from the air. My giggly friend went boom, blasting the man into the arms of the stars and beyond, my air shield only just snapping over me in time to protect me from the flames and accompanying spray of body parts.

"Sin!" Ethan barked from behind me and I whirled like a ballet dancer, hurling a fistful of flames into the surrounding marketplace. Stalls were set ablaze, the many cursed and dangerous wares exploding in flashes of colour, and screams swirled through the air like choir music while blood flew and chaos descended. This was exactly how I pictured Christmas morning, flash-bangs and adrenaline galore.

"*Sin*." Ethan grabbed me by the shoulder as my gaze locked on a woman who was clutching a selection of dried-up fingers in her arms, racing for freedom. Where did she get those fingers? There weren't any nice people who touted fingers about like that so she had to be bad to the bone.

"One second, my old chum," I said to Ethan then bowled my latest fire bomb after the woman, the little explosive bouncing at her heels then going bang with an explosion that made my ears ring. "Damn, I love that sound, the way it shakes and shudders my eardrum is a special kind of treat." I stuck a finger in my ear and Ethan grabbed me by the shoulders, forcing me to look at him.

"Did you take these bombs from Rosalie?" he snarled.

"I didn't *not* take them. But don't worry, sugar, I left her something better in their place. She'll thank me for it later. Now let's get inside and blow this shit hole to kingdom bum."

"*Come*," he corrected me.

"Later baked potata, I can't just go blowing my load right now, I'm saving it for the after party." I skipped away from him, racing toward a doorway where a few guards were gathering their wits. They turned to us, magic crackling at their fingertips as they prepared to fight, but I'd already rolled one of my friends between their legs and as I pointed it out, their eyes bugged a second before they were blasted to hell. I raced inside while pieces of them rained down around me like dandelion seeds caught in a summer breeze.

"Where's Hastings?" Ethan cursed, looking around for our little guard friend.

"Hiding under a table probably. Let him be. He's just a babe. We'll fetch him later," I said and Ethan nodded, not wasting any more time as we forged on.

Magic blasted our way from the fleeing crowd in the entranceway and I wrapped a tight air shield around us, their strikes of air, water, fire and earth not nearly powerful enough to break through. Ethan started blasting Fae with water, sending them flying into walls and freezing them in place to clear our path.

I cast a fire-nado into existence, sending it out to sweep through the crowd and cause untold destruction. The Wolfy boy's strikes were efficient and brutal where mine were wild and unpredictable, making us an unstoppable force united. I tossed a giggly bomb onto the stairway that people were fleeing up and the whole structure groaned as I blasted a hole in it.

"We have to get our goods," a pretty boy with fluffy gold hair called to an older gentleman, grabbing his arm and towing him towards a concealed door. He shoved it open, revealing a set of steps heading underground and they slipped away down it like moles down a hole.

I caught Ethan's arm as he stabbed an ugly man with an ice blade who had made a bid to kill him, tossing the body away and shaking my friend. "I am feeling very squid-like all of a sudden."

"What?" he blurted, trying to turn from me to engage a group of Fae who were running at us with roars of anger and magic building in their palms. I tossed a blast of fire their way and their screams zig-zagged through the air while my eyes remained on Ethan's shiny blues.

"I have an inkling, see?" I shoved him toward the open doorway. "Down there's where they keep the good stuff, I reckon." I tossed him through the door and cast an air shield behind us so no one could follow before sprinting down the stairs into the dark. And it *was* dark. As dark as an unwelcoming asscrack, but my inkles were growing and I knew we were going to find ourselves somewhere real interesting in a moment or three.

As we wound through tight corridors, a sound grew up ahead, a cacophony of sorts, birds and monkeys and shrieking animals I couldn't put a name to. All kinds of wild things waiting for me to reach 'em.

My heart pumped harder as I burst through a door, finding cage upon cage, stacked as high as high could go. There were rows of them, stretching away into the nevermore and I growled ferally as I took in the magical creatures contained within bars. I saw me in there. That crow-looking thing, I could see my own eyes in its eyes. Its struggle my struggle. I'd been right where he'd been. A crow-thing in a cage, all sad and yearning to be free. To do what crow-things did best and be crow-like.

"Fuck these fucking fucklings," I hissed, aiming my ire at the people who had done this. Not my crow-thing. Or that horse-goat over there. Nor that group of three-legged celery-looking birds in that corner.

The snap of a lock made me turn and I found my Ethy-baby breaking open a cage with a wedge of ice in his hand.

"I knew I liked you for a reason, Wolf boy," I purred. "You see in these creatures what I see. You're just like that pygmy shrew-thing over there. You resemble him and he resembles you."

Ethan's gaze slid to the shrew in question. It had four bucked teeth protruding from its mouth and eyes that stared in different directions.

"You're one and the same," I whispered, then clapped his scowly face on the cheek and turned to start breaking open cages.

I broke my crow-thing free first and he squawked his thanks, flying up to land on my shoulder. I smiled my biggest smile at him. He had a beak that was brightest gold and his eyes were a dreamy pool of violet, but the rest of him was jet black, his feathers as smooth as silk.

"I love you, Crow-thing, I truly do." I kissed him quick then turned to release his friends. My friends. *Our* friends. We were an army now. An angry army of animal-things with Ethan and I mere soldiers in their battalion.

"Rise!" I called as I cracked another cage open with air magic and released a bunch of mini-pony-cat-things. "Be free. And kill – kill your captors! Kill them all!"

Our system was efficient, the cages snapping open time and again until the corridor was alive with running creatures. I ran with them, skipping and spinning as I went, as majestic as the magical animals I danced with. We turned a corner and found a line of guards running our way, shouts of alarm escaping them as the hoard of animals galloped their way.

A group of winged monkey-things slammed into the first guard, shrieking and clawing at his face. The next was mowed down by a horned tiger-thing and the last met with my own fury, fire swirling away from me and consuming the woman's head, eating her up until she was gone, gone, gone.

Ethan started cracking open more cages and I helped him, focusing on my air magic and sending it spiralling down the narrow corridor, ripping the doors clean off to free our new friends.

Crow-thing squawked on my shoulder and I squawked in response, following a line of rabbit-things towards the next turn. The corridor we stepped into was darker here, the cages bigger. Things leered out of them, big dangerous beasties with hungry eyes and sharp teeth.

"Not these," Ethan said, catching my arm.

"Oh but these are the killers of the crop," I purred. "They mirror our souls so very well. We can't leave them here to rot."

I paused before a bear-like creature with antlers and curved canines that hung from its mouth.

"That's a corlash bear," Ethan breathed in warning, telling me this animal was deadly.

It growled at me in warning and my shivers were timbered.

"Oh yes," I whispered. "I wouldn't leave you here in the dark, new friend." I broke the lock on his cage, opening it wide and stepping back.

Ethan gripped my arm tighter, tugging me aside as the bear-thing stepped out into freedom, sniffing the air and assessing the two of us. He towered over us both, his eyes full of rage, but he didn't turn it on us, an understanding passing from one monster to another. He turned and raced away up the corridor and I blasted more cages open, letting the bigger beasties run after him, beasts with claws and fangs and feral needs that would be unleashed upon the wicked Fae who lurked in this here hell hole.

"Wilder," a voice rasped behind me and I whirled around with Ethan, finding a cage I'd missed. A big one. One that was as dark as the pits of death and I wondered if the thing inside it was eating the light around it.

I squinted into the gloom, my goosebumps goosing as I sought out the monster within which knew my name. He lunged, a hairy arm with a clawed hand swinging for me through the bars and slashing against my air shield. I saw his face as he stepped out of the gloom, this hulking creature like a yeti, only worse than that. Far worse with his gnarled face and long limbs. But I knew his features, recognised them from the depths of my mind.

"Gustard?" Ethan balked, recognising him too. "What happened to you?"

If this had happened to Gustard then what the fudge had happened to our Lion boy? I glanced at the surrounding cages but didn't spot a yeti-Roary anywhere so that was good. Unless it was bad.

"Shadowbrook," Gustard hissed, his eyes snapping onto him. "Open."

He seemed to be capable of only one word at a time, his voice altered too, deep and growly, like it belonged to an animal instead of a Fae though he looked just as wicked and twisted as always.

"Open!" He bellowed, shaking the bars of his cage.

I reached for it, but Ethan slapped my hand away and I pouted at him.

"He deserves to rot in there for what he did to Rosa," Ethan snarled.

"I know," I said, turning my gaze back on Gustard. "I was only going to make his living space a little less comfortable." I touched the bars, bending them with my air magic and turning them red hot too as they buckled in on him, making Gustard roar in agony.

"Looks like the punishments of death are finding you in the living realm, Gussy," I hissed. "You'll rot here. Rot like an apple in a well and no one will look for you."

I gave the space one more look in case Roary was lurking in a corner but there was no sight of him here or anywhere.

"If that's Gustard," Ethan breathed fearfully looking around too. "Then what-"

"I learned a long time ago that there ain't no worth in worrying about the could-bes, kitten. Right now we know nothing and we won't know it until we know it. So let's not get all tangled in the could-bes. Okay?"

Ethan arched a brow at me like he was surprised. "That's actually pretty smart," he admitted, all surprised. Rude. I was known for my cunning plans and wily mind. But right now we had better things to do than squabble over his lack of faith in me.

"Then let's get back to the chaos, eh?" I turned from the still shrieking Gustard, petting Crow-thing and following Ethan into the dark, twisty-turns of the passages beneath this forsaken place. And I knew with a certainty that set my blood alight, I would see it fall before I left its shores.

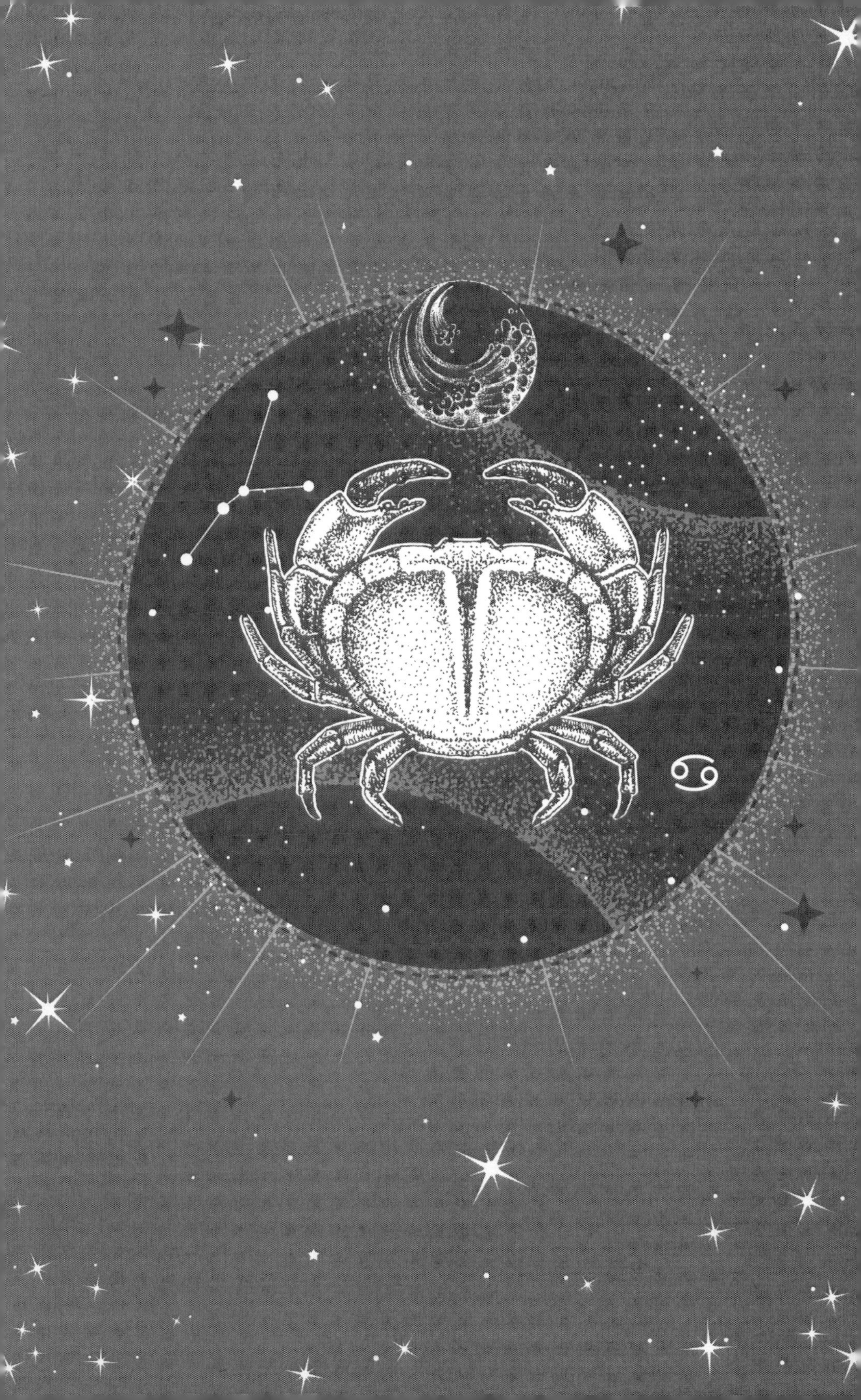

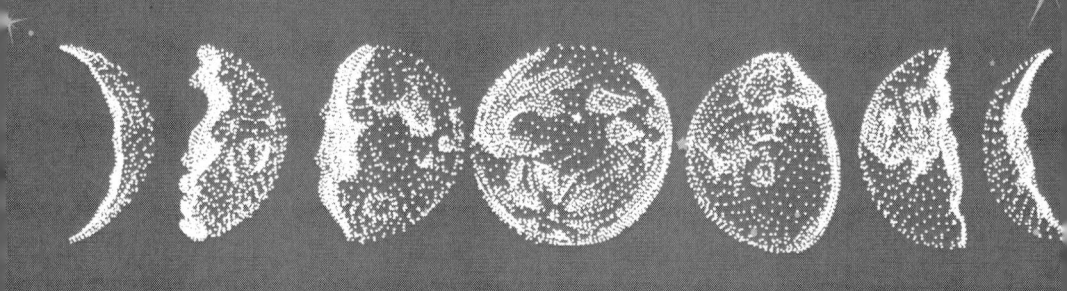

Hastings

OFFICER

CHAPTER FIFTEEN

The table I was crouched beneath was burning, the crackle and pop of the heavy wood combining with the growing heat and billowing smoke to force me from my place of refuge.

I'd lost track of Shadowbrook and Wilder in the mayhem and now it was down to me to cause the distraction Rosalie needed.

I steeled myself, flattening my palms to the dirty flagstones beneath me in an attempt to stop them from trembling. I expelled a harsh breath and rolled free of my concealed spot, throwing myself into a series of rolls. Whatever might be lurking out there wouldn't be able to get a lock on me.

I threw myself to my feet with a feral cry, raising my arms over my head to appear bigger and more intimidating. It was one of the tactics I'd been taught during my guard training at Darkmore and though the one time I'd tried it in there I'd received cat-calls and raucous laughter, I felt like I had it down now.

But there turned out to be no one there for me to intimidate.

The ramshackle marketplace which had been full of nefarious vendors and buyers alike was now abandoned, flames licking at several stalls, holes blasted through the walls and into the floor. Debris littered the ground and a few bodies were strewn over tables and under heaped rubble. Aside from that, I was alone.

"Err…guys?" I called out, turning to hunt for a sign of Sin or Ethan anywhere. They were probably in danger, desperately in need of my help but I had no idea where to find them.

The last time I'd been with them we'd been headed towards the east side of the stronghold so I turned that way and took off, water magic coiling around my fingers, my senses sharp in anticipation of anything.

A high-pitched shriek broke through the air ahead of me and I stumbled over my own feet as my heart leapt in surprise. I hesitated for a moment but my team were relying on me and I knew now that it was time for me to step up and embrace the call of the dark. I had to keep on this path.

I broke into a jog, the groans of some poor bastard reaching my ears, but I couldn't spare any time for him. He'd figure it out. My boys needed me.

On I ran through the near-abandoned building, a few vendors scrambling in the opposite direction with questionable wares clutched in their arms, some of them bleeding, others cursing the stars for their ill fortune this night.

Another shriek ruptured the air followed by a baying cry which made the hairs stand up along the back of my neck.

An open door stood ahead of me, the wood hanging awkwardly from one set of hinges, more chaotic sounds echoing up from the darkness within it. I could make out the start of a stone staircase leading down into the bowels of this place and I edged closer as more squawking and chattering reached my ears.

I leapt back in alarm, water spraying from my palms as a beast leapt up the stairs and burst out into the light.

I tripped over some loose rubble and went sprawling onto my back, something sharp cracking in my back pocket and jabbing me in the ass cheek.

My eyes widened as the beast leapt at me and I cried out, raising my arms to ward it off. But the savage thing passed between my waving hands, its small body around the size of a rabbit, though it was more rodent in its features with bucked teeth sticking out of its jaw at odd angles.

More whooping, shrieking and howling was rising from within the depths of that staircase and as I shrieked and flailed, knocking the small beast off of me, the thundering footfalls of many feet raced closer, making the floor beneath me tremble.

I scrambled back across the ground as the stampede of feet raced closer, the walls rattling now, terror pounding wildly through my heart.

I blinked and the room turned purple.

That wasn't right.

I blinked again and it was green.

The pain in my ass cheek sharpened as I scrambled back across the ground and I shoved my hand into my pocket, yanking out a syringe, the needle wet with my blood, the potion inside it gone.

I blinked at it furiously, my eyelashes like fluttering butterfly wings, ready to take off and leave my face behind forever.

"Don't go," I whispered to them, the syringe wafting around in front of my eyes. My jazzy, snazzy eyes.

I leapt to my feet with a surge of energy, the syringe tumbling from my fingers in slow motion, bouncing across the flagstones. One. Two. Three. A kind of flopways roll next, then four. Seven. It was slowing now and…

My gaze rose to the doorway where a hoard of beasts had appeared from nothing and nowhere. Birds flip-flapped into the air, critters scrambled over my boots, and big, bad beasties looked me up and down like they might crunch my bones to dust.

"Ca-caw," I whispered because they were here for me and I was here for them.

Something roared and it wasn't moving slowly anymore – it was fast, fast, fast and its limbs were long and tipped with razor sharp claws, its teeth bared in a hungry smile aimed right at me.

We were the same. Two feral creatures ready to roam these halls.

My blood was pumping all the way around my body and the room was blue in the next blink.

Blue means poo.

And I was on a roll.

No gnashers would gnash me.

The beast lunged but I dashed to the right, pirouetting by and leaping into a sprint. More monstrous things were scrambling from that open door and I wasn't going to be their meal. But I could lead them – they could be my pack!

"Come critters!" I roared and I broke into a run, turning back the way I'd come, my feet moving so fast that they were a blur beneath me.

The world was dancing and I was the drummer setting the beat. Jaws snapped at my heels, claws swiped at my spine and in it all I was running and leading the swarm.

I was the king of the beasties and they would answer to none but my call.

I released a yodel of command and they bellowed at my back, following me into the arms of destiny while my heart beat so fast I was almost certain it was trying to outrun me.

But no heart could run faster than I – for I was racing at the speed known only to the Creature Caller and I was *him!*

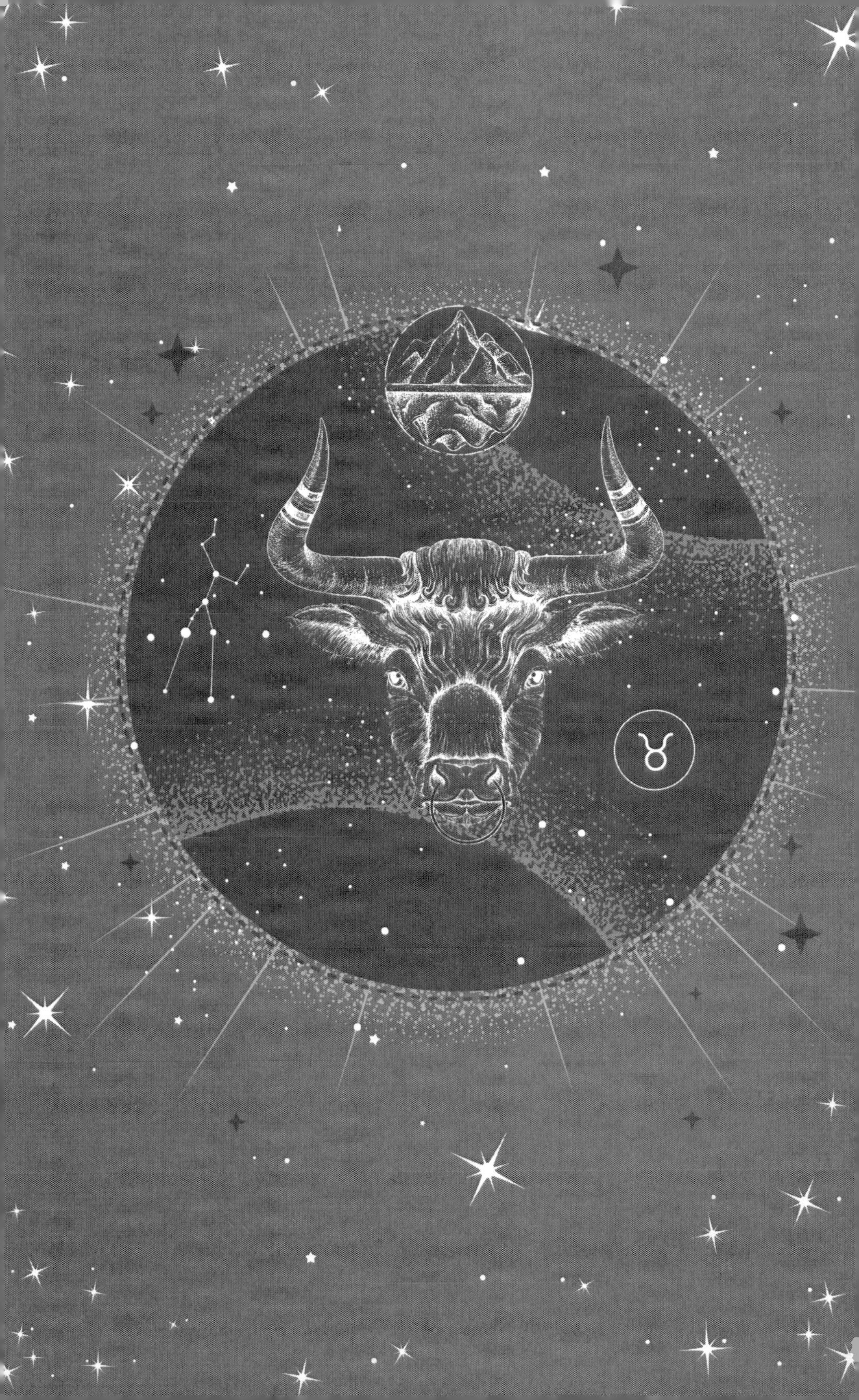

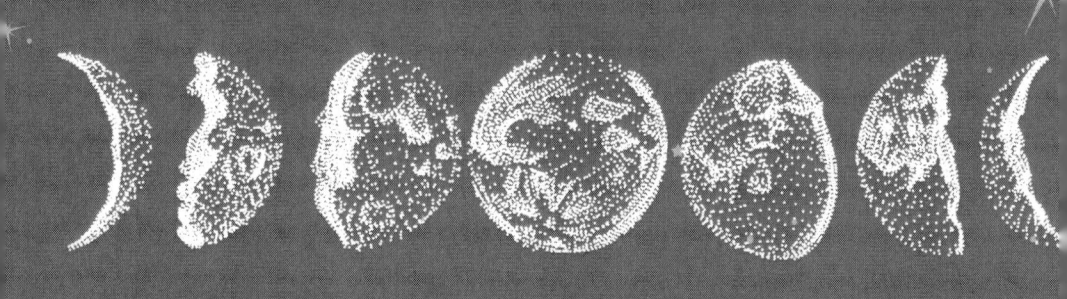

ROSALIE
PRISONER #12

CHAPTER SIXTEEN

The scent of smoke from fires burning above us was thick in the air, the dark in the tunnels beneath the main complex seeming more maze-like than ever the further we moved into them. When the bombs had begun exploding, the guards blocking our way on had run to investigate, leaving the way down here clear, but that didn't mean I'd forgiven Sin for stealing from me.

We'd passed a huge area of locked safes marked with symbols which I had to assume meant something to their owners because they were incomprehensible to me.

A faint Faelight hung in the air ahead of us but I was once again invisible while Cain stalked the shadows, seemingly alone with the dim light.

In any other circumstance I might have tried my luck cracking into those safes, figuring out what exactly these criminally-inclined Fae were hiding away down here. But I was on the hunt for something far more valuable than anything which might be stashed in those metal boxes.

There was an ache in my chest which called me onward and it was all I could do to maintain this cautious pace through the endless passageways beneath the compound.

"Are you still there?" Cain hissed from his position a little to my left and just behind me.

"We need to move faster," I said by way of reply, almost choking on the smoke as more of it filtered down here to torment us.

Cain cleared his throat too, grunting in agreement. "Come here," he commanded and I moved into his arms. "This is fucking strange," he muttered, lifting me into his grip despite being unable to see me.

"If we come up on trouble then hurl me away from you," I told him. "Give me a chance to come at them from behind."

"Yes, ma'am," he replied dryly before shooting onwards.

I buried my face in his neck, inhaling the raw scent of his skin, the tightness of his grip on me seeming to hold me together while fear of failure tried to creep up on me once more.

I couldn't make out a thing between the speed we were moving and the darkness but Cain never faltered, shooting down narrow corridors past crates of unknown goods and locked doors hiding illicit secrets.

We sped around a corner and my breath hurtled from my lungs in a sharp exhale as he threw me from his arms so suddenly that I almost screamed.

Vines sprung from my palms on instinct, lashing me to a beam hanging overhead and cradling me in their thick embrace while cries of agony and alarm filled the room.

I pulled a knife from my belt and cut through the vines that had saved me, landing on my feet and taking in the scene of panic as a blur of motion ripped through the circle of guards who had been standing before a barred cage.

Cain tore throats out, broke spines and caved in skulls with wicked ferocity, their screams ringing out and echoing all around us, but my eyes were on nothing aside from the man who stood behind those bars.

Roary's gaze flicked back and forth, tracking the blur of ruinous carnage which was Cain while I strode through the centre of the room towards him with my heart tearing straight down the centre.

In some ways he looked the same as he had when I'd last seen him on the outskirts of Darkmore, his golden eyes on mine, beautiful face written in agony as he let me go, except now that pain in him wasn't only for me. There was something else here. Something I wasn't seeing but could *feel*. Something had changed in him, some vital piece torn away and as I looked into his face I didn't feel the relief I had expected to at our reunion – I felt only a sucker punch of dread, knowing what he had lost, what had been taken from him.

I released my hold on my moon gifts, my body materialising before his eyes as I reappeared.

Roary exhaled a low groan as his eyes fell on me, moving to the bars of his cage, arms reaching through them for me unthinkingly.

"You came," he rasped as I took his hands in mine.

"Was there ever any doubt?" I replied steadily, my fingers curling around his while he gripped me so tightly it was as though he were checking if I were real.

A final scream punctured the silence and Cain fell still at my side, bloodstained and brutal in his beauty. I felt the overwhelming urge to kiss him as I looked his way, to take his mouth with mine and lay the claim which both of us had spent too long denying between us. But Roary needed me more right now.

"Cain?" he said in surprise. "You…you're helping…how - no fuck that - *why?*"

"You can blame your mate for that one, inmate," Cain grunted and the use of that term out here in this place was so ridiculous that I couldn't help but laugh. The sound fractured into a sob as I met Roary's eyes again, the pain I found in them not matching to what I had expected in light of his liberation.

"What's that on your face?" Roary asking, his eyes narrowing on Cain's pencil moustache and despite the urgency of our situation I snorted a laugh.

"Nothing," Cain snarled, dipping his head irritably.

"Let me get this cage open," I said. "I can try to-"

"No need." Roary released his grip on my hands and pushed the gate to his cage open with a hard shove. He reached up to the collar at his neck next and tugged it loose, tossing it to the ground alongside the magic blocking cuffs which had been around his wrists with a sneer of disgust.

"How?" I breathed, looking from Roary to the collar but as I glanced back to him I found him suddenly closer to me, so close that I gasped.

His arms closed around me and he shoved me back against the wall so hard that I hissed at the jolt of unexpected pain. Roary's hand slammed against the wall above my head, his whole body going rigid with tension and I stared up at him in alarm.

"What's wrong?" I asked because there was something so changed in him. There was something so alien about the way he had just moved, the way he had me pinned to the wall, the way his eyes clung to mine before falling to my neck, his chest rising and falling heavily.

Cain released a low growl from behind him and I looked up at him just as Roary lost control and lunged at me.

His body flattened me to the wall, his strength locking me in place but the gasp of alarm which escaped me was all aimed at the teeth he'd just driven into my neck.

My lips fell open but no words came as he began to drink, his body immobilising me against the wall, his muscles trembling where they pressed to me, stone crumbling above my head where his fingers dug into the bricks.

Cain shot for us but I lifted a hand, baring my own teeth. "Don't," I commanded, a horrifying realisation coming for me as Roary released a low groan and drank more deeply.

"This is so fucked up. How can this be happening?" Cain demanded, his body rigid with tension, the effort it was taking him to restrain himself more than clear. "He's a Lion," he insisted, pacing closer, seemingly unable to stop himself until his chest collided with my outstretched palm.

Roary snarled ferociously at his closeness but didn't withdraw, drinking deeper, his body driving me back more firmly.

My eyes locked on Cain's, my lips parted on the words which I couldn't bear to speak.

We'd discovered the sickening truth of the experiments which had been taking place beneath Darkmore all this time. We'd seen what they'd been trying to do but I hadn't dared let myself fear that fate would have come to Roary in the short time we had been separated. I hadn't allowed myself to fear this reality until it had slapped me in the face and forced me to look it in the eye. Roary, my Lion, my beautiful, prideful Lion. What he was was akin to *who* he was. And this...

"Where is it?" I breathed, a tear sliding down my cheek as I moved my hand up Roary's back and caressed his close-cropped hair. "Where is your Lion, Roar?"

With a savage jerk he withdrew, a noise of pure agony escaping him.

I cursed in pain myself as his fangs tore my skin with the sudden departure, blood spilling freely down my neck.

Cain was on me in moments, his hand at my throat, healing the wound but I pushed him off, closing in on Roary even while he backed away.

"Where is it?" I demanded, louder, firmer.

Roary's hand closed over his mouth, his eyes on my neck where the blood no doubt still stained my skin, horror written across his expression.

"I don't give a fuck about a little bite and a bit of blood, Roary," I snapped at him, flicking a vine his way to yank his hand away from his mouth, revealing bloodstained fangs in a mouth which never should have had them.

I tried to hide my shock, but his flinch said I'd failed in that.

"I'm not the man you fell in love with anymore," he rasped.

"Of course you fucking are," I snarled. "But that doesn't mean we're going to leave your Lion in this place. So where the fuck is it?"

Roary swallowed thickly, glancing away from me and looking towards a door to the rear of the space.

"Drav...or Vard, whatever the fuck he's calling himself. The motherfucker who did this to me has it. It was here though. He's been showing it off to those sick assholes who want in on this twisted bullshit. I heard him saying he was going to be taking a meeting with one of them but I don't know where he went after that. One of the Minotaurs he set to guard me didn't like what he was doing and gave me the key to my cell, collar and cuffs. He said to take that door once I got out. That's all I know."

"It's all we need," I swore to him because if it wasn't then I would make it so.

"Come on," Cain agreed, shooting past us and throwing his shoulder against the door. It burst open, revealing a long corridor lined with cages, the doors of which were all wide open, leaving nothing in their depths.

"These were full earlier," Roary muttered, moving to follow Cain.

I stepped beside him and took his hand in mine, winding my fingers through his and holding him tightly. He tried to pull back and I levelled him with a dark stare.

"I waited ten years to make you fall for me, Roary Night," I warned him. "Don't go thinking there's anything which might ever make me want you less."

"I'm not the man you-" he began but I cut him off sharply.

"Do you love me less for my scars?" I demanded.

"You know I don't," he replied in a low growl.

"Then don't go thinking a pair of fangs will put me off," I snapped. "Besides – you know I like it rough. And I've never been averse to a little biting."

Cain threw me a heated look over his shoulder and I gave him the hint of a smile before focusing on the task at hand and leading Roary after me into the dimly-lit passageway.

We made it to a fork in the rows of cages, the way to the right lit with the flickering glow of flames, the way to our left abandoned in darkness.

A burst of raucous laughter sounded in the distance and to our right and I recognised Sin's voice.

"This way," I said, indicating the opposite direction. "If they'd found it, we'd know already."

Ethan had his orders to send me a signal in pain if he happened to find Roary first and I was certain he would have extended that to the discovery of his Lion

– assuming he recognised it when he saw it. Either way, the moon was urging me to the left and my other men had their orders to keep the ruthless Fae in this place fully occupied while I worked.

Cain and Roary didn't question me, both of them presumably so used to my judgement being correct in these kinds of scenarios that they were beyond doubting me anyway.

The cages got larger as we headed through the darkness, the scent of blood and rot mixing with the animal stench which ruled down here. I eyed a cage large enough to hold two elephants, wondering what the fuck had been inside it.

Ahead of us lay a door, illuminated around its edges by the glow of light from within. I didn't fail to notice the corpse sprawled before it, the skin of the Fae's face torn off entirely making it difficult to tell if they'd been male or female.

I tossed a silencing bubble up over us before inching closer to the door and asking the moon to hide me from sight once more.

Cain and Roary hung back a few steps as I approached, watching my flank, having my back.

I reached out with my power, feeling the magical ward which stood around the door, blocking the entrance.

Vines crept from my fingertips and spread out before me, trailing swiftly along the edges of the ward, brushing against it gently, testing, tasting, just enough to let me know where it stood but not enough to inform whoever had cast it of my presence.

A smile tightened my lips as I found the edges of the ward less than a foot around the door.

"My cousin Dante has a saying about fools who only guard the obvious entrance point," I said, stepping to my right until I was looking at the wall beyond the outer edge of the ward. "They're asking to have their back door blown open."

Magic exploded from my palms, two pillars of solid stone crashing from me and into the wall before us. The thin skin of bricks were blasted apart, my magic taking hold of them and merging with them, ripping them aside and hurling them away over my head so that we were left standing before a wide hole, looking into a room where two men stood gawping at us in utter horror.

My eyes went straight to Vard who was gaping at us like a fish out of water – or rather gaping at Roary and Cain because he couldn't even see me where I stood directly before him.

I took a step forward, ready to launch myself at him, but before I could do anything, a roar of utter agony broke from Cain's lips and a rush of air swept past me as he launched himself at the huge blonde bastardo who I had barely spared a second glance for.

The two of them went crashing into a stack of crates and tumbling out of view and Vard blasted a ball of fire at us in the few seconds I lost to my shock.

Roary snarled ferociously, shooting after him as he turned tail and fled but he went crashing into the wall, seemingly unable to fully control himself at Vampire speed.

I broke into a run, not sparing any time on either of my men as I raced after Vard who had flung himself through a door at the back of the small room.

I hit the door, cursing as I found it reinforced with magic and coating my fists in iron as I began to pound on it to break through.

Roary joined me, using his newly heightened strength to attack the door too and we fell crashing through it as it finally gave way.

Vard was already at the far side of the cluttered space, a row of shelves between us that didn't quite hide the glass jar in his arms which glowed with a bright, golden aura.

"There it is," Roary gasped, shooting ahead again and slamming straight into the shelves, sending them crashing down on us and forcing me to throw a shield of dirt up over our heads to save us from being crushed.

"Come, Benjamin!" Vard bellowed and I cried out as what sounded like an explosion came from behind us where Cain had been engaged in his fight with the blonde bastardo.

I sucked in a sharp breath as Dragon fire bellowed from the jaws of a huge, bronze coloured beast which I had to assume was the bastardo in his shifted form.

Cain shot towards us and I threw my earth magic up again. This time my wall of dirt was joined by ice as Roary helped me, though even that was only just enough to shield us from the blast of Dragon fire which exploded over it.

I cursed in Faetalian, reappearing again in the midst of my men and gritting my teeth as the flames continued to blast over the top of us.

"Grab hold of me and hold your breath," I commanded, turning my attention to the ground at our feet and grunting as I forced it to bow to my command.

The moment Roary and Cain had grabbed my arms, vines sprung from me to tether them in place and the ground gave out beneath us.

We fell into the embrace of the soil, the dry particles all bowing to my command, dragging us through them beneath the ground, hurling us in the direction Vard had taken.

Dirt pressed to my face, clogging against my ears, nose, mouth, trying to suffocate us despite my hold on it until I finally launched us back up into the air.

I heaved down a thick breath as we emerged in another room, this one stacked with wooden crates, once again marked with random symbols.

I released Cain and Roary from my magic, the three of us hastily swiping dirt from our faces and taking stock of where we were.

Vard was racing for the exit, Roary's Lion still clasped tightly in his grip but before I could take so much as a step in his direction, a rasping, horrifying voice rattled through the air, a single word scraping from the throat of a monster which loomed above us, baring its teeth.

"Bitch," it hissed and my eyes widened as I recognised the lilt of that voice, the poisonous undertone, the unbridled hatred.

The thing bared its pointed teeth in what was undoubtedly a psychotic grin, and I only had the briefest of moments to recognise the beast which had once been Gustard before it was upon us.

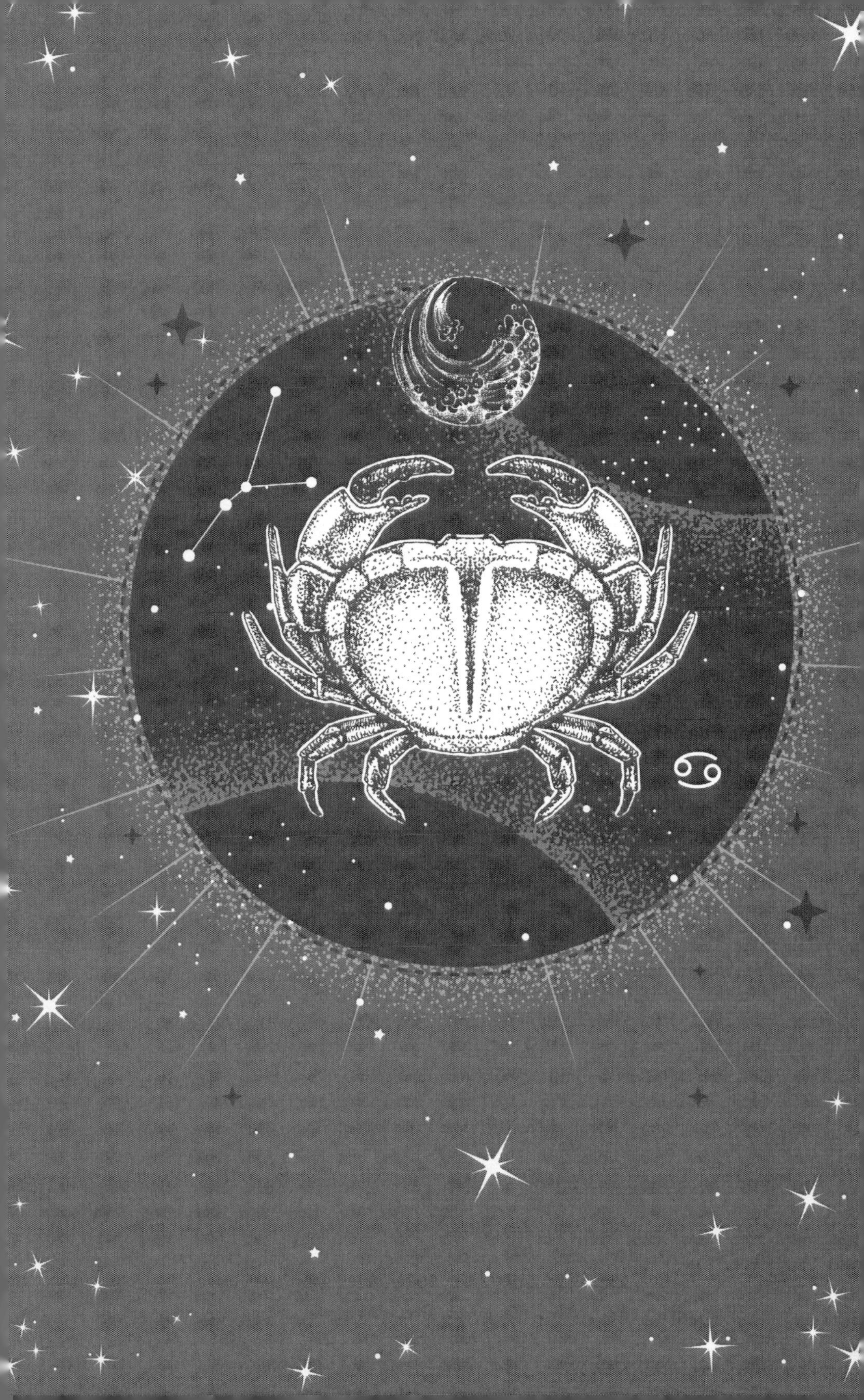

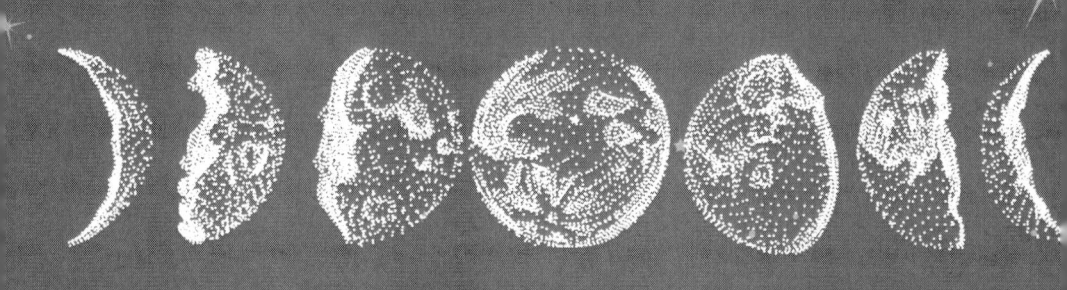

ETHAN

PRISONER #1

CHAPTER SEVENTEEN

"Are you sure about this?!" I called to my maniac companion as we ran side by side through the winding corridors of empty cages. We were going back the way we'd come, the last of the wild magical animals we'd released racing away behind us, urged on by a gust of wind at their backs that Sin had cast.

"Sure as a sea shore," Sin confirmed, the crow-like bird on his shoulder cawing its agreement, rigidly remaining with its saviour.

My heart was racing and I felt a thrill I hadn't felt in so damn long. It swam through my veins, singing the sweet melody of freedom. This was where I had once found myself, between the turmoil and disorder. I adored the hum of adrenaline in my blood, and I'd star damned missed this kind of madness. But Sin's wild streak was the type that could likely get me killed in countless insane ways. Somehow, I didn't care. I only forged on at his side, my pulse a keen drum in my ears, willing my movements to quicken as we delved into the dark together once more.

He turned a corner and came to an abrupt halt, his head snapping around to look at me.

"It's open," he whispered and I looked to the cage he gestured towards, realising where we were. Gustard had been here. And now a key was sitting in the lock of that cage, proving someone had let him out.

My shoulders tensed as I glanced up and down the passage and I felt Sin's air shield close tighter around us.

"What was your plan?" I breathed, then flicked up a silencing bubble.

"Start a fire in the belly of the behemoth," he hissed, fire snapping into existence on his fingertips. "One that catches, rises and burns it all to cinders."

"Rosalie's here somewhere," I growled.

His eyes sparkled at me, full of havoc, daring me to play his dangerous game. "You think our wild girl can't handle a few sparks? Her soul is made of a fire far hotter than any I can cast. She'll be out before the flames make it near her."

My jaw tightened as I took in the certainty in his eyes, feeling it too. Then I nodded and watched as fire spilled from his hands in a waterfall of hungry flames, pouring across the floor and rising up the walls to dance over the ceiling. It spread fast and thick, and I cast ice against my skin and his to shield us from the thickening heat.

"Run, pretty boy, run." Sin smiled devilishly then raced back the way we'd come while flames poured along behind him.

I cursed as they licked my legs and sprinted after him, knowing he could slow them down, but he was laughing like a madman again and making them chase us even faster.

The riot of fear in my chest gave way to that delightful thrill once more and I gave myself to the chaos, a smile of my own finding its way to my lips.

"You think fire is power?" I called to him and he glanced back. "Let me show you what water can do."

I willed my elemental power into the walls around us, letting it drive into the cracks and dagger up and away from us, as high as it could go, the water slithering through the walls, the pipes, every space it could find. It dug into every crevice, no gap small enough to stop it and my grin widened at the use of such furious magic. When I'd let it spread as far as possible, I yanked on the tether of it just enough to make the entire building shudder with the promise of destruction.

"Holy cow, Wolf man," Sin cooed. "I can feel your presence in the walls."

"The moment I want to, I can pull each brick out of place and bring it down on every asshole remaining in this starless place."

"And you'll get your chance, pretty boy," Sin purred. "But hold it while my flames rise."

"I'll wait until I'm sure Rosalie has made it to free air then she can watch it all fall at her feet."

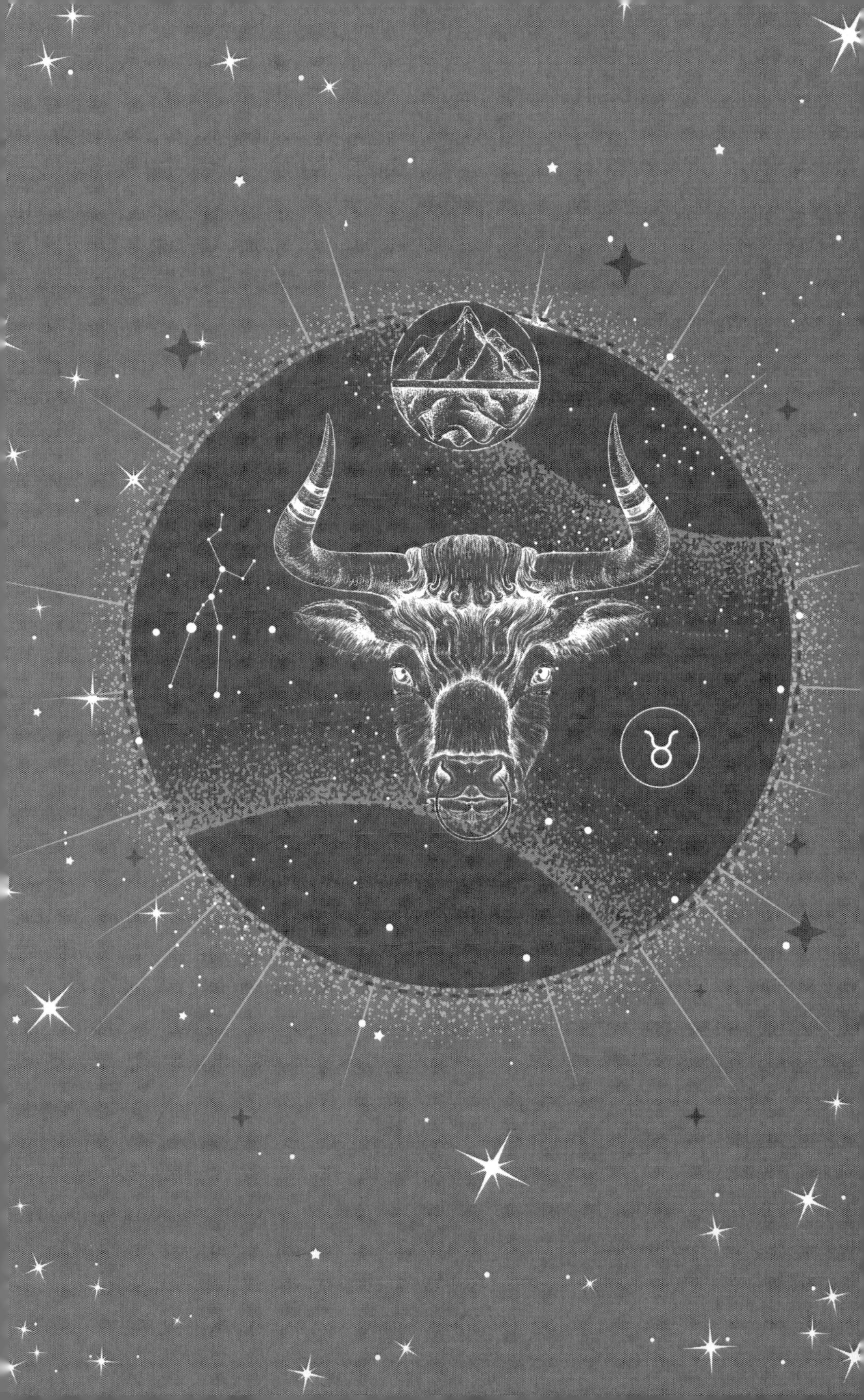

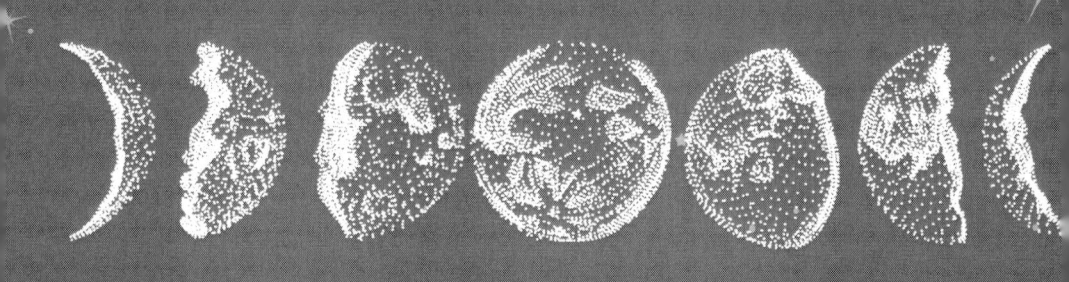

ROSALIE

PRISONER #12

CHAPTER EIGHTEEN

My back collided with the wall, a curse spilling from my lips as I forged an iron sword in my fist and tightened my grip on it.

The beast which had once been Gustard lunged at me but Cain shot between us, throwing up a wall of fire that forced the monster back.

"Here!" I yelled, tossing the sword to Cain who caught it neatly before speeding away again.

The smoke which had been seeping into the space was getting thicker and as I forged another blade for myself, I choked back a cough. It was getting hotter in here too and despite the massive, monstrous form of Gustard taking up most of my attention, I spared a glance in the direction we'd come from.

My heart leapt as I took in the flames racing towards us, spiralling through the empty cages and moving at a speed which had to equal magic.

"Roary!" I yelled, hurling myself away from the fire and he looked my way as he leapt out of reach of one of Gustard's flailing arms.

His eyes widened in alarm, his hands going up and hurling a wall of ice out between me and the raging inferno that was headed our way.

I threw myself towards him, raising a hand to send a row of wooden spears straight at Gustard and force him back towards the flames.

The door where Vard had disappeared was wide open, its emptiness looming and taunting.

I shouted a command for the others to aim for it and broke into a sprint myself.

"He's getting away!" I yelled.

Roary's head snapped around, his body going rigid with tension, a sound of pure grief spilling from his lips before he shot away from us.

Cain collided with me as I called out for Roary to wait, lifting me off of my feet and shooting after him at Vampire speed.

Gustard roared behind us, the sound of the roof caving in meeting with his furious bellows and for a fleeting heartbeat I gave in to the call of hope that he had met with his end.

But of course the nasty bastardo wouldn't go down so easily and as I looked back over Cain's shoulder, my red hair tumbling around me, I found him lurching from the heaped rubble and taking chase with the flames of the burning compound at his back.

Cain cursed as he ran and I turned in his arms, hunting for a sign of Roary ahead of us.

"He's given in to the hunt," Cain grunted as we turned sharply and started up a set of stairs, Gustard falling out of sight behind us though his howls of fury followed on. "He doesn't know how to stop himself. If I can catch him then I can try to get him to come back to his senses but if he's lost to it…"

"Put me down," I demanded.

"What? No. I'm not just going to-"

I punched him in the jaw, snarling furiously as we sped from the stairwell and back into the ramshackle marketplace where so many Fae had been congregated with illicit intent what seemed like moments ago.

"You swore not to get in my way, Cain. Now put me down before I make you."

Cain skidded to a halt, fury etched into every piece of his face but I ignored him, shoving out of his arms and looking around wildly in search of Roary or Vard.

A wild giggle drew my attention to our left where flames burned bright and Sin Wilder was clearly having the time of his damn life.

Hesitation halted me. This place was done for and we needed to get out. Sin and Ethan didn't know we were here but I could make up for that.

"Catch up to Roary and help him get his fucking Lion back," I commanded, stepping right up to Cain and meeting his glare with one of my own. "You're faster without me and I need to find the others. We'll be right behind you."

Cain hesitated, his word and his wants clearly at war.

I pushed up onto my tiptoes and kissed him hard, my hand fisting in his shirt, and a groan of pure need escaped him before I shoved him away forcefully.

"I'm right behind you. Go," I commanded and with one last, furious look at me he finally conceded, shooting away in a blur of motion in hunt of Roary and the man who had stolen his Lion from him.

Smoke stung my eyes and the heat in this place was near suffocating but I held my ground, tipping back my head and howling in call of my mate.

Ethan's reply sounded in the distance within moments but even as my heart soared with relief, it spilled away again just as fast. Because at that precise moment, the floor collapsed beneath me and Gustard leapt from the rubble, intent on delivering me to my death.

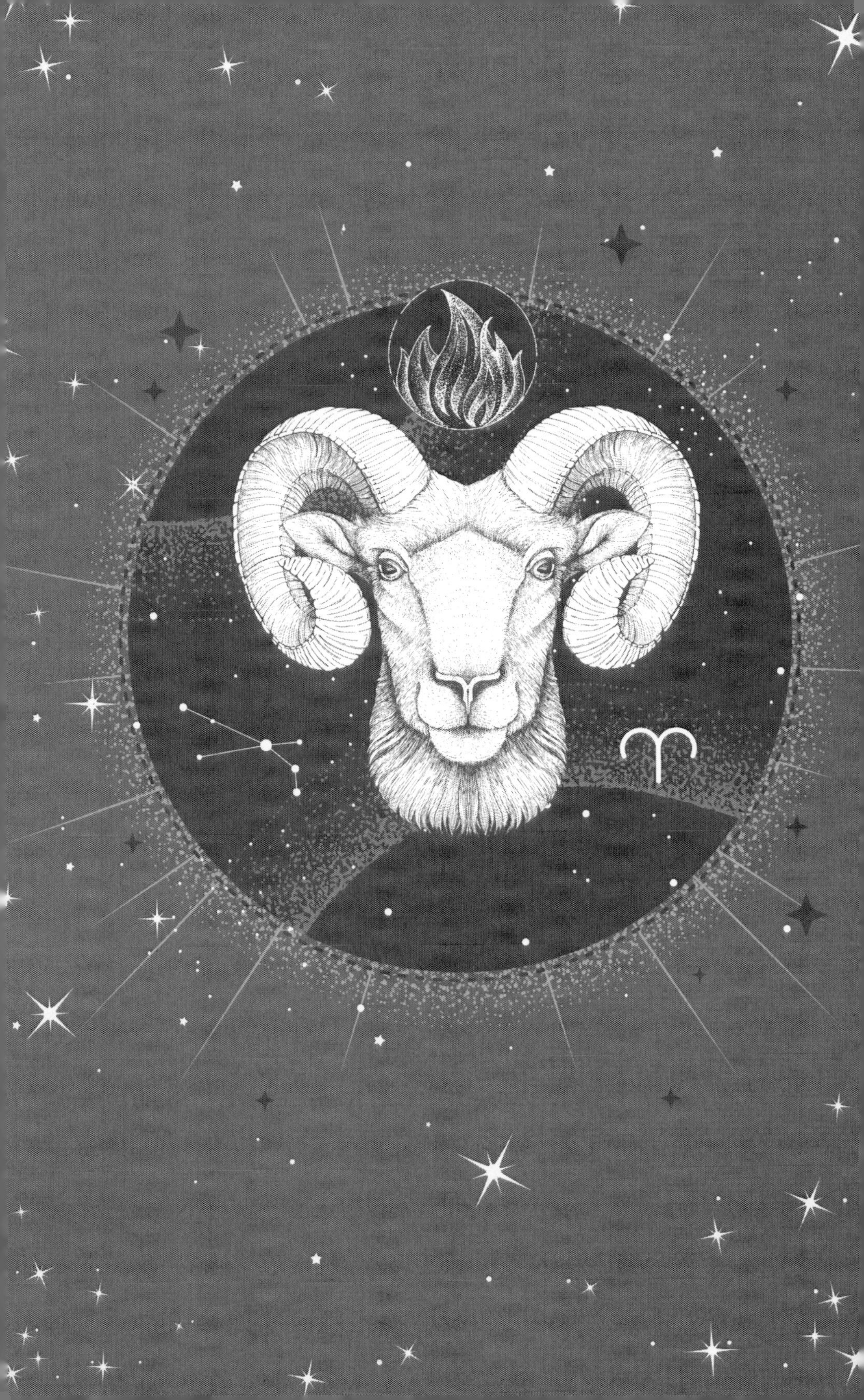

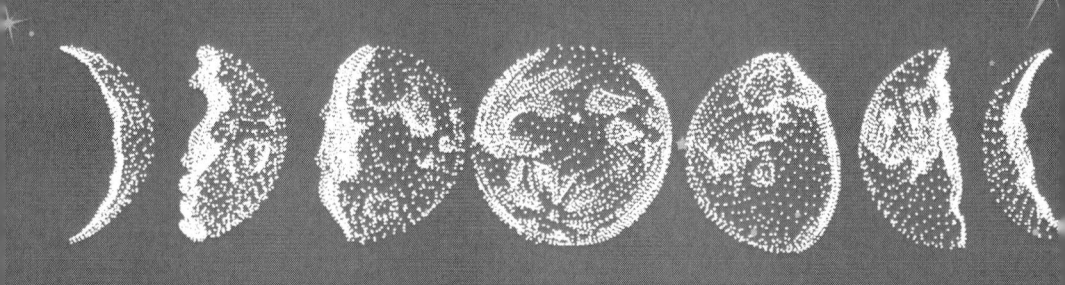

CAIN
COMMANDING OFFICER

CHAPTER NINETEEN

I raced through burning halls, fire flaring in every direction, both Dragon and elemental. My mind was latched onto the man I'd seen with Vard, a thousand childhood memories ripping through my skull like a shot of ice. My blood was cold with it, the sight of him churning up a storm of emotion that I'd long pushed down inside me. He was the reason for my friend Merrick's death, the reason for so many kids' deaths. He had been sending them off to 'Bliss', a promise of nirvana, but it had been a sick lie. And now I saw him standing with Vard, a man who was responsible for the twisted experiments in Psych, I had a feeling I knew where those 'lucky' kids had ended up.

I broke through a burning wooden wall and sprinted up a stairway beyond, the almost imperceptible sound of fast footfalls ahead of me telling of where Roary was. With the speed we were moving at, it didn't make sense that we hadn't caught up with Vard and my bloodthirsty tormentor Benjamin Acrux until I glanced up, jarring to a halt as I spotted the huge hole Benjamin's Dragon form had ripped into the roof.

A glint of bronze scales and the sound of a bellow spoke of his position on top of the building, the debris cascading down to where I stood.

I could still reach him, destroy Benjamin for all he'd done to me and take Vard down along with him. I could climb fast, I could get hold of them. But the sound of screams made my head whip back to look at the passage Roary had taken.

He was lost to the hunt of our kind, unable to draw himself from it. And I knew Vampires who had spiralled into that instinct and never come back. If he lost himself to it now, there would be little left of him remaining. His priority would be blood, no longer Rosalie.

I cursed myself and sprinted after him, the heavy beating of Dragon wings filling the air and warning of Benjamin's escape.

But my mind was set and as I raced up a stairwell, I found myself in a ballroom of destruction. Fire bloomed up the walls and people screamed, running for their lives while Roary ripped through the heart of them, tearing out the throats of any Fae he could get his hands on. I didn't care for these wretched souls who had a hand in this place of sin, but my love for Rosalie Oscura had me running for Roary, determined to bring him back from the brink of oblivion. He was like a newly Awakened Vampire and Roary had no one to teach him our ways, no one to show him how to control the urges or harness the bloodlust.

"Roary!" I shouted, racing for him as he sank his fangs into another victim's throat.

His eyes locked with mine, a feral need filling them, one I remembered the burn of. I had been there and I knew the only way to pull back was to hold onto the things worth keeping your head for. And he had a hell of a lot more to hold onto than I had back when I'd faced these challenges.

He turned and sprinted from me, chasing down his next target, but I was hot on his tail, not letting him escape me this time. He was a fast motherfucker, but he was clumsy too, his body not yet adjusted to this new way of moving. I put on another burst of speed and slammed into him from behind, taking him to the floor and pinning him there with the bulk of my weight. I rolled him onto his back beneath me as he struggled and forced my arm across his chest, shoving him down.

He snarled at me and the natural rivalry between our kind flared inside me, making me bare my fangs right back at him. Blood stained his mouth and chin, his eyes wild as they slid away from me to a woman racing past us. He thrashed, frantic to get to her but I reared back and punched him in the face. He snarled, dazed by the blow as he met my gaze again.

"Think of Rosalie!" I barked. "Your mate." I grabbed his arm, yanking it up to make him look at the mark that bound him to her. "She's yours and she's waiting for you to return to her."

He snarled a second longer but then his gaze fell on the mark on his wrist and a frown creased his brow.

"For her," I pushed. "Come back from hell for *her*."

Slowly, the darkness in his eyes faded and his muscles slackened. "Cain?" he rasped like he was seeing me for the first time.

"Yes, asshole," I muttered. "Now get up." I pushed off of him, rising to my feet and offering him my hand.

His throat rose and fell then he slapped his palm into mine and I yanked him upright.

"Don't go thinking this means more than it does," I muttered, tugging my hand free.

Warmth coiled around my left arm and I found the leaves of the rose vine receding a little. Just a few inches, but enough to tell me I'd pleased the curse in my actions today, and for some reason, I felt more like myself than I ever had in my life.

A flash of bronze scales caught my eye through the window and a growl built in my throat as I spotted Benjamin swooping past it in his Dragon form with Vard clutched in his talons, gazing down as if searching for something or someone they had left behind. I could still get to them. There was still time. I sprinted off across the ballroom toward the exit, determined to destroy them both.

Roary raced along at my heels and we tore through passages filled with debris before finally making it outside. Inhaling deep, I tasted the fresh air washing into my lungs and turned my gaze to the sky, seeking out my enemies and promising them a bloody death.

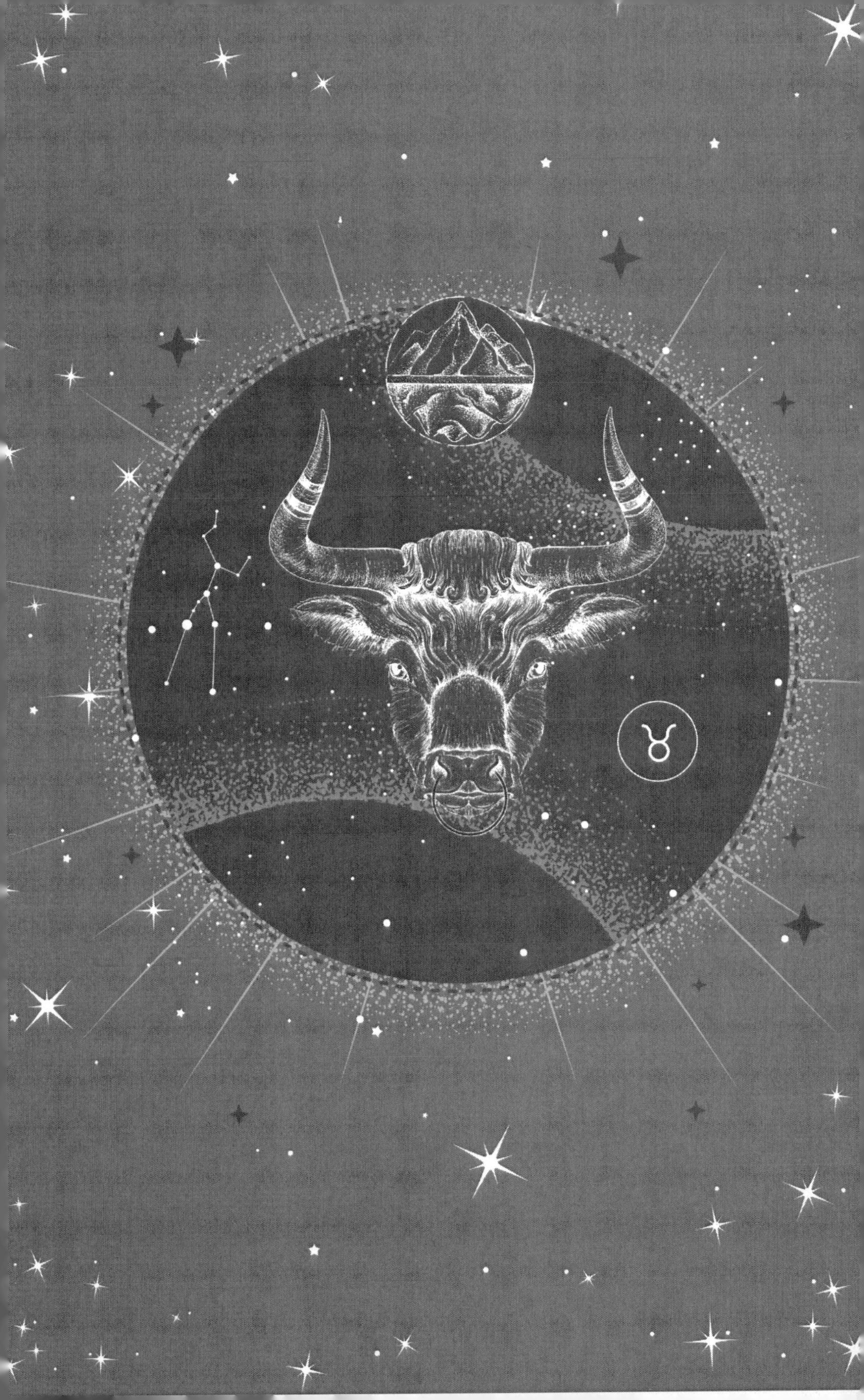

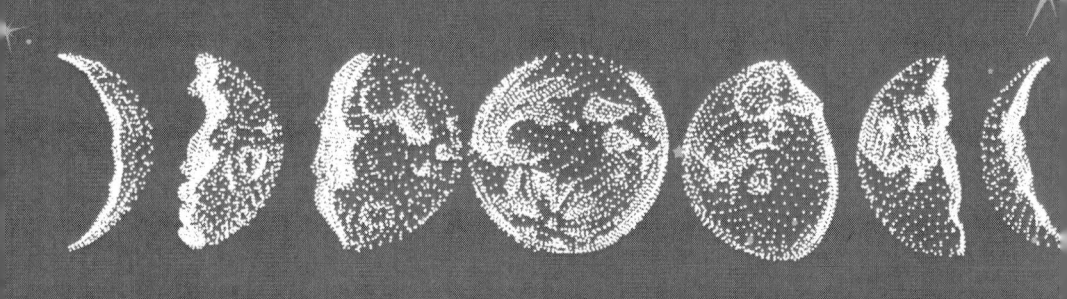

ROSALIE
PRISONER #12

CHAPTER TWENTY

I wasn't sure if I'd been knocked out or if I'd simply hit my head so hard that it seemed like I must have done. Either way, I was brought back to reality with a jolt as Sin yelled a battle cry, leaping through the cavernous hole above me and shifting mid-air into his Belorian form. A dark feathered bird squawked as it took off from his shoulder and circled above us and I realised it was a rare talian corvid.

I blinked up at the monstrous beast as he collided with Gustard, my ears ringing from the impact of my skull against way too many hard surfaces on my fall down here.

I cursed as I rolled to my hands and knees before gripping a piece of metal and heaving myself to my feet again.

"Give me your hand, love," Ethan called and I turned, finding him leaning down into the hole behind me, his arm extended towards me while Sin and Gustard fought ferociously at my back.

I took a running jump, ignoring the way my head rang at the movement and caught Ethan's hand in mine. He hauled me up and into his arms, tugging me away from the crater in the floor and pressing his hand to my cheek, healing magic flowing into me at the contact.

"I've got you," he swore, going all mushy and shit but I pushed him aside, my focus on Sin who was still locked in battle with Gustard.

I had no idea what Vard had done to make the piece of shit I'd known in Darkmore into this terrifying beast, but I did know that we were wasting time here with him.

"I have this place ready to collapse," Ethan said. "As soon as we're clear we can bring it all down on that motherfucker's head."

"Sounds like a plan," I agreed. "Sin – jump!"

The Belorian which was Sin twisted its head in my direction, slammed its pincer into the side of Gustard's monstrous face then took a running jump in our direction, shifting as he did so into his Harpy form, long, white hair flowing down his back.

He sailed over our heads and I threw a shelf of rock out over the hole before us, containing Gustard in the bowels of the building before turning and running in the direction Roary and Cain had taken.

Ethan kept pace with me and Sin landed, shifting back into himself to run with us as well. He was butt naked, having lost all of his clothes when shifting into the Belorian but his bouncing cock was the least of our concerns at the moment. The talian corvid that had been with my Incubus followed close, squawking as if urging us on.

"This is the most fun I've had in years," Sin cooed, tipping his head back and howling in a good impression of a Wolf.

I howled with him, Ethan joining us as we let the others know we were coming.

I coughed as the smoke rose around us, the corridors blurring around me, concealed within the blackness. Sin threw a hand out, casting a strong wind to blow it away from us and I sucked in a ragged breath of clean air with relief.

"Look," Ethan said, pointing at a hole in the roof big enough to admit a-

"Shit," I hissed as a bronze Dragon swept through the sky overhead, blotting out the sight of the moon for a moment. The moonlight glimmered off of the beast's immense body, illuminating a man who was clutched in its claws. Vard. And I had to assume that golden glow against his chest was Roary's Lion still clutched in his arms.

"I can take him," Sin said, grinning wickedly and cracking his knuckles.

"You think you can take on a Dragon the size of a fucking bus?" Ethan asked, not bothering to hide his disbelief.

"A bus?" Sin chortled. "How about two buses and a bonus elephant?"

"What?" Ethan questioned but hope sparked in my chest as I realised what he was suggesting.

"Your Lionel Acrux form?" I gasped excitedly, remembering the way Sin had shifted into the enormous green Dragon and flown me through the Order yard back in Darkmore. And he was right – he was far bigger than that bastardo out there.

"Yeah, sweet cheeks. Wanna go for a ride?" Sin purred.

"Fuck yes," I agreed.

Ethan looked like he had more questions but I caught his arm, forcing him to back up with me so that Sin could shift.

A roar bellowed from Sin's lips as he shifted, his skin splitting apart to reveal the huge Dragon form which would no doubt ignite terror in all who laid eyes on it once he took to the skies.

I wasted no time, sprinting for him and casting a blast of dirt beneath my boots to launch myself up onto his back. Ethan followed using his water magic, murmuring in low appreciation as he took up position behind me and locked his arms around my waste.

Sin leapt into action the moment my hands had fisted one of the giant spikes which protruded from his back, leaping for the roof and ripping into the edges of the hole which the bronze Dragon had carved into place, widening it for his bulk.

I threw out a hand, encasing me, Ethan and that ever-following talian corvid in a lump of rock, like a barnacle stuck to the Dragon's back, protecting us from the crumbling roof as tiles and wooden beams slammed down on us.

My gut lurched as Sin launched himself into the sky and I threw the stone casing off of us, howling wildly as a rush of wind collided with us.

Sin bellowed a challenging roar at the bronze Dragon who turned in midair, his wings stalling as he took in the immense beast now racing for him.

Vard shrieked like a newborn babe.

"The King has come to claim his vengeance on me!" he screamed, kicking and flailing where he was still grasped in the bronze Dragon's claws, almost dropping the precious cargo which was clutched in his arms. "Go!"

"Don't let them escape!" I bellowed as Sin tore through the sky, closing the distance between us and our quarry, but Vard was fumbling a small pouch between his hands and the Dragon was racing away from us, flying with a roar which was clearly laced in terror as it raced for the open ocean. And worse than that – the edge of the anti-stardust wards.

"Sin!" I commanded, ducking low, urging him on.

I threw vines after them and Ethan hurled whips of water, trying to snatch the Dragon into our grip, slow it down. I wanted to tear Roary's Lion from the hands of that stronzo Vard but I was afraid of missing, of knocking it from his arms and the jar smashing or sinking into the sea below.

We were closing in on them now, only twenty feet dividing us and Sin roared as he lunged but a flash of glimmering stardust sparkled in the moonlight. Despite my screams of despair and Ethan's howls of protest, the stars ripped our prey into their grasp and snatched them away from us in the blink of an eye.

Sin bellowed mournfully, a thousand bubbles exploding from his mouth and washing over us in the balmy sky as he swung back around towards the beach.

A sob caught in my throat at how fucking close we had come to stopping them, how near we had been to reclaiming what they had stolen from my mate.

Ethan gripped me tightly, his own pain at our failure clear as Sin dropped towards the shore with a mournful cry which sent even more bubbles tearing over us.

We landed heavily and I was almost thrown from Sin's back as he crashed into the sand, clearly not used to navigating the enormous form the way Dante was.

I slipped from his back with the balmy night air clinging to my skin, and I stumbled to a halt at what I found before me. Cain was gripping Roary's arm while he stared horror-struck at the dark sky, his eyes locked on the place where Vard had slipped out of reach.

"They got away," Roary rasped, still staring at that spot of nothing.

My gut lurched, heartbreak threatening at the raw emotion in his words, but we had no time to dwell on it.

The sound of Gustard battling with his confinement was growing louder, thumps and roars from within the burning compound filling the air and now that Vard had taken Roary's Lion away from this place there was nothing left here for us.

Sin shifted back into his own form behind us and the talian corvid landed on his shoulder with a mournful ca-caw like it sensed the weight of our loss. The four of us drew together, each of us looking to Roary with hurt and sorrow written across our expressions.

"We'll get it back, Roar," I swore, taking his hand in mine and tugging him in the direction of the beach. "But right now, we have to run."

He nodded emptily, letting me pull him after me as I broke into a sprint and the five of us set a course for the dock where our boat remained anchored – one of the last remaining in place.

The sea was full of retreating Fae, their vessels making a fast pace out onto the ocean as they escaped the carnage we had brought to their door.

A furious roar echoed from the compound at our backs and Ethan turned to look at it, raising his hand in the air before closing it into a fist.

All at once, the compound collapsed in on itself like the hand of some giant had swept it from existence. Flames billowed towards the moon above as the bricks and beams all caved in and the sky was illuminated in blazing orange before us.

We kept running, our group racing back onto our boat, my hand never once loosening its grip on Roary as I drew him onboard.

Sin cut the tethers holding us to the dock and Ethan worked with him to launch us out to sea.

I watched the burning rubble of the compound as it retreated from view and a lump thickened my throat as a huge figure burst from the ashes, screaming furiously at the sky.

But we were already too far for Gustard to reach us, and as Grimolda Isle faded away into the distance, I finally let myself breathe again.

I turned to face Roary, pain spearing me at the hopeless expression on his face and as he met my gaze, he flinched.

Roary dropped his head, trying to tug his hand from mine and backing up a step towards the cabin in the centre of the boat.

"Don't you dare run from me again, Roary Night," I growled, matching every retreating step of his with a pace of my own.

He moved back into the cabin and I followed, never once releasing him and kicking the door shut as I stepped through it to afford us some privacy.

"Rosa," he rasped and I surged forward, kissing him hard, forcing him to do nothing at all other than feel the truth of my love for him in the simple press of my lips against his.

Tears slipped from my hold, the salt of them tracking between our mouths as they moved as one and his hands slowly slid around me, gripping my waist and holding me tight.

"You are *mine*, Roary Night," I said into that kiss. "My love for you withstood the walls of Darkmore. It persisted in the years which parted us and grew with every moment I have claimed in your arms since. Don't you dare try to shut me out now. Lion or not, you're mine. Do you understand that?"

I took his arm in my hand, my thumb pressing down on the mate mark which proved the truth of my words beyond all doubt.

"I am yours," he said helplessly, his voice ragged and broken. "But I'm not all I should be anymore."

"Yes you are," I disagreed, my hands moving to the buttons of his shirt, fingers tugging them free while our kiss deepened and his tongue sank into my mouth.

Roary seemed to resist for a few moments before finally giving in, his fingers knotting in the back of my top before tugging it up and over my head.

My bra followed as I pushed his shirt over his shoulders and slid it down his arms, caressing the thick swell of his biceps, forearms, wrists and finally lifting his hands to my breasts.

Roary groaned as he massaged my skin, one thumb scraping over my nipple while he tugged the other between his fingers.

I moaned for him, the heat of his body so familiar, so intoxicating, and nothing in this world or any beyond it could ever change that about him for me.

I unbuckled his belt, pushing his pants and boxers down, freeing the thick shaft of his cock and moaning again as I slicked my thumb through the bead of precum which crowned his tip.

"I want you inside me, Roary," I gasped against his lips. "I want your cock so deep in me that I can't breathe for the feeling of it consuming me. I want you to take me and remind yourself that there is one thing in this world which you will always own no matter what."

I stepped back for a moment and let my eyes roam over him hungrily, from his sculpted abs and broad shoulders to the mouth-watering perfection of his solid cock.

Roary groaned hungrily, his lips dropping to my throat as he tugged at my belt in turn while kicking his boots and socks off so that he could remove his pants completely.

I licked my lips while he undid my pants, moaning loudly as his hand pushed beneath my waistband and into my panties. I was so wet that it took nothing at all for his fingers to be inside me, the heel of his hand grinding down on my clit and making me cry out with pleasure.

"How can you want me so much like this?" Roary muttered, his eyes on the movement of his hand as he drove his fingers in and out of me.

"I want you like this with fur or fangs, Roar," I panted. "You can feel the truth of it. I'm so wet for you. You have no idea how many nights I lay awake thinking of you while you were locked up in Darkmore, my hand where yours is now, your name on my lips as I made myself come for you."

Roary groaned with desire, kissing me again and moving his hand more forcefully inside me.

I whimpered with need, gripping his biceps and digging my fingers into his flesh as he brought me to the edge so easily.

But as I sank into the taste of his mouth against mine, the rough scrape of something sharp rolled over my tongue and Roary jerked back so suddenly that I almost fell at his feet.

I blinked at him in surprise, my body primed for pleasure, his hand now absent from my core and my pants hanging open and caught on my ass.

It took me a moment to realise that he was covering his mouth with his hand while still backing up until his legs hit the single bed in the cabin.

I tilted my head to one side, slowly pushing my trousers and panties down and removing them along with my boots and socks so that I was just as naked as him.

"You think I mind if you bite me, Roar?" I breathed, licking my fingers as he watched me before trailing them down my body, rolling them over one peaked nipple, then my ribs, navel, and finally finding my clit.

He released a strained noise as he watched me, still apparently intent on restraining himself but that bullshit wasn't going to fly with me.

I moaned as I sank my fingers into myself, my free hand tugging on my nipple as I let my head roll back so that my red hair tumbled down my spine.

"I used to lay in the dark and do this every night with your name on my lips," I panted, driving my fingers inside my cunt again, moaning louder, my hooded eyes on his. "Are you going to make me do it again, Roary? Or are you going to come here and show me how much better your fingers feel than mine? How much better your cock feels than my imagination ever could have predicted? You can have me any way you want me, amore mio. On my knees with your dick sliding down my throat or on all fours while you take me from behind – You're the only Alpha I think I've ever fantasised about like that, you know? The only one I ever *wanted* to overpower me."

And just like that, he shattered for me.

Roary slammed into me and whirled me around so fast that my spine hit the bed before he even met my lips with his own. His hand found mine where I was still toying with my clit and he guided my fingers back inside me, his own joining them so that I was stretched wide, gasping his name.

He kissed me harder, growling against my mouth, his fangs catching on my bottom lip and tearing it open.

Roary groaned in pleasure as that small dose of my blood rolled down his throat and I moaned loudly while he drove both of our fingers inside me again.

He took complete control of the motion, the pressure of his hand over mine making the friction against my clit so rampant that it only took a few more powerful strokes before I was coming for him, calling his name out to the heavens as I did so.

"Every night?" he questioned, his eyes searching mine while I panted beneath him and he slowly pulled our joined fingers from my core.

"Every fucking night," I agreed. "And not once did my fantasy ever come close to the reality of claiming you."

He groaned hungrily, rearing over me and licking a drop of my blood from the corner of his mouth before stilling again as he realised what he'd just done.

"Bite me," I urged, baring my throat to him and he swallowed thickly, knowing what it meant to have an Alpha Wolf offer themselves up in such a way.

"I love you, Rosalie," he murmured before hooking my thigh over his waist and sinking his cock into me with a slow and languid thrust which stole the breath from my lungs and had me moaning with need.

He dropped his mouth to my throat, kissing the pounding pulse point, hesitating there. I knew he was thinking about the ragged tear he'd left in my skin when he'd bitten me before, but I wasn't afraid of him. He could take what he needed from me as roughly as he liked and I'd still offer up more.

I gripped the back of his head, my fingers tightening in the short strands of his hair as I pressed my neck to his lips and tilted my hips up in the same motion, taking his cock even deeper.

Roary breathed my name against my skin, drew his cock back out of me and then drove it back in again in tandem with his teeth puncturing my throat.

I cried out, my heels digging into his ass, encouraging him deeper, harder and he gave in to me as he slammed his dick in and out of me with a feral possessiveness which had my head spinning.

He drank deeply, fucking me even harder, the strength of his new Vampire Order form awakening in his limbs, combining with the already powerful might of his body until I was utterly consumed by him.

I came hard, my fingernails biting into his flesh, his cock ruining me entirely and still he didn't slow. My body felt like a tool for his pleasure, his teeth falling from my throat before sinking into the fullness of my breast as he lifted me into his arms, bending my spine so that he could take me deeper still.

I came again, gasping his name and he flipped me over beneath him, rabid in his claiming, my name a curse and prayer on his lips. He lifted my ass and sank into me once more, his teeth finding my neck from behind as he pinned me beneath him and fucked me so brutally that it was all I could do to knot my fingers in the sheets and take him.

My body tightened again, pleasure burning through me so hot that I was afraid I might combust in it, my need for him, every fantasy and desire all coming to this truth – I was his and he was mine.

And as he finally came deep inside me, a roar leaving him which was all Lion despite what had been stolen from him, I knew that everything it had taken to bring us to this place was worth it. And that whatever was needed from this moment on would come.

Because I had dreamed of Roary Night for far too long for fate to ever allow us anything other than our happily ever after.

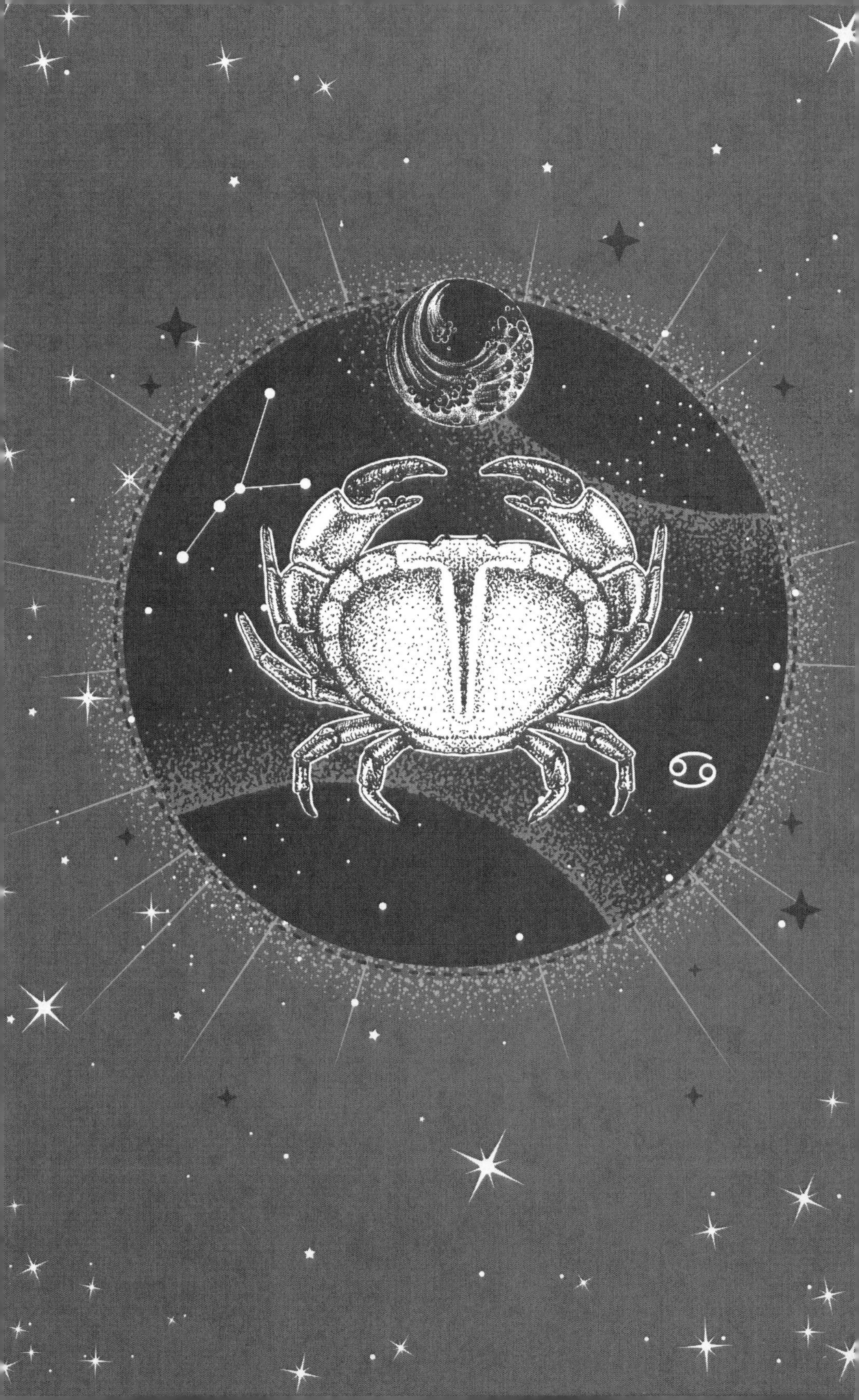

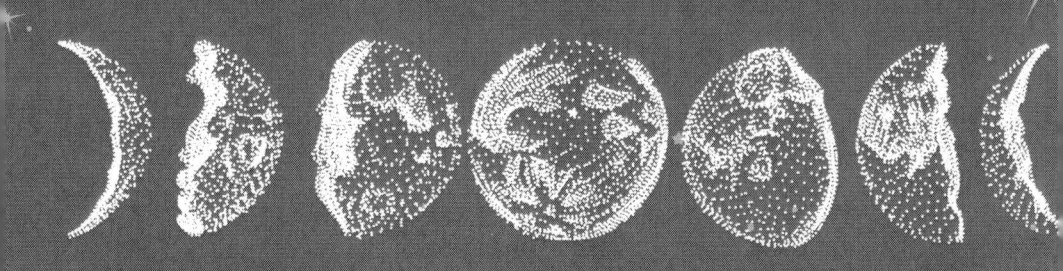

HASTINGS

OFFICER

CHAPTER TWENTY ONE

Through the tumble down remains of the housey-pie, we ran like a raucous circus of beasties and baddies. My dark hair fell in my eyes and bounced up and down like a cricket on my crocket.

I was leading the charge, the chaotic rush of dangerous animals all following me to their destiny which just so happened to be a feast of bad guys.

They didn't bite me though – no, I was one of them, their own, king of the creatures, man of the mammals, fae of fiends-

"Ahh!" I yelled as a heavy weight collided with my spine and sharp teeth sank into my right buttock.

I whirled around, punching the serifius monkey in the face and causing it to fall back with a cry of alarm.

It looked at me and I looked at it, my eyes wide as saucers and its full of accusation.

Oh no. I'd gone and marked myself as its enemy.

The beastie raised a hand and pointed at me before releasing a furious whoop of challenge.

I squawked in fear as a hundred hungry eyes swivelled my way. It was like being in the mess hall back at Darkmore. But these weren't convicts without access to their magic, and I was no superior with a shock baton.

"Oh crickets," I breathed before turning and running as fast as I could in the direction of the beach which sung my name in the distance.

Fae were running, screaming, blasting magic in every direction, carrying their goods or simply sprinting for their lives as the hoard of angry monsters charged after us.

I didn't have to be the fastest. I just had to be faster than…that guy.

I grabbed a man who held a box of what looked like orange-capped mushrooms in his arms. Probably some kind of illegal whatsit. He was a bad guy for sure. And he was smaller than me too.

He cried out in alarm as my grip on his arm tightened and I spun us around before launching him straight at the group of hungry looking animals.

Snarls, cries, screams and the crunching of bones followed but I was running faster now because his strength had just become my strength and I was a four legged Larry on the path to redemption.

I made it to the sand and saluted the terrifying looking bull which depicted Taurus on a rock as I passed. I could have sworn he winked at me as I made it past him to where the ocean kissed the sand and my name was Mandy all over again.

I tripped over my own feet, yelling in alarm and throwing my hands out before me. My palms struck the sand and ice sprung from them, coating the beach ahead of me and sending five Fae skidding to the ground.

I was up and running again, an unknown source of screaming and curses following me as the beasts chased me on.

The sea loomed ahead.

I could see boats on the dock too but as I looked their way I could make out teeth and angry grins on their prows.

No. I needed the water to wash me away. It was my only choice.

Something leapt onto my leg, that first critter digging its claws into me and scurrying up the inside of my pants.

I howled as I kicked out, trying to dislodge it but it moved beneath my clothes, biting and scratching.

I couldn't stop, so on I ran, a huge beast like a fanged gorilla at my back, almost upon me.

Salvation called my name in a sultry purr as I set eyes on the prettiest looking barrel I'd ever seen and I raced for it with wild abandon, opening my arms wide in greeting.

She beckoned me closer and I sprinted for her, throwing myself onto her back just as the sand met with the waves.

The beast which pursued me hollered in rage, swiping at me with razor claws, splashing out into the tide at my heels. I waved my arms at it wildly, spraying water from my palms, shooting my vessel out to sea where I collapsed in a heap of exhaustion and sighed in utter relief.

My trusty barrel sighed my name as I bobbed out into the ocean on her back and I turned to look at the beach behind me. The compound was burning and the animals which had run with me so peacefully were feasting on the bad men. It was a truly horrifying spectacle to behold but as I bobbed away, I lifted a hand and waved.

I was forgetting something important. But Bobby bobbed on so I clung to her, riding her to a sanctuary of the unknown while the world changed colour with every blink I took and euphoria tingled through my limbs.

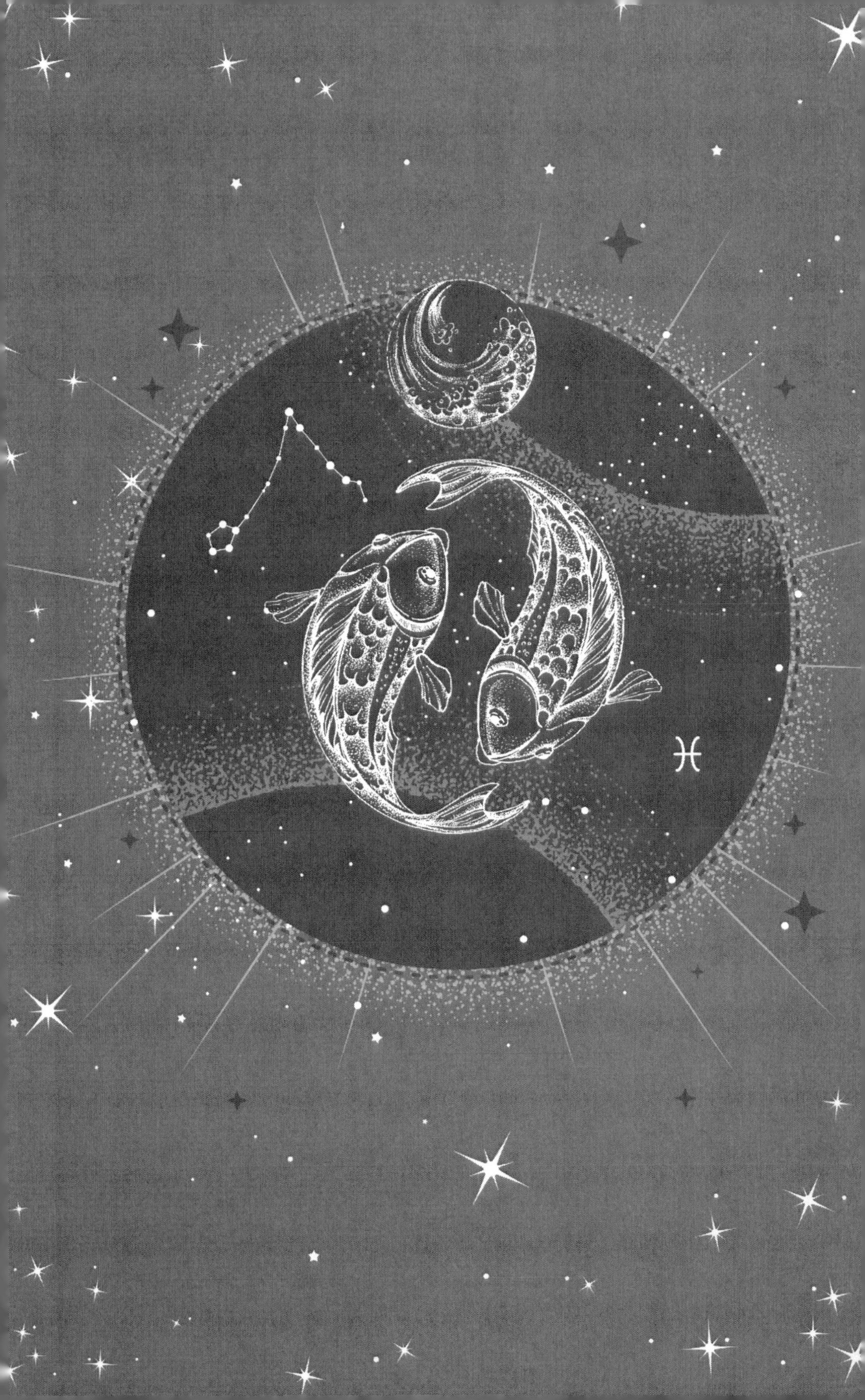

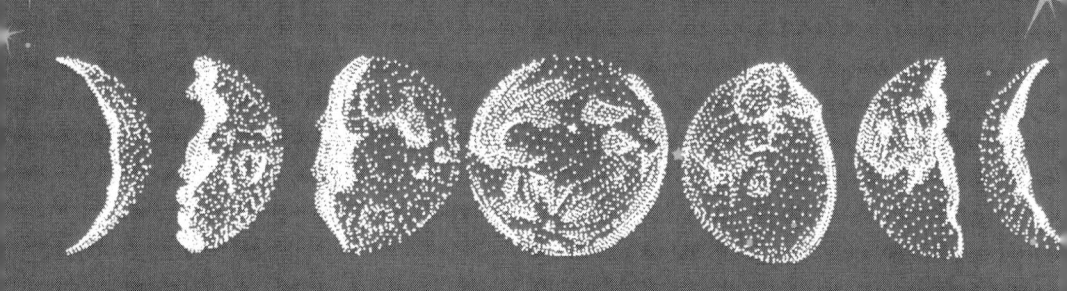

Roary

PRISONER #69

CHAPTER TWENTY TWO

I could barely feel the movement of the boat as Ethan propelled us along with water magic while Sin cast air at the sails up on deck. In this cabin, it was quiet, so quiet that my thoughts were all too loud. Rosalie had gone to check on our progress across the sea, and with her absent, I could feel the demons of my mind rearing up.

Flashes of waking on that cold, metal operating table kept flickering through my head. I pressed my fingers into my eyes, trying to banish them and when I dropped my hand, I stood abruptly in alarm.

Cain had entered the room, silent as the wind and imperceptible even to my heightened hearing. I guessed Vampires couldn't detect other Vampires so easily. He observed me curiously, frowning as he looked me over and my fangs extended, a primal kind of rivalry building inside me.

"So your instincts are in line with mine then," he muttered. "Seems you are one of my kind through and through."

"I'm not your kind," I gritted out.

He cocked a brow. "Denial won't do you any good here."

I pressed my lips together, seeing the truth in his words and wanting to refute them still, but my shoulders dropped in defeat. "I'm aware of that. I just...don't know who I am anymore."

"I'm not sure I've ever figured that out myself, so your situation isn't so unique," he said.

I released a breath. "If you've come here to goad me, Cain, you can-"

"I'm not here to goad you," he cut in. "It's fucked up what happened to you."

"I'm well aware of that," I clipped.

A long pause passed between us and I had the feeling he was going to leave, but instead he stepped closer. "I don't care for much in this world. But I've seen a lot of twisted things, and this tops the list."

I frowned at him. "Why are you here?"

"I'm a Vampire."

"And?"

"Now you are too," he grunted.

"Still not seeing your point," I said.

"Our kind don't mix all that well together, but there's mutual respect between most of us. So...if there's anything you want to know, I suppose I might be willing to advise you on it."

"Did Rosa send you in here to say that?" I asked suspiciously.

"No," he growled. "Just forget it." He headed for the door but Rosalie entered before he made his escape.

"We forgot Hastings," she blurted, her eyes bright with concern.

"*Jack*," Cain cursed, trying to move up the stairs to exit the cabin, but Rosalie pressed a hand to his chest.

"We'll turn back. We'll find him," she reassured him then hurried back up the stairs with Cain in tow.

I shot after them, moving so fast that I crashed into Cain on the deck, my foot catching on a rope and sending me flying. He caught me by the collar before I could faceplant and righted me then snatched his hand back and stalked away before anyone noticed what he'd done.

I followed Rosalie along the deck to where Sin was sitting on the railing, humming a song and casting wind at the sails.

"We need to turn back," she called to him and Ethan looked up from his spot further down the deck. "We forgot Hastings."

"Isn't that Hastings?" Sin pointed at Cain.

"That's Cain," Rosalie said with a frown.

Sin barked a laugh. "Oh right yeah, he looks like a totally different man with that moustache drawn onto his upper lip. Perfect disguise."

Cain glared at him, prowling forward like he planned on punching Sin, but Rosalie placed a hand to his chest to stop him.

"Wait, I think…I can hear Jack," Cain said and I realised I could too as I angled my attention towards the sea.

"Yeah, we all hear the echoes of his death cries," Sin said morosely. "Long shall we remember little Hastlings."

"*Hastings*," Cain snapped at him, then hurried to the rail and looked over the side. I shot over to join him, peering out too and blinked in surprise as I spotted Hastings far out on the water clinging to a barrel and propelling himself along with water magic.

"Guysss!" he called. "I'm heeeere!"

Cain pulled off his shirt, drawing Rosalie's attention then he kicked off his shoes, dropped his pants and dove overboard. He powered through the waves, swimming for Hastings and rounding him up, using his Vampire speed to increase the pace his friend was moving at.

When Cain hauled him on deck, I took in the bedraggled Hastings who looked like he'd been through hell and back. He fell to the floor, panting then rolling onto his back and giggling, kicking his legs.

"What's wrong with the bub?" Sin asked, butting in between Cain and Rosalie to inspect Hastings. Ethan came hurrying over to look too and Hastings started laughing again.

"The sea went awoosh and asplash. Saw a sharky out there who nipped at my toes, but I'm the king of the critters now. They won't harm me. I led them all to safety, you know? It's their island now. Their haven of wilderness. Boom and a splash I went. I saw the fire, oh it went burn, burn, burn it did." I noticed some scratches and small bite marks beneath the torn, dirty shirt he was wearing.

Sin nudged Hastings with his toe. "He's broken. Better put him out of his misery." He took a damn machete from his hip which he'd gotten from the stars only knew where but Rosalie swore at him in Faetalian until he stowed it at his hip again.

"Did you…use the jazzy eyes by any chance, Jack?" she asked softly and he grinned up at her.

"You're pretty like a strawberry cake," he sighed.

"Thanks. But, the jazzy eyes? Do you remember taking a shot of it?" Rosalie pressed.

"It stabbed me in the…ass," he whispered.

"Oh that sounds all kinds of accidental," Sin said, winking at him and Hastings blinked back very slowly and intentionally.

"Is that the shit your great uncle Marco swears by?" I asked Rosalie in a low tone. "You know, the one with the twitches and that weird, faraway smile who always kinda smells like cabbages and-"

"The side effects are only permanent in him because he used it too often," Rosalie cut me off, giving Hastings a wary look. "Jack probably just needs to rest and I'm sure he'll be back to himself in no time," she said. "Ethan, carry him into the cabin."

He did as she asked, scooping him up and carrying him away while Cain took a syringe of jazzy eyes from his pocket and tossed it overboard with a scowl.

"How far from shore are we?" I asked Sin who was twisting his syringe between his fingers while his eyes skipped from me to Cain then Rosalie as if he was making a very important choice.

"Two plops and a skippity hop," he answered and I plucked the syringe from his fingers with a whip of water magic while he was distracted, tossing it overboard after Cain's. He scowled at me in outrage and I gave him a dry look before turning to Rosalie. "Translation?"

"A few hours," she said, stepping closer to me and pressing a kiss to my lips. "You should rest too."

"I'm not weak," I growled.

"I know," she said firmly. "That's not what I meant."

I nodded stiffly, looking to the horizon but she caught my cheek and turned me to look at her. "Se io sono la luna, allora tu sei la forza che mi sostiene," she purred.

"What does that mean?" Sin blurted, stepping close and smiling between us.

"It means 'if I am the moon then you are the force that holds me up'," Rosalie translated then flicked Sin on the chin.

"Oo," he shivered. "Give me some pretty words, honey pie. I want you to call me something hot and filthy in your fancy language."

"Sei un dolce piccolo idiota," she purred and he shivered again as she petted his head then walked away with Cain toward the cabin and I smirked at her words.

"What did she say?" Sin demanded of me, moving to pick up his newfound bird friend where it was perched on the rail at the edge of the boat.

I shrugged, pretending I hadn't understood Rosalie's words.

"She called me a big-cocked bandit, didn't she?" he called, stroking the bird's head as I walked away to join my girl in the cabin. "Didn't she?"

I said nothing, disappearing down the steps, knowing I would soon be back on the shores of Solaria, heading for the main Oscura residence. I was nervous to say the least, my return sure to bring a thousand questions and judgements on my head for what I'd become. But for now, the path was set. And all I could do was keep journeying towards the horizon and praying to the stars that the Fae I was dying to see would still love me when they saw the new and ugly truth of me.

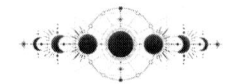

I let the others go ahead up the driveway to where the Oscura manor perched on the hill while Rosalie stayed with me. Its white walls and swing-around porch were so familiar to me that it hurt. The vineyards swept away from it, the evening sunlight colouring the grass gold, but I stood in shadow, none of that glow finding its way to me. The gates rose up at my back and I was still lingering in the fact that they had let me through, the touch of my magical signature enough to open them like they had been waiting for me to return all this time.

"It's okay," Rosalie said, stepping closer, her fingers curling around mine. "You're home now."

Home. That word had always meant this place, but it had belonged to my family residence too. What were my father and three mothers thinking about the reported news that I had escaped Darkmore? Were they proud of such an impossible achievement? Would my father find admiration for me again, or was I too far past the point of his affections? And even if he offered them, could I really forgive him for turning his back on me?

Too many questions hung in the air with far too few answers accompanying them.

As Sin, Ethan and Cain made it to the door, a chorus of howls sounded keenly in response to their arrival, the noise making my mind pool with memories. I'd spent so many days and nights here, endless parties, feasts, games and festivities all blurring into one feeling inside me that felt a lot like love.

When you were in with the Oscuras, you were family. And to them, family was the most important thing in the world. These Wolves would run into battle at my side, they would celebrate the smallest of my achievements and none of them had ever cast a dot of judgement my way. But now I was returning to their door as a wholly new creature. I wasn't the Lion Shifter so many of them shared those fond memories with. I didn't even look like him without my mane, and I had a sense that the torment in my eyes would be easily noticed by the Wolves.

They would know I went to Darkmore whole and came out broken. And it felt like a failure to the people I loved best. My brother…how was he going to react to this? How was he going to accept it?

My throat thickened and the urge to turn back made me retreat a step, but Rosalie was there, fingers squeezing mine, her eyes so big and wide, drawing me in and promising me she was here no matter what.

"Non scappare mai da cuori e braccia aperte," she whispered, moving closer and reaching up to cup my cheek. "Never run from open hearts and wide arms."

"I'm afraid," I admitted gruffly. "I'm not who I was."

"You are more than you were," she said fiercely. "They tried to destroy you but here you stand, Roary Night. A free man who survived the impossible. That's all I see when I look at you. Well, that and the Fae who owns my heart. Who was worth every struggle it took to return him to my side."

"You confound me," I said in a low voice, though there was no denying the burning love in her eyes. I cherished that love more than anything I had claimed in my life.

She smiled like a cat. "Come on, Roar. Let's go home." She tugged on my hand, leading me up the driveway and I found it easier to move now that I was walking in her footsteps.

Sin, Ethan and Cain had been drawn inside, the door wide open and a frantic crush of bodies surrounding them. Some of the pups were in their Wolf forms, yapping and howling excitedly while racing between everyone's legs. Amongst them all, I picked out a flash of blonde and my throat tightened.

Leon appeared, muscling through the throng of bodies and made it onto the porch, his gold eyes seeking and his usually carefree expression twisted into a frantic desperation.

Rosalie released my hand just as Leon's gaze fell on me, his recognition followed by confusion and concern as he took in the loss of my mane, the changed man I'd returned home as.

"Leon," I rasped, my feet falling still though the need to run to him crashed through me. But it was his choice. He might reject me over this alone, but he didn't know the half of it yet.

"Roar!" Leon bellowed, leaping off the porch and sprinting for me, his eyes bright with emotion.

He slammed into me, nearly knocking me to the ground as his muscular arms wrapped around me, gripping me tightly as he buried his face in my shoulder.

I hugged him back, his long, golden hair sweeping around me, the scent of citrus on his skin which was deeply linked to my childhood. He was the light to my dark, my little brother who had been born to love the world while everyone in it loved him back. He was the boy I'd played my first game of Pitball with, the kid I'd shared everything with, who had followed me on adventures, trusting me blindly while leading him through rivers and caves. There was no bond in the world like ours and to reunite with him now with free air in my lungs and no chains in sight or guards barking at us to keep apart, was a thousand times better than I had imagined it to be. But the relief at finding my way to this future was tarred by the truth of what I was now.

Leon finally released me, smiling so big it lit up every corner of his face. "You're here. Fuck, what happened to your hair?" He reached for my short hair mournfully and my chest tightened.

"It's a long story," I muttered, batting his hand away and he frowned deeply.

He looked to Rosalie and snatched her into a hug before she could escape, crushing her into his chest and scrubbing his knuckles against her head. "You did it, you little hellion. You freed him."

She struggled her way out of his arms, smirking at him and shrugging like it was nothing. But she knew it was everything. I'd seen what she'd gone through to get me out of there and I had no doubt that the Oscuras would pull every damn detail from her tongue and repeat it to the whole world until it was pure legend in the family.

"Come inside, everyone's waiting to see you." Leon beckoned me after him.

"Leon...we should really talk," I said darkly.

"But-" he started but Rosalie cut him off.

"Go talk to him, Leone," she insisted, giving him a push toward me and heading up to the house where a bunch of Wolves swarmed her.

Silence fell between us and I ran a hand over my short hair self-consciously.

"It'll grow back," Leon offered. "Did someone cut it?"

I nodded and he growled angrily. "Are they dead?" he hissed and I nodded again. "You're still more of a Lion than anyone I know. They've all been talking about you. Our moms are so excited to see you. And Dad, holy shit Roar, he's telling everyone about what you did. Escaping Darkmore. It's the most he's spoken about you in years. He can't shut up actually. He says he always knew his great Lion son couldn't be kept chained. Not even inescapable Darkmore could keep a Night contained."

My frown only deepened at those words and Leon's smile fell.

"I know he's been an asshole," he added. "The worst damn kind. But maybe there's a chance for you two to make it right now?"

I scored a hand down my face, shaking my head. "Leon, you don't understand. Dad won't want anything to do with me when he finds out..." My throat wouldn't release the words, my tongue weighed with lead. What if I lost Leon because of this? What if he couldn't handle it?

"Finds out what?" he pressed, his concern rising.

"You remember Vard, right? He used to be the king's Seer. He was into experimenting on Fae."

"Yeah," Leon said grimly. "I remember that asshole. He was Lionel Acrux's Royal Seer."

I nodded, not that I'd been out of prison at that time. I'd had to hear about it from him mostly. "Well, he's back."

"What do you mean?"

"I mean he's been undercover for some time, and he was using prisoners from Darkmore for his experiments."

"But he died in battle. His body was found," Leon insisted.

"Then he must have faked it," I said fiercely and Leon's gaze bored into mine, a thousand protests dying on his lips as he saw the truth in my eyes. Vard hadn't died in battle; he had made everyone believe he had then snuck away like a rat down a hole.

Leon's face paled as I told him about everything we'd discovered in the Psych Ward, but when it came to the next part, I stalled.

"Tell me," Leon urged, clearly sensing where this was going as his golden gaze trailed over me.

I cleared my throat, my eyes falling from his face to land on a grape vine as I forced myself to tell him the rest. "He's been perfecting a procedure that enables him to...to exchange one Fae's Order for another."

He sucked in air and I made myself barrel on before he said anything.

"He did something to me at Drav Enterprises, drugged me, forced me to go through some twisted procedure and when I woke up, I…" The pressure in my head was growing and I felt painfully dizzy as I recalled what it had been like in that moment. "I was on an operating table and my chest was wide open. Vard was there and him and his surgeon, they…they took my Lion."

"Roary," Leon said, fear lacing his words. "They can't, it's not…how could they?"

"I don't know," I breathed, still not looking at him, shaking my head as I tried to process what had happened to me, still in shock from it all. "But that wasn't the end of it. When they took it away, they replaced it with a new Order. They changed me. They forced that change upon me. And they said none have survived that transformation until now. I was the first, but I won't be the last."

I looked up at him, making myself do it and expecting to find him recoiling from me, but I only found rage and sympathy written into his features.

"What Order?" he rasped and in answer, I let my fangs extend and bared them at him.

His throat bobbed and he nodded before throwing his arms around me, hugging me firmly and speaking into my ear. "We'll destroy them for this. And we'll get your Lion back. I'm so sorry this happened to you."

I gripped him tight, the feel of his embrace like a balm to my soul, soothing its jagged edges. I'd been so sure he would reject me for this. Our kind were proud and being Lions was so ingrained in who we were as Nights. Relief and gratitude swept through me for this man who hadn't abandoned me at any point. Not when I'd been arrested, not when I'd brought shame on our family, and not now when I stood before him as a wholly changed creature.

"I thought you'd want nothing to do with me," I admitted as we pulled apart.

"We're brothers," he said passionately. "If you'd returned here as a swamp rat, you'd still be *my* swamp rat. There's no form you could take that would change that."

"I don't deserve you, but I'm fucking grateful for you," I said.

"You deserve more than me. Come on, Aunt Bianca is preparing a feast. Let's celebrate the good and forget the bad. Everyone's dying to see you, swamp rat or otherwise, two Fae most of all."

"The kids?" I rasped, a keen need filling me to meet my niece and nephew at long last. I'd seen pictures and heard so many tales from Leon, I had such an image of them in my mind that it was as if I knew them already. But I didn't really. I had been denied them and that, above all my punishments, had been the cruellest.

Leon nodded, smiling excitedly as he led the way up the house, my body humming with anticipation, but trepidation too. I wasn't the Fae I'd hoped to be when I met them. I was more scarred than I'd planned on, more damaged and altered. But my love for them transcended all that, guiding my feet forward as if fate was coiling me close to them by a thread.

There were Oscuras milling on the porch, trying to get back inside to see the newcomers and as we made it to the steps, two kids squeezed through the crowd of legs and came flying at us.

The eldest boy Luca led the charge, but the little one RJ put on a burst of speed to catch him, a fiery determination sparking her eyes. Leon stepped aside and they let out little gasps of excitement before launching themselves off the porch steps with complete faith that I'd catch them.

"Uncle Roary!" they shouted in unison as I lunged, grabbing them mid-jump before they face-planted the ground. Their little arms came around my neck and RJ placed a kiss on my cheek before pulling my hair.

"I missed you," I told them with a grin, hugging them tight, the relief at finally uniting with them making the weight on my heart lessen.

"Dad says you broke out of prison!" Luca said excitedly. "Did you punch a guard in the face?"

"Or the butt?" RJ piped up and I laughed.

"The face *and* the butt," I said.

"Told you!" RJ squealed, then the two of them wriggled out of my arms and leapt at Leon, tugging on his trousers.

"Can we show him the thing we made now?" Luca whispered keenly and my sharp Vampire hearing picked it up.

"I'll bring him to the kitchen, you two go get it ready," Leon said excitedly and they dashed back into the house with cries of excitement.

Leon rested a hand to my shoulder and I smiled at him, my chest full of light. "You have no idea how good it is to see them in the flesh."

"They'll never leave you alone now, bro. You're like a celebrity to them, they haven't stopped talking about you since the breakout."

I breathed a laugh and let Leon lead me into the house where the Oscuras were bustling around and chatting keenly.

The sight of all those people was strangely off-putting, like my inner desires for company had shifted, and I realised it must have been to do with my Order. Vampires were notoriously solitary and as I stepped into the manor and was overrun by excited Wolves, my gaze caught on Cain where he stood by a grandfather clock, escaping the bedlam.

He was the epitome of all their Order stood for and I knew he held the answers to a lot of the questions I had about my newfound desires. But he was also an asshole with an attitude problem that had been very much pointed at me during my time at Darkmore. It was hard to forget about the times he'd shouted orders at me or punished me for disobedience.

Ethan was in the thick of the masses, soaking up the attention as he pushed a hand through his blonde hair. A bunch of Wolves cooed and praised him for his bravery as he retold the story of my breakout. Hastings was close by in a crowd of his own, his cheeks turning a little pink as the Wolves pulled details from him.

"Dalle stelle!" Dante boomed as he pushed through the throng of Oscuras. "Let me get to him." The Wolves parted to let him through and he clapped me on the back of the neck, pulling me to him and kissing me on both cheeks before embracing me. The Dragon born of Wolves was one of my favourite people and I smiled at him, letting the joy in the space infect me at last. "Good to see you, Dante."

"Better to see you, mio amico," he said then he whispered in my ear. "Rosa told me what they did to you, and I assure you we will gut every last enemy who is responsible for this. A morte e ritorno. Now come! Eat, drink, celebrate with us. For the night is still young, the FIB left here empty handed and the dawn waits for no Fae."

Rosalie caught my eye from the stairs as I was swept away into the lounge, the Wolves crooning, all desperate to greet me, but also to touch me like doing so would grant them eternal luck. There were arguments breaking out over the need to get closer to me, and Leon was being swept away on a tide while being asked a thousand questions about me at once.

Bianca all but shrieked when she spotted me in the lounge, barking at the Wolves in Faetalian to let her through and they leapt aside like they'd been struck with a frying pan. I had to bend right down to embrace her, and her kisses pressed all over my face before she let me go. There was no escaping it either because she had damn strong arms on her.

"Your mommas call here daily," she told me. "Whenever you are ready for them, let me know. They're welcome here any time."

I nodded stiffly, unsure when I'd be ready for such a thing. Facing them like this, telling them what had become of my Lion didn't seem like an option, though I felt guilty for leaving them in the dark. I just wasn't ready to face it yet.

Bianca grasped my hand and tugged me along. "Come, come. I've made your favourite dessert. Brambleberry pie with fresh whipped cream."

"You shouldn't have," I said, though hell if I hadn't dreamed about Bianca's brambleberry pie in Darkmore.

She led me into the kitchen where the huge pie was waiting on the counter, but my attention was drawn away from it to Luca and RJ who were standing up on the long dining table with a paper mâché Lion standing in front of them. It was as tall as the little one, RJ, and she hugged its neck, the painted face of it grinning at me.

"Is you!" she announced.

Luca did a little dance around it, showcasing the beast and despite the pain in my soul over the lack of my Lion Order, I couldn't help but smile at what they'd made for me.

"It's purrrrfect," I said and RJ squealed a laugh as I petted the beast's head.

Bianca wasted no time in dishing me out a slice of pie, soaking it in cream and handing it to me in a bowl with a spoon. "Buon appetito, leone mio."

I spooned a piece into my mouth and damn well groaned at how good it tasted. "Nothing compares to your baking, Bianca."

She swatted a hand at me but grinned all the same.

"I want pie," Luca said hopefully.

"Then pie you shall have, nipote," Bianca said, heading over to grab some for him while RJ begged for ice cream.

The Wolves were pouring into the kitchen, some looking hopefully at the pie while others crowded around me again, asking questions about Darkmore. Someone put music on and Dante's Uncle Lafeto started up a conga line, shoving a set of doors open and leading a bunch of the Wolves out onto the porch. I'd never known any Fae who could descend into a party faster than the Oscuras.

The celebrations were quick to escalate, the family wine was passed from hand to hand, bottles uncorked and glasses filled with such efficiency that it was a marvel in itself. Rosalie found me again and I tucked her under my arm, holding her close while a song broke out about her, like they'd been waiting for this moment to present it.

"There once was a Wolf that shone like the moon,
Her fur so sleek and as bright as a spoon.
She was daring, brave and gave what-for,
When she went deep down into Daaaaarkmore."

"Per la luna," she cursed, embarrassed as the song grew in momentum, everyone around us seeming to have learned it. Rosalie tried to escape, but I held her tight, a grin finding my lips as I stared down at her.

"You earned your legendary status, pup," I said. "Now stand here and endure the repercussions of your greatness."

Sin pushed into the room with two glasses of wine clutched in his hands, one red, one white and he sipped intermittently between them. He tried to sing along, mumbling when he didn't know the words then making up his own in places, but catching onto the chorus quick enough. He loudly introduced the talian corvid on his shoulder as 'Crow-thing' and the pups at the party howled excitedly, half climbing him to pet the creature.

Between the music and the wine, it was easy to forget our problems and fall into the lull of safety and joy this house was known for. The Oscuras had a way of banishing the woes of the world and brightening all the dark shadows of the night. And as Rosalie pulled me into a dance and I held my girl against me while the music swallowed us up, I knew nothing could shatter this moment of rapture while the moon was rising. Not until the dawn came. And for now, that seemed like an eternity away.

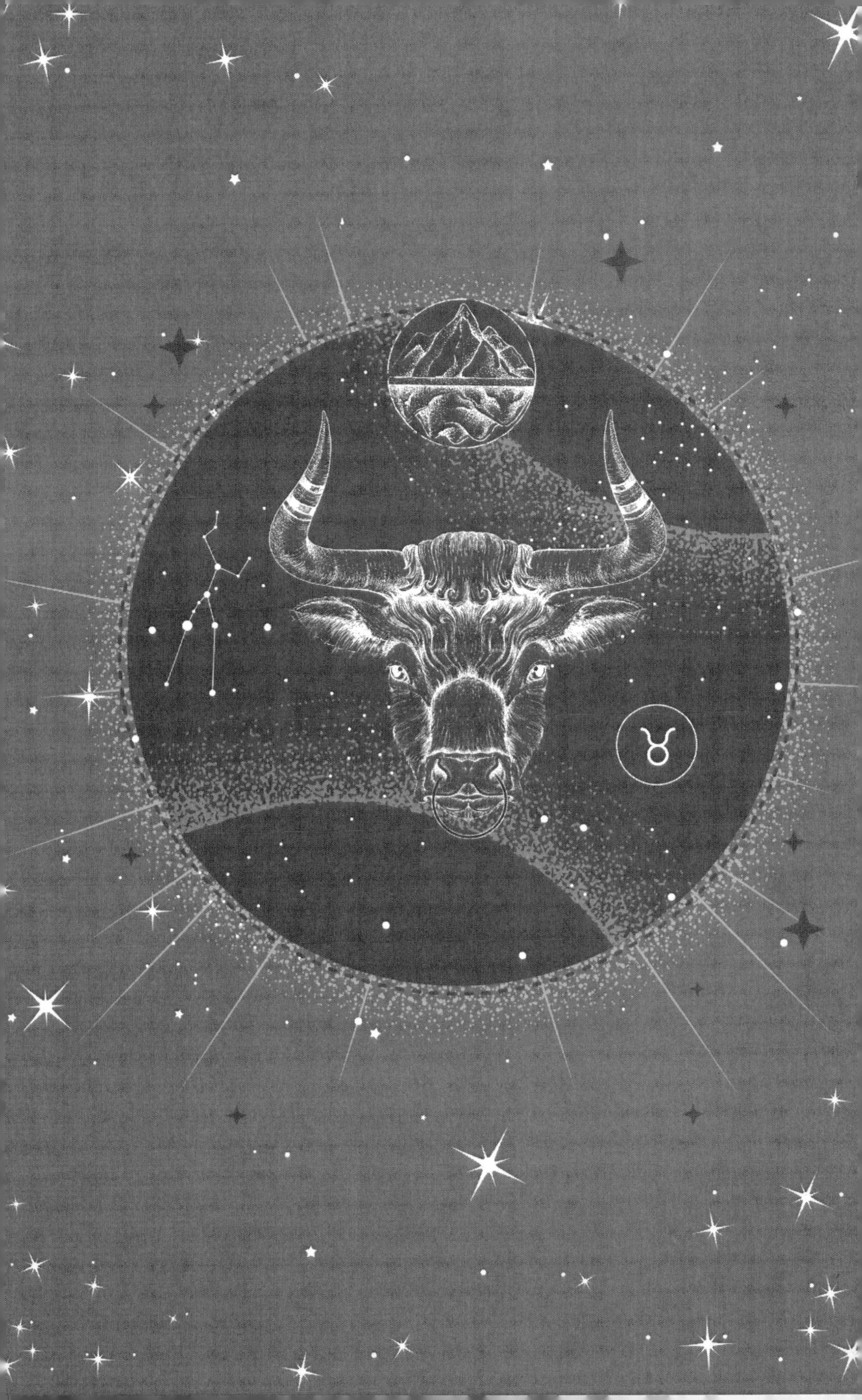

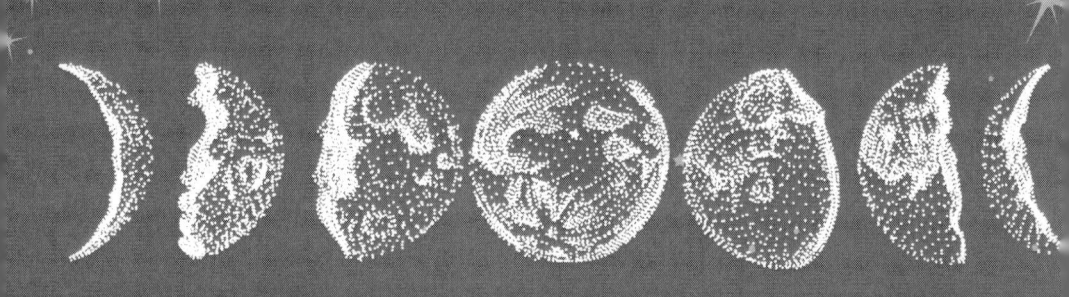

Rosalie

PRISONER #12

CHAPTER TWENTY THREE

No one could party like the Oscuras. It was a fact, pure and simple. The Wolves were going all out and finally having the celebration they had planned on giving me when I'd first returned here – Roary's appearance meant it was time to indulge at last.

I stayed close to him as the festivities grew louder and more chaotic, the party moving outside onto the sweeping lawn above the vineyard where the moon could watch over us in our revelry.

Drinks were passed out, toasts made and though the aching loss of Roary's Lion and the bastardo who had escaped with it still hung over us, we were in desperate desire of a little reprieve.

The Oscuras gathered around us, seeking stories from Darkmore, every detail of our escape, the full tale of my mating to both Roary and Ethan, and they demanded every scrap they could get.

Hastings caught my eye as he lingered at the edge of the group while Sin recounted the mayhem he had caused rescuing Roary from Grimolda Isle. Guilt stirred in my gut once again for having forgotten him. But damn, he was just kinda forgettable sometimes.

"You're leaving out the most important part," I interrupted loudly while Sin reenacted a moment where he had supposedly wrestled eighteen alligators by hand. I wasn't certain when the story had turned so fictional but I did have an idea of how to say sorry to Hastings for treating him like a stronzo. And for accidentally unleashing jazzy eyes on him too. "Hastings over there saved all of our asses by leading the wild beasts and monsters away from us when we needed him the most. He saved my damn life out there then swam half way across the ocean to reunite with us for good measure. He's a motherfucking hero! And he should be rewarded for such loyalty and bravery, don't you think?" I raised my glass to him and the Oscuras all whirled his way, calling his name out in a toast and howling in celebration of him.

The last I saw of Hastings was his reddening cheeks as around twenty of my cousins and other Oscura clan members descended on him, purring compliments in his ears, reaching out to caress him and cooing over his heroics. I doubted he'd be having a night of dim lighting and quiet love-making tonight, but if he let his inhibitions drop, he might just find himself the centre of a pack orgy dedicated to his pleasure.

I slipped away while they were distracted, catching Ethan's hand and leading him onto the dance floor, wanting to feel the hard press of his body against mine as I let the music have us.

He had no objections and moved onto the writhing dance floor at my side. I soaked in the bare grass beneath our feet, the moon hanging low in the sky above and the feeling of my clan all gathered around us. One song turned to two, five, ten. I lost count as I moved with my Wolf, my breaths coming heavier, our dancing laced with lust, our hands never leaving one another, the world practically fading around us.

Ethan took my lips with his, the dancing Fae who surrounded us fading out of existence as he sank his tongue into my mouth and moved against me in a way which begged for fewer clothes.

My skin was slick with sweat, my dress riding up as his hands caressed the backs of my thighs and roamed up the bare skin of my spine. I trailed my fingers down his chest in turn, the buttons of his shirt hanging open, exposing lines of hard, inked flesh for my enjoyment.

"I could dance with you forever, love of mine," he growled in my ear, the rough scratch of his stubble grazing the sensitive skin beneath it.

"But then we'd never get to the real fun," I teased, my fingertips catching in his waistband and tugging lightly.

He growled, drawing me closer, pushing his leg between my thighs as we danced. I moaned at the rough friction his jeans offered against my clit, my teeth sinking into my bottom lip.

One of us was going to break at any moment. This tension between us had to explode, the way it was mounting was utterly infuriating. My body ached with need, my nipples hard and pressing through the fabric of my dress, my skirt riding higher with my movements and Ethan's fingers gliding up the backs of my thighs to encourage it.

His cock was rock hard between us, grinding against me as we danced, the promise of it alone enough to make me sigh his name as sweat made my hair cling to my cheeks. Our panted breaths merged between us, the way we moved together this beautiful sin which I never wanted to stop committing.

My lips fell to his neck, teeth raking across his skin, the taste of salt and freedom clinging to him and making me inhale breathily.

I gasped as rough fingers skimmed down my spine, turning my head to find Roary at my back, a darkness in his expression which made me blink in surprise.

"Roar?" I questioned while Ethan dropped his mouth to my throat and began to paint a line of kisses down to my collarbone.

"Sharing isn't coming as naturally as it used to, little pup," he growled, his hand curling in my hair as he wrapped it around his fist.

Ethan's head rose just as he reached the top of my dress, his lips barely skimming the rise of my breast and I groaned in frustration as my peaked nipple ached with longing for him to finish that descent.

"You just need practice," I told Roary, tipping my head back so that I could claim his mouth with mine.

Ethan gripped my waist, holding me in place with his leg still firmly between my thighs.

"Let's go somewhere a little more private," Roary growled, taking hold of my wrist and tugging.

I kept hold of Ethan as I followed obediently, my body aching with want, desire rioting in every inch of my flesh.

Roary knew this house almost as well as I did and he led us straight through a side door before tugging me up the back stairs. He hesitated at the top, clearly uncertain which was my room, and I kissed him hard before breaking free of both of them and running ahead to the door at the furthest end of the house which opened onto the stairs to my attic room.

Roary slammed into me as I stepped into the room, launching us across the open space to the bed and hurling me down onto it beneath him, his mouth on mine before I fully took in what he'd done. It was so strange to have him move like that, to feel the rake of fangs against my bottom lip while kissing him and yet it didn't feel like some alien element. It was still him. My Roar.

He shoved my dress up, fingers hooking in the edge of my panties and dragging them down my thighs slowly.

He reared over me, his eyes between my legs as I parted them for him, Ethan moving to stand at his back and enjoy the view too.

Roary took my ankle in his hand, tugging my shoe off as he dragged my panties over my foot before repeating the process on the other leg.

He dropped to his knees by the foot of the bed and Ethan sank down beside him. Even the thought of what they were planning had me moaning and as they moved closer together, hooking my ankles over each of their shoulders. I couldn't help but whimper in anticipation.

Ethan's mouth met with the skin on the inside of my left knee and Roary echoed his movements on my right. I reached out to push my fingers into their hair, encouraging them closer while they worked their way down, Ethan murmuring praises about the way I looked between kisses, lamenting how much he was aching for a taste of me.

I growled as they took their time working down the insides of my thighs, my hips bucking against the mattress, heels digging into their spines.

When their mouths finally met at my core, I cursed, the soft caress of my fingers in their hair turning to a rough grip.

I rolled my hips as their tongues met, one gliding over my clit, the other ducking lower, circling my opening.

I lost track of who was doing what as my head fell back against the sheets and I simply surrendered to the ruin of their mouths on me, panting their names into the dim light of my room.

I rocked against them, fucking their mouths, taking my pleasure in greedy, hungry doses until I was coming so hard that I didn't even recognise the ragged cry which broke from my lips as my own voice.

Ethan moved on top of me, crawling over my body, pushing my dress up as he went, unbuckling his pants with his other hand. I tugged at the fabric of my dress to help him, hauling it up and over my head and he was inside me before I'd even gotten it off.

His name fell from my lips in a curse as he slammed into me, fucking me roughly, using the tangled fabric of my dress to pin my arms above my head.

"More," I gasped as he slammed into me hard enough to steal my breath and he laughed darkly before flipping us over, positioning me on top of him.

"You heard her, Roary," Ethan panted. "Our girl needs more."

Ethan gripped the back of my neck and tugged me down to kiss him while driving his cock up and into me from below with that same, punishing rhythm.

The sound of Roary moving close behind me had my body tensing to come with the mere thought of taking them both at once.

"Lean forward, beautiful," Roary commanded, his rough fingers rolling down my spine.

Ethan slowed a little as Roary came to kneel at my back, and I sighed in pleasure as he pressed his mouth to the side of my neck, his bare chest warming my spine.

I could feel the hard press of his cock against my ass, and I released a ragged exhale at the promise of that touch, but as he moved over me, he guided his cock lower to where Ethan already filled me and lined himself up there.

I cursed, fisting the sheets and pressing myself more firmly to Ethan who took my mouth with his and kissed me slowly, languidly, like he was exploring the shape of my lips, determined to commit every rivet and facet to memory.

I lost myself in that kiss while Roary tilted my hips into the position he needed and slowly slid his cock into me too.

I tensed as he stretched me, then forced myself to relax, exhaling heavily as his dick found its place within me alongside Ethan's. A ragged moan fell from my lips and as they both began to move together, my entire body feeling like it was engulfed in flames of wicked bliss.

I gasped at the exquisite feeling of them owning me like that, their bodies sandwiching mine, hard muscles surrounding me, pleasure driving me towards ruin.

Ethan murmured praises against my lips while Roary groaned his own desire along the side of my neck.

It was so much, the intensity burning me alive, and though I fought against it, wanting to prolong this euphoria, I couldn't help but come with a feral cry as they thrust into me again.

My pussy clamped tight around them, forcing them to shatter with me, and the hot spill of their cum combining within me made my head spin at its perfection.

Roary rolled off of me and I collapsed between him and Ethan on the bed, panting riotously.

"My turn," Sin said darkly, my heart jolting at the sound of his voice and I pushed up onto my elbows, blinking at him through a haze of lust as he pushed off of the doorframe where he had clearly been positioned to watch us.

Sin stalked into the room, stripping his clothes off as he came for me and I wound my fingers in the bed sheets, biting my lip in anticipation and parting my thighs for him in offering.

Sin moved over me slowly, his eyes shifting between Roary and Ethan who lay spent on either side of me, their fingers reaching out to brush against my flesh, caressing me and watching hungrily.

I leaned up in anticipation of a kiss from my incubus, but Sin smiled darkly, dropping to his knees at the foot of the bed instead and tipping down to claim my core with his mouth.

"By the stars," I murmured as his tongue rolled up the length of my opening, tasting the combination of Roary and Ethan's claim on me, our mixed pleasure coating his tongue.

Sin rounded my clit with his tongue, groaning as he tasted me, my already heightened senses buzzing wildly while he worked me over.

I tipped my head back, supporting my weight on my elbows and a ragged gasp fell from me as I took in another figure standing in the doorway, his gaze heavy with lust as he watched us.

Cain held my gaze as I met his, watching Sin devour me while Ethan and Roary rolled onto their sides, trailing kisses over my flesh, claiming my breasts and toying with my nipples to deliver me even closer to nirvana.

My thighs clamped tight around Sin's head as he fucked me with his mouth but he gripped my knees, forcing them wide again, baring me to him completely so that he could enjoy his feast.

I came at a rough flick of his tongue, crying out, gasping his name and then he was on me, in me, his cock sinking into the slickness of my cunt, a low groan leaving him as he drove slowly to the hilt.

Sin fucked me slow and deep, his mouth finding mine, hands roaming up the lengths of my arms until he had them pinned above me.

I moaned as I took the thick length of his cock, each thrust slow, languid and impossibly deep like he was striking a drum so far inside me that its low tone rattled through the darkest parts of my soul and made them ache.

I couldn't see Cain anymore but I could feel him watching us and the thought of that only turned me on more.

Sin groaned, his cock thrusting in again and again, Roary and Ethan kissing and caressing me, finding every zone of pleasure on my body and using it against me until I was little more than an aching ball of need between them.

I cursed in Faetalian, begging and pleading with them for a further release and Sin laughed wickedly before giving me what I wanted, fucking me faster, rolling his hips so that his pubic piercing claimed my clit.

Within moments I was coming again, seeing stars in the darkness behind my eyelids as I shattered between my men, gasping their names and descending into a well of utter bliss.

Sin fucked me harder, taking his pleasure from my spent body while prolonging the ecstasy in mine.

When he came I fell with him once more, the roar of release which bled from him staining my soul in a riotous sin which matched his name.

He rolled off of me and my eyes fluttered open, the door still wide before us, Cain's rabid gaze on mine.

I bit my lip, hesitating short of beckoning him into the room with us because I wasn't even certain what he was to me or what I was to him.

He took a single step closer then froze, swallowing thickly before shooting away again.

Sin sighed dramatically, flicking his fingers towards the door so that a gust of wind slammed it.

"All the more for us then, wild girl," he purred, rolling me over and hoisting my hips up so that I was on my knees. "Now be a good girl and take Shadowbrook's cock between those pretty lips. I wanna hear you choke my name out around it while I fuck this untouched ass of yours."

His fingers slid into my pussy, before slicking up, coating my ass with all the lubricant he would need before driving the tip of his cock against my ass.

Ethan smirked at me as he got to his knees and offered me his dick as requested while Roary moved into place beside us, fisting his own cock in hand, his eyes blazing with desire as he watched us.

The empty space on my right had a small twinge of regret kindling in my gut and I wondered if I should have commanded Cain into the room with us. But as Sin's cock drove into my ass and Ethan's slid between my lips, I found other things to occupy myself with. Like finding my destruction between the arms of my three antiheros and coming for them more times than I could count before dawn could end our tryst.

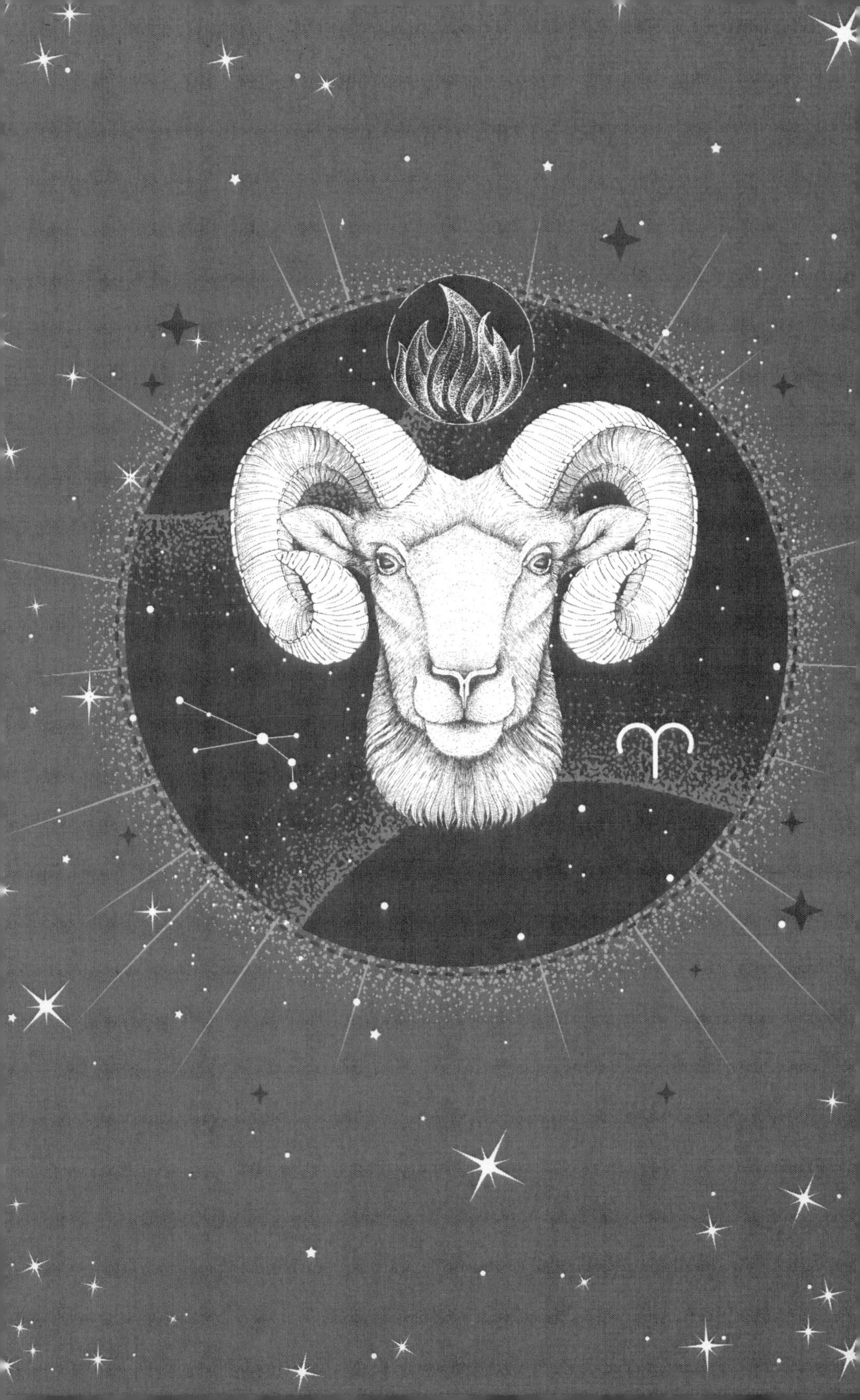

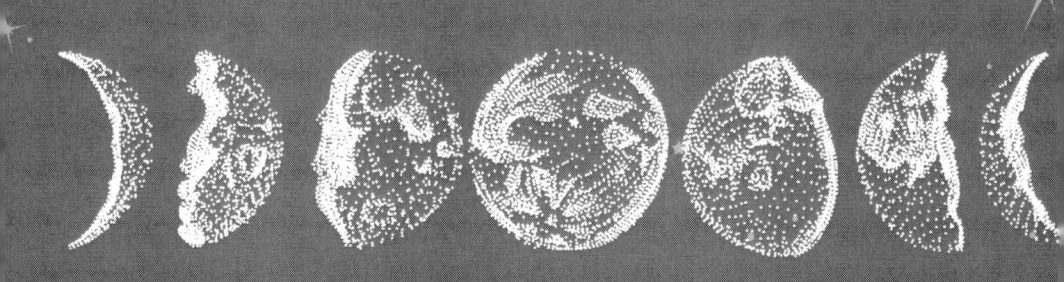

CAIN

COMMANDING OFFICER

CHAPTER TWENTY FOUR

The moon was a blur above me as I swayed, standing in the long grass. I'd run away from the house with a burst of speed, the wine I'd drunk making me unsure exactly how far I'd moved, but it had to be pretty damn far.

My chest was cracking, letting all the twisted pain of my past slip out and ooze through me like poison. Darkmore was done with me, Rosalie didn't need me and the moon was hell bent on destroying me. This curse likely had no answer. It was set on my death and I was fooling myself if I really thought there was a way out.

A hiccup drew my attention and I turned as Jack stumbled towards me, his shirt on backwards and torn at the collar, his still black hair standing up on one side and lipstick smeared across his mouth.

"Mason," he said by way of greeting and I nodded, glancing over his shoulder to the vines he'd emerged from where soft moans and giggles were spilling into the night from at least three female voices.

"I see you've made some new acquaintances," I said a little frostily because my own dick certainly wasn't seeing any action and I couldn't get the vision of Rosalie Oscura being worshipped by three other men out of my mind, the imprint of it seared onto the backs of my eyelids and taunting me with every blink.

"Umm...yeah..." Hastings shuffled awkwardly and I found myself blurting an apology at him before I could stop the words from spewing from my lips.

"I'm sorry," I said. "For...not being the Fae you thought I was. For letting myself get embroiled with Twelve and falling for her tricks. I should have been someone you could rely on, look up to, but really I was just her pawn, falling for every sweet word, gentle caress, drop of blood..."

Hastings pursed his lips, considering my words then shrugged. "I fell for her too," he admitted. "Tried to kiss her once." He cleared his throat and glanced back to the giggles which came from the vines before going on. "Not that she allowed it. And honestly I can see now that I don't fit with her. The Incubus was right about that – I'm not a match for the wildness in her. But...I think you are...sir," he added hastily as I shot him a sharp look.

"She has her harem well stocked with three other-"

"But she still looks at you like she's waiting for you," he said. "She is clearly a lot of things that neither of us realised back in Darkmore but not all of those things are bad. I think she freed me when she freed herself from that place...and I think she wants to free you too, Mason. You just have to let her."

I frowned at him, the alcohol I'd consumed making his words sound all too alluring but the curse mark on my arm and the three men she was probably still fucking - even though it had been hours since I'd run from them - spoke of a different fate for me.

"Jack!" called a seductive voice from within the vines. "I need you, come back to us!"

Hastings turned bright red, opened his mouth to say something, closed it again, cleared his throat then saluted me before striding back into the vineyard to answer that call.

I gritted my jaw, shooting away at speed so that I didn't have to listen to any part of what he was getting up to and rounding the house before stumbling to a halt near the foot of the sweeping lawn.

My vision steadied as I managed to stop swaying, the moon coming into sharp focus above me. Every rivet and shadow was like a taunting smile that was turned my way, mocking my futile hope that there was a chance for me yet.

"Fuck you!" I hollered, my rage spilling out all at once. "If you want me dead, then take me now – why make me wait?!"

The moon was quiet in answer and a growl fell from my throat. I released a tide of curses at the celestial being that had afflicted me, letting out my fury until my voice echoed off the hillside.

"Cain," a gruff voice made me turn and I found Roary Night at my back, reaching for me.

I looked to his outstretched hand and he dropped it, his brow drawing low. "You're riling up the Oscuras." He gave me a shove as a chorus of howls sounded from the direction of the manor and I realised I hadn't run all that far from the house. "Move before they come out here and gut you for speaking about the moon that way."

As the howls gathered in momentum, I turned and raced for the trees marking the border of their land, not wanting to deal with that shit while my mind was thick with a haze of alcohol. Roary came with me, keeping up, but stumbling over a log as we made it to a clearing. He crashed to the ground, carving a line in the earth as he skidded to a halt at my feet like a half-blind mule with three legs.

He huffed angrily, shoving himself upright and half-heartedly wiping at the dirt covering his jeans.

"You're the clumsiest Vampire I've ever encountered," I muttered.

"I'm not a fucking Vampire, that's why," he hissed and agony flared in his eyes, telling of how much he yearned for his Lion.

I regarded him with a pit opening up in my chest, the thought of losing my Order too vile to consider.

"Mm," I grunted. "Well it's your focus that's the problem. You're trying too hard to see where your feet land rather than watching where you're going."

"My legs are moving so fast, I can't help but look to make sure I don't fall and fucking break them," he sighed.

"You'll only fall if you don't watch what's ahead of you and listen to the world around you. Your legs will take care of themselves if you focus on where you're damn well going."

"It's impossible to adjust to how quickly the world comes at me," he said, shaking his head.

"Not for our kind," I said. "You need to trust your Order."

"It's not my Order!" he bellowed and a few birds took off from their roosts in the trees around us.

Silence fell and the branches above us swayed in the breeze, making the moonlight ripple across us both. Roary's hands flexed at his sides, the muscles in his arms tight.

"I feel invaded," he said at last, his voice lower, hollower. "This thing inside me isn't mine. It doesn't belong to me."

"It's yours if you embrace it, but shit, I can't even begin to imagine what it might take to do that mentally."

"Embracing it feels like betraying my Lion," Roary admitted.

I nodded stiffly.

"Anyway, I came to find you because Rosalie is worried about you," he said and my walls flew back up.

"What does she have to worry about?" I scoffed. "She has her two mates and her psychotic plaything to keep her happy."

"You're a stubborn motherfucker, aren't you?" He shook his head at me as if I was the problem and my fingers twitched on instinct, the urge to scold him for talking to me that way still ingrained deep. But stars be damned, he had a point.

And we weren't on uneven ground anymore. Out here in the real world, it was every Fae for themselves.

"My friend Merrick used to say the same thing," I said, the memory of my childhood friend cutting open an old wound. It was why I forced all thoughts of him from my mind as often as I could.

"The boy you grew up with under Benjamin Acrux's rule?" Roary confirmed.

"How'd you know about that?" I clipped.

"Sin told me everything."

"Of course he did," I huffed, glancing away from him, unsure if I wanted to go any further with this conversation.

"Lionel Acrux was the one who sent me to prison. Gave me a sentence that was far longer than any thief should have gotten. And he forced me to make a death pact to ensure I was never released early. That's why Rosalie came to Darkmore. She felt responsible for me ending up there – even though that's bullshit – but she knew the only way I'd walk out of there as a young man was by breaking me out. Anyway, my point is, I know what it's like to be on the receiving end of an Acrux's wrath. Their favourite kind of power is one built of cruelty."

I nodded, easily agreeing on that. "I thought I'd put my past to rest, but seeing Benjamin again showed me how damn foolish I was to think that. I am my past. Just a walking wound who lashes out at the world because of the anger I feel inside. That anger lies with Benjamin, but he wasn't there to receive it, so I offered it to everyone else. I am so very filled with hate, Roary, and I think it's mixed with my blood like venom. There's no antidote, no cure. I am this heartless creature because of him, but there's no undoing that now."

"You're a fool if you believe that, Cain. And I think you're a lot of things, but a fool is not one of them." Roary's eyes glinted silver as the moon caught in them and I found myself stepping slightly closer to him.

"I'm a miserable fuck who deserves everything he gets." I tugged up my left sleeve, revealing the curse mark and Roary regarded it, moving nearer. "She told you about this?" I guessed and he nodded, reaching out to trail his index finger over the rose vine that was crawling over my skin.

"I've never seen magic like it," he said. "Rosa holds gifts that go beyond any normal Wolf, perhaps any normal Fae."

"Not even she knows how to undo this." I tugged my sleeve back down. "The moon has decided my fate."

"No fate is ever set. You could still break the curse. Stranger things have happened, Cain. Don't lose faith just yet."

"Why are you on my side all of a sudden?" I asked suspiciously.

"Because I'm starting to see what Rosalie sees in you."

"An easily manipulated guard who now trails around after her like a hungry dog?" I sneered.

"You discount yourself so simply," he tutted. "Maybe if you tried noticing your good deeds, you'd find more to count than bad."

"I highly doubt that," I said bitterly.

"Rosa is forming a pack out of us. You should be a part of that. She wants you to be," he insisted.

"No, I'm not part of the pack, Roary. But I have decided on something. I'm hers now. Whatever she seeks, I will be in service to her until she secures it. I will follow her commands and do as she bids me to."

"Well if that's not the definition of being part of her pack, then I don't know what is." Roary quirked a grin at me and I blew out a breath of dismissal.

"The moon marked you as good for her, while it marked me as *bad* for her. If that's not proof of our differences, inmate, I don't know what is."

"Inmate?" he mused. "I don't see any bars out here between these trees."

"Old habits die hard."

"True. But let them die, Cain," he said, the smile dropping from his face. "Embrace the new world."

"Only if you do the same," I said, arching a brow at him.

"I might need some help with that," he muttered.

"I thought you'd never ask," I taunted. "You need someone to teach you the ways of your Order, and the rules that come with keeping our urges in check. The Vampire Code. You almost fell into the hunt before, and I know

218

better Vampires than you who have lost themselves to it entirely. They don't come back. And you won't either if it happens again."

"Teach me then," Roary urged, grabbing my hand. "Swear you will."

I hesitated, knowing the responsibility this would be. He should have been taught by the best of our kind, a role model that could teach our ways with patience and understanding. I wasn't exactly the poster child for the position, but then again, Roary wasn't your everyday newly Awakened Vampire. So maybe I was exactly who he needed.

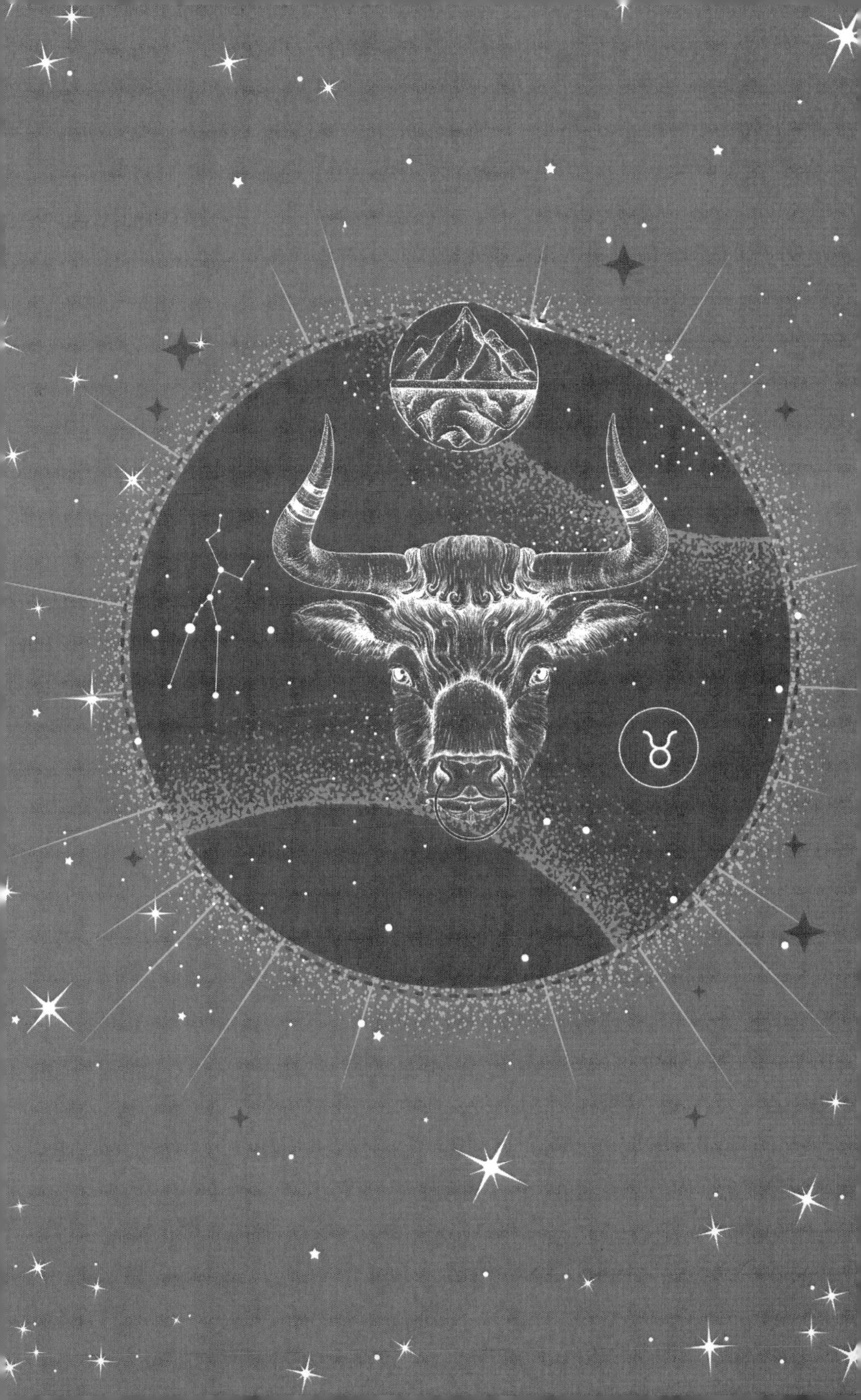

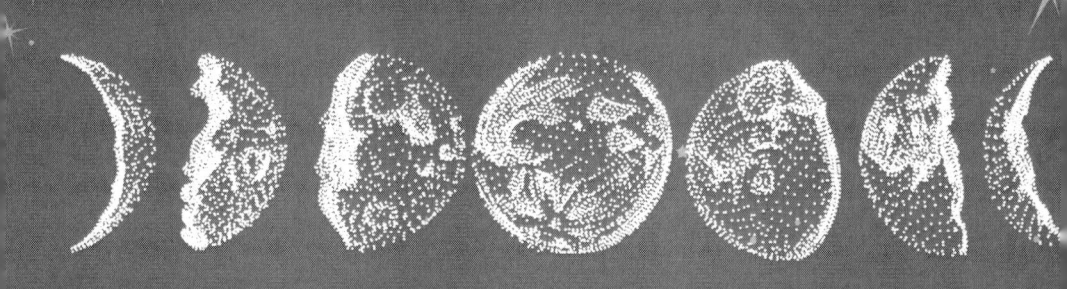

Rosalie

PRISONER #12

CHAPTER TWENTY FIVE

I'd never been one for sleeping in a pack huddle, but I had to admit there were worse places to wake up in the morning than tangled between three excruciatingly gorgeous men. My body ached in a blissful way which spoke only of our carnal claiming the night before and I sighed as I nuzzled Ethan's chest, Sin's arm banding around us tightly.

It was tempting to remain in place there all day but I had things to do and places to go. I wished this shit was over but there was still a victim in need of escape who we had to reclaim and I wasn't going to rest until we had returned Roary's Lion to him. What we would do with it and how we would go about returning it to his body after the fact would come next. For now, I knew what was needed of me.

I eased myself out of my position between the men I had spent the last night claiming, wriggling free of them and pushing to my feet at the foot of the bed. Roary was still absent after crawling from our tangled limbs several hours into our tryst and I frowned as I took in the empty space on the bed where he should have been.

I knew that sex was only a distraction for him from his grief at the moment but it still stung that he hadn't returned to us to sleep. Of course that was on the assumption that he had slept at all.

I ran a hand through my tangled hair, a cool breeze raising goosebumps on my bare skin and a delicious ache resonating through my bones. I grabbed some clean clothes and a towel, leaving Sin and Ethan snuggled up in bed, the two of them closing in on one another now that my body didn't divide them, and I headed for the shower.

I glanced in the mirror after locking the door at my back, the red in my hair glaring at me like a bruise that needed healing. It wasn't a bad look exactly, it just wasn't me.

I flipped open the cupboard beneath the sink and rummaged around until I found the dye removal potion lurking in there and headed to the shower with it.

I cranked the water up to scalding, sighing as I stepped beneath the flow, allowing the rush of liquid to soothe the throbbing ache in my muscles, the tender flesh between my thighs. It was almost a shame to heal it all away. But I needed to focus today and having a constant reminder of how good it felt to be pinned between my men likely wouldn't be very helpful.

Magic tingled from my palms as I washed myself clean before dumping the dye removal potion into my hair and standing beneath the rush of water until the water ran clear again around my feet.

I dressed in a pair of stonewashed jeans and a black crop top, my wet hair dripping down my spine as I padded downstairs on bare feet to the delicious scent of my aunt Bianca's cooking.

I strode into the kitchen, finding several of my cousins looking up at me and smiling widely as I arrived. Dante was lounging in his seat at the head of the table which took up the heart of the huge room, his eyes on a newspaper though he tipped a nod my way that told me he was aware of my arrival.

"Let the Alphas eat in peace," Bianca shot at the Wolves who were edging closer to greet me and they grumbled as she hustled them out of the room with violent swats of her dishcloth and loud hissing sounds.

I snorted in amusement, dropping into my spot at the opposite end of the table to Dante and thanking my aunt as she piled pastries hot out of the oven onto a plate before me alongside a bowl overflowing with fruit, a steaming mug of coffee and a tall glass of orange juice.

"Your food might just be the thing I missed most while I was locked up in that hellhole," I admitted, reaching out for a cinnamon bun and sinking my teeth into it with a prolonged moan of pleasure.

"Oh hush," Bianca chastised though the smile biting into her cheeks made it clear she was pleased by the compliment.

She washed her hands off and bustled out of the room, murmuring about the state of my hair as she went and I smiled into the next bite of my food.

"Fourteen hours," Dante mused, turning a page in his paper.

"What's that?" I questioned.

"That's how long the FIB spent sifting through our things, trampling around the vineyards, abusing Mama's home."

A sourness twisted my gut at his words and I set my pastry down with a sigh.

"Any arrests?" I asked.

"Fernando couldn't help mouthing off and Clarissa threw a punch. Both have been released on caution already. Surprisingly most of the others managed to behave themselves or at the very least clear out of here rather than hang around to make trouble."

I nodded, my relief clear and Dante set his paper aside, his gaze boring into mine.

"I know the famiglia is suffering because of what I brought to our door-" I began but he waved me off.

"There isn't a Wolf among us who would have wanted you to do a thing differently, piccola regina. I only want to be certain it is all worth it. I don't want any of you getting caught – not even that Incubus who's been swinging from the lemon tree and riling the pups up relentlessly. I want this done so that we can all move on."

I nodded, my mind fixing on what it would take to achieve that.

"I need to get Roary's Lion back and kill the motherfuckers responsible for taking it. That kind of knowledge can't be allowed to spread. If the idea of swapping and trading Orders catches on then this is only the beginning of the fucked up lengths some Fae will go to just to be able to claim their pathetic desires. Poor and underprivileged Fae with powerful or prized Orders will be hunted or convinced to part with them for a pocket full of gold. There will be kidnappings, murders. It will lead to all kinds of further depravities and it will hit the Fae with the least the hardest. Alestria itself could fall."

"I know," Dante said, his voice a rumbling growl, his eyes flashing into reptilian slits as his Dragon raised its head and peered out at me. "Which is why this needs doing quickly and quietly. Before more depraved assholes set their sights on it. The less who know about it, the better."

I nodded my agreement. "I have someone whose speciality is finding people who don't want to be found. I'm going to meet with him today in the hopes that he can point me to Vard."

"Good." Dante picked his paper up again, his attention swallowed by it and I returned to my meal, resolution steeling my soul in iron.

Aunt Bianca returned and I relaxed a little while she brushed and braided my hair, the soft tug of her fingers through the silken strands making some of the tension in me subside. The moment she was done, I pushed to my feet, heading for the door without another word and calling for Sin to join me.

Ethan appeared with him and I gave him a lingering look in the black sweatpants which hung low on his hips, his blonde hair still mussed from sleep and whatever other activities had occupied us for the night.

"Down boy," I said, pressing my fingertips to his chest and halting him where he was. "This is something I only need Sin for and I think it's best we avoid being out in public in too large a group for now."

Sin whooped, throwing his arm around my waist and hoisting me against his chest before twirling us around. His new bird pet was on his shoulder again, having slept stars knew where last night, but the creature looked happy enough.

"Tough luck, kitten," Sin purred, patting Ethan on the head as he backed us towards the front door.

"Don't be too long," Ethan called after us, his brow furrowing as he watched us leave.

"Aww, are you worried about me?" I teased.

"Always. Which is in part because I'm hopelessly in love with you and in part because you see danger and just stride right on up to it. You're hazardous, Rosalie."

"You wouldn't want me any other way," I replied, giving him a taunting smile.

Sin lifted Crow-thing from his shoulder, placing him gently on Ethan's and petting his head before kissing it. I swear the bird crooned at him and Ethan glanced at it uncertainly.

"Er, what am I supposed to do with him?" Ethan asked.

"He'll have a plate of fried worms for breakfast followed by some Fae-chewed mealy bugs, If you could get right on that, Ethy-pie." Sin clapped him on the cheek. "Chew the mealy bugs *slowly* so he doesn't choke on them, and can you let him feed from your mouth too. It'll remind him of his nesting days, thanks. Byeee."

"*What*?" Ethan barked, but Sin led me out the door and snapped it shut behind us so Ethan's confused cries were more muffled.

"So where are we going?" Sin asked, grabbing my hand and swinging our arms between us as we started the descent down the porch steps. "To the beach? Or a fair? Or an opticians? Oh I love a good squinty at the bottom line and a rage row when the scrangly bitch with the pointer stick tells me I'm wrong and it's a W, not a penis-"

I opened my mouth to reply to that but the visual image he had just given me had a snort of laughter falling from me instead.

"We're going to see Jerome so that he can help us locate Vard," I explained, tugging him so that he followed me down the long drive.

"Right…right. Because Vard can see the future and you want to find out whether or not you and me will be mated too or if I'll forever be the third wheel, only able to make myself feel better by loudly fucking you when I know Cain is near enough to listen so that I can console myself with the fact that there is a lower position in your pack than mine-"

"What? Sin, no – we need to find Vard because he has Roary's Lion."

"Oh."

I rolled my eyes at him, jerking my chin towards the huge barn where the Oscuras kept our cars and leading the way towards it.

Sin pouted as he followed me and I sighed.

"I've told you clearly enough that I want you, Sin. Why do you keep falling back on this nonsense and making out like you're not good enough for me?"

"It's not that I don't believe you. It's that the moon doesn't like me. She hasn't given me a sparkly moon mark and I can't help but think it's because of all the times I've looked her dead in the eye while taking an outdoor piss. It was disrespectful and she's getting her revenge now."

"The moon sees everything that takes place at night and you taking a piss has got to be the least of the depravity she's witnessed. Hell, you were an assassin – don't tell me you never killed anyone while she was watching."

"Of course I did. But she liked that, the saucy minx. All the blood and screaming and death got her going, just like it did you. It was the pissing that pissed her off. I know it."

I paused with my hand on the door to the barn, the magical wards tingling against my palm as they recognised me, parting to let me in. "The moon doesn't hold grudges, Sin," I said.

"Except against Cain," he pointed out. "She gave him that curse which is gonna make him die a death bleeding out of his asshole and she won't break it."

I pursed my lips. The idea of that fate for Cain was a whole lot less enjoyable than it had once been and I flicked a glance up in the direction of the moon in question over that but I couldn't spot her lingering in the morning sky and she clearly had her reasons for maintaining that curse upon him anyway. Who was I to question her?

"And yet you're curse-free," I said, brushing my fingers up Sin's forearm. "So drop the little lost boy bullshit and stop comparing yourself to Ethan and Roary. What you and I have is ours alone, Sin. And I'm not giving you up or playing favourites, am I?"

"No," he exhaled and I tiptoed up to brush a kiss against his lips before opening the door to the barn and leading him inside.

"Ho-ly cow on a cornflake," Sin cooed as he took in the cars all lined up within the huge space, our family garage pretty impressive on first look.

There was…well, yeah it was awesome. I grinned as I watched Sin dive into the space, touching all the vehicles from the gleaming sports cars to the SUVs, convertibles, ATVs, dirt bikes, super bikes, the small battalion of electric scooters which Dante had surprised the pups with last Christmas, the pair of monster trucks which honestly caused more chaos than they were worth, to the twenty-three golf buggies, most of which bore evidence of being used as battering rams when they were being raced across the valley en-mass.

"You have a fluffin' helicopter," Sin called from within the depths of the barn and I weaved between the cars to find him grinning up at it.

"Yeah, there are a couple of light aircraft and gliders too – my uncle Fabio got his pilot's licence a few years back so that he could chase Dante through the sky. We however need to take something which will draw less attention." I beckoned for Sin to follow me and led him towards the front of the barn where a set of huge doors stood and most of the more practical vehicles were lined up and he booed as I selected a pickup for our chariot.

"We can play with the fun ones another time, Sin. We need to be incognito at the moment, remember? Also, the FIB are watching the roads out of the estate in hopes of catching some of us – so I need you to shift and drive while I hide in the footwell."

"Drive?" he asked, moving around the truck and slowly climbing in behind the wheel. "Yes. Drive a vehicle. Like an everyday Sam."

I gave him a dry look. "You can't drive, can you?" I asked.

"Pfft. I can drive you crazy. I can drive my cock into anything, anywhere. I can drive a goose to gander and I can drive-"

"But you can't drive a car?"

Sin narrowed his eyes at me then shrugged. "Maybe I can or maybe I can't."

Suspicion clawed at me but then I remembered him telling me that his hobby had been to do up cars while we were back in Darkmore and I relaxed.

"You almost had me there," I admitted, settling into my seat and reaching over to take the keys from the sun visor above the driver's seat.

Sin grinned innocently, taking the key from me and starting the engine.

"You need to shift," I reminded him and he sighed before shifting into a perfect lookalike of Dante.

"Shit," I breathed, blinking at my cousin in surprise. "When did you pick up his form?"

"At the party," Sin replied, his voice now laced with Dante's accent. "Sooo many of your pack wanna bone him, poppet. Luckily, I think it was mostly the ones who aren't actually blood related to him, but if you wanna try a little filthy fantasy…"

"Ew, fuck no," I said, crinkling my nose and recoiling from him. "Shift into someone else – Dante is under too much suspicion anyway. His alibi is barely holding up on account of there having clearly been a Storm Dragon there when we escaped. Him being the only one of that size currently on record as living in Solaria is pretty damn incriminating. But as they can't prove for definite that there aren't any others and there are so many witnesses and so much CCTV footage of him elsewhere they can't make charges stick. Besides, Dante and our famiglia have a few friends in high places who might have helped us out a little. But the FIB *know*, Sin. They know and they're pissed. So be someone else."

He sighed like I was a total buzzkill then shifted again appearing as a man about twenty years older with a slim frame, salt and pepper hair and a smouldering depth to his gaze as he turned it on me.

"So are you my sugar daddy in this roleplay?" I asked him, my lips twitching in a smirk which he returned with a far filthier version.

"I'm whatever kind of daddy you want me to be, kitten," he purred. "Now where to?"

I programmed the satnav with our destination and leaned back in my seat as I pressed the remote for the barn doors and they slowly began to swing open.

Sin started the engine then revved it, sighing appreciatively as he flexed his fingers against the wheel.

"How long has it been since you drove?" I asked him.

"Too long," he groaned, revving the engine again.

I dropped my hand onto his thigh as he eyed the opening doors like they were a chequered flag and the moment they were wide enough, he slammed his foot to the floor and launched us through them.

Laughter tumbled from my lips as he yanked on the parking brake, swinging the back end around in a cloud of dust as he lined it up with the main drive before racing down it at speed.

The smile on his face was infectious and I kept my eyes on it as I dropped down into the footwell of the car to conceal myself as we reached the main gates to the estate. They swung wide just in time for us to blast through them and Sin howled as we made it to the open road.

"I see the piggies," he called loudly, waving out the windscreen at what I had to assume were the lurking FIB in their car. "I think they're gonna give chase!"

"Maybe you should stick to the speed limit then?" I called over the rush of wind which was billowing in through his open window.

"Nah. Where's the fun in that? Those motherfuckers can't catch me!" Sin threw his hand out the window, a blast of air magic erupting from his palm and sending dust up into the air in an enormous cloud beyond our rear wheels.

I pulled myself up into my seat again, fastening my seatbelt as he showed no signs at all of slowing down and looking out the rear window where a horn was blasting and sirens wailing from within the cloud.

The truck roared as Sin floored it, rocketing us up the road and towards the sprawling metropolis of Alestria in the distance.

I gave up on any attempt to rein him in, instead lowering my own window and grinning out at the open road ahead of us while my hair was whipped around my face and the FIB were left far behind in our dust.

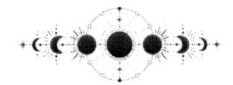

・(・(・●・●・)・)・

The streets of Alestria weren't quite the horror-filled alleys and criminally ruled hell holes they had been during my childhood, but the people here were wary of newcomers all the same. Peace had been achieved in this place thanks mostly to Dante and all the shit he went through ten years ago when Dark Fae ruled these streets and a war between the Oscuras and the Lunar Brotherhood seemed never ending. Of course the darkness of the war for the throne had touched this place too and though that had been a perilous time for many I was proud of what Alestria had achieved then too.

When the Order persecutions had taken place and Fae had been hunted simply for being a Tiberian Rat, Minotaur or Sphinx, Alestria had used its criminal network and hive of underground cells and secret places to hide those in need. Our city was one of the few which had managed to successfully protect the majority of its citizens from the wrath of Lionel Acrux right until the end of the battles.

"I heard it was as bad up here as it was in Darkmore for a while," Sin said in a low voice, bobbing his chin at a spray-painted symbol of two Phoenixes rising from the centre of a crown on the side of an apartment building. It wasn't the first we'd passed.

"It was," I agreed, the pain in my heart where members of my famiglia should have still resided twisting sharply as I thought back on the carnage of war.

"Did you fight in it?" Sin asked, his eyes on me though I turned my gaze steadily out of the window.

The clash of battle and screams of dying Fae filled my ears for a moment and I swallowed thickly before banishing them again. "I did. Dante and I led our pack into battle in the army of the True Queens. I…killed a lot of Fae that day. Sometimes I swear I can still taste their blood coating my tongue."

Sin was silent for a long moment but he reached across the seats and took my hand in his.

"My wild girl," he murmured softly. "I'm glad the moon had you in her protection."

"Me too," I agreed.

"We're here."

I blinked out of my reverie, the roar of battle, stench of death and endless screams abandoning me and landing me in a warm truck with Sin at my side and a whole ocean of time between now and then.

I smiled tightly, grabbing a baseball cap from the backseat and pulling it low over my face just in case any of the CCTV cameras around here were working and jumped out.

Jerome lived in a fancy penthouse suite on the top floor of the tallest building in the heart of the city. He'd moved into it a few years ago from his hometown of Iperia, spreading his criminal dealings further – though of course he had to bow to the rule of the Oscuras here. I'd often thought he liked it because the view from his windows made the Fae below appear as irrelevant as ants – his ego ripe for stroking at all times.

Sin slung his arm around me, the lighter weight and shorter length of it in this form feeling unfamiliar as he drew me close to him.

We passed a Fae dressed as a doorman - though I figured henchman was more accurate as he leered at us threateningly, but he made no move to slow our access. No doubt Jerome already knew we were here even if Sin was in disguise, my face was obscured by the hat and we were driving a truck he'd never laid eyes on before. That was why I wanted him for this. He was the best.

The elevator slid open as we approached it, a mirrored cube welcoming us inside. The doors closed at our backs the moment we embarked and it began to sail upwards.

Sin shifted beside me, sighing like it was a relief to shuck that skin and rolling his shoulders as he settled back into his own flesh.

"Better?" I questioned.

"Always," he agreed. "Unless you wanna play out the sugar daddy fantasy-"

"No," I said firmly, that little crease appearing between his brows saying he still believed he'd catch me out on some hidden fantasy I held over the real him one day. I stepped closer, taking his hand and trailing my fingers along his jaw as I made him look at me. "No, Sin," I repeated and that frown smoothed out, his mouth closing on mine as he offered me a kiss far sweeter than his usual desire-ridden claiming. There was relief in that kiss, honesty and hope and…love.

"And there was me thinking your tastes were more singular," Jerome's soft voice coiled around us and I broke from Sin to step into his apartment, realising the elevator must have stopped while I was distracted by the taste of his kiss.

"How so?" I asked, striding into his pristine bachelor pad like I owned the damn place and earning myself an appraising look.

"Your obsession with the Night boy-"

I breathed a laugh. "I can assure you that Roary is no boy," I said.

"No Lion anymore either if the rumours I've heard hold merit."

The smile slid from my face to puddle on the floor like acid and I took a step closer to Jerome who held his ground, a cup of coffee held in his hand where he surveyed me from a position near the huge windows which looked out over the city.

"Hello, brother." Sin strode across the space which divided me and this stronzo as if the floor hadn't just coated itself in ice and embraced him fiercely, Jerome in turn patted Sin half-heartedly on the back. For someone who had been so desperate to see Sin released from prison, he certainly didn't appear to be overwhelmed with emotion at his return. "We need to find that Lion."

Jerome extricated himself from Sin with a smile before stepping away again and moving into his open plan kitchen. The whole thing was black, with dark marble countertops and accessories to match.

"What makes you think I know where it is?" he asked as he placed his empty cup down and set his coffee machine working.

"Because you sit up here all day looking at your little screens, nosing into business which isn't yours but which will benefit you the best. So just name your price, bastardo because I don't have time to waste on this."

Jerome considered me for a long moment then his eyes flicked to Sin.

"I don't need money," he said dismissively, as if I hadn't already known that.

"What then?"

Jerome scowled at me, clearly not liking my tone. He thought himself an Alpha but in truth he was all Omega, a lone stronzo too big for his boots, howling at the moon as loudly as he could as if shouting and stomping his feet might force her to listen. So if he wanted to find out what would happen if he went up against me then I was ready but the truth was, I needed his help if I wanted this done quickly.

"There's a job I need doing," he said finally, his eyes cutting to Sin. "Someone important who is mouthing off and causing my organisation issues. I need him out of the way."

"Sin needs to lay low until the heat of our escape dies down," I growled. "Name another price."

The air crackled with tension as Jerome's coffee machine spat liquid into his cup with a hiss and a splutter.

"No," Jerome said firmly, a challenge in his eyes which told me this wasn't about the price; it was all above proving he still had some hold over Sin which

I didn't. He was swinging his dick around in an attempt to make me back off and bow to his command but that really wasn't my style. Besides, my skin was prickling with some darkness which lurked beneath the surface of this pristine place and my moon senses were warning me not to back down for a moment. Something was off here and I'd never ignored the moon before.

"Fine," I said and Jerome smirked triumphantly before I could go on. "We'll do it another way. Come on, Sin. We're leaving."

Sin blinked in surprise, his head wheeling from me to Jerome then back again before he pushed off of the window he'd been leaning against and strode over to join me as I headed for the elevator.

"Sin," Jerome growled, a low command to his voice but I spoke before my Incubus could.

"He doesn't jump through your hoops anymore, Jerome," I said tightly. "He's not your little bitch boy and I'm not dancing to your tune either. You might think you're all powerful up here in your tower but really you're just a lonely man hissing orders to the wind while the moon laughs at your petulance."

The elevator arrived and I stepped into it, Sin only hesitating a moment before following.

Jerome scowled furiously as the doors closed between us and Sin gave him a cheery wave before they shut out the sight of him entirely.

"I thought we needed him to find Roary's Lion?" Sin questioned but my skin was still prickling with my gifts, telling me to find another way.

"The moon will help us," I said firmly, my skin glimmering a little as if in confirmation of that and I smiled. "We don't need him."

Sin gave me a look which said he was clearly questioning my sanity. "So the moon decided to join the Daring Anacondas, did she?"

"I'm not sure. But my powers have never led me astray before. She led me to you, hides me from my enemies, hell, she even let me converse with the dead once or twice."

"And what did death have to say to you, kitten?" Sin asked curiously as the elevator arrived in the sparkling foyer and we headed back out to the street.

"Oh where's the fun in telling you that, amore mio?" I asked him with a smile. "Some secrets are best left beyond the grave."

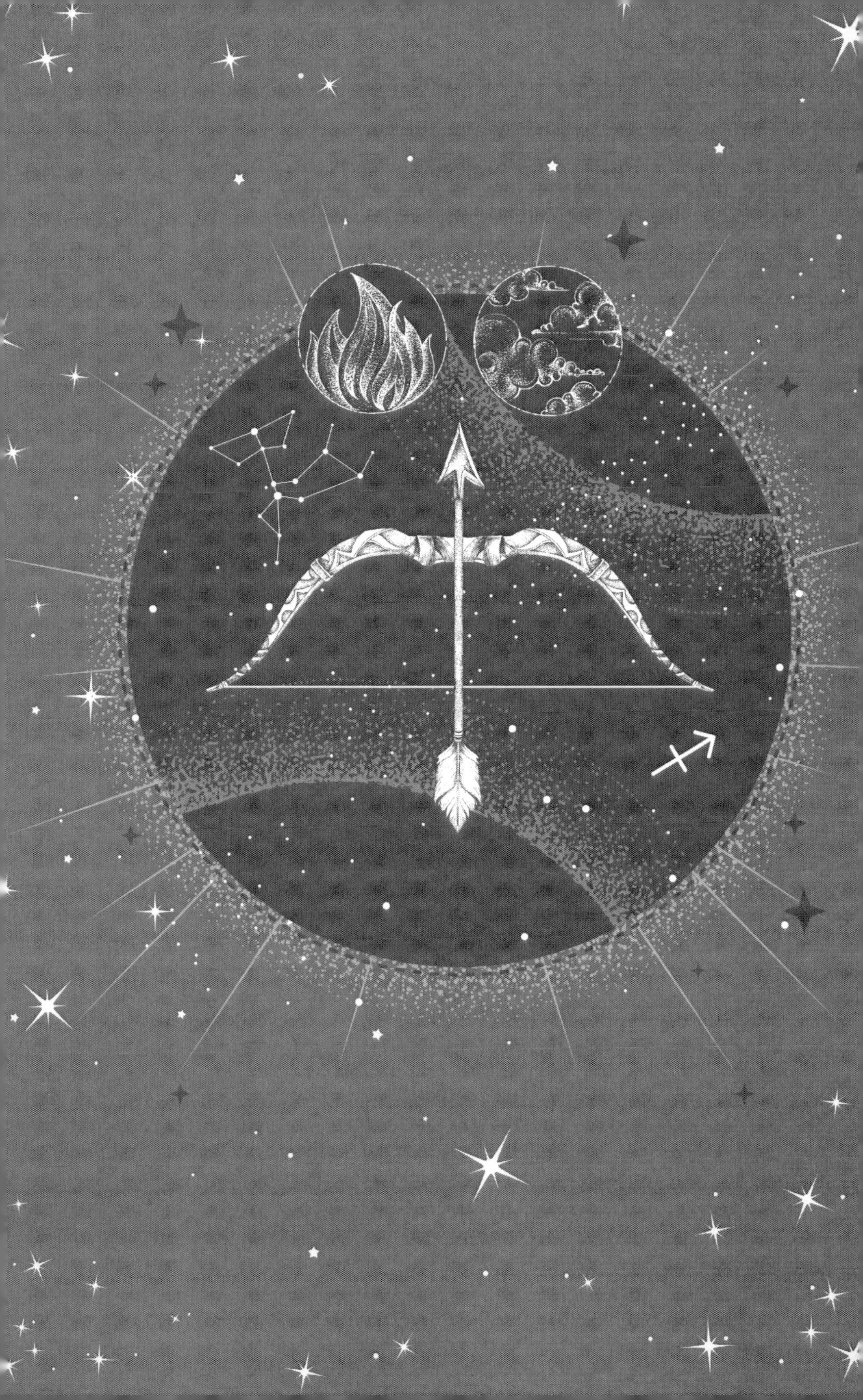

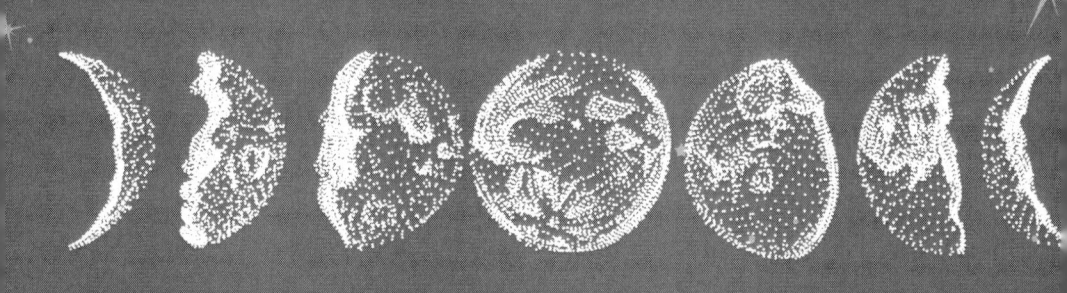

SIN
PRISONER #88

CHAPTER TWENTY SIX

The day had passed me by like I was a hamster caught in a whirlwind. I was just a small rodent being tossed waywardly though the air as we returned to the Oscura household, ate the best food I'd ever tasted and played games with the pups until the early hours of the morning. I'd finally been lured away from an intense game of tag by Rosalie nibbling on my ear and that had been enough to draw me into an hour-long fuckfest with my girl and her mates before we'd finally passed into oblivion.

It felt like I'd only just fallen asleep when I was rudely awoken by an ass cheek driving into my hip, and it wasn't the perfectly round kind I wanted to sink my teeth into. It belonged to a long-lost Lion who had taken up the middle of the bed with Rosalie while Ethan manned the other side of her. Now usually, I wasn't averse to a more masculine ass cheek on occasion, but my heart was pounding tonight and it didn't want anything or anyone but the girl currently being held captive between two donkey dicks.

I pushed to my feet, stalking to the end of the bed that was nowhere near big enough for the four of us – let alone Cain who was no doubt peeking in the window with a silent tear tracking down one cheek – not his ass cheek at least.

I'd had enough of those unless they belonged to a feral Wolf with eyes as big as the moon and lips that could make rose petals wither with envy.

I snatched her ankle and yanked her out from between them like I was ripping a tablecloth out from under a bunch of items in my way. She squeaked in surprise, nearly hitting the floor, but I caught her and tossed her over my shoulder in the next second. Disgruntled shouts came from the other men who had claimed her, but I was already gone, kicking the door closed and taking the twisty-windy halls this way and that through the manor house so they couldn't easily follow.

When I found an empty room – after opening several and causing a ruckus in the house – I finally carried Rosalie inside, ignoring her ongoing questions as to what the fuck I was doing.

I planted her ass down on a dressing table, stepping between her thighs and taking a kiss that silenced all of her words. Her hand coiled around my throat after indulging me a few moments, and I laughed headily as our mouths parted.

"Wanna be my dominatrix for the night?" I asked, wiggling my eyebrows suggestively.

"I want to know why you stole me from my bed?" she asked.

"Too many cocks," I stated. "I want you to myself for once. Or does our great Alpha not approve?"

Her fingers curled a little tighter around my neck and my smile grew. "Would you really let me play dominatrix with you?"

"I'd let you put on a strap-on and ride me raw if it pleased you, baby."

"But is that what *you* want?" she pushed, her eyes narrowing.

"Me?" I frowned.

"Yes, you, Sin. How often do you think about what *you* like sex to be?"

That one stumped me right there. I was a tree one second, then I'd been ruthlessly cut down.

She lowered her hand from my throat and I leaned in to kiss her jaw; nibbles, then bites, then licks until she laughed throatily, pulling me closer.

"Give me a second to think that one out. My brain moves in twenty-seven directions at once, sometimes I need a minute to find my own answer."

"Maybe you don't need to think about it. Maybe that's the problem," she suggested breathily as I made it to her neck and bit down there, marking a trail of ownership along her bronze skin.

"Things get dangerous when I stop thinking. There's not much of a rational rail service in my brain, but if I buy a ticket I have a chance of making it to a less psychotic stop."

"You make a weird kind of sense," she sighed, tipping her head back as I made it to her breasts, sucking, licking, pulling her silken night top down and freeing her tits for my hands to grab. They filled them just right and my tongue circled one nipple then the next.

"What do you like? Just follow your instincts," she urged.

"Those get me into trouble, wild girl," I laughed into her breasts then squeezed and nuzzled them. Fuck I loved her tits. They were a perfect nest for the flightless bird of my hungry tongue.

"The best kind." I could hear the smirk in her voice and my lips tilted to mimic it. "Do what you want, Sin. Be who you really are with me. That's all I desire."

I groaned into her soft skin, pulling away and stepping back to look down at her. "I don't know where that'll lead, but if you let me set my demons free I just know they'll play nice with you, even if a little rough too."

"You don't seem like a man who keeps his demons locked up," she teased.

I leaned down to speak into her ear. "The darkest ones lay deep. That's the risk, pretty one. If you want to dance with the devils in me, be ready to face the worst my soul has to offer. It's where the predator inside me waits, where the reaper within sits with patience, where the hungriest pieces of me await their next meal."

She shivered, leaning into me instead of away. She knew what I was. She had seen so much of me, but perhaps not all of it yet. And I didn't want any part of me hidden from the eyes of my Moon Wolf.

"Give it to me. All of it. The good, the bad-"

"The downright atrocious," I finished for her, leaning back and offering her a twisted grin.

I let her take in my bare chest and watched her expression shift as my body changed, my Incubus powers sliding over my skin to reveal what lay mirrored inside me. I could taste her desire in the air and it unveiled this new form in me, showing what my soul looked like in Fae form. It was this she wanted most, to see me as I was, but deeper still. I was the most naked and the most powerful creature in that moment. A potent kind of energy flooded my veins, the magic I drank into my flesh more than I had ever tasted at once.

My skin was drenched in blood, soaking me through, and jagged black spikes had grown along my arms and curled up over my shoulders. I had horns like daggers and skin as tough as iron. But I was still me. Still Sin Wilder. Or even fucking Whitney Northfield beneath it all. There, she had it. The Whitney in me. The root and the shoot. The way I felt inside manifested upon my flesh.

"Shiver my fucking timbers, baby," I growled, staring at this perfect incarnation of my deepest wants before me. She was it. The stars hadn't made her for me, oh no. Nothing this pure would have been gifted to me. She was mine because we were drawn to the jagged pieces that our pasts had placed in us, corrupted parts that the stars had no hand in crafting. That was where we connected, within the wreckage of our truths.

"I'm a monster," I said darkly, wondering if she would shrink from me now, but she only slid down from the dresser and pulled her top over her head, tossing it aside. Her silk shorts went next, revealing her naked flesh to me and making me groan with want.

"You're *my* monster. And the way you look now is how I feel on the inside too. It's dark and twisted and drenched in the blood of the past, but it's so beautifully real, Sin. *You* are so beautifully real. Have me now, how your soul wants me. Let it be brutal and let it be everything."

I lunged for her, my cock so hard with need that I didn't even bother to take the time to drop my boxers, I tore them clean off of me and threw them away. With a surge of desire, I grabbed her arm and threw her onto the bed, her back hitting the clean sheets as I leaned over her and spread her thighs wide. I feasted on her skin, licking my way along her tight pussy until I found her clit, letting her feel the way my tongue had split like a snake's as I slid it over her. She cried out, gasping when I did it again and pushed her legs even wider as I drove three fingers into her at once.

She moaned, clawing at the sheets while I fucked her with my mouth like only a heathen knew how. She was coming on my lips within a few seconds and I pushed another finger into her, stretching her and making her hips buck to meet the rhythm of my hand. I was rough and firm, pushing her to her limits as those sultry eyes met mine, my tongue riding her clit again and again, demanding her body bow to mine once more. The blood coating my skin didn't mark her pretty flesh, the apparition of it not real enough to do so, and I liked it better that way. Her this perfect, untouchable goddess while me the manifestation of all the ruin she had ever felt, bestowing pleasure upon her without mercy.

Her pussy clamped tight around my fingers and my laugh came out in a throaty chuckle as her thighs locked around my head. When she finally released me from the cage of her legs, I kneeled up between them and forced her to roll over, slapping her ass and leaving a clean handprint marked on her skin. I gripped her hair and angled her head to the mirror to the side of the bed.

"Watch as I destroy you, honey pie," I commanded and she sucked her lower lip as I fisted my cock and ran my thumb over the piercings adorning it.

"Ass up," I commanded and she angled her hips higher as I released her hair and splayed my hand down over her shoulder blades, pushing to keep her pinned there. The feel of this Alpha submitting to my desires made my head spin. She was my whirlwind on a calm day, my chaos in the boredom. We would always seek each other here in the crux of our madness.

I fisted my cock tighter and slicked the tip through the wetness of her pussy before driving myself fully inside her with a hard thrust of my hips. She cried out and I roared as she took every inch of me and I started pounding into that sensitive place inside her, not holding back, giving and giving to the brink of insanity. But I'd been beyond that brink, I lived out there in the sea of wildness and I wanted her to know how good it could be to swim in its waters.

Her eyes met mine in the mirror as I fucked her with the full power of the fury that lived in my bones. She moaned my name, *Sin, Sin, Sin,* and that one word was the embodiment of all we were in that moment. It was nirvana, but it wasn't enough. Not yet.

"Keep looking at me, don't break eye contact," I gritted out and she nodded, her brown eyes locked on mine in the reflection.

Incubuses could be lost if they changed forms too many times, if they forgot to come back to their own form enough. Sometimes I had felt close to losing myself, but Rosalie Oscura had not only grounded me in exactly who I was, she was now unveiling pieces of me I'd never seen in myself. I'd heard rumours of this. That an Incubus could reach a state of lust that gave them utter control over the sensations of their partner's body, and I felt our souls connect with an abruptness that rattled me to my core.

I could feel what she felt, could heighten it, make it ten times more powerful, and as I thrust into her again, she let out a sound that was as close to bliss as I'd ever heard. I made her feel it all, made her skin come alive with pleasure until she was hardly able to do anything at all but take what I gave her. I fucked her with a purity that blinded me, her lust feeding my magic to the point of overflowing.

"Sin, oh my stars," she groaned, fisting the sheets, but there was no strength in her grip, because I was wringing her of it all. I held her hips and drove in even deeper, pulling on the connection between us and making more pleasure spill through her than I had ever delivered to anyone before.

We were united in a way that transcended this realm, our bodies, all of it. We were one and as I stared at her in the mirror, transfixed by this beautiful creature of mine, I realised there was no more blood on my skin, no more spikes or horns. I was me, wholly me and my body was shimmering as if I was a star damned Pegasus.

My cock was thick and so hard, I was losing all grasp on everything in this world but her. She was all that existed. All I wanted to exist. And as one, we came apart, the noise that left me a pure, carnal sound that went on and on while she echoed it. I finally stilled inside her, coming so hard I was close to blacking out. Rosalie's body relaxed into a puddle beneath me and I slowly withdrew from her, falling down at her side.

My hand landed on hers and our fingers wove together as she curled into me, panting and laughing.

"You're it for me, wild girl," I said breathlessly. "Whatever that was confirms it. I didn't know love like this could exist in me, but it's there regardless, you perfect peachy thing." I turned to find her lips, and they were already there, meeting mine.

"I love you too, you perfect peachy thing," she echoed and my smile was surely branded on my mouth, etched too deep to ever be removed.

We lay there, breathing each other in until the night deepened and sleep stole her from me. That jealous bastard had come calling, luring her away like the Pied Piper he was.

I knew what I had to do now. There was no sleeping for me tonight.

I slipped out of bed, gently lifting her and carrying her back to the arms of the men who adored her so well. Her Atlas lay on the nightstand and I picked it up, casting a silencing bubble around me as I made a call to Jerome, my gaze fixed on my softly sleeping girl within the clutches of her pack.

It wasn't long before I had a name and location for the job, then I left her there, showered and dressed before slipping away like a moth through a crack, my pulse drumming everywhere beneath my skin. One little message to Jerome promised that his deed would be done, and I continued on through the hallways of the Oscura manor with a new hunger rising.

The thing about me was, when I wanted to dance no one could stop me. And when I looked for it, I could find rhythm in all things. From the hum of the wind to the percussion of the rain. Tonight, there wasn't much of those, but there was a creak in the floorboards as I crept through this big old house. The corridors were dark, but the dead of night didn't bring total silence. I could hear low chatter beyond doors, whispering, giggling pups that reminded me of my childhood with Jerome. Always breaking rules and curfews.

Then our games had turned to brutality and I knew how that rainbow of bloodshed tasted. It was as sweet as it was bitter. It wasn't actually the killing that I enjoyed the most; it was the thrill of the hunt. And tonight, I could feel that thrill swing-dancing through my veins and singing *oh murder, oh my.*

My sex pot had refused Jerome's job and I'd seen the rage in his eyes, known the danger she was putting herself in by doing so. I couldn't let it lie, so I was a bull in a meadow now, my horns pointed at the sunburnt ass of a naked nincompoop, and soon that nincompoop would fall to satisfy Jerome's desires.

Oh my, the music was really thumping tonight. I could hear it in the walls, in the sky. The stars were twinkling at me as I made it out a window and landed as light as a feather on the porch roof outside. Carefully, dandy-footed and surefooted, I climbed down and took in the swing seat on the porch where two sleeping Fae remained undisturbed.

The bigger of the two was Roary's brother with his golden hair and ever-grinning lips. A cat he was, but the creature curled up in his arms was no cat. Though small, I'd seen her bite, seen her turn her predatory gaze upon more than a handful of men in this house. Mmmhmm, Leon Night's sugar-lipped sweetheart was my real challenge here as I carefully drew a silencing bubble around me and crept toward my target.

"Oh little Lion, just sleep and see," I whisper-sung. "You think you win at stealing but you haven't met me." I slipped my index finger into his trouser pocket, hooking out the key to the shiny orange Mustang GT he'd been bragging about stealing from some stripper dude in the mortal realm. "Mine, mine, mine. Doesn't she just look so fine, fine, fine?"

I turned, racing away into the night with a giggle escaping me and a manic smile borrowing all of my happies to make it grow and grow.

The GT was waiting there like a fancy flan in a hat and I gave it a little bow before pressing the button on the key. The lights winked at me and I winked back before sliding into the driver's seat and settling myself in for the ride. I could drive like an expertito. I started her up and she purred like a dream as I slammed her into gear. When she roared, so did her Lion.

"This is where you learn that I am the greatest felon in the land, kitty cat." I smiled at him as he came charging toward me across the lawn. His sweetie pie ran into view and that was when I turned the car around and raced for the gate at full pelt. A little device on the dashboard made the gate open for me and I laughed harder as I made it beyond the gate and onto the open road. When I passed the FIB, I shifted to look like a wholly different Fae to fool them, driving slowly past them before driving fast, fast, fast again, taking hairpin turns at a speed that pressed me back into my seat, losing anyone that might be chasing me into the night.

The stars were aligned for my hunt, because Jerome had told me my target was staying in his summer retreat not far from here.

"You foolish fool," I grinned. "Tiberius Rigel, I'm coming to get you."

He sounded like a bore of a man, some government official or maybe he wasn't even in that role anymore, who fucking knew or cared? But I had no doubt that old Tibs had lived a good life setting his laws and talking his talk at least for a while, being the big boss man and making sure there was no room in this kingdom for Fae like me. Miscreants and mayhem-makers. We wouldn't get to express our true nature if it was up to people like Tibsy boy. But the thing about fancy men in fancy hats was that the world always caught up to them. And tonight, retribution was headed his way in the form of a blackhearted villain who knew how to make death into one hell of a party.

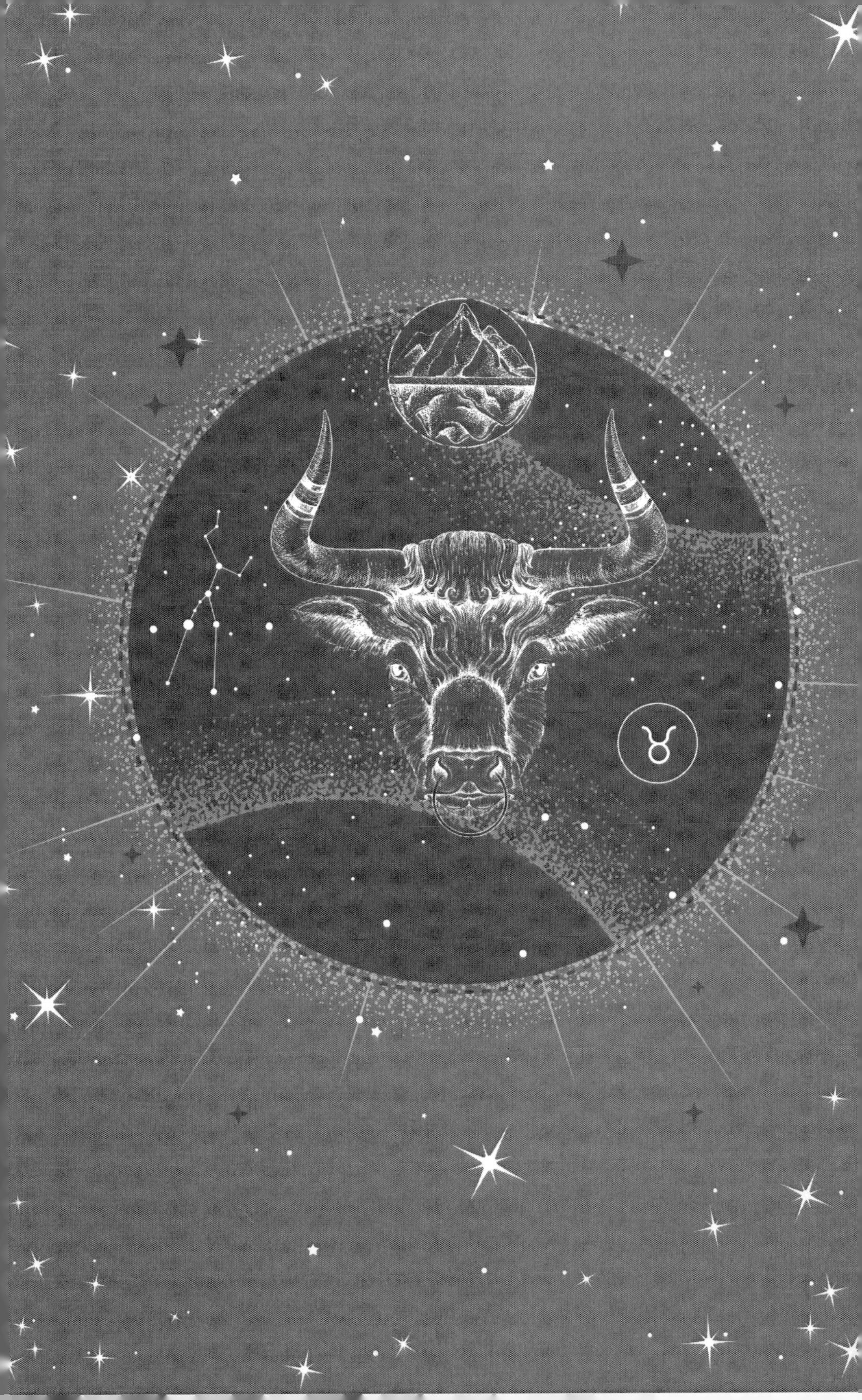

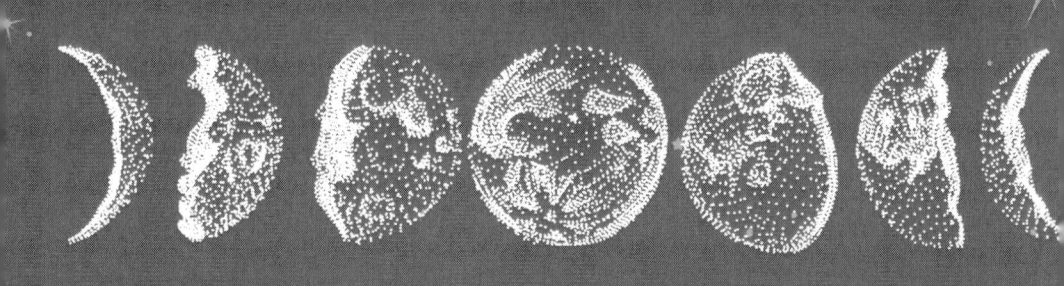

Rosalie

PRISONER #12

CHAPTER TWENTY SEVEN

I sighed, rolling over in bed and trying to ignore the strange itching feeling which had started up beneath my skin and seemed determined to drag me from sleep. It was no good.

I sat up, gently moving Roary's arm off of me and untangling my legs from Ethan's.

Moonlight poured in through the window above my bed so brightly that I squinted up at it as I blinked my eyes open. A frown dug rivets into my brow as that discomfort increased, the itching intensifying, urging me to get up.

"Alright," I murmured sleepily. "I'm listening."

The moon was urging me to move faster so I stole out of bed, scrubbing a hand over my face and taking stock of the room. Sin was missing.

"By the stars," I groaned, irritation puncturing my sleepy haze and bringing me fully awake at last. I gave the room a sweeping look, finding Sin's clothes gone and a crumpled note left in their place.

I crossed the room and picked it up, expecting him to have left some kind of explanation. Instead, I found a drawing of a lemon, a squid and a thumbs up.

"Fucking Sin," I muttered, tossing the note aside and grabbing a pair of jeans and a black t-shirt. I didn't wake the others as I headed out of the room. This was something I needed to deal with myself.

I slipped through the house, the sounds of my sleeping famiglia coming from within many of the rooms I passed where pack huddles were the norm and my often solitary existence was more than unusual. Though I supposed I was conforming now that I had my men sharing my bed more often than not.

I passed the room that Cain was sharing with Hastings, hiding my passage in a silencing bubble so that even his Vampire senses wouldn't detect me.

When I made it downstairs, I headed to the cloakroom just off of the front door and hunted around in it until I found my leather jacket and a helmet hidden in the back. I quickly laced a pair of boots onto my feet, scowling at the mud coating them, making it clear one of my family members had made use of them in my absence.

Outside the moonlight was even brighter, illuminating the world in lines of silver and making my skin tingle with the rush of the celestial being's power.

That sense of urgency only increased and I broke into a run at her command, racing down the track to the barn and selecting a motorcycle from the lineup. I could hear Leon's voice carrying from somewhere close to the house, cursing out Sin for stealing his car and knew it couldn't have been long since he'd left.

I tucked my hair up into my helmet and muttered several colourful swear words about my Incubus as I started the engine and roared out of the barn, though I hid the sound within my silencing bubble so only I could hear it.

The drive was illuminated in a river of silver light far brighter than that surrounding us, the moon offering me a path to follow, leading me to where I needed to be. I sent up a word of thanks to the moon as the power she had gifted me flared in my blood, the path becoming all the clearer.

The gates swung open, allowing me to exit and I raced out onto the road beyond. My eyes fell on the FIB vehicle which was parked up to watch the exit to our stronghold and I grinned as I found the pair of agents inside it fast asleep, no doubt the work of the beautiful being hanging low and fat in the sky above me.

I made it down to the crossroads where I expected my path to lead me back into the heart of Alestria, to Jerome's apartment if I was being entirely honest about it, but instead the glimmering trail of moonlight directed me south towards the coast.

I frowned, but only hesitated for a beat before following the guidance of the moon and tearing away towards the sea at high speed.

The road was clear and open the entire way, either by design of the moon herself or maybe it was just because it was the middle of the night and no other motherfucker was travelling this way.

The prickling within my skin was growing fiercer, the sense that something truly awful might come to pass if I didn't make it to my destination in time eating at me.

I headed further south, the world slipping into a rugged terrain around me, nature left to keep hold of this wild expanse of open woodland before I broke free of the trees and found myself up on the cliffs overlooking the sea.

There weren't a lot of properties out this way but there were several hulking mansions owned by rich and famous Fae and used for summer getaways. We tended to leave them alone and they left us alone in turn but I knew that every one of them were powerful, important people. The kind who even the Oscuras avoided messing with.

"What the fuck have you gotten yourself into, Sin?" I growled.

The moonlight veered off of the road, leading me onto a well maintained track which speared out towards the sea, descending rapidly with the cliffs rising up around me and the trees thickening once more.

The bike ate up the distance to the foot of the cliffs and I dismounted as I found a pair of heavy iron gates barring my way on, making sure I left the track far enough away for any CCTV cameras to be able to pick me up.

I cursed in a low tone as I spotted a bright orange sports car dumped in the trees at the edge of the path, barely concealed within the greenery, the engine still running.

I closed in on it, unsurprised to find it empty and I shut the ignition off before straightening and looking around for another clue from the moon.

Patches of silver light puddled in spots throughout the trees to my right, the moonlight punching holes through the canopy and leading me around the perimeter of the property.

I reached out with my earth magic and guided the plants and greenery aside as I crept closer, giving me a clear path which eventually led me out of the trees to the side of a stunning beach house set back from the glimmering sea beyond.

A low picket fence ringed the property though clearly it was protected by powerful wards which were the real security in place. I reached out tentatively with my magic, feeling for the wards and hunting for some way around them but as I began to work my will into the solid wall of magic, the brush of fingers down my spine made me jerk around in alarm.

I snarled a warning, an iron dagger forming in my fist as I twisted to look all around me, finding nothing and no one there.

An unnatural breeze rustled the swaying leaves closest to me and as I glared out into the darkness, a breath of pleading reached my ears.

"Stop him, Moon Wolf."

My heart leapt at the words, the tumbling echo of them seeming to span the ocean and beyond while still being so quiet that it was hard to make them out at all.

The leaves rustled faster, the crash of their tiny bodies against one another forming a chorus of words which I couldn't pick out, but the harder I strained my ears to listen for them, the more of them spilled over me.

Lies. Concealment. Falsehood.

"Shit," I hissed, moving closer to the wards again but I was forced to turn as that same brush of fingers ran down my spine.

I eyed the space around me warily, not seeing anyone there but I could feel them as if their presence had laid an imprint on the world around me like the shape of a body nestled into blankets.

"Speak," I commanded, leaning into my connection with the moon and feeling the rippling fabric of The Veil flickering around me as if someone were trying to push through it from the other side of death.

"Whitney cannot follow this path," a voice called to me in desperation and I almost flinched at its proximity. "He is headed towards a fate that can't be undone."

"What fate?" I demanded, my eyes scouring the nothingness though the presence seemed closer than ever, the impression of a beautiful woman with wide, deep-set eyes which were filled with pure terror, filling my mind.

"His father resides in that house. The man who never knew he existed. In life I was forced to forget my son but in death I see it all…"

Her voice trailed away and I cursed in Faetalian as I rounded on the house again, pushing my will against the wards. There wasn't time to be subtle. So I threw everything I had at them and hoped I'd be able to find a way through before Sin Wilder made a mistake that might ruin his entire life.

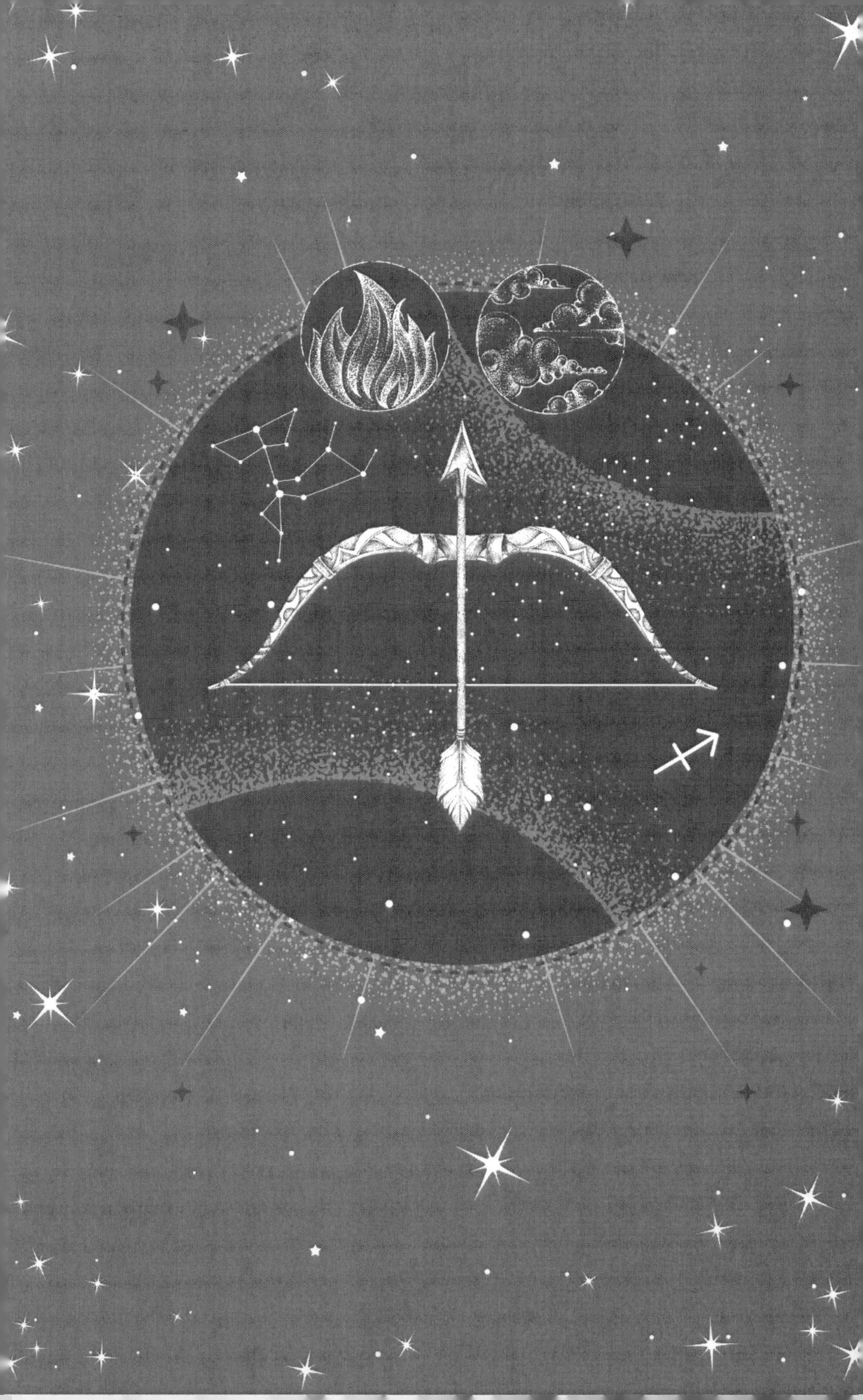

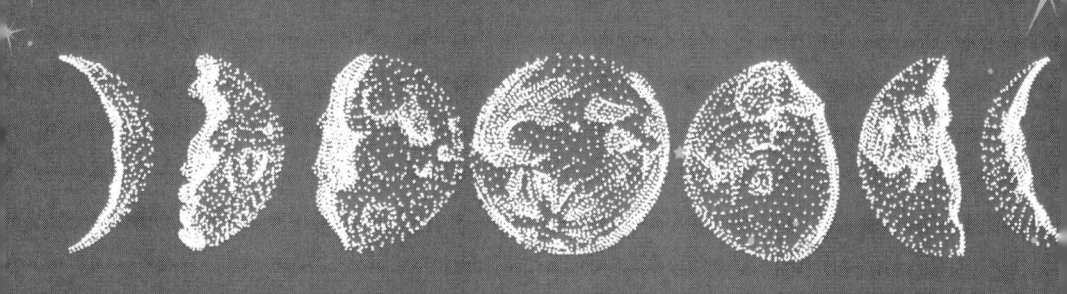

SIN

PRISONER #88

CHAPTER TWENTY EIGHT

A mansion overlooking the sea. How cliché, Tibsy boy.

My muscles were primed for action as I slinked through the darkened halls of this fancy man's house, passing by his fancy trinkets and even fancier décor. Oh yes, old Tiberius Rigel liked his finery. I'd have bet he was born with a silver spoon stuffed up his ass, unlike me who had a rusted toothpick shoved in there before I was tossed away like trash in the nearest garbage can. It would probably have fucked up a weaker Fae than me. Done something to their mind, cracked 'em good and turned them into a real reprobate.

Lucky for me, I could shrug off stuff like that. One good shrug was all you needed to get through a childhood based on a foundation of trauma. Yup, there were no scars left on my mind, baby. I was different, sure. Quirky, definitely. But it was around about the time people started whispering the word 'crazy' at me when I got stabby. A perfectly reasonable reaction, actually. It was just that society tended to frown on that kind of thing. But society-rule-makers were just a bunch of Fae in top hats attending balls and haw-he-hawing at pretentious jokes about governmental things that couldn't interest me even if

I was paid big bucks to listen.

Tibs here was one of those Fae, or at least, he had been. Whichever it was, I didn't much care, but I did have a bit of a bug to bear with him. A jiggy little bug that kept doing a jive in my bear's ear. Because all in all, I couldn't say the stars had been particularly gracious to me in life. They tended to favour swanky cocksure rich dicks like Tiberius Rigel from the moment of their conception to this here moment of their death. His demise would include a nice healthy dose of stabby glory in payment for all his good living, but he had done a damn lot of good living. It wasn't exactly justice in my books.

I wasn't against wealth exactly; it was the hoity-toity attitude that came with it. The privilege, the bluster and most of all, the entitlement. They took it for granted, all this. Their shiny shoes shimmying along their shiny halls, never suspecting that bad omens would come creeping in their back window. I had a knack for breaking through magical wards and Tibs had had some seriously hard nuts to crack, but I'd cracked them alright. And now here I was, fate-bound to deliver him his end, like I was sent by The Ferryman himself, ready to ship his soul off beyond The Veil.

It didn't matter who he was or what he'd done, I was on this job because I had a sixth sense when it came to Jerome, one that could feel his rage in the air. He hadn't taken kindly to my wild girl refusing him and I knew how to settle that matter. The best way to solve all matters. With death and dancing.

I paused where the moonlight fell in a pool over a table facing the window. There were photos lined up on it in gilt frames, family pictures, Tibs beside a teen boy with a mohawk, his arm slung around his shoulders and big ass grins on their faces. So he had a son. And one glance to the left showed him on a boat trip with a girl that just had to be his daughter. My gaze lingered on those happy faces, the memories alive with joy and good feelings.

I hooked up the photograph of him with his son, a frown burrowing into my brow like a hungry mole. Was Tibs a good father? Had he considered tossing either of his kids into the trash? Had he beat them? Belittled them?

My gaze fell on another photo of the teen boy, but he was older now. A man with strength in his eyes. I pursed my lips and placed the photo down, adjusting it back into position while my heart cracked and old, ancient, childish desires poured out. If I'd had a childhood like these kids clearly had, would I be this…different? Would the world want me if I'd been raised in privilege, inviting me to its swanky balls and hailing my name from the hills? Would I be the felon I was today if my mother hadn't tossed me into the trash?

I headed on, finding a kitchen and coming to a halt by a block of knives. I hadn't brought my own, and there was something poetic about him dying by a knife that had recently chopped a tomato for his fancy man salad. I picked the largest one and twisted it in my grip, the cool steel kissing my palm in greeting. Darkness swept through me, my demons awakening, urging me on, whispering of blood and chaos. I might need to use magic too, the asshole was one of the strongest Fae in the kingdom after all, but I was one powerful motherfucker myself, and I had a lot of experience in bringing bad men to their knees. Was he bad though? I hadn't done my research on this one. I usually liked to know their crimes by heart, liked to pick them for those very reasons and whisper the names of their victims in their ear as they died, sometimes accompanied by a lovely little lullaby of my own creation. But this was the first time I found myself out on a job for one reason that went beyond whether the man in this house was a cretin who deserved his death.

I was here for Rosalie. Because she didn't yet understand the danger my brother posed. She didn't grasp the lengths to which he would go to get payment from her in light of her refusal. She didn't know. But I did. I'd watched Jerome pluck a man's eyes out for less than Rosalie's refusal, I'd seen him peel skin from the bone with a smile on his face, I'd watched him gut people for less than a hundred auras debt to him. He was beautifully, dangerously monstrous, but I had never before felt the threat of him until my honey pie had painted a refusal upon his door. That threat of him to her had ignited a spark of wild fear in me, and I didn't subscribe to feelings like that often. But his eyes on my girl with a no sliding from her tongue had set my nerves aflame. So here I was, doing the deed he'd set and not questioning a thing about it, because better

Tibs died tonight than my wild girl died tomorrow.

So whether he was a good daddy or not, whether he had lived a supreme life, saving baby kittens and building orphanages with his bare hands, it didn't matter. Because his number had been called and the king of death was going to hand deliver him his order.

I moved deeper into the house, finding a stairway, climbing up the cream carpeted steps and seeking the floor above for his room. He must have been sleeping. All was quiet and still, no sound of a headboard thumping away while he railed his girlfriend, boyfriend or paid hooker. I'd seen no other Fae in those photographs downstairs, no mother or other father smiling proudly in those pictures. But as I made it to a white door, I paused to take in a portrait beside it of a woman whose beauty had my head cocking. She was regal, her eyes bright, yet oh so dark. Her name was written in calligraphy at the bottom and it was a name which fit her impeccably. *Serenity*.

You could see the love in the strokes of the brush. Whoever had painted this had adored this Fae and had tried to immortalise her for all to witness. I knew with a strange kind of certainty that Tiberius was the culprit, and it was so clear to me that this was his room before I even opened the door.

My hand fell on the knob, my silencing bubble extending to cover the noise as I twisted it and pushed it wide.

The moonlight shining through the window at my back cast my shadow across his floor, right up to the end of his bed. The shape of him lay beneath his comforter. He was sleeping so soundly, I considered not waking him before I slid my knife into his temple. But that was too easy, no fanfare or splatter. Besides, I liked them looking me in the eyes when they went, so they knew who their maker was in the end.

I took a step forward but a hand snatched me from behind and I whirled on my attacker, bringing the knife up and throwing my weight at them. My knife kissed the bronze skin of a delicate neck and brown eyes narrowed as they met mine.

"Rosa," I gasped, yanking the blade away from her throat as I pushed my silencing bubble out around her.

"Stop," she growled, the word a command. "You can't kill him."

"Oh yes I can," I snapped, offended that she thought I was incapable of killing this rich fucker. "In a hundred ways before he wakes."

"That's not what I meant." She gripped my hand and I noticed there was something about her that was off. She was feeling something that I couldn't place, but I knew it was important.

"What is it, sex pot? Speak quick before he wakes and I have to get knife-happy."

"It's just, I…the moon…" She shook her head then her eyes moved past me to land on the painting. "It's her." Rosalie moved away from me, ethereal in her movements as she raised a hand and placed it upon the woman in her picture frame.

"You're kinda giving me the heebies, baby. Are you playing a game? Do let me know the rules so I can play too," I urged eagerly, following her to the painting and taking in the woman with her flowing black hair and gleaming brown eyes.

"I can hear her," Rosalie said, goosebumps rising across her skin.

I frowned, listening for some voice coming from the painting, but I heard nothing. "I really should be getting stabby, can we talk to the painting once Tibsy boy is dead?"

"No," Rosalie growled, all bossy boots again which, honestly, I fucking loved. It normally got me hard, but right now didn't feel like a good time to get hard. It felt like something important was happening but I was two buns short of a baker's dozen and no one felt like filling my bread basket.

"Sometimes, when the moon wills it…I can speak with the dead," Rosalie breathed, her whispery voice setting a chill in my bones.

I swallowed thickly as a net curtain fluttered away from the window at my back and caressed my arm.

"Er, honey bunch?" I said tightly. "What's happening?"

Rosalie whispered the word 'yes' in agreement to something then turned to me suddenly, her eyes as bright as moonlight, glowing at me with a burning silver luminescence. When she spoke, it wasn't her voice, it was deeper, without an accent, still feminine, but lilting in a way that didn't belong to Rosalie.

"I've waited so long," she croaked, stepping closer, reaching out and caressing my face. "Beyond The Veil where all answers are given. I was forced to forget you in life, but now I remember. You are my son. Mine and Tiberius's boy. I loved you so fiercely before you were lost to me – I *still* love you."

Something crackled around me and I was vaguely aware of my silencing bubble falling but I couldn't draw my gaze from Rosalie's glowing moonlit eyes. I knew in my soul that this was no trick, the moon was allowing this, letting words pass from The Veil through my Rosalie, and the one who spoke was…my mother.

Her fingers tracked my jaw and tears of silver slid down Rosa's cheeks. I was well used to madness and the twisted way of this world, so this truth wasn't something I dared deny. I leaned into her touch, wanting so badly to feel this caress, to know what it was to have my mother's love soaking into my skin. But then I withdrew, clarity punching me in the chest and reminding me that my mother had thrown me away. She had discarded me, and if what she said was true, if she was truly my mother, then the rest of it had to be true too. The tossing, the trash can.

I shook my head, backing up, retreating to the window until my spine was pressed to it and I felt boxed in. I could run. Left, right, dive out the window itself, but those glowing eyes wouldn't look away. They had me trapped and I suddenly felt like a young boy being scolded by the mistress of the orphanage when all I wanted deep down was to be held, to be told I was loved and it didn't matter that I liked to do strange things, because my mother would love me anyway. She loved me *because* of those things. But she didn't. Never had. She'd been the first to look at me and see something unwantable. She'd been the first rejection but far from the last. I had been so unwanted that they'd tried to hide me away in the belly of Darkmore, tried to pretend I didn't exist anymore. No one wanted me, least of all her. No one, no one, no one-

"Sin," Rosalie's voice broke through over my mother's, the light in her eyes fading. "Listen to her. Just listen."

I wanted to refuse, but for her, by the stars, for *her*, I would do anything.

I nodded, throat thick and limbs heavy as that warm voice came from my girl's throat once more. "I was so in love with your father, but I wasn't the one he was destined to marry. He had been betrothed to a woman of pure, Siren blood, of great power and from a family held in great esteem by the Savage King and his father before him. My Tiberius was destined to be bound to another woman in matrimony but his love for me made it impossible for him to give me up or I him, despite his planned union to her. So he kept me despite their upcoming marriage, our love a secret which she knew well - though she despised me for claiming his heart from her. But it wasn't his heart she truly wanted. It was his power, his prestige, his bloodline which meant that their child would be in line for the throne once they came of age. So she ignored his indiscretions with me right up until I found out that I was pregnant with you." Her voice cracked and I only stared into those moonlit eyes, drinking in her words even though this story held no happy ending. "I was a fool. I thought…I stupidly believed that she would allow me to take her place and be the one Tiberius married once she realised I was with child. So, without telling another soul about my pregnancy, I went to her and told her that you were growing in my belly. I told her that Tiberius loved me and that I was going to ask him to discard the arrangement between the two of them and marry me instead. I knew he would do so despite the scandal, despite the wrath of the king, because I knew his love for me would win through."

"So why didn't it?" I breathed, my words slipping past my lips as little more than an exhale as I held my breath against the answer which would spell out the tattered truth of my beginnings in this world.

"She was a far more powerful Fae than I," my mother admitted. "And she wasn't willing to give up her path to the power her wedding could offer. She used her Siren gifts on me, forcing me to feel hatred in place of the love I held for Tiberius. She made me leave a note to him, ending things between us, then hid me away in the basement of her home, concealing my pregnancy while pushing forward with her plans to marry the man I loved. She kept me tethered in the confines of my own mind, a slave to the power of her Siren gifts. I lost all sense of time, of the world, of myself. I don't even remember giving birth, only that she took you from my arms before I'd ever had a real chance to hold you. When she returned, she forced her way deeper into my mind, her Siren gifts so powerful that I lost all memory of ever having you at all. She kept me captive a few months longer, only releasing me after her marriage to Tiberius when my mind had been moulded and beaten into submission and I had no recollection of any of the time which had passed since the moment I had realised I was with child."

"Then why was I wrapped up in a blanket with the name Whitney Northfield stitched into it?" I demanded, hot-headed yet softening quickly again, feeling guilty for blaming her when the truth was such a wicked damn thing. "I just need answers."

"Some part of my mind must have clung to the hope that you could find me if I left a clue, a name… the name I'd wished to give you."

"I searched that name though, I never found anything," I growled, frustrated with the stars and most of all furious at the woman who had forced my mother to abandon me.

"Northfield is a common name," she said mournfully. "And I was no one special."

"You were to me," I croaked, then forced out my next words, needing to know it all. "What happened next?"

"She let me go. I was sent back out into the world with only a feeling of yearning left in my soul where you belonged that I could never understand until my death, when all clarity was gifted to me beyond The Veil."

"But why?" I rasped, knowing I had so many other questions, but that one clawed at me most of all.

"Linda wanted Tiberius for his power and she wouldn't let anything stand between her and that. She wanted me gone so that she could take him as her own and provide an heir to the throne herself. I'm only glad she didn't kill you as I fear she'd intended to do. But I suppose even her power-hungry heart couldn't bear to hurt an innocent babe."

"So what happened to you after that? If she let you go, then why aren't you alive?" I rasped, my mind a muddle with all she was telling me, the answers to so many questions flooding my brain to the point of overflowing.

"She had spent the better part of a year messing up my mind with her gifts to make certain I would have no memory of bringing you into the world and had left me with a false memory of a head injury to explain away my forgetfulness. But I don't think she paid enough attention to blocking out my love for Tiberius and within a few months of my release from her captivity, the hatred she had falsely given me for him fell away, my love for him breaking through once more and filling my heart until I found myself upon his doorstep one morning, begging him to have me back. Tiberius had loved me in all the time I'd been gone and despite his marriage to Linda, he couldn't deny his heart when we were reunited, and we fast rekindled our romance. He brought me into his household, gave me a job working in his manor to disguise the real reason for my presence and told Linda he would not let me go."

"You were his dirty piece on the side?" I snarled, hating the idea of that and she shook her head.

"It sounds so much worse when you say it that way, but it wasn't like that. Tiberius had always made it clear to Linda that his heart was already spoken for and once he got me back, he refused to lose me again. She wasn't happy, but she had little choice but to endure my presence. I may not have remembered my time with her, but being close to her after that always filled me with a fear I couldn't explain. I made certain to keep my distance, never once letting her get me on my own. She was focused on placing an Heir in her belly, though I knew that following my return, Tiberius refused to perform his marital duties to give her the chance of one. She got her wish of a child by him eventually, but not before my death and not before I birthed another son. Once

I found out about the pregnancy, I had this instinctual urge to tell Tiberius immediately, as if some part of me knew that if I kept the secret, something terrible might happen if I didn't. He protected me throughout it. Linda was furious when she found out, but Tiberius made it clear that our child would be his Heir. He couldn't divorce her without causing a huge scandal and the Savage King would have been furious if he alienated Linda's family, whose political sway was integral to his rule, so Tiberius convinced her to fake a pregnancy, to allow me to remain hidden in the shadows so that once my child was born she might pretend that our child was hers. To give our baby the legitimacy he needed to claim his position as Heir."

"Why would you agree to that?" I hissed, my mind reeling with the fact that I had a brother, born in blood and kept from me just as every piece of my bloodline had been kept from me until now.

"It wasn't an easy choice, but I wanted my child to be an Heir, not some scandalous secret. Power is everything to the Fae and I wanted my baby to claim their birthright more than I cared about stepping out of the shadows myself. Behind closed doors, I would have my family. What did I care if Linda pretended they were hers in the open when I could have that?"

I wrinkled my nose at her assessment of the choice she made, but I supposed I would have given anything to be able to claim a family for myself once too.

Serenity went on, still speaking through Rosalie's lips, my love's body a vessel for this communion through The Veil. "But after Max's birth…Linda grew more desperate, not giving up on her lust for power or her desire to place her own, legitimate child on the throne in place of mine. She tried to tempt Tiberius away from me, but our love was too deep for him to ever be swayed, and eventually she saw the only way was to…remove me from the picture."

"No," I gasped, seeing where this was heading all too clearly. Like I was standing in oncoming traffic, chained to the ground, knowing my fate before it collided with me.

More tears slipped down Rosalie's cheeks as Serenity continued. "After

Max's birth, it wasn't long before I became sick. So sick that there seemed to be no cure. Tiberius did everything he could, had healers from all across the kingdom and beyond come to me to try to save me from the plague in my bones. But...it was not to be. Linda had poisoned me so carefully, so cunningly that no one ever suspected it, and finally, she got her wish and I was taken out of the equation altogether. She managed to provide a potential Heir herself; Ellis, who she threw all of her efforts into in the hopes that she might one day challenge Max for his position and steal his title of Heir."

"Where is this Linda bitch right now?" I hissed. "Is she in this house? Tell me her location and I will bring a world of vengeance upon her," I spat, my grip tightening on the knife as emotion sliced through to my core. I didn't know how to handle it without the outlet of killing. I needed the screams of the woman who had stolen so much from me singing in my ears before dawn came. I would travel any distance, go to any lengths to find her tonight.

"She has been punished well," Serenity said, a bite to her tone. My mother reached for me again with Rosalie's hand. "I cannot stay much longer. Please. Let me embrace you, just once. Let me show you how much you are loved."

I remained still for several seconds before nodding stiffly and she moved forward, her arms winding around me, her hand coming to the back of my head and pulling me into the crook of her neck. I melted, nothing but a boy in the arms of a mother who I had been so sure despised me that it was almost impossible to accept that she adored me after all.

"Tiberius must know the truth," she whispered.

"He does," a deep voice cut through the air, and Rosalie pulled back, her eyes blinking and the moonlight evaporating from them at once.

Tiberius stood in the doorway in a red dressing robe, his eyes wide with shock as he stared from Rosalie to me. "I heard it all," he breathed.

My heart thumped once, twice, three times and then I ran at him, arms wide for a hug, but before I made it, I slammed into a wall of ice he cast to stop me and staggered back.

"You're Sin Wilder," he gritted out, a note of fear to his voice that said he truly knew me. Well, at least what the press said about me. And they tended to paint me as one bastard of a criminal.

He looked down at the knife in my hand and I quickly hid it behind my back. "Just a little misunderstanding, Daddykins," I said, a smile lifting my lips.

"Don't call me that," he said warily, his eyes tracking over me. "Is this some trick?"

"You heard her voice," Rosalie said. "I don't go channelling dead people every day. So what she said was important enough for the moon to allow it."

"The moon…" Tiberius tracked a hand down the back of his neck. "Why have you come here?"

"Well, it's a funny story actually," I started, but Rosalie cut over me.

"The moon guided us here. Serenity clearly wanted this message unveiled. You know the truth now." She looked to me, wonder lighting her expression. "Sin is your son."

"Fuck, full body shivers right there," I said, looking at my arm as the hairs raised along it. "Do you feel it too?" I looked to Tibsy, but he didn't seem so excited. He seemed afraid, wary, like a goose about to lay an egg.

"No," he grunted, stepping back and eyeing me with caution. "You're not…you can't be…"

A boat sunk in my chest, holes punctured in its hull while screaming sailors threw themselves overboard in a bid to be saved. But there was no surviving the stormy sea in my heart as I watched this man shrink from me. My so-called father didn't want me. Of course he didn't want me. One look and he saw a dangerous felon, a madman, the type of Fae the rest of the world wanted nothing to do with.

"Serenity confirmed it. She and the moon bent the space between life and death to offer you this truth," Rosalie growled, stepping toward Tiberius in anger. "Your son stands before you and you dare deny he's yours?"

Tiberius's throat rose and fell, his gaze moving from Rosalie to fix on me. My face. Taking it in with a scrutiny that left me raw. Yeah, there were similarities alright. But I didn't need those to know the truth, my girl had already confirmed it. I was an orphan no more. But if he didn't want me-

He stepped forward, his hand rising to grip my jaw and I froze as he inspected me, looking into my eyes and studying every corner of my face. Something shifted in my chest as the weight of the stars fell upon us, their whispers tickling my ears.

"I guess I found my way home, Dad," I said, my smile growing, my most mischievous side on show.

I waited for him to reply, my smile not slipping on the outside, but inside it crumpled as I awaited his rejection. Me and all my inner monsters would be too much for old Tibs to accept. But I ached for him to know the true me. This man with his tidy hair and smile lines, I could tuck right into one of those smile lines just fine. Easy peasy. He'd let me though, right? Right??

"I've seen so much of life that I thought it impossible for the stars to surprise me any more," he muttered to himself.

I loved talking to myself too. We had loads in common already.

His hand dropped to rest on my shoulder and my heart lurched and jerked like it was riding a mechanical bull. "I see what we are, boy. There's no denying it, and I find I do not want to now that the truth has settled within me. You are Serenity's son. My son," his voice cracked on the last word, his fingers squeezing my shoulder.

Those words mended something in me that had long been left wrecked in the shadow of my soul. It was pieces of my childhood self, stitching back together and coming to life once more.

I dropped the knife still clasped at my back and flung myself at him, throwing my arms around him and hugging him tight, tight, tight. He gasped in surprise and when we parted, I blurted everything at him. I told him about my childhood, of Jerome, how we used to get into all kinds of trouble, how he would send me on jobs to kill his enemies – but I would always, always check if they were bad guys first – then how Jerome had sent me here and how it was such a funny coincidence.

"Jerome is going to laugh and laugh," I sighed, looking to Rosalie over his shoulder who was shaking her head frantically at me. Aw look, she was so happy for me that she couldn't contain it.

"Jerome Novius is a wanted man," Tiberius growled.

"As am I," I sang.

Tiberius fell quiet, probably because he was thinking about how great all this was. His fancy man brain needed some time to catch up with it. "I will return shortly. Remain here until I return." He took off down the hall at a fierce pace and Rosalie lurched forward, grabbing my arm.

"We need to leave."

"Leave?" I scoffed. "Why would we leave. Tibsy – sorry, my *dad* – has probably gone to make us cookies. I wanna be right here when he brings them back."

"He's not gone to make cookies, idiota, he's gone to summon the FIB."

"Psh," I waved her off, stepping into my dad's room and switching on the light. I let out a low whistle, taking in his finery. "Wow, am I like, an Heir to the throne now or something?"

"No," Rosalie gritted out, grabbing my arm again and tugging to try and make me leave. But I wasn't going to leave. I had cookies with my dad to look forward to. Then maybe we'd all go on a fishing trip together and I'd catch an old boot on my hook and Dad would say 'well son, at least the fish won't be able to run as fast now' and we'd laugh and laugh and-

"Sin." Rosalie rounded in front of me, slapping a hand to my chest. "Tiberius knows who you are and he's been on Jerome's tail for months. Do you really think this news is going to change those facts? You're wanted for multiple murders. The press are calling you the deadliest Fae in Solaria."

"Really?" My chest puffed out. "Little ol' me? Do you think Dad's going to get me a trophy with those words engraved on it? I don't have a shelf to put it on though, maybe I could make Hastings carry it around…"

"You're not hearing me," Rosalie snarled. "He's going to arrest us. We'll be put back in Darkmore."

I frowned down at her, thinking on that for a sec, then dismissing it. "Naahhhh. He wouldn't do that. He's my dad! Oh look he has a painting of a lemon tree!" I ran over to where it was hanging on the wall. "If that's not fate, I don't know what is."

I took out the Atlas I'd stolen from Rosalie, calling Jerome and holding it to my ear.

"I found the location of Roland Vard," he said. "He's in the Polar Capital, I've just forwarded you the coordinates. Is Tiberius good and dead?" he asked keenly.

"No, but listen, I have even better news! Turns out, Tiberius Rigel is my father."

"*What?*"

"Yeah, it was a shock to me too. First I was like woahh, then I was like woahhhhhh, then I was like wowee, then I was like-"

"Sin," Jerome cut in. "What the fuck is going on?"

I explained in all the detail I could and Jerome fell so quiet on the end of the line that I had to check if he'd hung up. But he hadn't, he was just playing little baby mouse with me. "It's okay, bro. I told him everything about you, from your dodgy friends to your many hideouts, to your kill list. He's a really good listener actually. And don't worry, he's my dad, he'll totally let you off. We're cool."

"We are not cool, you fucking moron!" Jerome bellowed.

I hung up, deciding to give him some time to mellow his jello. He'd understand when he realised what a funky fancy man my dad was.

Rosalie started pushing me toward a window across the room while I continued to admire the décor. "What's on your mind, sex pot?"

"Sin Wilder, if you do not start running for your star-damned life this second, I will knock you out and carry you away from here myself," she hissed.

"You're not leaving," Tiberius's voice boomed from behind us and we whirled around to look at him.

My arms stretched out for a hug, but he left me hanging, pulling someone into view in the doorway beside him. My eyebrows arched as I took in the man from the photographs with his jet black hair, handsome face and piercing brown eyes. Tiberius's son. Max.

"Baby brother!" I cried, running toward him, but he cast a whip of water that caught me by the wrist, yanking me back.

"Max," Rosalie said in a warning tone, something in the way she spoke to him saying she knew him already. "Let us go."

"Dad said…" Max shook his head, staring at me, then looking to Tiberius. "Some crazy shit, that's what he said."

"He is your brother," Tiberius growled. "And until I work out what to do with him, he will need an escort."

"Oo la la," I sang. "What does that mean?"

Tiberius shoved Max toward me, his mouth moving as he murmured some spell and his hands flicked as he cast it quickly. A glowing white cuff appeared around my right wrist and Max's left and I felt the sudden need to stay with him no matter what.

"You cannot go anywhere without Max," Tiberius announced. "And Max, you will have to stay with Sin until I summon you."

"What?" he balked. "You can't do that."

"I already have," Tiberius said firmly, then marched to a desk and yanked a drawer open. He took out a pouch of stardust and tossed it to Rosalie. "Go wherever you need to go. And do not get yourselves caught while I figure out how to handle this." He twisted his hand again and I felt the anti-stardust wards fall around us, allowing us to leave.

"We won't come back," Rosalie swore.

"You might not. But Sin won't have a choice," Tiberius said and I smiled big at him. Aw, he missed me already.

"See you soon, Dad," I purred, then I leapt on Max, kissing his cheek, and he shoved me back in alarm. "You and me are going to be best, best friends by the time he summons us."

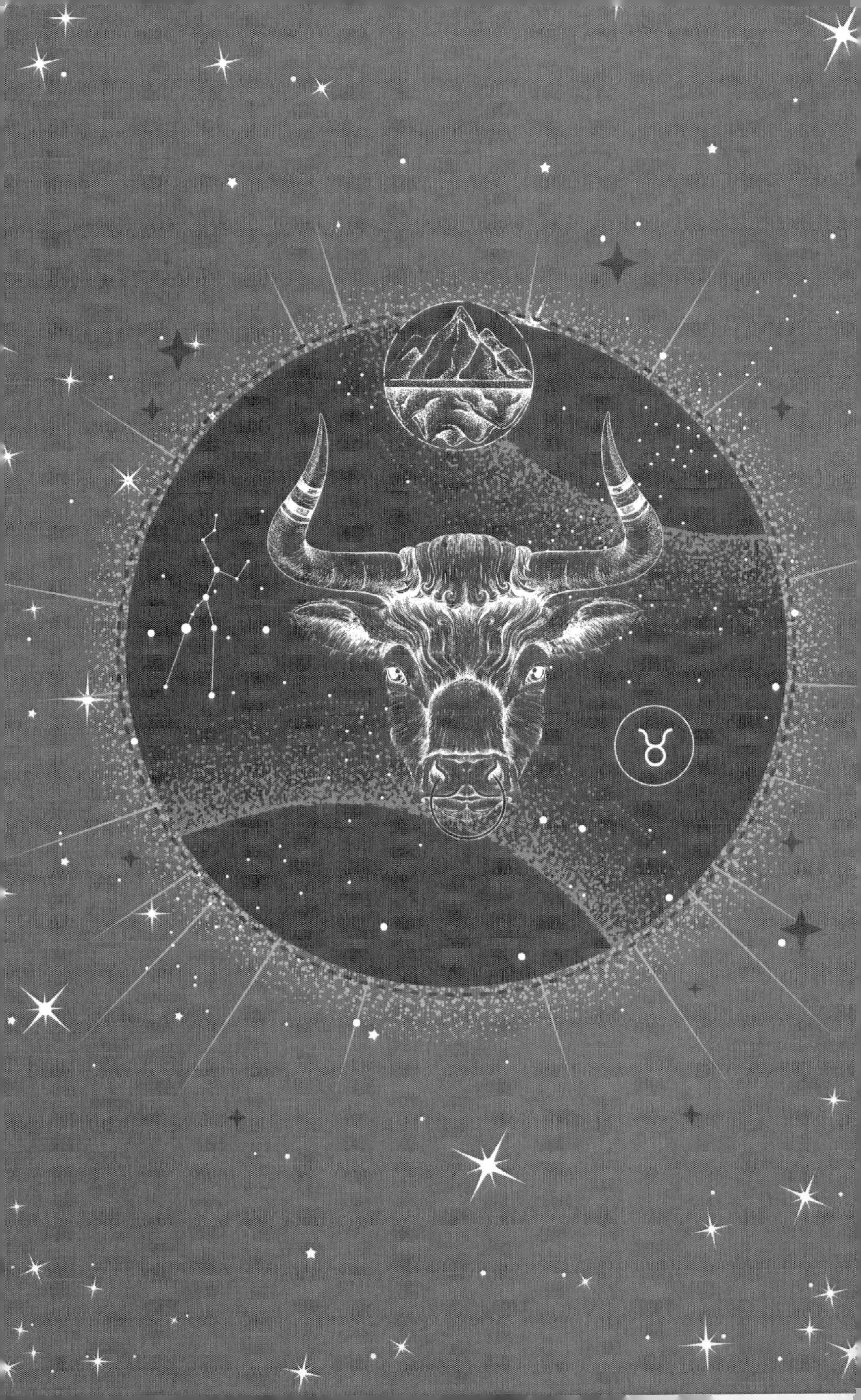

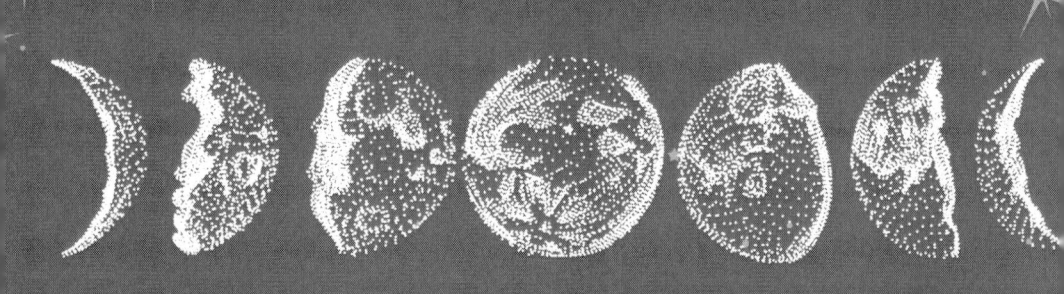

ROSALIE

PRISONER #12

CHAPTER TWENTY NINE

Filling in one of the most powerful Fae in the country about our less than legal enterprises and the pure carnage which had led us to this point had been something of a force of will. I knew Max least of the former Heirs - though perhaps that was for the best as I had slept with two of the others and him being Sin's brother could have been a whole lot more awkward if he'd been a part of that particular night of debauchery. But it also meant that it was a hell of a lot more difficult for me to guess how he might react to some of the more illegal details of our journey to this place, so I'd focused as much as possible on the heinous crimes Vard was responsible for.

To his credit, Max had listened patiently, looking every bit the well-groomed politician he'd been raised to become as he took in each fact, weighed and measured it and seemed to take notes despite not actually putting pen to paper or anything of the sort. But I got the feeling there wasn't a single piece of the story which he hadn't taken in in its entirety.

"So, obviously now there are two things left to achieve," Max said once we'd finished regaling him with the details where we sat clustered around my Aunt Bianca's dining table, a silencing bubble keeping the story between myself, Ethan, Roary, Cain, Sin and Max alone. I hadn't even wanted Hastings here for it because I knew there were parts of this that he not only didn't know but which would likely end up further scarring his more delicate mind if he was forced to endure the full details of them. He'd been distracted easily enough in the company of the pack after I'd reminded them once again of how gallantly he'd saved my life.

"Which are?" I asked, leaning back in my chair while Ethan and Roary leaned forward on either side of me, tension spiking around us as we awaited this assessment.

"We need to get Roary's Lion back then kill Vard, Benjamin Acrux and any other motherfucker who knows about this shit. Every piece of research, every scrap of evidence that anyone ever did about Order extraction and exchanging needs to be eliminated. The idea of this getting out into the hands of any evil bastard who might want to take advantage of it is completely unacceptable."

The entire room seemed to exhale, tension sweeping out the open windows and billowing away across the vineyards beyond as if snatched on the hands of the wind itself.

Ethan grinned darkly, leaning back and slinging his arm around my chair while Roary sagged forward in what was clearly a mixture of relief and fear. Because we might all be agreed on the fact that we had to reclaim his Lion, but we were all too aware that returning it to him might not be simple - if it was even possible at all.

"Can you get the FIB off of our backs, brother?" Sin asked from where he was sitting on the counter beside the window, his feet in the sink, three lemons bobbing about his ankles in the water he'd run to soak them in. His new pet Crow-thing was fluttering about in there too taking a bath.

Max tensed at the fraternal pet name, glancing at Sin and then back to me like he didn't even know where to begin unearthing that can of worms. Hell, I didn't know either. He was a grown man who had thought himself to have no brothers until a few hours ago but was now being told that not only did he have one, but that he had an *older* brother, the ramifications of which would have been truly world-shattering a few chaotic years ago, but now…

Well, between the way Solaria was currently being ruled and the fact that I couldn't think of a single person less suited to leadership on a grand scale than Sin Wilder, I wasn't sure it made a difference at all. At least not in the wider sense of the word. But for the two of them? Sin had been alone his entire life, abandoned by his mother, hating and resenting both her and whatever stranger had sired him, only to find out that the man who shared his blood never would have given him up had he known about him and that his mother too had been robbed of the chance to love and raise him – or even remember him while she lived. Not only that, but the woman responsible for tearing him away from the family he should have rightfully claimed was long past the point of revenge, her life having been thoroughly destroyed in the events of the war which had played out while he was incarcerated far beneath the ground.

Max blew out a low breath. "Let me make some calls. I can lay a false trail, have the FIB hunting the four of you elsewhere. Everyone thinks *you're* dead already anyway," he added, bobbing his chin at Cain who blinked in surprise.

"Dead?" he questioned.

"Sure," Max said. "You and that Jack Hastings guy I saw chasing a couple of Wolves up the stairs when I arrived. The FIB spoke out about it last night claiming the likelihood was that the two of you had been murdered once you were no longer needed as hostages for the escape. It's the most likely scenario I suppose – I doubt they'd ever guess that you'd actually fallen for an inmate and helped her esca-"

"I didn't help with shit," Cain growled. "I just…couldn't let her die."

I met his ruinous gaze while that declaration sat between us all like a bloody heart laid bare on the table, an offering if ever he'd give one.

"And I'm grateful for that," Roary said roughly.

Max cleared his throat then swept a hand over his face. "This is fucking messy," he grunted.

"Messy is my favourite flavour, little bro," Sin put in and I snorted.

Max straightened. "Alright…I think I need to make a few calls and then-"

"They'll send me back," Sin said darkly. "You call up your prissy friends and tell them any of this and they'll all say the same thing; that I'm bad to the bone, rotten to the core, corrupted all the way to my roots and that no matter how handsome I am, I can't be left free."

"You're a convicted murderer," Max muttered and I tensed, expecting Sin to leap at him, for lemons and water to fly everywhere and for Aunt Bianca's prized kitchen to fall prey to their collision, but instead a deep intensity fell over my Incubus and he replied in a low purr.

"Tell me, Maximus, how many Fae did you kill in that pretty little war you fought while I was rotting away underground like some forgotten turnip?"

"My name is Max. Just Ma-"

"Answer me!" Sin roared and Crow-thing squawked, leaping up onto the counter beside the sink.

I pushed to my feet, preparing to get between them even as Ethan, Roary and Cain stood, clearly planning to move in front of me in turn.

"Fine." Max held a hand out to us, asking us to stay out of it and I slowly lowered myself. If anyone understood the delicate and often combustible dance of family politics, then it was me. "You wanna know how many Fae I killed in the war? Well I can't answer you. It was utter bloodshed, brutal and horrifying in every way. I blasted my power across the battlefield in ferocious arcs and I couldn't possibly have kept track of my kills even if I'd tried."

"And can you tell me that every Fae who died by your hand deserved it, kitten?" Sin asked him. "Are you certain they were all rotten fruit? Hateful and evil in every way? Can you be sure that none of them were just caught up on the wrong side of that battle? Or maybe even forced to fight against you for fear of what might happen if they didn't?"

Max swallowed thickly but said nothing. A chill crept through the room, the horrors of war seeped over us, thickening the air and making me shiver as the screams I was usually so good at keeping at bay found their way closer. Sin's accusations could just as easily have been made at me. I fought in that war too. I tore out throats and blasted magic across the battlefield with wild abandon, caring only that those I killed fought for Lionel Acrux against me. Their reasons for joining his ranks hadn't mattered at the time. Only victory had.

"Because I can name every kill of mine if you'd like me to," Sin went on, the only one of us who seemed wholly unaffected by the horrors which had permeated the room and with a shudder I realised that I was feeling what Max was. His Siren Order gifts were slipping from him, his own memories and feelings about the war now spilling into the air itself until it threatened to choke us all. "I can tell you what made them bad, bad Fae. I can list off their crimes and tell you their stories and I'm certain even you would have to agree that their deaths were well earned."

"Stop it," I growled, my eyes on Max who blinked at me in surprise as he realised it, clearly having expected my berating to be aimed at Sin. "None of us need to feel your shit. We have our own demons to haunt us."

It took him another moment to take in what I'd meant and with a suddenness that felt like a rubber band snapping against the air, the cold horror of the war abandoned us, his emotions pulled tightly under his grasp once more and the balmy summer breeze washed around us again.

"Alright," Max sighed. "I get it. I won't speak to anyone other than making that call to lay the false trail for the FIB. But you aren't the only Fae who want Vard dead."

"He *is* dead," I pointed out. "If you think that they would want you to let them know he lives after they finally got to move on, after they were able to find solace in the knowledge of him parting ways with this world then go ahead and tell them. But you know better than I do if it would cause more harm than good."

If the others were confused by my declaration they didn't ask for more details on who I was referring to. Max clearly understood who I meant though and he nodded slowly, seeming to agree with me that Vard was best left dead in theory until we could make it the truth.

"Fine," he said. "I won't tell anyone else about any of this – for now. But if it gets out of hand-"

"It won't," I assured him. "But if we're all agreed, I think we should go now. We have a location and every moment wasted is another where my mate suffers without his Lion."

"We can't go yet," Cain said, surprising us all and I looked to him with a frown.

"Why not?"

"Because Roary is about as useless as a lemon in a prison riot," he growled.

"Hey," Sin barked while Max looked utterly confused and Roary scowled.

"He needs to get in touch with his Vampire. It doesn't matter if he wants it or not. It doesn't even matter if he won't *be* a Vampire for much longer. He needs to be able to use his speed and his strength to his full capabilities or he will just be a liability when we go after Vard and Benjamin and I'm not risking them getting away from us again."

I softened at the raw pain in his voice, knowing that this was as personal for him as it was for Roary.

"So what do you suggest?" I asked him.

His eyes flashed with darkness, reminding me that he was no law-abiding guard. "That we go to the Hellion Hunt."

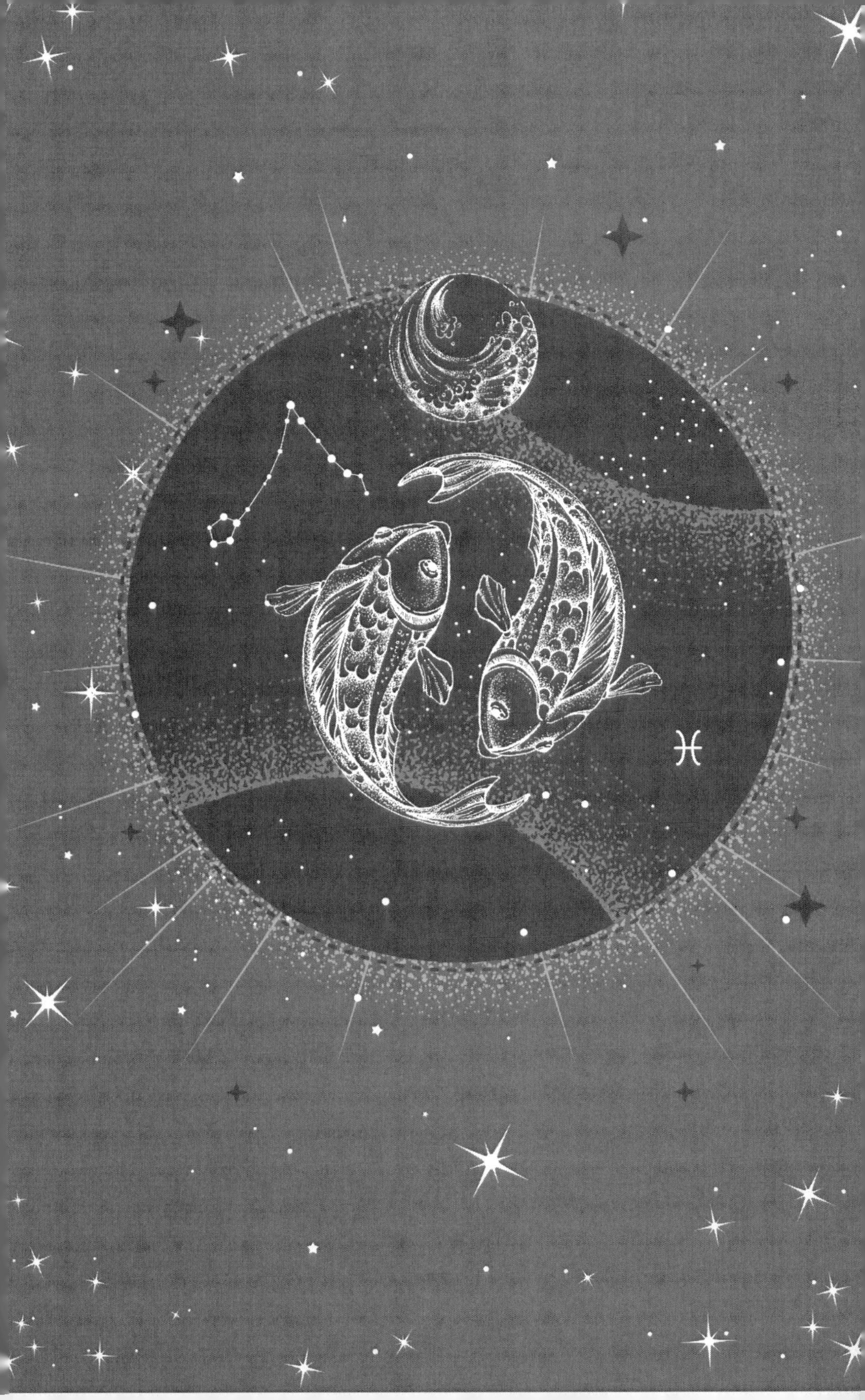

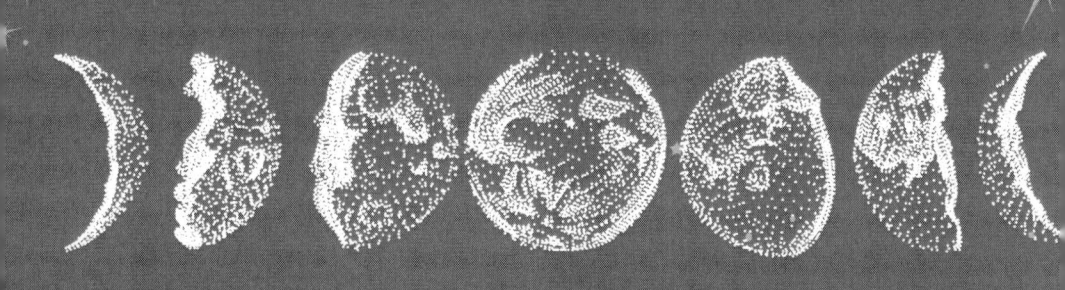

ROARY

PRISONER #69

CHAPTER THIRTY

The Hellion Hunt was a place so illegal that the atmosphere was like walking into Darkmore on the night of our escape. It was ripe with excitement, the air electrified as the masked members of this underground sport let out their inner fiends.

The masks all represented different predatory animals, hiding the identities of those in attendance and we each wore one of our own as we walked deeper into the sandstone cave system. I took in the wolf mask covering Rosalie's face, the thing carefully crafted by her earth magic with silver rivulets running through the painted fur.

She had made one for each of us, mine a bronze Lion that reminded me of my former self, while Ethan wore the face of a white bear and Cain wore a black snake with a shimmering jade gleam between the scales. Max wore the face of a savage-looking raven and Hastings hid behind the face of a donkey. Sin's was the most ostentatious of course, his vision for the mask driving Rosalie to snap at him several times while he'd crouched on the kitchen table and kept making wild suggestions while she forged it. The mask looked to be part crocodile and part eagle with sharp teeth protruding from a golden beak that were made from pure diamonds. It should have looked ridiculous on him, but between his easy swagger and endless confidence, he somehow pulled the thing off.

To enter any of the hunts, we had to use code names to keep the secrecy of this place. In fact, it was said if a true name was spoken here and the Vampire Hellions who ran this place heard it, they would happily cut out your tongue and force you to swallow it.

The passage we followed was lit by balls of fire that rolled along glass pipes in the walls, curving overhead and spiralling away underground, leading us deeper and deeper into the unknown. The crowd around us were whooping and chattering keenly, the masks on their faces doing nothing to hide the unsavoury nature of them.

Their presence spoke of danger and I found myself stepping closer to Rosalie, noticing the other members of her newly formed pack tightening around her too. She didn't seem to notice us protecting our Alpha, but as looks passed between us, I knew they were just as ready to fight as I was.

A drunken asshole came stumbling into me and I shoved him away with a snarl that warned him to back the fuck up. He muttered an apology as he looked up at me, taking in my height and the promise of pain in my eyes before quickly disappearing back into the crowd.

Finally, the narrow passage opened up and a roaring din of noise fell over us as we arrived on a carved balcony that ran around an enormous cave, overlooking a stomach-churning drop.

Sin pranced forward, shoving Fae aside and tugging Rosalie after him by the hand as the rest of us muscled our way after them, arriving at the very edge of the balcony. Far below was a view into a network of passages carved through red rock in a winding labyrinth. Some of the paths led underground or off into the chambers hidden beyond the outer walls, but it looked like most of the hunts could be viewed from up here.

There were balconies further down too, smaller, more private spaces where throne-like seats were filled with those who had likely paid for the privilege.

Rosalie rested her elbows on the stone railing, gazing down at the pit where all kinds of carnage was about to go down. "So how does this work?" she glanced Cain's way as he stepped up beside her.

"The Hellion Hunt is held down there," Cain explained. "But private hunts are held off in private chambers too. The main hunt grows progressively more savage throughout the night. Each round will have five volunteers who wish to be hunted and up to twenty Vampires will hunt them at once."

"Fuck me, twenty?" Ethan muttered. "Don't any of them get carried away and kill the volunteers?"

"Sometimes," Cain said darkly. "That's the risk the volunteers take. It's part of what draws them here. Fear of death is often the best way to feel most alive."

"Holy guacamole," Hastings murmured, his eyes roaming over the arena fearfully, and I gave him a bracing pat on the back.

"I suppose I'm pretending I never saw any of this shit then?" Max muttered irritably and I breathed a laugh.

Sin climbed up to sit on the railing, swinging his legs casually. He might have had air magic, but that shit still made me uncomfortable. "Can anyone play? I want to play!"

"If you want to volunteer, be my guest," Cain said, a smirk to his voice.

"Oh you'd just love an excuse to suck on my neck, wouldn't you Cainy bub?" Sin slung an arm around his neck and Cain knocked it off.

"So what's the plan?" I asked. "How is this going to help me get a hang of being a Vampire? Isn't this exactly what Vampires aren't supposed to do?" I shot Cain a look and he met my gaze over Rosalie's head.

"Yes, which is precisely why it's the perfect way to hone your skills. If you can keep your head down there and follow my lead, you'll learn more about being a Vampire tonight than I could teach you in a year."

"This sounds fucking dangerous," Ethan said, moving in to lean against the railing, but it wasn't a warning, he sounded star damned excited. "Are only the Vampires allowed to hunt?"

"There'll be a free for all later tonight," Cain answered. "The Vampires hunt alone because they tend to move so fast that there's no point in other Orders running with them. There's no chance of catching the prey before they will. It's pointless."

"The prey," Rosalie purred. "Dalle stelle, you'd have to be crazy to volunteer." She glanced Sin's way, but I couldn't catch the look that passed between them.

Cain moved to stand at my side. "Come on, we need to register. If we hurry, we can join the first hunt."

"Good luck," Ethan said, gripping my shoulder, a bright glint in his eyes. "We'll be watching."

I nodded to him and Rosalie purred well wishes in Faetalian, wiggling her fingers at us in goodbye before the five of them grouped closer together. Cain steered me away towards a stairwell and we circled endlessly down to the base of the cavern where a line of Vampires were queueing up to a stone booth to register for the hunt. There were snarls passing between them, a sense of rivalry thick in the air as we joined the line, and I felt that same rivalry burning through me too. My fangs lengthened and I growled at the assholes closing in behind us. Cain seemed surprisingly at ease in this situation, looking all too natural in this environment.

"How many times have you hunted here?" I asked.

"Lost count."

"Why did you do it?" I frowned. "You risked a lot by coming here. If the FIB ever caught you, your clean slate would have been pretty damn tarnished. You might have found yourself shoulder to shoulder with the convicts in Darkmore, and I doubt they would have been kind to a former guard."

"Mm," he grunted, ever the cagey bastard.

I figured that he had no intention of opening up to me, so was particularly surprised when he did.

"I might have to wear a mask here, but it always felt like taking one off whenever I stepped into the Hellion Hunt. I was free in this place. Free to be the monster I always knew I was. I was raised to fight, to unleash the cruellest parts of my being, and no matter how much I despise Benjamin Acrux for the upbringing he gifted me, I do owe him one thing. In his company, I learned how far I could push myself, I found out how strong I could be, how vicious. And there is something in that which I still crave even if I spent many years trying to crush it away. It's what I was drawn to in Rosalie, that damn wildness which knows no bounds. She has never changed who she is to fit anyone's demands, especially not society. I tried to be someone else for so long, that sometimes even now I don't know exactly who it is I am. I only know that the longer I spend in her company, the more I uncover it."

I stepped closer to him, noticing that the rivalry between us was present, but I didn't feel it as sharply as I did towards the other Vampires around us. And I was pretty sure it was because I respected him. I wasn't sure when that had happened, but it was impossible to deny now that it was staring me in the face. "Then that's where you belong, Mason. No one should be forced to be anything but who they are, not by themselves or anyone else in this world. You get to choose, don't forget that."

"Mm," Cain grunted again but something told me he had heard me.

We moved along the line and finally made it to the booth, securing our places in the first hunt under our code names.

"Okay Lawman and Nightkeeper, you're all signed up. You'll need to wear these." The woman passed us two simple white masks that would cover the top half of our faces. "Put them on just before the hunt. They will remain fixed to your face until the hunt is done and will allow ample room for biting your prey." She took each of our hands, casting a spell that made a silver fang glow on the backs of our wrists along with the number one. "Head through the gate to my right and make your way to the starting point where private rooms will allow you to change your masks in secrecy."

We followed her directions, passing through the iron gate, showing our fang marks to a bulky guard on the way and taking a winding passage onward.

"Keep close to me during the hunt," Cain said firmly. "Focus on my instructions. If you feel you are starting to lose your head, then tell me and I will direct you in how to refocus."

I nodded, my pulse quickening as the cry of the crowd rumbled through the sandstone walls. "And if I fuck up and lose my head entirely?"

"You won't," he said firmly. "Think of Rosalie, of your brother. Of all the reasons you have to remain rooted in your own mind."

I nodded again as we rounded into a chamber where doors led off into private rooms. Vampires were walking in and out of them then making their way on down another passage with their white masks in place for the hunt.

It didn't take us long to change into ours, leaving our masks behind and following the directions of another guard as we headed toward the start point.

We arrived before a long row of iron gates set into the wall, all of them leading out into a wide, brightly lit passage where the clamour of the crowd was loudest. There were Vampires already standing before many of the gates and a woman dressed in a leather jumpsuit waved us over, her mask that of a panther with glittering rhinestones around the eyes. She checked our marks then directed us to stand before two gates that were beside one another.

Cain gave me a nod as I stood in front of mine. I glanced at the Vampire to my left. Golden curls fell around the brow of his white mask and he casually flicked them back as he glanced my way.

"First time?" he asked smoothly, moving to lean his shoulder against the wall between my gate and his like he had all the time in the world to kill.

"How can you tell?" I growled, assessing him and trying to figure out if he was a threat. He was dressed in casual clothes fit for running just like the rest of us, but his voice suggested he was more highborn than most of the cretins here.

"You've got that jittery look about you," he taunted, his lips lifting into a grin.

"Leave him be, Hornrider," Cain drawled and I turned to him in surprise. "You know this asshole?"

"He's been running here the last year or so," Cain said with a shrug.

"Thinks he can take my place as the Elite Hunter, but I've been running this hunt since he was just a school boy with hopes and dreams that crashed and burned."

"You're just bitter you have a real challenge these days, old man. I'm faster than you by a mile," Hornrider said.

"Faster maybe, but speed doesn't equal skill," Cain clipped.

"You sound like my old professor, and he was always such a sore loser too," Hornrider said, his grin only widening.

"Nice name by the way," I commented and his casual smile dropped a little.

"Someone else signed me up when I first came here and you can't change it once it's assigned," he grumbled.

"Sure," I said like I didn't believe him and he opened his mouth to curse me out, but his voice was drowned out.

"Take your positions!" the woman in the panther mask shouted and Hornrider moved back in front of his own gate, readying to run.

I looked to Cain, preparing for what was to come, but how was I really supposed to do that? I had no idea what to expect beyond this gate.

"Follow me," Cain said firmly. "Do not stray. The volunteers will have hidden themselves in the maze already. Our job is to find and bite as many as we can *without* killing them."

"Got it," I growled, planting my feet, the energy in my blood building and building.

"Hellion Hunt – begin!" a voice boomed throughout the entire cavern and the gates flew open all at once.

I took off with a bolt of adrenaline making me move in a blur of motion. Cain was a step ahead of me and Hornrider proved his word about his speed as he kept pace several feet ahead of both of us. The three of us were the fastest, gaining momentum by the second as we tore out into the maze, winding left and right through the ten-foot sandstone walls. One glance up showed the roaring crowd staring down at us from the huge balcony high above, and though I sought Rosa among the masses, there was no way I could pick her out within the throng of faces.

Cain took a hard right, yanking me after him by the arm and we chased after Hornrider who was sprinting away with apparent ease, throwing a grin back at us over his shoulder before he swung a hard left. Cain took that turn too and I followed fast, nearly tripping as a series of stone steps led down into an underground chamber. It was pitch black inside and my eyes took a second too long to adjust before I nearly ran headlong into a wall. I stumbled to the right, spotting Cain sprinting off through the chamber, still hot on the heels of Hornrider.

"Listen to the change in the wind, the vibration in the stone, forget relying on your eyes first. They come second," Cain called to me.

I raced to catch him, attempting to do what he'd said and hearing his footfalls hit more stairs, telling me where they were. I didn't stagger at all as I followed him down them, listening again and hearing Hornrider's footfalls taking a turn to the right at the base of the stairs. I turned before I saw the wall looming ahead of me this time and a whoop of excitement left me as Cain picked up the pace.

We sprinted through the dark until finally making it back out to the brighter passages above where the crowd bellowed in encouragement at the sight of us. "Lawman, Lawman, Lawman!" a group were baying, and I glanced at Cain as I made it shoulder to shoulder with him.

"You're famous here," I jibed.

"I'm just an Elite Hunter," he said in answer, shrugging it off as always but it was clear he had more than a small fanbase. There were plenty of Fae calling out to Hornrider too and the golden-haired man took the time to throw a wave their way.

A howl carried from the right that sounded like it had come from a man and as we all turned that way, he came into view at the end of a long passage. His long, dark hair whipped out sideways as he turned and sprinted out of sight and Hornrider cried, "Mine!" putting on a burst of speed and making a beeline for his target.

Cain grabbed my shoulder, scrunching my shirt in his fist and yanking me down a path to the left. I heard the whoosh of a blade and ducked the same moment Cain did as a giant saw swung horizontally overhead.

"Fuck," I gasped, looking to Cain. "You didn't mention that shit."

"Thought it might put you off, inmate." He smiled wide, looking more at home in this place than any person should, then he sprinted away down the passage, leaping over a pit of spikes and ducking another swinging blade. I followed fast, making it through the path of death and chasing him down one where the floor was layered with ice. I raised my hand to melt it but Cain slowed, slapping my hand back down to my side. "No magic. It's against the rules."

I skidded on the ice, cursing as I fought to keep my balance but Cain just gave me a look that said he wasn't fazed by this then ran at the wall, sprinting up it, leaping to the opposite wall and doing that twice more before standing on top of it. The crowd went crazy for that move and I could tell he was lapping it up even if he didn't so much as look their way. I prepared to attempt the same move, hoping I didn't fall on my ass and make a fucking fool of myself in front of Rosa and the others.

I managed it though, releasing a laugh as I landed beside Cain and he braced me.

"Now, let's see if we can spot some prey," he said, his tone low and hungry as he gazed across the many passages spreading out around us.

"Awoooo!" a female voice made my head snap around and my heart lurched violently in my chest. Rosalie was standing up on a wall herself, gazing right at us with her wolf mask still in place.

"What the fuck is she doing in here?" I barked as I spotted several Vampires turning in the passages and heading her way with ravenous movements.

"That fucking girl," Cain growled in fury.

"That's *our* fucking girl," I hissed. "And we'd better get to her before those pieces of shit do."

Rosalie leapt off of the wall as a Vampire lunged up from the passage below, taking a swipe at her.

I leapt to the next wall, then the next, moving quickly as Cain kept pace with me to my left, my pulse rioting with fear. If they caught her, if they *touched* her-

Everything blurred in my head, my mind latching onto the hunt so keenly that there was no escape. I would catch her first. She was *mine*.

I made it to the passage she was running down, a female Vampire speeding along behind her, just seconds from reaching her. I threw myself from the wall with a roar of rage, landing on top of the Vampire and crushing her beneath me, making her scream as some bone broke from the impact of my weight.

Cain landed ahead of me, chasing after Rosalie who had darted away down another passage. I scrambled upright with a surge of rivalry in my chest.

"Cain!" I barked. "Get away from her!"

He didn't slow this time, not bothering to check if I was keeping pace anymore as he raced down a set of steps after my girl.

I chased him underground into the dark, hearing him move, the sound like the shifting of the wind. My hearing was alive with it, the way the air twisted ahead of me, showing me the way through the oppressive black.

Cain was right. I didn't need to rely on my eyes as much as this. I could hear my path far better than I could see it, and I no longer found my feet stumbling, no longer second guessed myself as I moved. This Order was so unlike my Lion, but I was starting to thrive within its shell. It offered me agility beyond bounds, my senses heightened in a way that was nothing short of a gift, and for the first time since this strange Order had taken possession of me, I revelled in its power.

I heard Cain stop a heartbeat before I was about to collide with him and came to a jarring halt behind him. I shoved him against the wall, pinning him there with a snarl. "She's mine."

"Listen," he hissed, ignoring what I'd said.

Slowly, I managed to focus, the warring desire of the hunt still sharp and

my mind clouding with the need of it, but I still had hold of myself. I closed my eyes, listening to the soft shuffling of a body somewhere close, just above us.

"She's up there," he breathed. "There must be a crawl space in the stone ceiling."

"Then I'll get her out." I tried to lunge away as the need to hunt rose in me again, but it was Cain's turn to get hold of me, shoving me against the opposite wall.

"Resist it," he snarled. "Resist its call and turn from here. That's how you'll know you have mastered the desire, Roary Night. If you can turn from her blood, you can turn from any Fae's."

"And leave you to claim the prize of it? *Never*," I spat, my fangs burning with the need to sink them into Rosalie's skin, to claim her as my own.

"There is no better test than this," he demanded. "Focus and turn from here. Do not seek her out."

"I…can't," I said breathlessly, but he released me as if I'd said the opposite.

I looked to the stone ceiling, hearing her moving there, so near I could have her in my arms in seconds, could sink my fangs into her and claim what I so desperately craved.

But there was an alternative. I could turn away. Leave and not follow this aching thirst. It would be painful, torturous, but not impossible.

Cain gripped my cheek. "You are strong enough to do this."

I nodded, and somehow managed to make myself retreat, backing away until that crushing need lessened. Bit by bit, until it was no longer a necessity but an option.

"I did it," I exhaled. "I controlled it."

"The first time is the hardest," Cain said. "It will only get easier from here."

A scraping of stone sounded then Rosalie dropped down into the passage lithely, casting a Faelight to see by.

"That's against the rules," Cain clipped but she just shrugged.

"No one can see us down here. Live a little dangerously, Mason," she purred, stepping into his personal space and placing a kiss on the corner of his mouth. "Thank you for teaching him the ways of your kind."

"You should never have come down here," Cain growled, though he pulled her closer to him by the waist possessively.

"What greater test than Roary resisting the hunt when it comes to his mate?" She looked to me, her eyes hooded seductively as she slinked out of his arms and walked in my direction. "You deserve a little reward." She slid the hair away from her neck, revealing the rose vine tattoo curling up it as she offered me a drink. "You must be famished after all that hunting."

Someone screamed out in the maze above us and the sound intensified the moment, the hairs on the back of my neck raising to attention.

"Rosalie," Cain warned. "He has only just managed to resist the hunt."

"Yes, and you said it gets easier from now."

"Yes, but-" he snarled and Rosalie whirled toward him.

"What is it you're really thinking?" she demanded. "Because I don't think your concern lies with his strength of will anymore."

Cain stepped closer to her, his hand sliding around her arm and gripping tight. The sight made my muscles tense and a deep growl rolled through my chest.

"Ah," Rosalie said in understanding, glancing between us both. "You're possessive of my blood."

"I wish to stake a claim on you as my Source," Cain announced and those words flicked a switch in my head. I lost it, tearing towards him with a furious snarl and colliding with him, forcing him away from Rosa and throwing a punch to his gut. He shoved me back with equal ire, our wrath mounting as we fought, throwing furious strikes and snarling in utter rage.

"Enough!" Rosalie commanded, forcing her way between us and planting a hand on each of our chests. "That's enough. You will share me. I will be a Source to both of you or neither of you. That is my offer, and I will not let either of you drink from me at all ever again if the choice is neither."

"Rosalie," Cain rasped. "You can't do this. It's not natural. Vampires choose a singular Source and no other Vampire can drink from them unless they fight for the right of that Source themselves. It is the way of our Order."

"You will share or you will both rescind your claim on my blood for good." She thrust her chin up and I met Cain's gaze over her shoulder, both of us growling in anger.

"You're challenging our very instincts," Cain snapped.

"Continue to point out the obvious if you like. But it's my blood, so it's my rules. Go find another Source if you like, but if you wish for it to be me, you will do so on my terms," Rosalie said firmly. "That's my offer. Take it or leave it. Five – four-"

"Wait," Cain gasped.

"Three – two- one more second and the offer is not on the table anymore," Rosalie sang.

"I agree," I said quickly.

"One," Rosalie said then Cain blurted

"I agree."

"Good." She ran her finger under Cain's chin then beckoned me closer by it. "Now come here and show me how well you can play together."

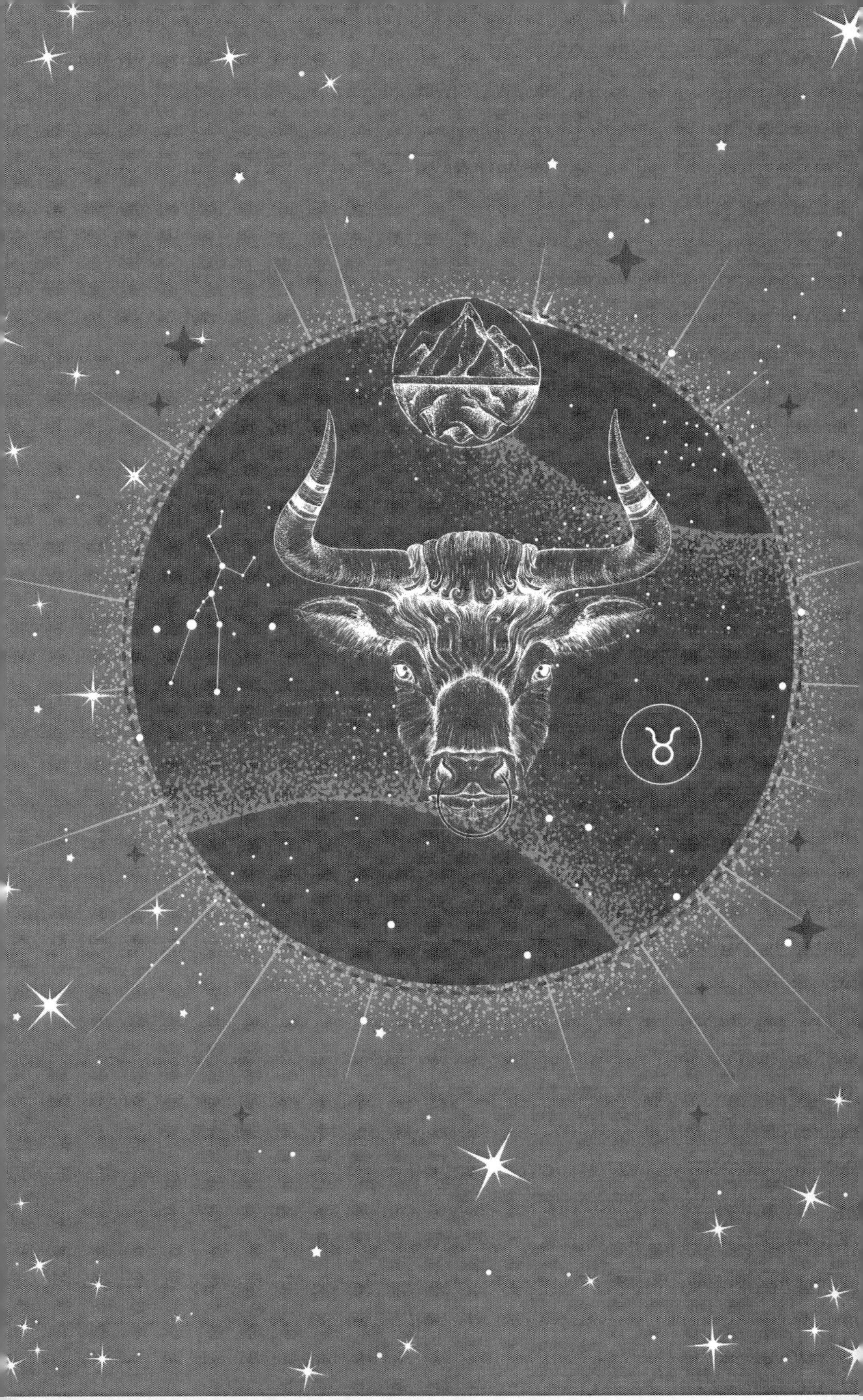

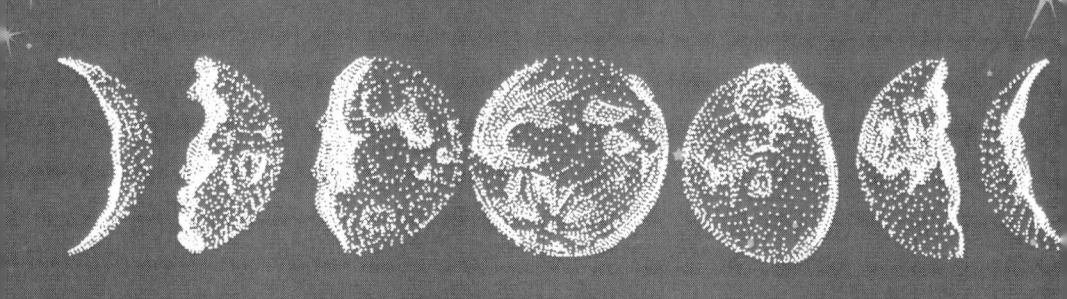

ROSALIE

PRISONER #12

CHAPTER THIRTY ONE

Roary closed in on me from one side, Cain from the other, their fangs bared, desire for my blood glinting in their eyes and I smiled darkly as I held up a finger to halt them.

"Good boys," I purred as they both stilled, that preternatural lack of movement which only a Vampire could claim holding them both entirely without motion.

Magic coiled from my fingers and stone rumbled as the walls of the labyrinth obeyed my call, closing off the exit on either side of us, sealing us within a chamber entirely for ourselves.

The darkness pressed in on us and I felt them moving closer to me once more, my blood heating with their nearness.

"What are you waiting for?" I teased, my eyes unable to pick out anything around us but my words unlocked their restraint, and I sucked in a harsh breath as they collided with me from either side.

Cain's fist tangled in my hair as he tugged my head back and Roary's arm banded around my waist to hold me up as I bared my throat to them and was rewarded by the rough heat of their mouths closing over my flesh.

I moaned as their teeth punctured my skin, their venom sliding into me and stalling the magic in my veins.

"Leave enough for us to escape this place," I panted as they drank deeply because I was the only one among us with the earth magic we would require to leave this pit of sin once we were done debasing it.

A snarl parted Roary's lips as they pressed closer to me, their arms driving against one another, their hands clutching at my clothes.

My body hummed with their proximity, my nipples hardening to sharp points which dragged against the confines of my shirt, begging for their touch.

I ran my fingers down the side of Cain's face, the edges of the mask he wore smooth above the roughness of the stubble gracing his jaw.

I scraped my fingernails over that shadow of hair, gripping his chin hard and pushing in a demand for him to withdraw his fangs from my neck.

He growled in defiance and I growled in return, pushing harder until he conceded, lifting his head as I turned mine, our noses grazing, breaths merging and then I claimed his lips in a kiss which shattered the walls that had already been crumbling between us.

Cain groaned as his tongue pushed past my lips, his hold on my hair tightening as his body pressed to mine more firmly, the solid ridge of his cock impossible to ignore, the feel of it making me slicken between my thighs.

My fingernails grazed his jaw as I held him there, kissing him deeply, telling him with the press of my mouth to his that I claimed him just as certainly as I had claimed the rest of my men. I ran my hand lower until I was gripping the fabric of his shirt, twisting it between my fingers and tugging in a command for him to remove it.

Cain stilled, pulling back so that our lips barely touched, hesitation filling that small space between us while Roary continued to feast on my blood.

"Stop lying to yourself about what we are," I hissed at Cain, my eyes fixed in his direction though the pressing dark made it impossible to see any part of him. "Give yourself to what your heart has already decided for you anyway."

"You mean that?" Cain asked, his voice ragged around his restraint.

"Despite everything else you've claimed, you still want-"

"If you make her wait a second longer I'll take her for myself and refuse you all part of it," Roary snarled as he ripped his teeth from my throat and pushed forward to claim my lips with his own, the taste of my own blood coating my tongue.

Cain snarled, releasing his hold on my hair then tugged his shirt from my grip as he ripped it over his head and tossed it aside, the whisper of the fabric hitting stone making my body thrum with anticipation.

Roary kissed me deeply, his fingers unbuttoning my jeans before he pressed his hand beneath my waistband and sank it inside my panties.

I moaned as he discovered my wetness, a noise of utter satisfaction escaping him as he drove two fingers into me with a slowness that had me whimpering with a desire for more.

"She's so fucking wet for us," he growled as he broke our kiss, his face turning towards Cain and I wondered if their keener eyesight could pick out more in the darkness than mine could. "Come and feel her for yourself."

Cain moved closer again and I reached for him, my hand finding the solid ridges of his abs and roaming over the taut muscles hungrily.

He pressed close to Roary again, though this time they didn't shove at one another but allowed each other the space they needed to consume me as one.

Cain's hand roamed down the front of my shirt slowly, his finger toying with my nipple while Roary pumped his fingers in and out of me with a languid pace which had me panting in need for more.

I stumbled back a step as they pushed closer to me, my back colliding with cold stone as I found myself trapped at the mercy of these beautiful monsters of mine and utterly content with my fate at their hands.

Cain's fingers rode down my body, over my navel and finally pushed into my jeans, the tight fabric tugging against my ass as his hand pressed over Roary's and he slowly – so fucking slowly – pushed two fingers into me as well.

I moaned, low and needy, my own hand riding down over Cain's cock while my other tugged at Roary's shirt in a demand for more of his flesh too.

My jeans pulled tight again as they fucked me with their hands, the fabric restricting their movements and making me growl in frustration. A murmur passed from Cain's lips, the words so low I didn't catch them but Roary's dark chuckle told me his Vampire ears had picked it up just fine.

"What are you plotting?" I hissed but instead of answering me, the two of them began to move their hands faster, the pumping of their fingers inside me gaining in speed as they used their gifts and found an alternating rhythm which had me cursing as the vibrations of their fingers took hold of me.

I swore in Faetalian, my spine arching against the stone wall, my thighs widening even as the denim of my jeans cut into me, still restricting their movements and yet the intensity of them being held in that one position was making me gasp for breath.

I came with a ragged howl, euphoria exploding through me and making my head spin with the rush of it.

The two of them withdrew, moving in such rapid motions that I was barely aware of them hoisting me from my feet and ripping my clothes and the mask from me until my bare feet hit the stone and I stumbled back against the wall once more, naked and panting for more.

They were on me again in a heartbeat, both of them naked too, their cocks driving against my skin, the heat of their flesh surrounding me.

For a moment, I didn't know which one of them was before me as their mouth came down over mine and I was hoisted into their arms but then I recognised the rough bite of Cain's kiss.

He groaned my name while Roary's mouth found the edge of my jaw and began working down it, his hands caressing my skin and sending goosebumps rushing over it.

Cain gripped my ass and I knotted my ankles at the base of his spine as he finally sank his cock into me with a feral growl which said he was done hiding from this, from me, from us.

I gasped his name as he filled me, my nails biting into his shoulders as his cock drove right in to the hilt.

"Make her scream," Roary urged, his hand roughly grasping my breast, his mouth on the shell of my ear.

I reached for him, my fingers curling around his cock and he growled my name as I began to pump it in time with Cain's thrusts deep inside me.

Cain was as rough as always, his body crushing mine to the wall, his fingers digging into my ass where he held me against him. I was brutal with him in turn, my heels driving into his ass, adding force to every thrust, my grip on his shoulders bruising.

Roary pushed closer to me, his teeth once again sinking into my neck and I panted his name while Cain filled me so perfectly that the space around me seemed to spin.

The cavern I'd created for us echoed with the sounds of our rampant breaths, the strike of flesh against flesh, ragged curses and moans of bliss.

Cain thrust into me harder and faster, driving another orgasm through my flesh so that my pussy tightened around his thick length. He cursed, fucking me harder still, driving deeper, his release so close that I could feel it in every strained muscle of his body as he tried to stave it off.

"Give in," I panted against his hungry lips. "Be mine."

Cain bellowed as he exploded inside me, forcing my body to shatter in pleasure once more and I gasped his name into the world like the claiming it was.

Roary groaned as my fist pumped him harder and the moment Cain's fangs pierced my flesh once me, he came for me too, the hot splash of his cum rushing over my thigh where it was still wrapped around Cain's waist.

We sagged against the wall in post coital bliss, the two of them drinking slowly, their fangs retracting and kisses replacing the bite of teeth on my flesh.

A smile drew my lips upward and I let my head fall back against the cave wall, knowing in my soul that I had finally gotten what I needed, that my pack was complete.

We untangled ourselves slowly, the dark pressing in more firmly as the feeling of their bodies fell away.

I flicked my fingers, tossing up a Faelight so I could find my clothes and a ragged gasp fell from me as my eyes landed on Cain's naked flesh.

His entire torso was stained with the rose vine mark of the curse, the mark extending from his arm and travelling over his back, down his thighs, spreading towards the far reaches of his body and painting a picture which was utterly undeniable.

"Why didn't you tell me it had gotten this far?" I demanded, stalking towards him, not caring that I was as bare as the dawn.

"You have no control over it," he grunted, reaching for his clothes with intent but I snatched his wrist into my grasp and denied him the opportunity to cover up the marks.

"Do you think that means I don't care for your fate?" I demanded, staring at the mark in horror, remembering what he had found out about it and knowing that it had to be nearing its conclusion.

"It's withdrawing," Roary said, moving to stand beside us and pointing at Cain's elbow where the mark was slithering beneath his skin, fading away.

"It does that sometimes," Cain grunted and the dismissive way he spoke of it told me that it didn't offer him much hope.

"Why?" I questioned.

"It…appreciates it when I do what is best for you," he admitted, his eyes moving from mine within the mask which still clung to his face, but I caught his cheek in my hand and drew them back to me.

"Non nasconderti da me, amore mio," I murmured. *Don't hide from me, my love.*

Cain swallowed thickly, his hand coming down on mine, holding it against his cheek.

"You shouldn't look at me like that," he muttered.

"Like what?"

"Like…I matter. It's not…this curse-"

"The moon is a mystery unto herself but I have a key to unlocking her heart," I told him and as I spoke the words, I reached out with my gifts, calling to the moon and begging her to see that Cain was no longer the man who had deserved this curse. That it wasn't my wish to see it fulfilled.

My skin began to glow with a silver luminescence, Roary swearing softly as he took it in, the cavern glimmering around us as it was bathed in its glow.

Brighter and brighter it grew and the marks on Cain's body lit with it too, the silver tainting them so that they stood out in glimmering lines all over his skin.

The glow grew so bright that I was forced to close my eyes against it and when it finally faded and the presence of the moon slipped from my grasp, I opened them in keen expectation.

My heart sank as I found Cain just as he'd been before, the marks still covering so much of his skin that he couldn't possibly have much more time left before the curse consumed him.

Cain barely even glanced down at himself before releasing his grip on my hand and stepping back, forcing my arm to drop between us.

"There is still hope," I told him because I had felt that in the weight of the moon's power. "But she wants it to be your task alone."

He nodded though he didn't seem to take any heart from my words and in a flash of motion he stood before me fully dressed again, the curse marks concealed beneath his clothing.

"Then I can only try to prove myself worthy of her mercy," he said. "And make the most of what time I have left if I turn out not to be."

I wanted to protest his words but I had felt the decision in the moon's magic and I knew that this wasn't my battle to face, so I simply nodded at him, hiding my own fears and burying them with my faith in the moon. If she wanted to test him then I could only put my trust in the fact that he would be able to pass.

Roary cleaned me off with his water magic then finished dressing himself and Cain helped me locate my own clothes and the mask I'd been wearing before I reopened the tunnels around us.

Blaring voices sounded, the noise of the crowd pushing in on us again and I hitched on a smile as I looked between my two Vampires.

"Looks like the hunt isn't over," I purred. "So how about you count to one hundred then see if you can catch me again."

I grinned at the way their eyes lit with the offer then turned and sprinted away once more, letting myself fall into the rush of the game and trusting in the moon to see me right in the end.

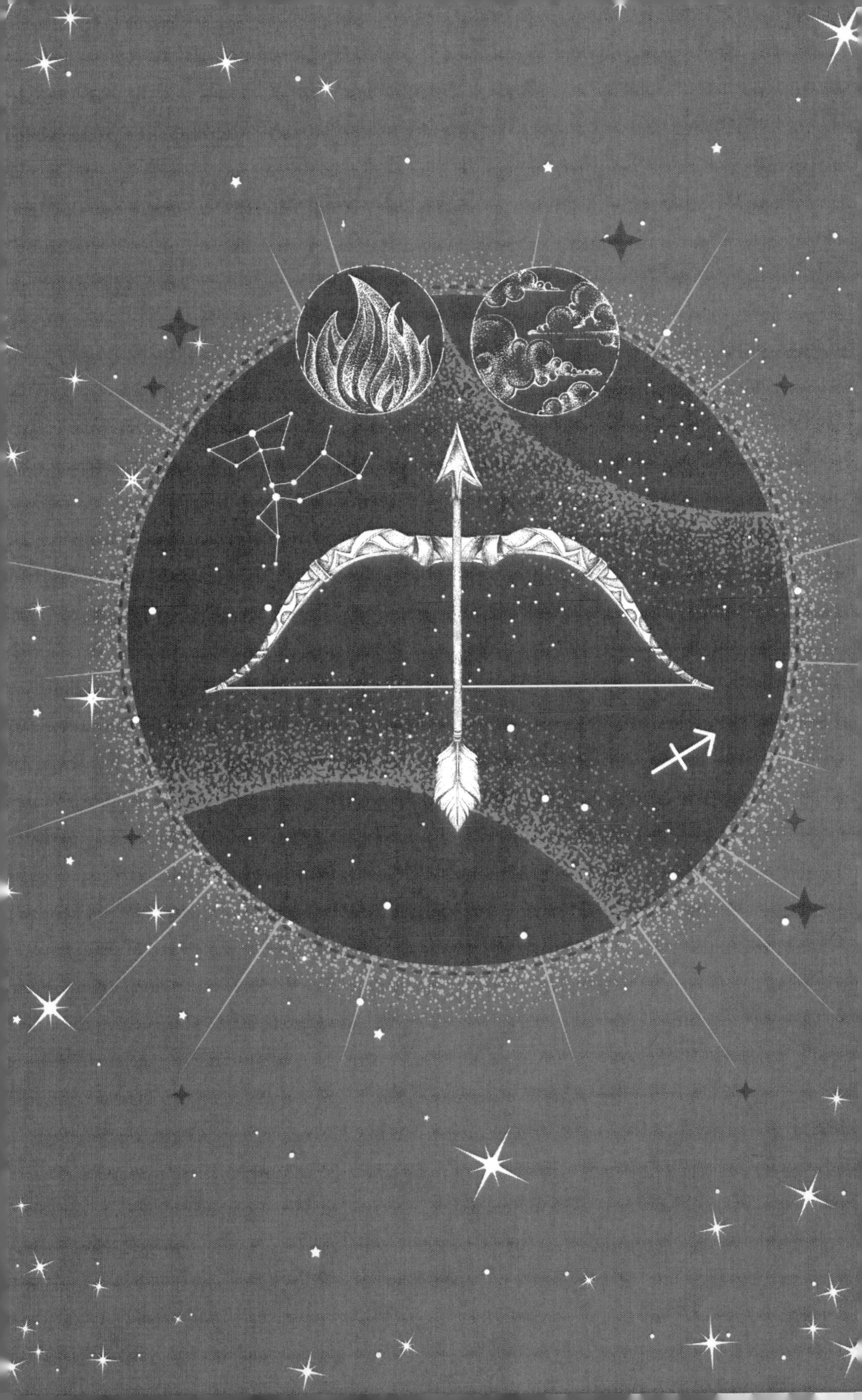

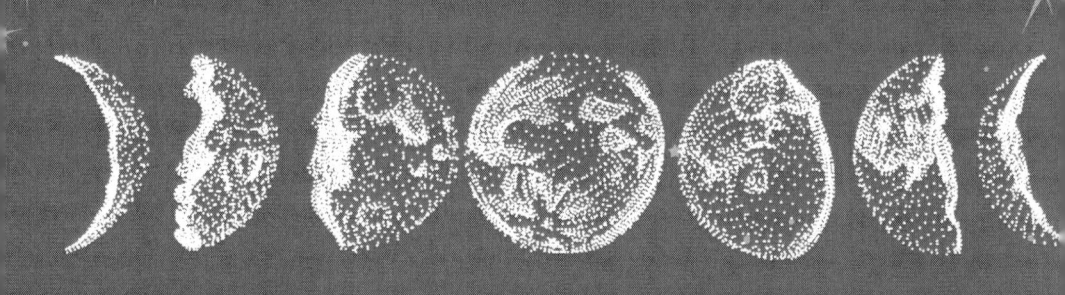

Sin
PRISONER #88

CHAPTER THIRTY TWO

"Well this has been fun, see ya." I clapped my little bro Maximus on the shoulder and shot Ethikins a wink as I leapt away into the crowd. I cursed as Max came barrelling after me, crashing into my back and knocking a couple of Fae over in the process.

"You can't go anywhere without me, idiot," he gritted out.

"Riiiiight yeah, totes forgot about that, kid."

"Don't call me kid," he warned, power sparking in his eyes.

"What else shall I call you then? Young whippet snapper? Little bud? Tiny bro?" I suggested, marching off through the crowd so he was forced to follow.

"None of those things," he hissed.

Little bro had the grumps, but I didn't know why.

"Rosalie told you not to wander," Ethan's voice carried to me as he followed too.

"Meh meh meh meh whipped-bitch meh," I mimicked his voice perfectly then started up the tunnel we'd entered through, weaving between the Fae still walking in and making Max chase after me.

A giggle left me as I picked up the pace and Max swore at me as the magic between us kept him on my heels. "Slow down. Where the hell are you going?"

"I have places to be and stuff to do," I sang. "Come on, chase me!" I ran faster and Max sprinted after me while Ethan fought to keep up, my feet taking me in diagonal lines through the crowd.

Fresh air hit my lungs outside and I went skipping down the hillside, my gaze locking on a gang of posturing dicks wearing tank tops, their muscles shining with tattoos loitering around a black SUV. They were the unsavoury flavour of Fae I'd often been around in Darkmore, and the biggest one didn't see me coming as I leapt at him, headbutting him in the face and breaking his nose.

"Ah!" he cried, fire magic exploding from him in defence, but I was a far stronger creature of flames and I quickly caught hold of them, sending fire bursting towards his friends, urged on by my own magic. They ran for their lives, splitting apart like ducklings lost on a raging river and I snatched the keys of the black SUV from Mr Breaky-nose and hurried into the driver's seat.

"Stop!" Max cried, but I just smiled my most twisted smile, dropped the back window and used air to snatch both him and Ethan, dragging them inside so they fell in a tangled heap on the back seats.

Max's Siren powers exploded over me and I gritted my teeth against the tsunami of strength spilling from him. He was trying to capture my emotions, make me feel all submissive and nicey-nice, but I didn't have the usual kind of mind to master. His Siren powers lashed onto me but my emotions danced and jumbled, taking him on a tailspin.

"What's with you?" Max called, giving up on trying to get hold of my emotions as his Siren powers fell away.

"He's Sin Wilder, there's no controlling him," Ethan answered for me and I bared my teeth at my brother in the rear-view mirror.

"That's right, baby bro," I said keenly. "I'm as wild as my name. Did you ever feel like something was missing all these years? Something full of mayhem, sweet bedlam to shake up your candy cane of a life? Well I'm back, crumble cakes and I'm here to stay. We'll rule the world, me and you. Brothers and bros, besties and baddies, am I right?"

"Watch where you're going!" Max yelled and the car bumped up in the air as we hit a ridge on the hill.

"There's gotta be a road around here somewhere," I muttered as Ethan clipped his seatbelt into place. Ever the worry worm.

"It's back that way," Ethan said firmly. "Where are you going?"

"To the past, my friend. To the middle of it all, not the beginning but the centre. Where my story pressed pause before I was snatched away to Darkmore by a hundred Fae in uniform."

"I highly doubt it took a hundred Fae to capture you," Max scoffed.

"Oh-ho, he wants to challenge me already, are you feeling threatened, smalls?"

"Threatened?" he laughed and there it was, the beautiful insanity in him too. Yes indeed, he was powerful alright, just like me, and that wasn't where the similarities ended. I'd bet if I could tempt out the madman in him, he'd be up for playing with me in the dark. "I'm an Heir, I've faced bigger threats than you and seen the whole world change before my eyes. You don't scare me, Whitney."

"Whhhhhhitney he calls me!" I laughed, howled really, then smacked the steering wheel to set the horn a-blaring. "Damn he has good comebacks. But oh Maximus, you're not an Heir anymore, I heard."

He shrugged, but maybe it bothered him, maybe it didn't. Hard to tell when you were driving a hundred miles an hour across terrain so dark you couldn't see your butt from your ankle. Oh headlights. Right. I switched them on along with the windscreen wipers and found me a road, turning onto it with a crack that fucked up the front of Mr Breaky Nose's car real good.

I got my bearings then sailed off into the night, taking my stowaways with me and singing a ditty at the top of my lungs, making up the words as I went. "There once was a mutt who put things up his butt and he liked it more than he would say."

"Shut it," Ethan barked, but I just sang louder.

"He liked things round, grown from the ground, as big as a tree or as small as a flea, and shoved them up, up, up his butt, butt, butt."

"Sin!" Ethan snapped and Max gave him the side-eye.

"What?" I smirked. "I never said it was about you, Wolf boy, you must just relate to the lyrics."

Ethan pouted and I continued my song at full-volume, taking roads at high speed and finally arriving in the nearby town where I had once planned on putting down roots. It was surrounded by trees, the birdsong here like no other place I'd ever found.

I pulled onto my land, following the drive through the woodland and coming to a halt in front of the cabin that belonged to me. It wasn't much, but it had once been everything.

"I'll be back in five minutes," I said then climbed out my open window and went swaggering up onto the porch in front of my house.

There was a tea cup turned over by the door and I flipped it up, finding a slug hanging out with my key. I tipped him a salute for protecting my property and tossed the teacup back over him before heading inside.

It was just as I'd left it. With my favourite wooden chair sitting by the window, the extra legs I'd screwed onto it giving it the look of a bug, especially with the horns I'd added to the back. I patted it in greeting and took stock of my things. My sack of bottle caps sat proudly by the fireplace and the collection of hats I'd taken from all kinds of fair folk were hanging on the walls alongside a selection of photographs I'd snapped of interesting things. Like an array of cakes, a man with a half-burnt eyebrow, a donkey eating a shoe, a crab in a handbag, and all other kinds of amazing stuff.

My odd shoe selection was lined up by the door and – holy shit! "Ganderstein," I said excitedly, kneeling down to wave at the spider I'd befriended years ago. "You've gotten bigger, and browner and more gangly."

"Sin, what is this about?" Ethan stepped through the front door with Max a pace behind him, the two of them looking around my living room curiously.

I left Ganderstein to his ganders, standing up and feeling suddenly exposed with my little brother's gaze picking apart my house. Ethan was cool with weird stuff, but Maximus? I didn't know what he saw when he looked at my less than usual possessions. Was he going to do what most people did and cringe away from my oddness?

"Where are my manners?" I said, a little jittery as I grabbed some napkins from a basket hanging from a hook by the kitchen door, doing a little twirl and tossing them out at their feet. "Welcome to my abode."

I bowed, then twirled some more and was pretty sure that was enough etiquette. I'd brew them tea and put on one of my fancier hats or some shit when I was finished with my business.

"And in answer to your earlier question, it's about a lot of things, Wolf boy," I purred. "I have a lot of valuable things in my house and I'm here to collect them. I didn't know the Hellion Hunt was held so close to my pad, but here we are." I swept over to my sack of bottle caps, picking it up and tossing it to him.

He caught it, looking inside with a frown. "How are these valuable?"

"How are they not?" I tsked and headed into the kitchen where a toy bat was floating in a bucket, still paying the price for the reason I'd put him there. "Alright Batticus, you've paid your dues." I took him out the bucket and placed him by the pile of gloves I'd stuck googly eyes on.

I picked up a flowerpot and tipped out the tape recorder which I'd used to give myself reminders.

Max took the device with a curious look and played the last recording. "Don't forget to climb that tree in that place where that judgemental shrub is."

"Oh yeah!" I said excitedly, throwing a few precious things into my flower pot – like bubble gum and un-popped popcorn – then I raced for the back door. I threw it open, running up the garden path that was lined with gnomes – all of which had been planted face down in the ground – then I raced away into the woods.

"Sin!" Ethan called as he followed and I felt the magic linking me to Max yanking him after me too.

I didn't have to go far to find the judgemental shrub in question, though it had grown a whole bunch since I'd last been here, the judgemental vibe it gave off more of a welcoming uncertainty now.

"Someone humbled you," I said, nodding to it then walking up to the big oak tree beside it, looking for a foothold. My gaze fell on an old shovel beside it and I gasped with my remberings, quickly sticking it in the ground and starting to dig. My stashed wooden box wasn't too far down and it wasn't long before I yanked it from the ground and tossed it at Ethan. "Look after that. Go put it in the car, flitwit."

"We should really get back to the hunt, Rosa will be looking for us," Ethan pressed.

"Nahhh she's probably being boned by the Vamp patrol right now, she's not missing us," I said, waving a hand at him.

"They'd hardly have sex down in that pit," Ethan dismissed me, but I knew my wild girl liked a danger dong when it came dinging.

"Nah, I think we have time." Max swept past me, nudging me aside and started climbing the damn tree, finding a foothold with ease. He went up and up and I stared after him with the biggest smile on my face.

Ethan sighed and headed back to the car with my box while I followed Max up the tree, moving in his footsteps as he taunted me about being too slow to keep up. He made it to the very top and swung his legs over a branch, sitting there and gesturing to the place beside him.

I pulled myself up, taking in the view over the valley, the trees rolling away for miles and miles beneath the luscious moon.

I exhaled a breath, reminded that I was free. Gloriously, endlessly free. "I used to dream of views like this down in Darkmore. Sometimes it would feel like you're choking down there. The air isn't pure like it is out here." I inhaled deep and tasted the pines and the summer breeze. "Oh to be a bird, I'd think. Fluttering its wings and sailing into the eternal sky."

I felt Max's eyes on me and turned to him, finding a frown creasing his brow.

"How long were you in there?"

"Too long, little bro. Too damn long."

"I don't know what to make of you," he admitted in a low voice.

"Most Fae don't." I shrugged. "Most don't hang around long enough to find out either. Will you stay or will you go, I wonder?"

"I'm undecided," he murmured. "But I think I'd like time to know you outside of what the world says about you."

"What they say is mostly true, Maxy boy. I'm a deranged, unusual creature. I don't know if they represent me as I truly be, all I know is I am what I am and most of the world don't have time for different."

"I have time," he said, his arm brushing mine.

I looked at him and he looked at me. There was no denying our parentage, we shared the same eyes, same hardness to our jaws. But would Maximus really stick around once he knew what I was? It took a special kind of Fae to do that. Jerome and Rosalie being the shining examples. Max Rigel didn't look like a man who could be easily spooked, but spook him I likely would.

A glint in my periphery made me turn a moment too late and I growled as a dart lodged in my neck at the very same moment one lodged in Max's. My eyes widened at the familiar feel of Order suppressant slithering through my blood and my Incubus went bye-bye.

The tree shuddered and the branches around us coiled around us like giant arms, snaring my limbs as fire blazed from my hands, trying to burn them away.

Max tried to wrangle the wind and I joined him in his efforts, the whips of air wrapping around us and attempting to yank us from the branches banding around us. But the bark bit deep and dragged my hands back time and again, knots of leaves winding around my fingers, and every time I burned through them, more took their place. The tree was bending, bowing as if to the forest itself and we descended rapidly to the ground, slamming into the mossy dirt with force.

My head connected with a rock and my magic faltered as a daze took hold of me, noises sounding like echoes. Someone slapped cuffs onto my wrists and my magic locked down in an instant, the cold feel of them reminding me sharply of Darkmore.

The muffled sounds of a struggle made me turn my head, and I found Max being shoved into the back of a black van, magical cuffs glinting on his wrists and a wild look in his eyes. Ethan was on his knees beside it, his hands cuffed too and his mouth gagged with a vine.

The branches of the tree forced me to kneel and one slid under my chin, making me raise my head to the Fae who had done this.

Jerome stood over me, my dear brother giving me a look that left my brain confused. Behind him were a group of Fae, his followers all clustered close to Jerome with their hands on his shoulders, power sharing to gift him unspeakable strength.

I glanced around, sure he had come to save me from whoever had made this tree attack me, but his fingers moved and the branches holding me did too, telling me without doubt that it was him controlling them.

A wild laugh escaped me, my grin so very wide. "No fair, you didn't give me a chance to fight back! Let's go for round two but this time you can't go sneaking up on me, you cheeky chappy."

Jerome didn't smile, regarding me with all the coldness of deep winter snowfall. He was playing a real good game here, committing to the bit and I wanted to play too. So I'd have to accept being the helpless prisoner.

"Please! Please don't hurt me!" I screamed at the top of my lungs then laughed and laughed. Jeromeo didn't crack. My foster bro still looked all murderous and shit. He was good at this game.

"Sin," he growled and the branches around my limbs tightened enough to bruise. "You had a chance to return to me. More than one in fact. But you chose that Wolf time and again. You've abandoned me."

I frowned, not seeing the glint of fun in his eyes I was waiting for. It was all serious Simon in those eyes, and I suddenly didn't feel like laughing anymore.

"Abandoned you?" I scoffed. "Never, J man. I'm just in love, that's all. My heart's gone and made itself a home with someone else. You can't undo shit like that. Least, I don't think you can. And anyways, I don't want to. Not ever."

"That's precisely the issue," he said cuttingly and even the birds in the trees fell quiet.

I was feeling a sense of the uh-ohs that I was pretty sure I needed to pay attention to. But this was my Jeromeo, what could there be to worry about?

"Okay untie me now, it's my turn to play big bad boss man," I insisted.

"You're a fucking fool," he barked and one of the branches punched me in the face, splitting my lip open.

My gaze settled on the earth, my frown deepening and the cogs whirring in my head as I was left with the confused feeling that something wasn't right about all this. I just couldn't say what exactly. I looked to Ethan who had rage in his eyes as he glared at Jerome, and I got the sense that I should trust that anger.

"You think all those years I would have put up with your incessant chatter, your mindless, crazy bullshit if you didn't hold value to me?" Jerome demanded.

"Crazy?" I echoed in a whisper, that single word among his sentence sticking in my head like a needle.

"Yes, crazy. Fucking moronic too. You took a pittance for the hits I organised for you while I pocketed the real cash."

"What do you mean? I have two million auras and this really cool cabin," I said, trying a laugh, but Jerome didn't break character. He was really committing to being this angry, bitter man with a stick up his ass.

"You killed Fae across Solaria whose heads were worth millions, Sin," he said, shaking his head at me like I was so very idiotic.

"Pfffft, you're making stuff up now," I said. "That's my brother in the van by the way. Do you want to meet him? I think you guys will really get along."

"That's Tiberius Rigel's son?" Jerome's head snapped up to look at the van and I guessed he was super excited to meet him.

"Yeah, come on. Get this tree off of me and let's go have a cup of tea in the house," I urged.

Jerome leaned down to stare me in the eyes. "Listen to me, hear this and know it is the truth, Sin Wilder. You are a pawn to me, nothing more, and now you have shown that you will no longer play by my rules. You will not take the jobs I need you to take, and now you have betrayed me by revealing my dealings to Tiberius Rigel. The FIB are hunting me from Alestria to Iperia and there is no stronghold that is safe anymore. So I have done the only thing I can and made a deal with a man you delivered right to me. Do you know how valuable an Incubus Order would be to one of Roland Vard's clients?"

My frown was so deep now that I could feel it in my eyebrows. There was a darkness pressing in on me, whispering to my demons and urging them awake. *Enemy*, they purred. *Danger*, they warned. "The price he's offered me is generous indeed, and he is going to triple it when your Moon Wolf bitch comes coaxing for you along with that Lion Vard is hunting for. Now you have delivered me the Rigel boy too, no doubt he will pay me a hefty sum for his Order and I will get some well-deserved revenge on his father for the headache he has been causing me of late." He wielded the tree, making it hurl me into the van and I cried out to Ethan in alarm as the door was slammed shut in my face.

"Cut him free. He can tell Rosalie Oscura where to find us and we'll soon learn whether she'll risk everything for her Incubus like she implied," Jerome said and I relaxed marginally, relieved to know Ethan would be freed.

But my mind was spinning too fast and emotions were warring through me that I'd never felt before. I tried to place them. Tried to understand this turmoil, but I couldn't find the right word for it. It didn't matter anyway. I had no use for words anymore, only blood. The demons inside my mind were wide awake and baying for carnage, and I would reap it in the worst ways I knew how.

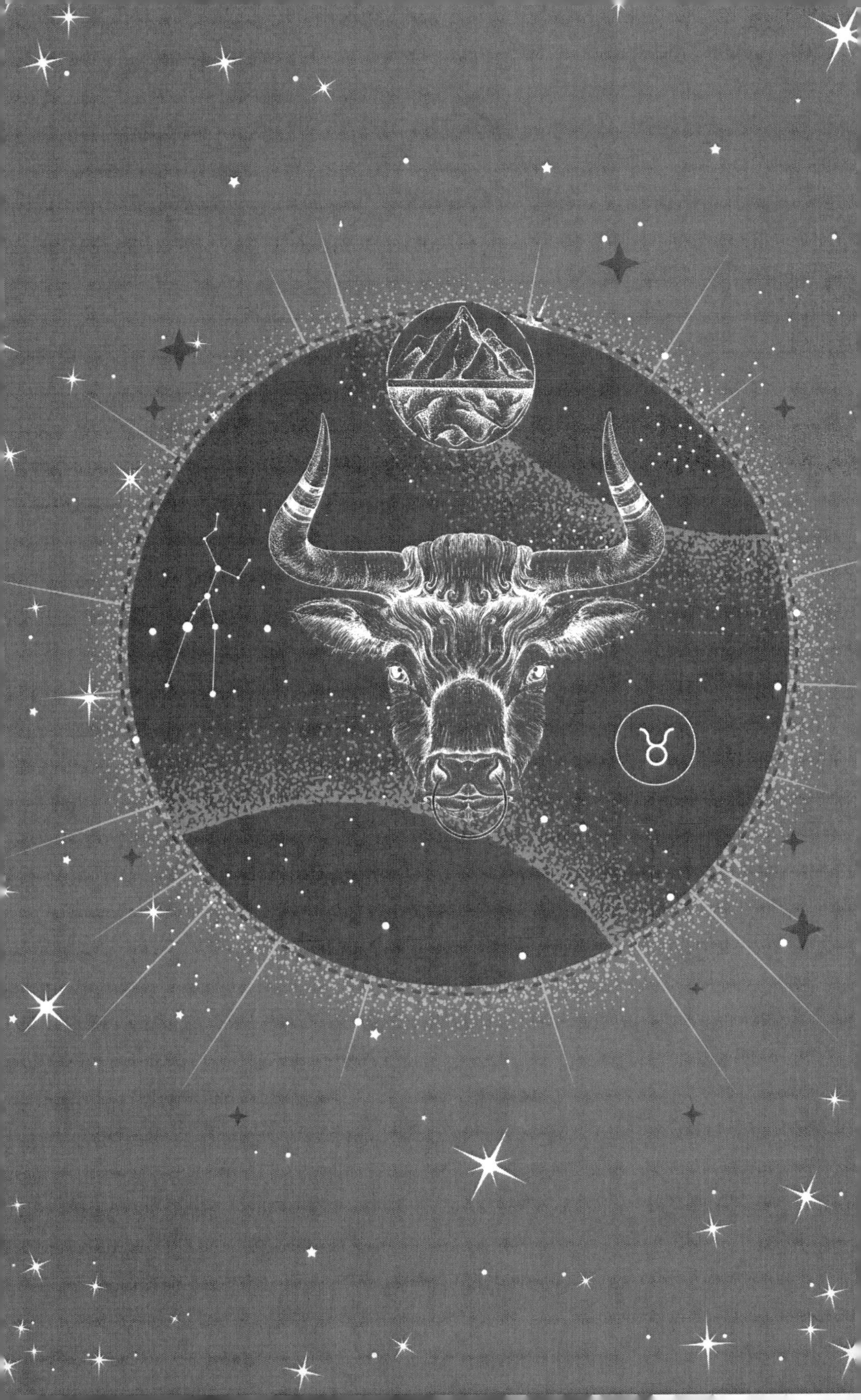

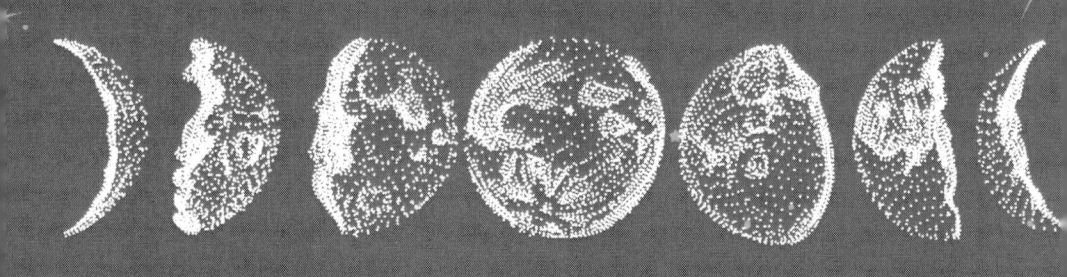

Rosalie

PRISONER #12

CHAPTER THIRTY THREE

The upper levels of the Hellion Hunt were a feast of debauchery and drunken revelry. The hunters and prey who had finished up their round were celebrating heartily, drinking deeply from potion-laced cocktails and smoking illegal substances. Fae fucked in dark corners or openly sprawled across the tables in pairs or groups, their masks still in place and offering them the anonymity some Fae preferred for such behaviour.

Wolves tended to fuck like that regardless of prying eyes so it wasn't much of a scandal to me, but as I spotted Hastings standing immobile by the bar, a tray of drinks clutched in his hands, his knuckles bleached white from the tightness of his grip and his eyes wide within his mask, I chuckled.

"Oh my poor choir boy," I purred, slipping through the crowd with Cain and Roary at my back like twin shadows.

"How can I see that he's blushing when he has that mask on?" Roary laughed.

"I thought he might be a little less green after spending his nights with those Oscura girls," Cain muttered, shaking his head.

"I think he had several drinks to build up his nerve and even then only took two of them to bed at once. The way my cousin Maria tells it, he blushed the whole time then too but he has a big cock so they made good use of it all the same."

Cain hissed in disgust and I chuckled but my gut twisted with unease as I looked around the room and failed to spot Ethan, Sin or Max.

"Where are the others?" I asked Hastings as we reached him and he flinched in surprise, jolting the drinks on his tray so they sloshed down his front while ripping his eyes away from the sight of a woman who was pinned between three Fae at once while loudly begging for them to come in her face and call her a bad little bunny bitch. One of the men surrounding her stuffed his cock in her mouth and she was silenced, breaking the spell the vision had had on my choir boy.

"Sorry," Hastings gasped. "I...went for drinks and then when I turned back the hunters and prey had returned and that guy over there asked me to erm...do something to him like the pathetic little toad he was. I don't want to mention the exact phrasing he used, but I lost track of the others while trying to escape him."

"And did you?" Roary asked.

"Did I what?"

"Did you punish him with your cock like the pathetic little-"

I jabbed him in the gut with my elbow as poor Hastings turned utterly beetroot, his ears, neck and the small amount of skin we could see around his eyes betraying his embarrassment.

He started spluttering, denying it with such vehemence that I couldn't help but feel sorry for him and I took the tray of drinks from his hands before setting it on the bar and patting his arm understandingly.

"Ignore the stronzos," I told him, narrowing my eyes at Roary and Cain who were snickering like badly behaved children. "They turn into asshats when their dicks have been wetted."

Hastings frowned then blinked in understanding, stumbling back a step as he nodded aggressively and seemed to find himself unable to look at me at all.

I sighed heavily, realising I'd only made it worse while Cain and Roary laughed even harder.

"So you lost track of the others?" I pushed, knowing that this conversation would only descend if I kept on down the route it had been taking.

"Erm…they were here…" Hastings looked around in confusion and I exchanged a look with Roary and Cain who seemed to have realised that something more serious than their juvenile sniggering was going on.

"How long ago did you last see them?" I asked.

"Well, we were watching the hunt and the three of you had just gone underground after being up on the walls. We lost sight of you so I figured I'd grab some drinks and the others said they'd stay right there." Hastings pointed to the railing where the view of the labyrinth was most easily visible and I cursed as I quickly surmised that the three of them were nowhere in sight.

"That has to be over an hour ago," Cain said.

"Were you just standing there staring at that girl getting fucked all that time?" Roary asked Hastings.

"No!" he protested. "There was a Pegasus who kept squirting glitter all over a Lion's mane and then a group of like ten Fae blocked me in the corner for ages and they didn't seem to hear me when I was saying 'excuse me' so I just had to watch the wall until they were…umm…done. Then I got to the bar and got the drinks but this guy accosted me and kept trying to get me to buy a vibrating butt plug from his Celestial Heir collection and he wouldn't take no for an answer so eventually I had to buy four of them and-"

"Wait, you bought four vibrating butt plugs?" Cain asked sharply and I couldn't help but snort a laugh too.

"He wouldn't leave and he kept showing me all kinds of videos about how they could be used and I just needed him to stop," Hastings protested and I patted his arm again.

"Okay, we get it. But that doesn't help us figure out where-"

The door in the corner of the room burst open with a heavy bang as it bounced off of the wall and my eyes widened in alarm as Ethan stumbled through them, his expression wild as he hunted the crowd for us.

I broke into a run, hurrying over to him, taking in the mud and blood on his clothes, the twigs in his hair.

"What happened?" I demanded.

"Sin said the three of you were fucking and we had some time to kill. He wanted to go back to his house and get some of his stuff before we went hunting for Vard but it was a trap – Jerome was waiting, he attacked us. He took Max and Sin, but he let me go so that-"

"Jerome took them?" I gasped, wondering what the fuck that stronzo had to gain from doing such a thing but the worst blow was yet to fall.

"Jerome took them to Vard," Ethan panted. "He said because Sin won't work for him the way he used to, he'd get the money he needed by selling him off instead and an Incubus is one of the rarest Orders of all."

"We have to go after them," I snarled.

"They'll know we're coming, it's what they want," Ethan warned though he didn't make any attempt to deny that we would be going all the same. "Jerome said Vard wants your Order too and Roary back under his control. They'll be waiting for us to strike."

"Good," I growled, pushing my way past him and leading my pack out of the caverns where the hunt was held. "Because it's time we finished this shit."

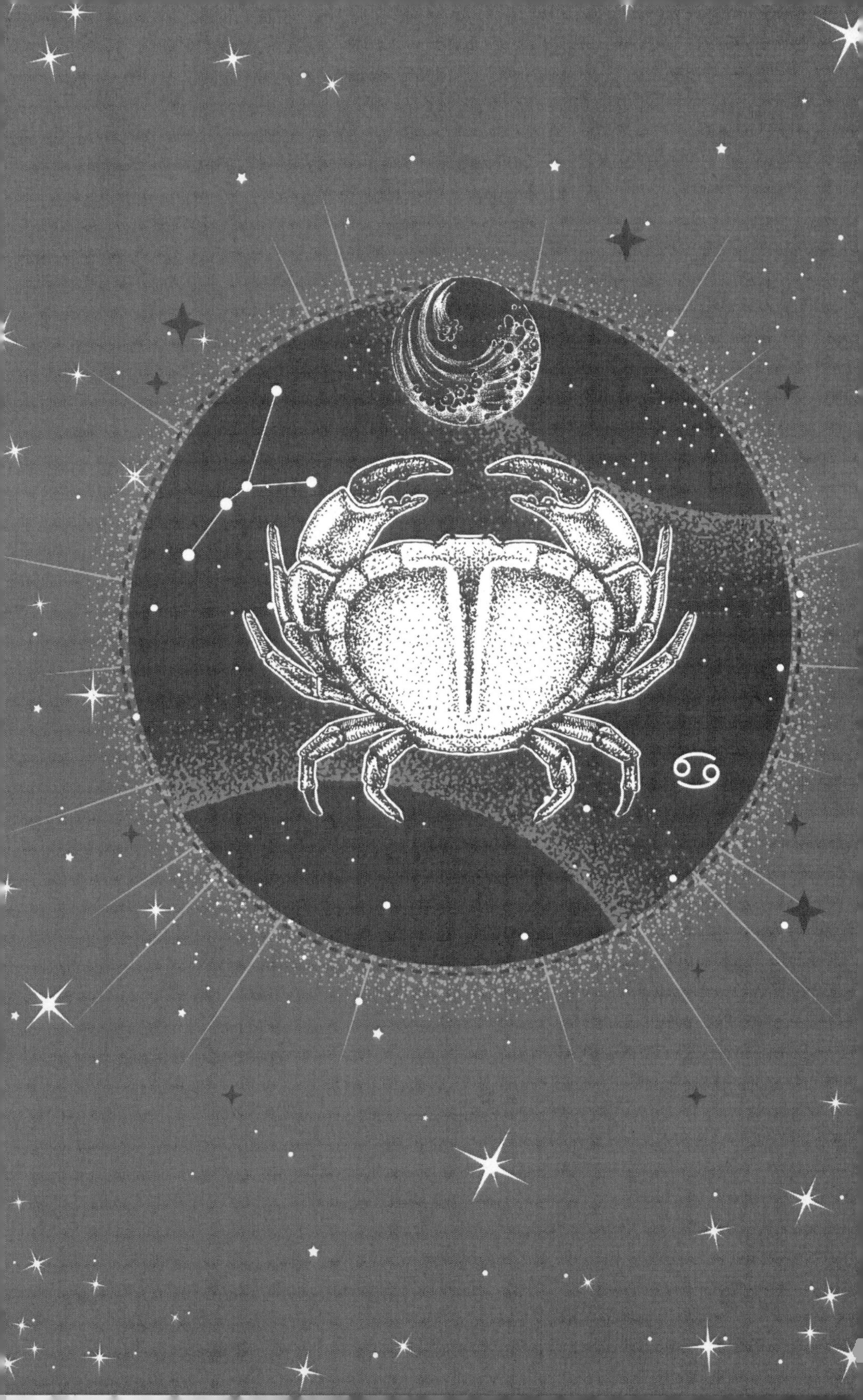

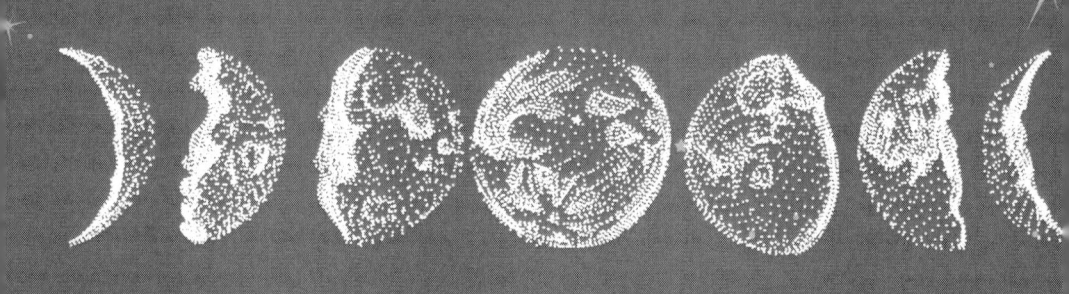

Ethan

PRISONER #1

CHAPTER THIRTY FOUR

We had enough stardust to get us to the coordinates where Vard was located, but I wasn't prepared for the freezing wind that battered me as the stars spat us out in the Polar Capital. We sank into the snow and took in the dark tower that rose up from the white ahead of us, reaching toward the moon and the shimmering green and pink of the northern lights.

"Cain, Roary, go around the back, Ethan take the front entrance," Rosalie demanded.

"What about you?" I asked with a frown.

She gave the tower a savage look. "I'm going to take a more direct route while you keep the guards distracted." Rosalie called upon her moon powers, turning invisible and I swore as she raced off across the snow, leaving tracks as she went. But with it being so dark out here, I doubted anyone would notice them, especially once the carnage started.

"What about me?" Hastings asked, smoothing down his fringe and giving the tower a determined look.

"You keep watch, bud." I clapped him on the shoulder then gave Cain and Roary a nod before they sprinted away across the plain, heading around the tower in a flash of movement. A roar and clash of battle broke out as they found targets to fight and I started off across the snow.

"Wait, I want to help." Hastings hurried after me.

"You wanna help? Find a way inside and get to Sin and Max then," I said then started running, setting my gaze on the large wooden doors that led into the stone tower.

"Wait!" Hastings called, but his voice was lost to the rumble of my power as I pushed my magic into the snow that led all the way up to the entrance, gathering it in a giant wave, building it up and up and up then hurling it at the door.

The thundering wall of snow impacted with the tower with a boom that rang out into the sky, the walls shuddering and the door blown clean off its hinges. A group of guards were sent crashing backwards with screams of agony as the weight of the snow crushed them.

Once it settled, I took in the passage inside, now layered in white, a glimpse of a stairway beyond promising me a path to Sin. My friend. Family really. At this point I could hardly deny what he'd become to me. He was part of Rosalie's pack which made him *my* pack, a brother in arms that I would do anything for. And I would retrieve him from this place come hell or high water.

I padded over the drift of snow that had mounted up in the doorway, casting a sword of ice in my grip and seeking out enemies in the dark. All was still and far too quiet, the sound of battle carrying from the direction Cain and Roary had taken, but nothing stirred in here.

The silence should have been encouraging, but my hackles raised, my instincts telling me not to let my guard down.

The snow shifted to my right and I raised my sword half a second before a monstrous beast burst from the bank of white. Gustard's sharp teeth were bared and his clawed hands outstretched to grab me.

I swung my blade, scoring it across his chest as he collided with me, knocking me to the ground and sending us skidding back outside. I tried to drive my sword into him as he screeched in my face but he lurched off of me as blood poured from the deep slice in his hair-covered skin.

I scrambled to my feet, my limbs bruised but no further injury slowing me down as I ran at him again, swinging the blade and preparing to cut his head from his shoulders.

He released a horrid, high-pitched noise that seared into my skull, making me stumble mid-stride and go crashing to my knees. The noise intensified, drilling into my head and making it impossible to do anything but throw my hands to my ears to try and block it out, my weapon landing uselessly in the snow beneath me.

Gustard's monstrous shadow fell over me, blotting out the light of the moon as he advanced, his large hands reaching out to end me for good.

I scrambled away, trying to put distance between us, but that sound only found its way deeper into my mind and I started to black out. The power of it was too fierce to fight off and fear found me as I realised I was going to be stolen from Rosa all too soon. This death wasn't worthy of me. I didn't deserve to die here on my knees. And something in the knowledge of that gave me the strength to keep my head just long enough to have an idea. I cast bubbles of water over my ears, the sound instantly muffled, keeping the disabling power of it at bay.

Gustard continued to screech, prowling forward and I let him come closer, pretending I was passing out and subtly casting a shorter blade in my grip, hiding it beneath my body. As Gustard's claws swiped at me, I acted fast, twisting up and slashing my blade at his hand, cutting it clean off.

Blood spurted and Gustard shrieked in pain, staggering back while I gained my feet. It took only a second for him to recover, charging at me again with a bellow of rage, his eyes pinned on me and demanding my death.

It was him or me, and I vowed on the moon above that I would win this fight.

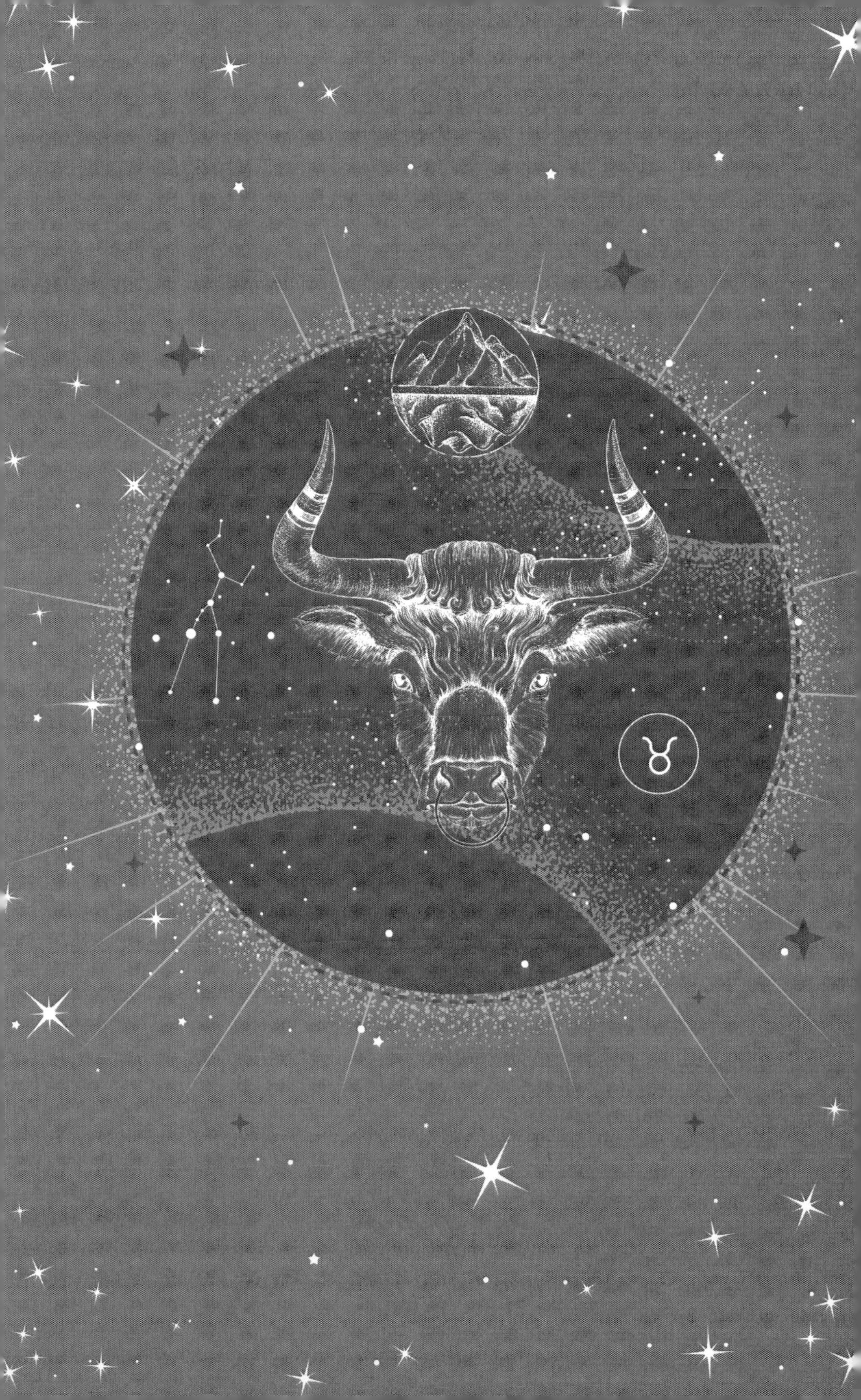

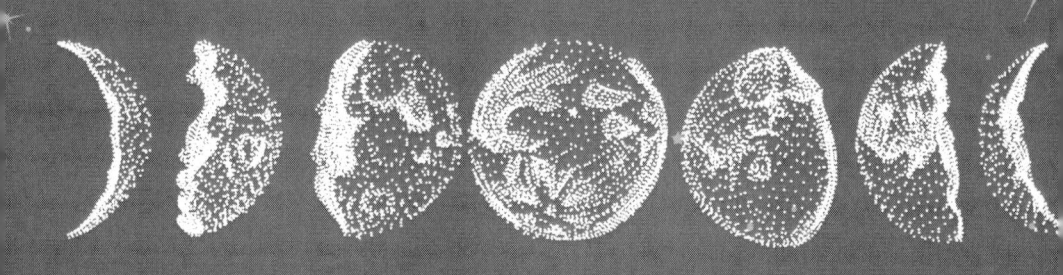

ROSALIE

PRISONER #12

CHAPTER THIRTY FIVE

I took a running jump and grabbed hold of the side of the tower, my fingers digging into the bricks and forging handholds as my magic flared from me. The moon was out and I had sprinted across the ground to get here meaning that my magic was blazing to its fullest extent.

My gifts had shrouded me from sight once more so while Ethan, Roary, Cain and Hastings all drew the eyes of anyone inside the compound to them, I went unnoticed as I heaved myself up the wall to find them.

Ethan howled and I flinched as an echo of his pain slammed through my side, making me wince before I gritted my teeth against it and heaved myself higher.

I looked up, not caring that the ground was getting more and more indistinct beneath me because my destination was ahead and not below.

A flash of movement made me glance to my left where Cain and Roary moved in bursts of Vampire speed, tearing into the line of guards who had run from the compound to confront them.

Higher. I had to move faster.

I reached up again, my fingers grasping at the stone and forcing perfect handholds into place with every movement. I was travelling fast enough to regenerate my power too so all I had to do was focus on the climb.

Sin was close, I was certain of it. And I had to hope that he hadn't been here long enough for anything untoward to have happened to him yet either. Vard's operations took time and it had been little over an hour since he had captured my Incubus and his brother. Surely he couldn't have started operating on either of them yet.

A blast rattled the tower and I cursed as I slipped, losing my grip on one hand, my feet swinging wildly beneath me as a dangled precariously by the tips of my fingers.

Magic flared through me even as the dizzying drop below swayed through my vision and I snarled at the tower, the world and the fucking stars for planting us into this tumultuous fate. But the moon had my back. Always had, always would.

I punched the tower with my free hand, my magic carving into the bricks like they were made of sand, until I could steady myself firmly enough to repeat the motion for my feet.

I panted as I clung to the wall, getting control of myself and letting the surge of adrenaline subside so that I wasn't shaking as I reached upwards again. I was about halfway to the top where glimmering windows spoke of a way in which none of the bastardos hiding away in this place should have suspected.

Moonlight illuminated the pale walls before me as if once again my favourite celestial being was lighting up a path before me. I could hear her whispering encouragement to me, promising that I was on the right track.

Higher I climbed, the cries of my enemies and the howling screams of Gustard's monstrous form fading away as I focused on nothing but the solid beat of my own heart.

My pack were fighting to buy me this chance. I wouldn't let them down. And as the moonlight shone brightly on the windows high above, I felt certain that victory would soon be within my grasp.

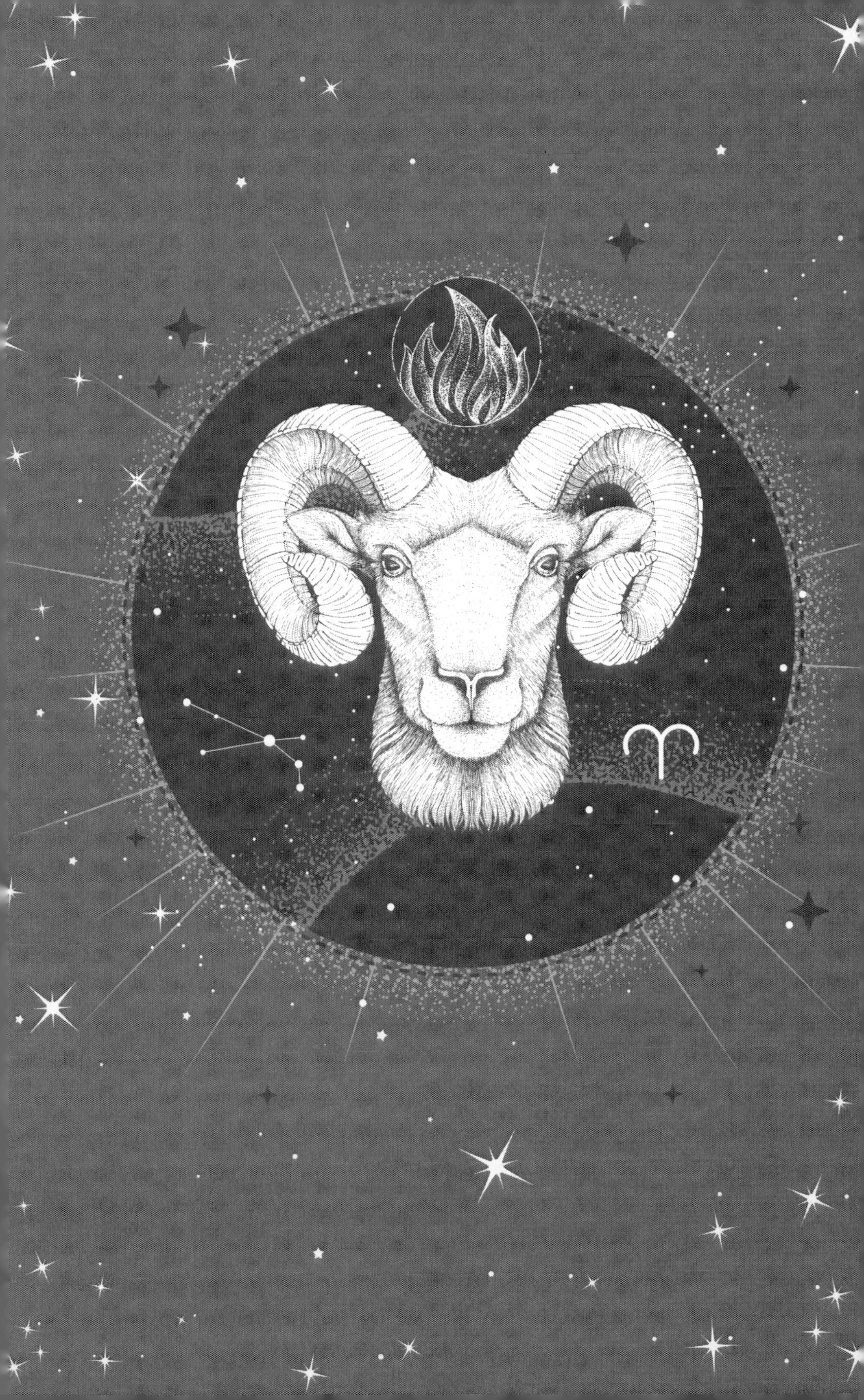

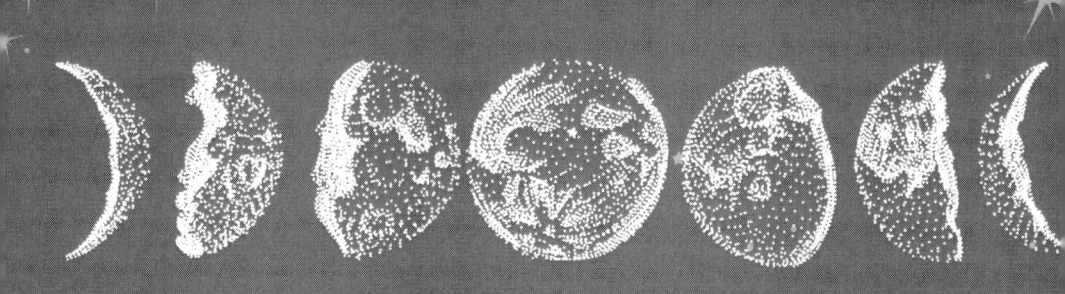

Cain
COMMANDING OFFICER

CHAPTER THIRTY SIX

The guards swarmed at us in a tide, but Roary and I cut through them like a storm of death, racing between their ranks and killing them with magic. My fire flared out around me, carving through their ranks, consuming them before they had a chance to cast back at me. Roary's attacks were equally fierce, blasting shots of ice at our enemies so they dropped like flies.

A Medusa lunged at me with snakes bursting into life from her head, each of them snapping at me and trying to get their immobilising venom into my veins. I burned them all, moving fast enough to avoid the strikes and those snakes screamed along with the Fae they belonged to before her whole head was swallowed in flames and she fell dead at my feet.

I was already moving on to my next opponent. The man cast vines at me, one latching around my throat and trying to choke me. He had enough strength in his magic to make me stagger to a halt and two of his friends came at me from the sides.

I blasted fire at the unFae fuckers while simultaneously burning away the vine at my neck and putting on a burst of speed, tearing towards the earth elemental and ripping out his throat with my fangs.

His screams cut off in death and I tossed him away from me, seeking out Roary as the last of the guards fell prey to his shots of ice. Bodies lay around us in the snow, the deep crimson of their blood staining the white red.

"That's it?" Roary said, looking to the iron gates they had exited through at the base of the tower.

Heavy footfalls carried from the twisting stairway beyond the gates and I lit fire in my palms, preparing to face whoever was coming our way. My throat tightened at the sight of Benjamin Acrux stepping out into the moonlight, casting fire just as I was and narrowing his gaze on me.

"Mason," he said in his deep voice. "This fight has been long fated. I've owed you death for far too many years."

"I almost killed you once. This time I will ensure the job is done thoroughly," I hissed, glancing at Roary and giving him a nod. "I'll handle this."

Roary hesitated only a second before sprinting past Benjamin in a blur of movement, causing a wind that made Benjamin's hair flutter. He glanced over his shoulder then back at me, cocking his head to one side. "He won't get far."

"He's not your concern," I growled, stepping to the side as I readied to face him. He took a step in the opposite direction, eyeing me up like a meal to be devoured, but I was no such thing.

"You promised those kids a real life, but all those years you were sending them to the butcher," I hissed.

"And I made a pretty price out of them too," he said with a grim sneer. "You think a bunch of dead runts gives me any less sleep at night?"

"No," I said coldly. "Cowards like you couldn't gain any true power in the world, so you sought to control and abuse kids who didn't even have magic to fight back with. You think that makes you a big man? It makes you a fucking weakling."

"How dare you," he snarled. "I'm an Acrux, a Dragon, a-

"Cunt," I finished for him then lunged, sending fire spiralling towards his face to blind him while circling around the back of him at speed, readying to snap his neck with my bare hands.

Before I got close, his Order form burst from his skin, his Dragon knocking me to the ground as bronze wings flexed above me and hellfire burst from his jaws.

I raced for cover inside the tower, hiding in an alcove as the heat of that almighty fire scored into the stairwell, racing up and away, but not finding its way to me in the shadows.

I waited for it to die back and Benjamin let out a roar of victory, clearly believing his fire had done the job for him already, but I wouldn't be put down so easily.

I turned and threw my weight into the wall, sending bricks flying as I leapt from my hiding place and pouncing straight onto his back.

He roared in utter fury as I built a spear of flames in my hand and drove it toward his skull. He bucked and I was knocked onto my front, clinging to his scales as he beat his wings and took off into the sky, climbing vertically and making me hold on for my damn life.

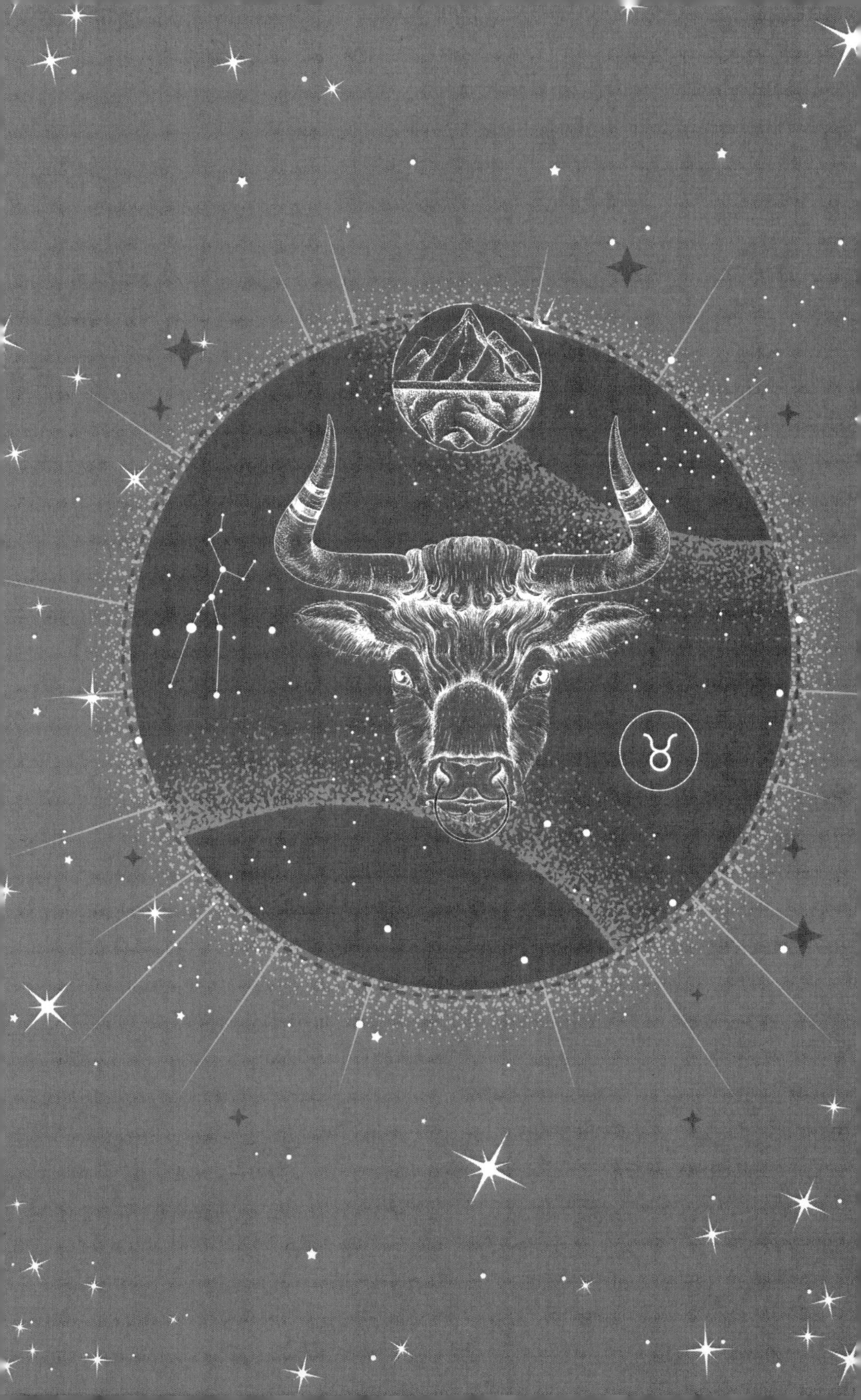

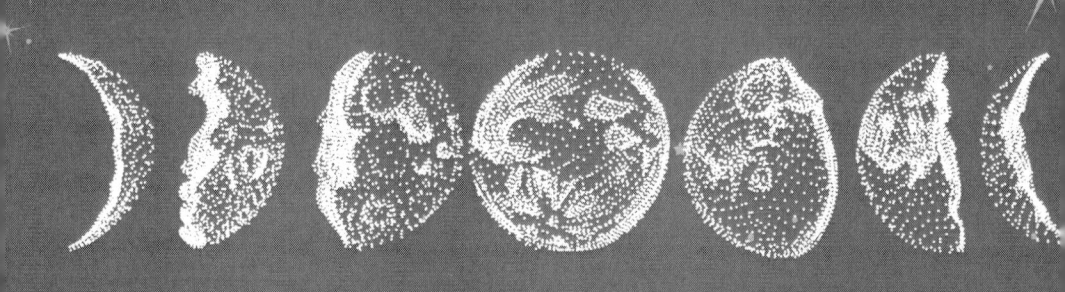

ROSALIE

PRISONER #12

CHAPTER THIRTY SEVEN

I couldn't focus on the bellowing roars of the Dragon who had joined the fray, Benjamin Acrux's fate was down to the stars and my men to decide. And in a way it was fitting too. Cain deserved his vengeance on the man who had stolen not only his childhood and innocence from him, but also profited on the suffering of the children who had been desperate enough to seek out the questionable care he offered them.

I hated to think of Cain and those other small Fae so in need of a home that they had been willing to endure the punishment and cruel 'training' of a monster in plain sight just to be able to survive. I hoped that Solaria no longer held places of poverty and desperation like the streets Cain had clawed his way through life on, and that those in need now found the safety and help they were due.

I gritted my teeth as the bronze Dragon bellowed a roar at my back, refusing to turn and look at the fight which was taking place far beneath me. Every moment I wasted was another where my men would be forced to fight on. We were up against a viper and that meant victory would only come once I had cut off its head. And Vard's beheading was the first priority on my list.

My muscles trembled with fatigue as I dug my fingers into the brickwork again, sweat slicking my skin and rolling down my spine as I climbed ever higher. Above me the windows were winking in the moonlight, beckoning me closer with every foot I climbed.

I was so close. And if I was lucky then Vard would be right there, up at the top of the tower looking out over the world below as stronzos like him so often enjoyed. But if not, it didn't matter. Once I was in, I would delve through every layer of that tower, scouring its innards and ending all of the sick bastardos I came across who were complicit in the fucked up devilry they were practicing within those walls.

Max had been right. No knowledge of this could be allowed to survive for another psychopath to pick up and continue. No scrap of information could be left once this was done. We would burn it all and end every piece of shit who was involved in its production.

I dug my fingers into the bricks again, my magic flaring, but as I pulled myself higher, a high-pitched shriek cut the air in two and I flinched, my head snapping around despite the promises I'd made myself to focus on nothing but my climb.

I sucked in a sharp breath as I spotted the huge doors at the base of the tower which had been torn clean off and from within the bowels of the building hunched shapes were moving out into the moonlight.

I froze, staring down in horror as I was transported back to the war, to the monstrous creatures which had joined that fight. Fae experimented on and tainted with dark and terrible magic, forged into monsters which were near impossible to kill, frighteningly intelligent and blessed with magical weaponry.

Monsters like the Belorian who Vard himself had created. Monsters like the thing he had twisted Gustard into. Monsters which had wings.

My heart leapt in alarm as a brutish beast launched from the depths of the tower, leathery wings snapping out and hurling it skyward. It was as big as Benjamin in his Dragon form, its face disconcertingly humanoid and eyes a piercing yellow as they locked on me.

I shook my head, trying to dislodge the notion that it was coming for me. I was invisible. I could feel the rush of the moon's magic and knew that there was no way it could see me.

But the beast did not sway from its path, racing through the sky towards me, and I cursed as I watched its nostrils flare.

No, it couldn't see me. It could smell me.

"Fuck," I gasped, reaching upwards as I tore my gaze from the beast which was flying for me at such speed that it defied physics.

I wrenched myself skyward a heartbeat before it collided with the tower where I'd just been, bricks crumbling away to scatter to the ground far below and the entire structure vibrating so forcefully that I was almost knocked free of it.

The beast shrieked again as it kicked off of the stone tower and launched itself back out into the sky, its wings beating hard as it swung in a tight circle, nostrils flaring as it hunted for me once more.

I gave up on keeping myself concealed; anyone would be able to see the beast attacking the tower anyway and though I remained invisible, I hurled vines out above me, aiming for the metal lightning rod which topped the tower.

The beast shrieked as it dove for me again, aiming true, its speed formidable.

The vines snapped tight and I threw myself off of the tower a mere moment before it crashed into the bricks where I had just been for the second time.

The vines snaked around my wrists at my command then wrenched me skyward, hurling me towards the windows.

My destination loomed but the monster threw itself after me, its eyes on the vines above my head, serrated jaws snapping wildly.

I yelled out in alarm as it collided with my vines, calling on my magic to save me but I wasn't fast enough and my stomach swooped like an anvil had just dropped straight to the pit of it as my lifeline was severed and I tumbled from the sky.

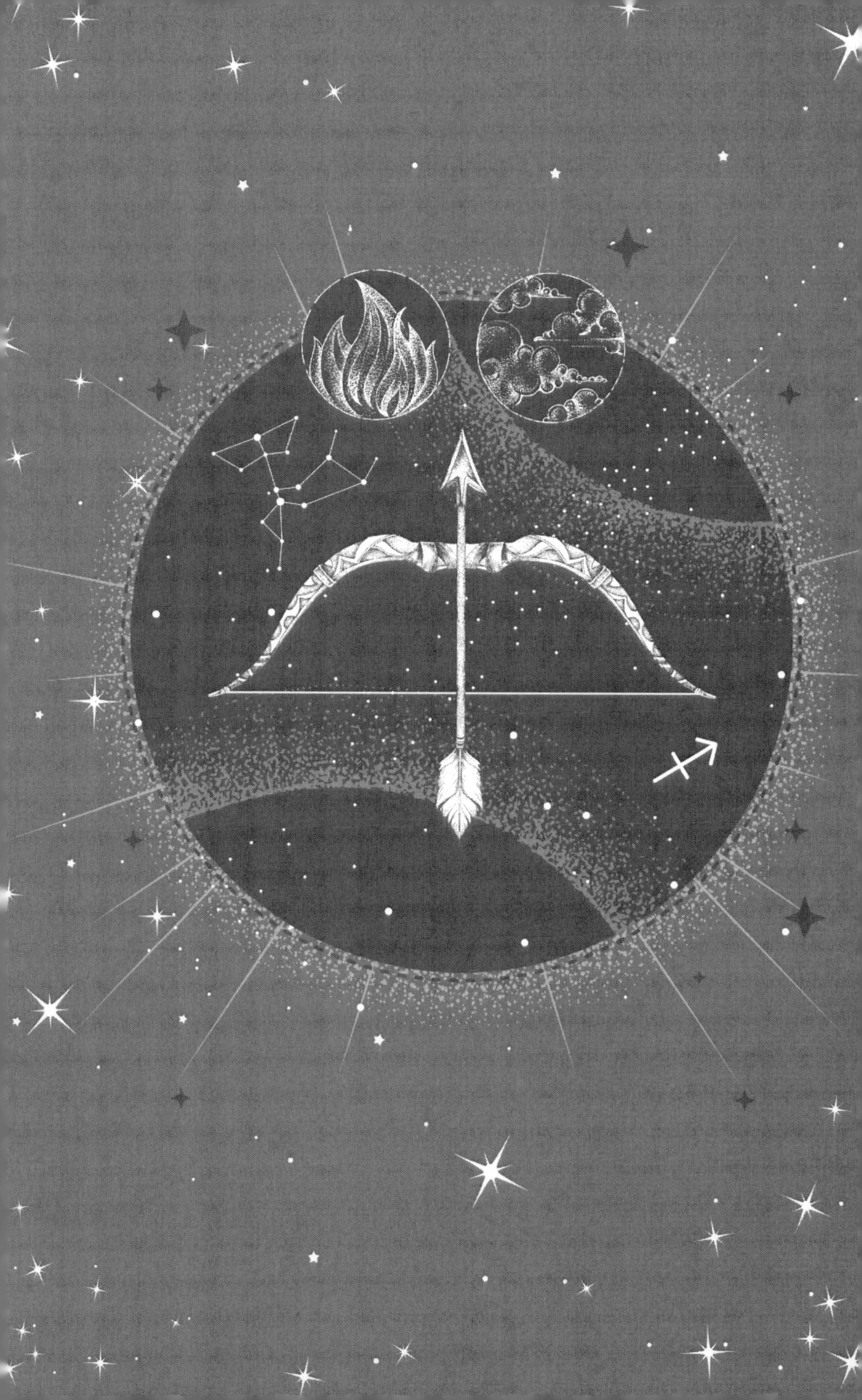

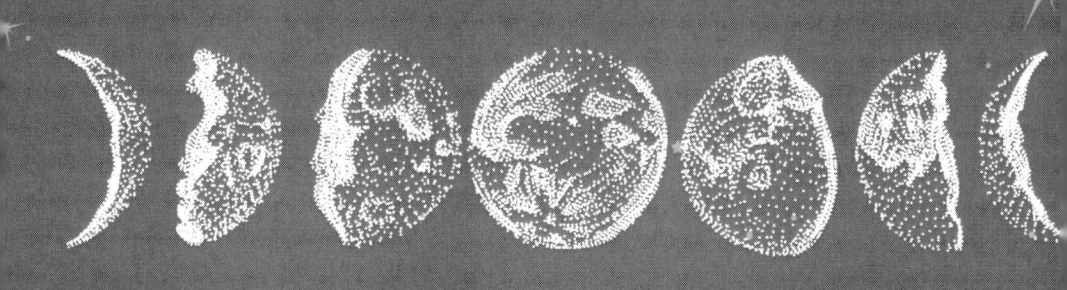

SIN
PRISONER #88

CHAPTER THIRTY EIGHT

My mind was torn in two like an unwanted envelope, the ripped edges causing me untold confusion as I tried to piece my halves back together. One side of me was laughing at Jerome's little game, the prank that he was taking to levels beyond anything he'd done before, and the other side of me was a twisted hunk of betrayal.

I had no idea which side was the truth. For surely my dear, dear foster brother of all these years hadn't actually betrayed me? He was the only thing in my past that had been a point of foundation, the rest of my memories just a sea of turmoil that never stopped churning. He was my brother, maybe not in blood, but through a bond forged by life itself. So why was I strapped to an operating table, shirtless and waiting for my skin to be sliced into?

My brother Max was on the table beside me, his muscles bulging against his restraints as he fought to break them. The room was cold, bland, lacking in colour like someone had stuck a sap tapper in it then bled it dry.

I'd been muttering to myself for a while, loud then quiet, laughing intermittently before spewing curses into the frigid air. Max kept telling me to remain calm, to find a way out, but there was none. I could see it plain and clear. With magical blocking cuffs on our wrists and Order suppressant in our veins, we were little more than mortals in this tower of murderous magic.

"Is this irony, Maximus?" I called to him. "One brother betraying another, only to capture his real brother in the process and tie us both onto cold metal tables. I never did understand the meaning all that well, but I think there's some ironing going on here."

"Just focus," Max insisted. "See if you can get a hand free."

"I think I want to believe in something different. That Jerome is going to jump out of a cupboard any second and start laughing and laughing, telling me I'm such a fool for doubting him, that of course he'd never drag me away to a tower in the middle of the Polar Capital where a dodgy scientist can extract my Order. Yeah, I'm gonna go with believing that."

"Sin," Max said heavily and I rolled my head to look at him beside me. "Jerome Novius has done unspeakable things to other Fae his whole life. He uses his allies and slides a knife in their backs the moment they're no longer useful to him. Me and my father have been heading the FIB hunt to find him for years. I've seen the images of what he's done to people, I've been sick to my stomach with it. Do you really think you're an exception to his ruthlessness?"

I fell quiet, all too quiet, quiet enough to hear the buzzing of the bees inside my head. I wouldn't care to listen to most Fae's opinion on things, but Maximus was my little bro. I had to try and hear him out.

"If I let that truth slip in and rip its way through flesh and bone, I fear I won't be the same Fae once it permeates my blood. My demons are already crowing in the back of my skull, they're riled up Maximus, riled up real good."

"So they should be," he gritted out. "He's used you, Sin. He's made his money off your back and now you're done dancing to his tune so he's sending his piggy to market."

"I'm Mrs Piggles," I rasped.

"What?"

I thrashed and bucked, fighting my restraints as rage coursed through me. "I'm Mrs Piggles!"

The door flew open and Vard swept into the room with a jar under his arm that glowed with a strange golden light. A group of nurses in scrubs walked at his heels and my ticker ticked up at the sight of Jerome in their wake.

"There they are!" I hollered. "The farmer and his flock! Oh and the butcher is here too, well I'm ripe for the picking, sugars. Come on then, cut me and gut me. I only ask for one itty bitty final request first."

"And what is that?" Vard drawled.

"Let me out of these chains and give me a fair fight. Scrap that! Make it unfair. UnFae too, if you like. But give me freedom and a chance to go down swinging, without magic or my Order if you really prefer." I gnashed my teeth at Vard. "How's that for an offer?"

"We have an operation to get started. Two in fact." He glanced at Max who sneered at him. "And we are suddenly under a little time pressure."

"Would that have something to do with the Dragon roars that keep carrying from outside?" Max asked and I glanced at him, finding a glint and a glimmer in his eyes.

"We have a minor inconvenience at our door, that's all," Vard said dismissively. "Now." He directed his nurses towards us. "Get them prepped. We'll do them at the same time."

"Anything to add, Jeromeo?" I called to my foster brother and his features hardened. "Any tricks up your sleeve? Laughs in your laugh-hole?"

"No, Sin," he said coldly then nodded to Vard who was glancing between us curiously. "Continue."

My jaw gritted, teeth grinding and cogs whirring in my ears. "Jerome!" I bellowed as he turned to leave. "This is all I'm really worth to you then?" I breathed, my voice cracking, betraying my pain.

"You've been a meal ticket for me, Sin Wilder. But it had to expire eventually."

"I dare you to watch then," I hissed. "Or are you not Fae enough to face the consequences of your decisions?"

Jerome's jaw ticked then he pressed his back to the wall and raised his chin, telling me he was going nowhere. The nurses placed their hands on me, starting their work and I let out a manic laugh that sounded like a witch's cackle. "Take me then! Cut me open and see what's inside but beware, little fiends, for once you open the cage of my flesh, you'll find nothing inside but a curse waiting to deliver itself upon your sorry souls. For I am Sin Wilder, creature of candied chaos and all those who cross me end up in bloody pieces."

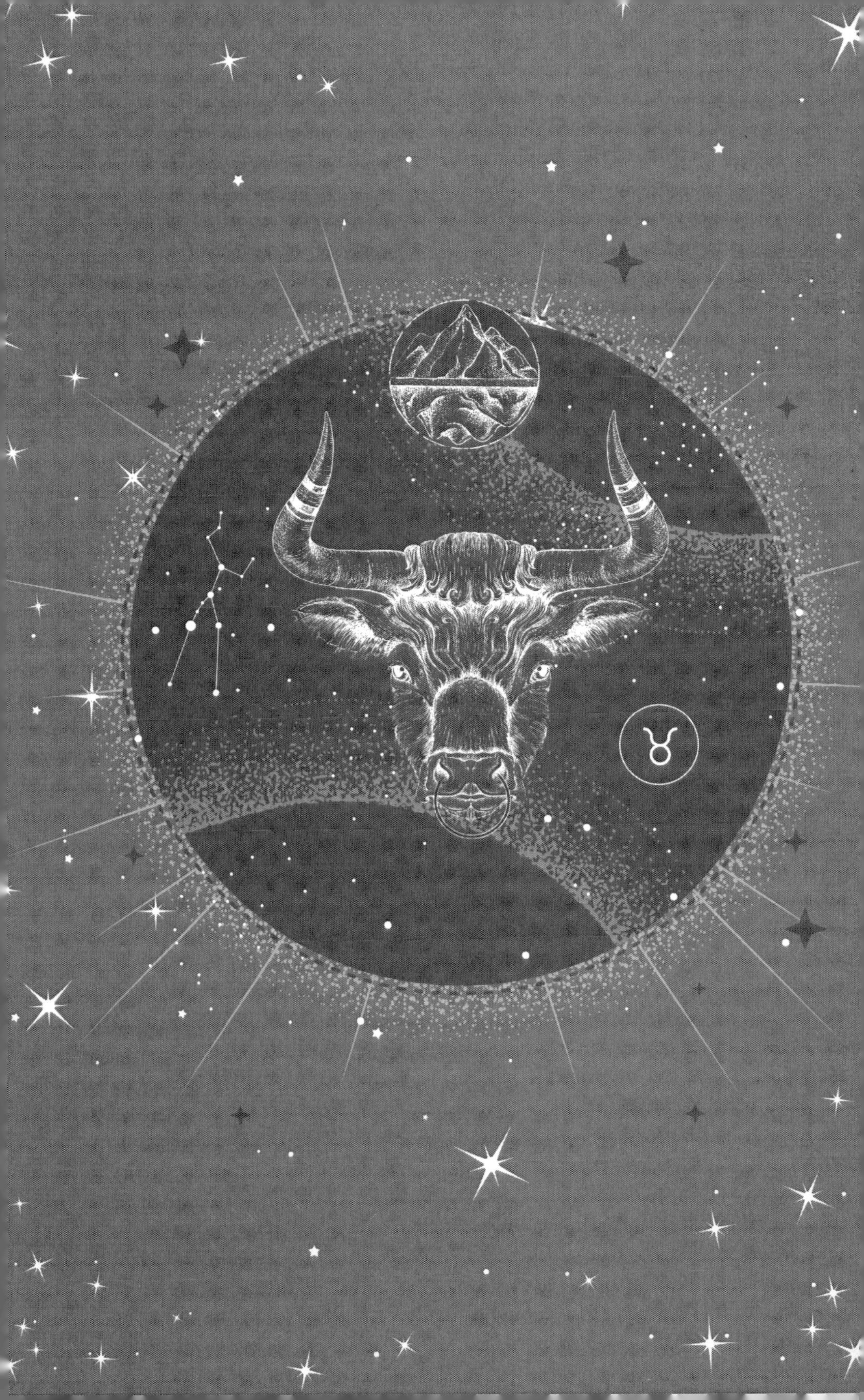

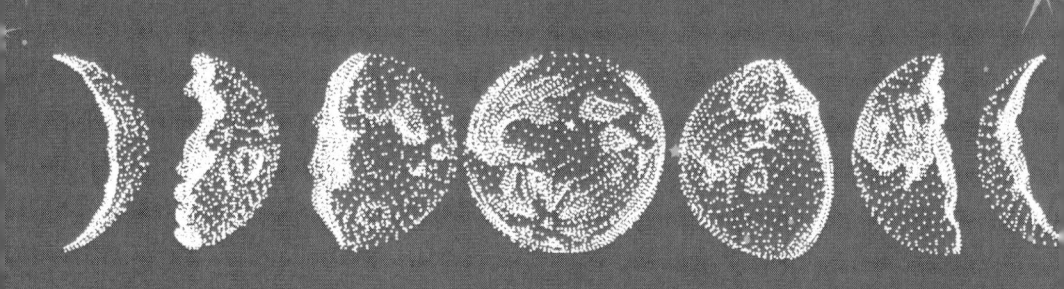

Rosalie

PRISONER #12

CHAPTER THIRTY NINE

Bricks slammed into my back as the vines I'd used to catch myself forced me against them so viciously that they crushed the breath from my lungs.

The beast that had sent me tumbling from the tower had thrown itself into the sky once more, circling, scenting, hunting.

Air magic would have been all kinds of helpful around about now to cut off the scent I was offering it, but I had long believed that earth was the far superior element.

With a twist of my wrists, a platform sprung from the side of the tower and I severed the vines holding me so I fell to my feet, perching upon it.

The monster was still circling, its head snapping in my direction as it locked onto my scent once more and I set my feet as I called on my magic in anticipation of its attack.

Power brimmed within me, the shape of it taking form in my mind and I gritted my teeth as I looked the beast dead in its yellow eyes and dropped my hold on the magic which kept me invisible.

The monster bellowed triumphantly, tucking its wings and diving for me with talons outstretched and fangs bared. My pulse hammered in my ears as I stood my ground, watching as it sped for me, holding off with each passing second, magic making my limbs tremble before I released it in a blast which rocked through me so powerfully that my knees buckled.

Spears of wood exploded into existence surrounding the monstrous creation, iron-tipped points driving at it from all directions with the full force of my power.

The beast bellowed as it was impaled, blood spraying from it as its death howl shook the sky.

I threw myself to the platform as its corpse hurtled from the sky, a shell of rock blazing into being a breath before it collided with me.

The rock cracked, shards of it tumbling over me, but the shield held and the weight of the dead beast tumbled over me before falling towards the ground far below.

I banished the magic containing me and shoved to my feet, pushing black hair out of my eyes as cries for the warring Fae below me drew my attention.

I spotted the carnage left in Roary's wake after he'd ripped through the guards and made it inside, my heart squeezing with concern for him. But as my gaze skipped to the other side of the tower, I found Cain clinging to Benjamin's back as the beastly Dragon whirled through the air. Benjamin barrel-rolled low to the ground and Cain was shaken off of him, hitting the snow and leaping back to his feet.

The Dragon sped off around the side of the tower and Cain's head tipped upwards, his gaze snapping to mine and beyond, my name tearing from his lips in a panicked cry.

I whirled as a powerful wind blasted my hair over my shoulders, steel blades forming in my fists as I moved but I was already too late.

Benjamin Acrux charged through the sky, circling around the tower in his bronze Dragon form, fire spiralling from his jaws as he bellowed at me and my death rushed in on rapid wings.

I had no choice but to run, to hurl myself from the stone platform and dive into the open embrace of the sky beyond.

Heat washed over me as the flames scorched the side of the tower where I'd just been, the scent of singed hair filling my nostrils as I fell.

I dropped the blades I'd crafted, magic ripping from me as I hurled vines out in all directions, my fall too fast to allow me time to aim. I just had to catch hold of something, anything and I-

The breath crashed from my lungs as Benjamin collided with me, his sharp talons snatching me into his grasp and squeezing so tight that it felt like he might crush me.

Cain roared my name again, a fireball tearing past me and colliding with Benjamin's scaled face but the Dragon barely flinched, his body immune to the effects of simple fire.

Benjamin dove for Cain, a roar spilling from his lips which shook the clouds in the sky above us.

My flesh began to glow with the power of the moon as I fought to get free, but the gifts I had claimed from her were no use in battling a Dragon.

Pain exploded through me as his talons squeezed tighter, a sharp crack telling me he'd broken ribs. The agony was near blinding but I fought through the haze of it, knowing the taste of pain far too well to let it immobilise me.

Magic tore through me, a spear forming between my hands and with a cry of effort I drove it up and into his armpit where the strength of his scales was compromised to allow the movement of his limb.

Benjamin howled in pain, hurling me from him as we closed in on the ground.

I threw my arm out, trying to soften the earth before I could collide with it, but Cain launched himself into my path with a snarl of fury.

His arms latched around me as I struck him, the two of us crashing down onto the softened dirt beneath the snow and rolling across it at speed.

We slammed to a halt and I wheezed out a breath around the pain in my ribs as I blinked up at my Vampire with a smile on my bloody lips.

Cain pressed his hand beneath my shirt, healing magic sliding into my body and taking the agony from me as he repaired the damage to my bones. But as I looked over his shoulder at the Dragon which spun through the sky before once again aligning itself to attack us, I had to think that he had wasted his time.

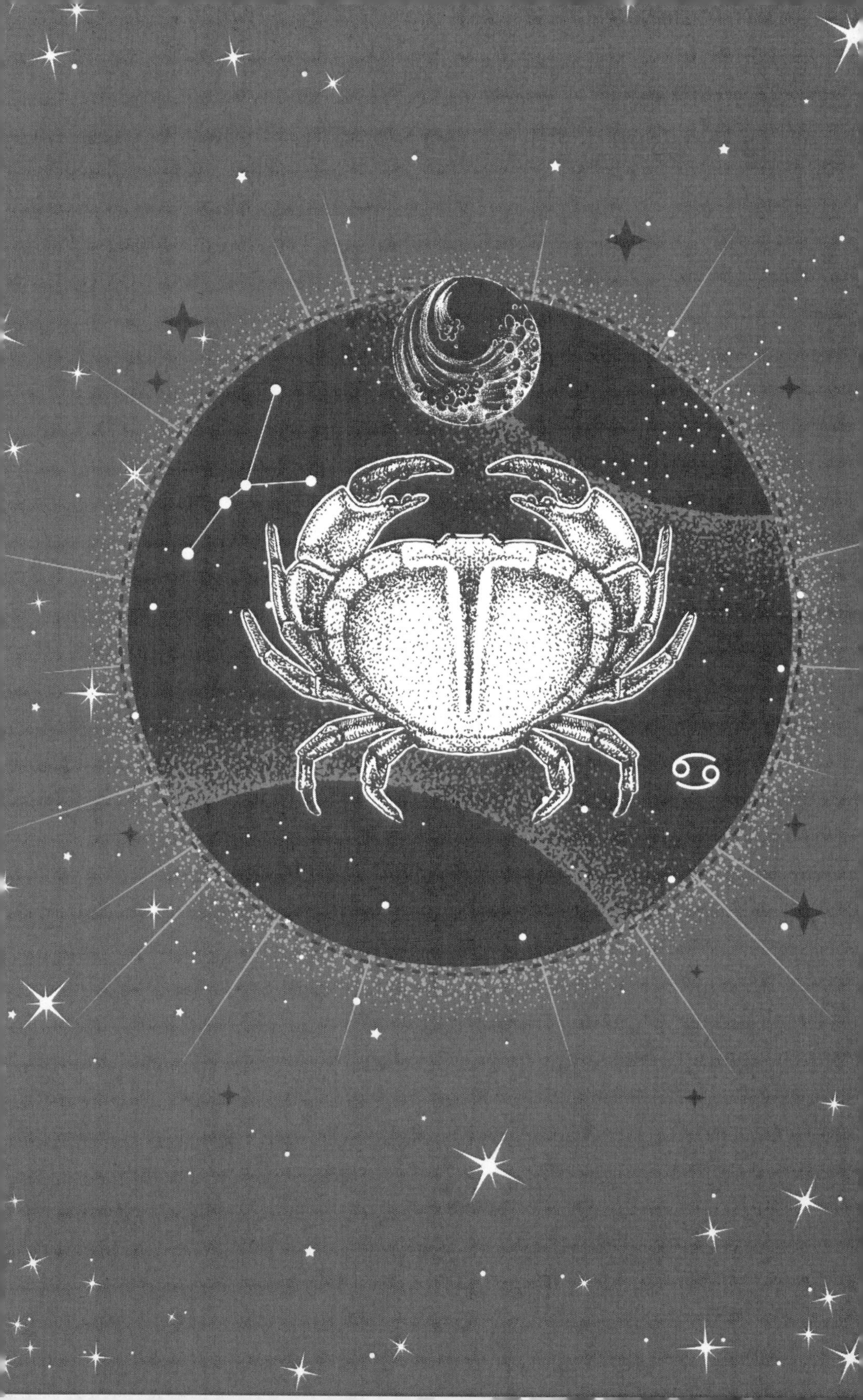

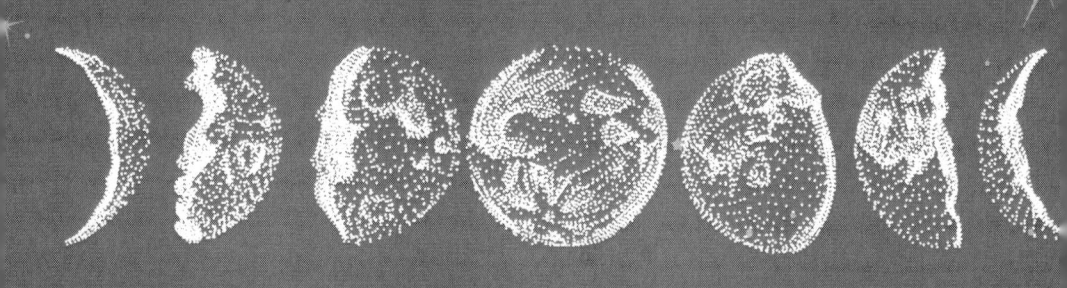

Hastings

OFFICER

CHAPTER FORTY

I ran faster than a bobcat on a bobsleigh, my arms pumping, legs whirling as I raced past Shadowbrook and the monstrous thing that had once been Gustard as they fought. I glanced at them as I passed into the tower, taking in the way Gustard lunged at Ethan, how the Wolf had fallen to his back beneath him, the bloodlust in Gustard's eyes as he raised a hand tipped with wicked claws.

He'd be fine.

I ran on, charging into the dark and baying like a bloodhound as I formed a whip of water in my hands and started circling it over my head.

I found myself in a dimly lit atrium, stairs spiralling upwards from the centre of the tower but doors led off to the right of the structure too.

I stalled, uncertain which way to go.

A loud bang made me shriek and I lost my hold on my water-whip, the magic falling apart and crashing down over my head, drenching me through.

I cursed, drawing the water back out of my clothes and scuttling towards the closest door as another loud bang came from up the stairs.

It was probably better to check behind the quiet, unassuming doors than to barrel on up the stairs where the sounds of carnage and death called out to me anyway. Far more likely that Wilder and the other fellow who he had forgotten to introduce me to were simply hiding away down here in the warmth of these rooms.

"Holy gobnuts," I squawked as I snapped the door closed at my back and lights flared to life overhead automatically, illuminating an operating theatre. There was only a single occupant in the room. A man was strapped to the table, face down and butt naked, his ass in the air where he had managed to push himself onto his knees, the underside of his hairy balls and short Johnson waggling in the direction of my face.

I slapped a hand over my face to shield me from the sight but quickly dropped it again as I heard the door lock at my back.

"Come back, have ya?" a familiar voice crooned and I gasped, my head whipping back and forth between the locked door and the man on the table.

"Twenty-four?" I hissed in astonishment.

"Who's there?" Plunger hissed, waggling his ass so that his balls slapped the insides of his hairy thighs.

I grimaced and side-stepped around the table to see his face and confirm my suspicions.

Plunger's eyebrows rose as he looked at me, one side of his face squashed to the metal bed he lay upon where he had pulled himself back as far as he could manage to allow him to thrust his ass into the air.

"Well wobble my jelly beans," he purred. "Is that my knight in shining armour I see before me?"

"What are you doing here?"

"That is a long and lingering tale which started with a wild night in the company of a lonely lemur."

"Erm…" I took a step back, glancing around and wondering if I should just move on, find Wilder and his brothers and forget I ever found this particular specimen lingering here.

"I always knew you were one of the good ones," Plunger crooned. "You always did me gently on the cavit-ah searches. You have a tender soul."

"I really need to find Sin Wilder and-"

"I seen him!" Plunger called. "I can lead you to him. Set me loose and we can find him together."

I winced but truthfully I couldn't come up with an excuse to leave him there like that so I looked around the room instead. "Where are the keys for your shackles?" I asked, moving towards a cabinet by the far wall.

"They took them when they left me here," he sighed. "But worry not. You see that bottle of oil over there?" He gestured with his chin towards a shelf and I nodded hesitantly. "Baste me up good with it and I can shift and slip free of these binds in a wink of an excited bum hole."

"I dunno…" I hedged, not liking the sound of that at all but there was a loud bang and a howl from beyond the door and a small yelp escaped me before I scrambled over to grab the bottle of oil. "Why do they even have this?" I asked as I moved back towards Plunger who was waggling his ass from side to side more forcefully now.

"I had it with me when they captured me," he explained. "I don't never go nowhere without something to get me slippy in a jiffy."

I wrinkled my nose, unscrewing the cap and squirting the oil at the shackles binding Plunger's wrists.

"More!" he cried as he shifted, swathes of excess skin appearing over his bones, the rolls of it bunching around his wrists and ankles as he tugged on them.

I squirted some oil at his ankles, trying to stay back but the bottle was hard to squeeze and the oil only dribbled out of it so I was forced to move up to his side.

"More!" he howled louder, his voice muffled around the star-shaped nose which now dominated his face.

I squirted again then cried out as his ass slammed into my chest, knocking me from my feet.

"Tug me!" Plunger yelled in time with a wild roar coming from the far side of the door and the thing rattling on its hinges as some beast collided with it.

I yelled out, scrambling upright and grabbing hold of Plunger around the waist, tugging with all my strength while my boots slipped in the oil which had puddled on the floor from the dropped bottle.

The beast roared again, Plunger's ass slapped me in the face and I screamed as the doors threatened to give way, death racing for me with increasing certainty, my final moments a nightmare which I would never be able to purge from my memory.

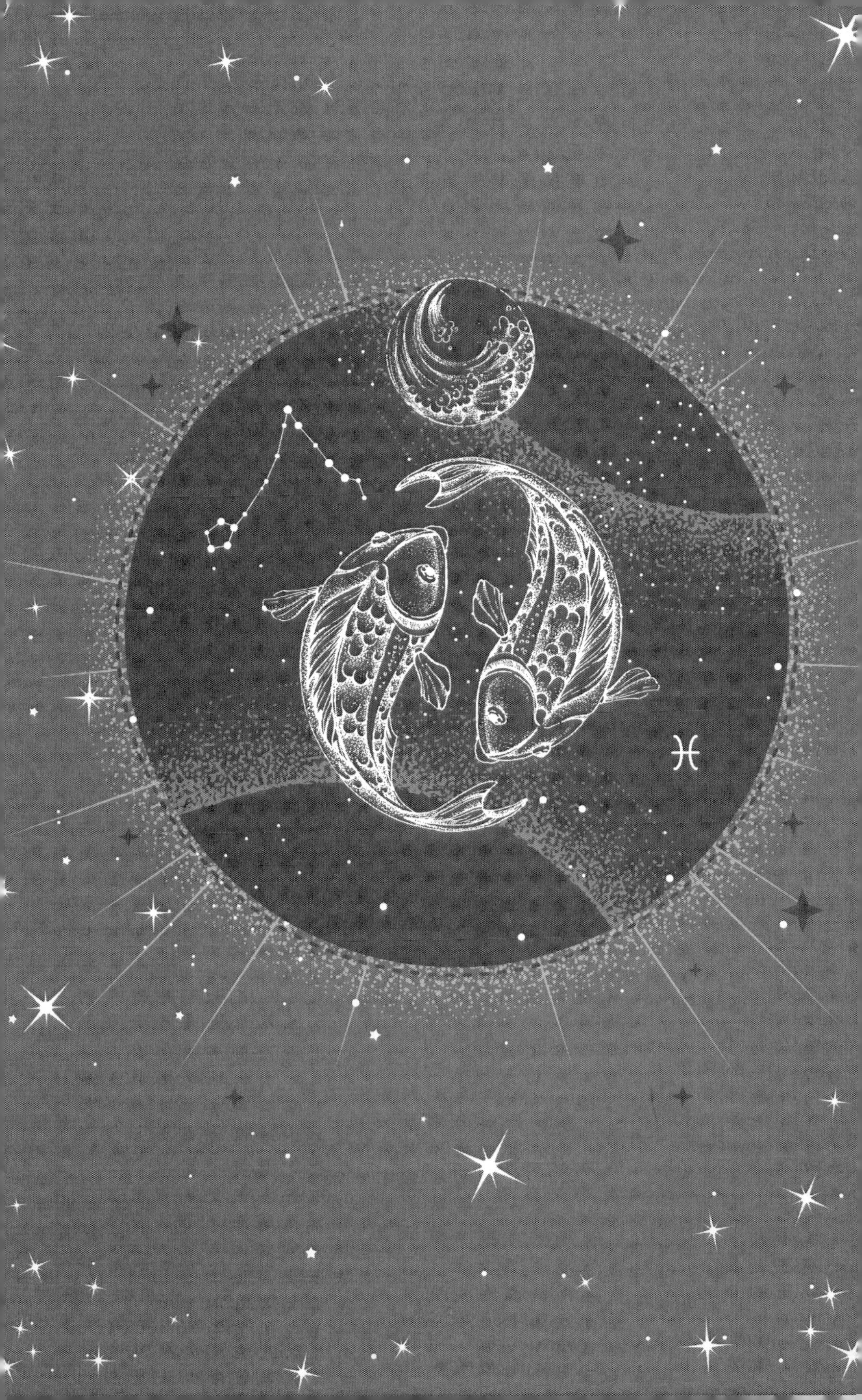

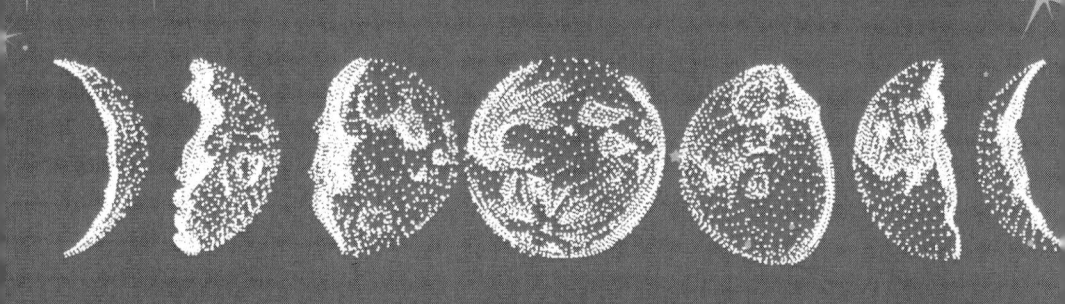

Roary

PRISONER #69

CHAPTER FORTY ONE

I'd only made it up a couple of flights of the twisting stairway when more guards had flooded down them to intercept me. They came at me in droves and I was forced to defend myself time and again, my Vampire speed not much good to me here when they were packed so tightly together that there was no chance of me cutting through them and killing as I went.

Instead, I had to dodge and duck the barrage of magic crashing my way and I was sporting plenty of burns and cuts thanks to these assholes. I killed as swiftly as I could, the ones I'd taken down piling up on the stairs and causing more of the guards to stumble, giving me an opportunity to kill them. But this onslaught couldn't go on forever and I had to be running thin on luck.

A fireball went whooshing past my ear and scorching the very ends of my hair in the process. I had to change tactics before I made one too many mistakes and ended up dead.

Summoning the force of my power, I cast water into existence further up the stairs, creating a torrential flood that blasted into them from behind. Cries of alarm went up, the cascade happening so quickly that even the water elementals among them could do little to stop it. They were sent smashing into each other with the water slamming into their backs and I leapt for the closest window. I broke it with my fist and swung myself outside as the flood sent them all tumbling away down the steps.

A dragon's roar split the air apart and my thoughts went to Cain.

"Stay alive, brother," I muttered under my breath then I hurried along the soaked stairwell, shooting up it in a burst of speed.

I checked the corridors I passed, seeking out any sign of Sin or Max and praying it wasn't too late for them. My hearing didn't pick up anything of note in these passages so I doubled backed to the stairs and kept climbing. My ascent slowed each time I found a door or corridor to search, but if this forsaken tower had belonged to me, I knew exactly where I would keep my most prized possessions. And that was at its very peak. So I forged on, climbing higher still only to find another line of guards racing my way.

I bared my fangs, more beast than Fae as I prepared to intercept them. Somewhere in this building my Lion was waiting for me, but while it anticipated my arrival, I would show my enemies what a bloodthirsty Vampire I could be.

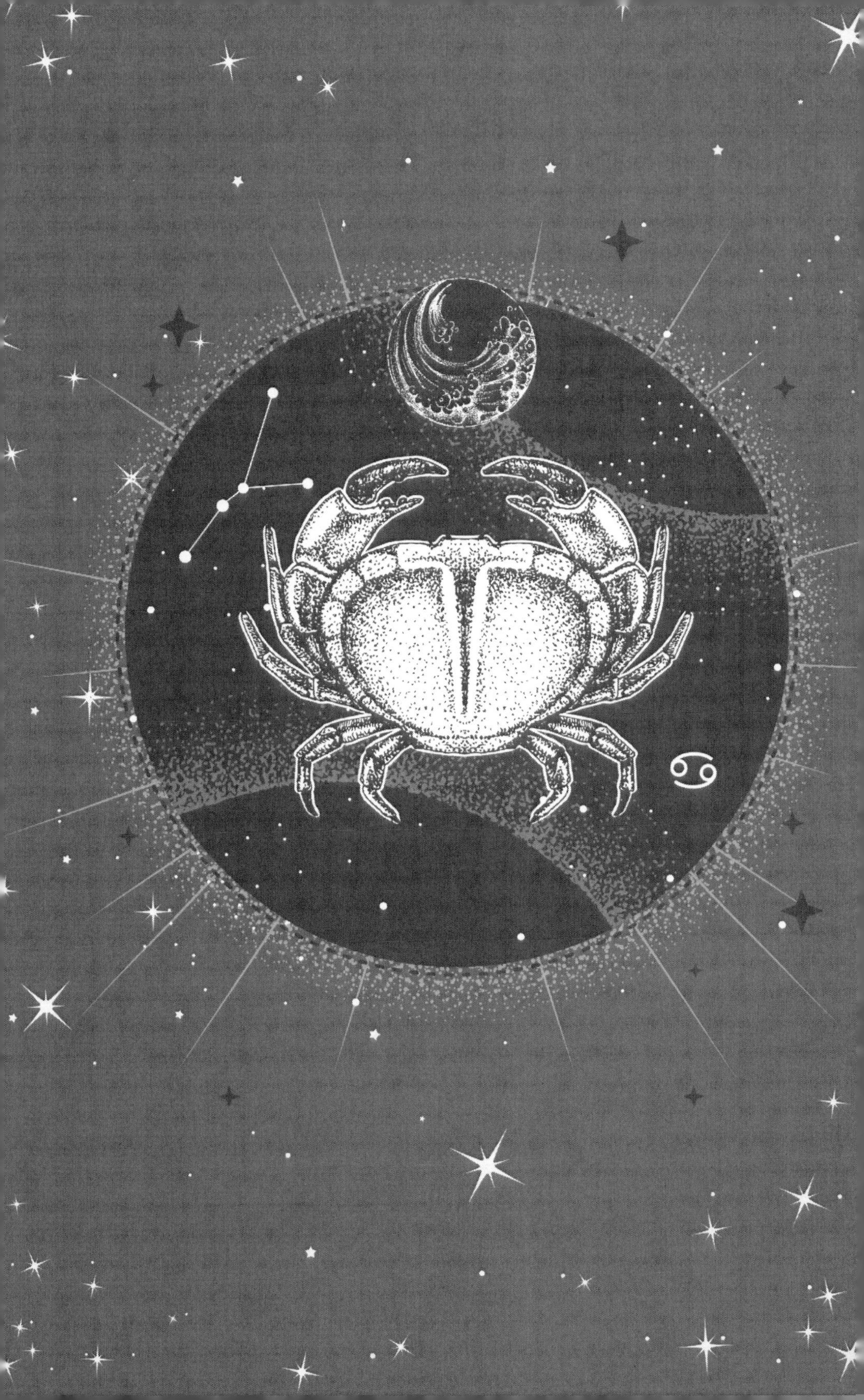

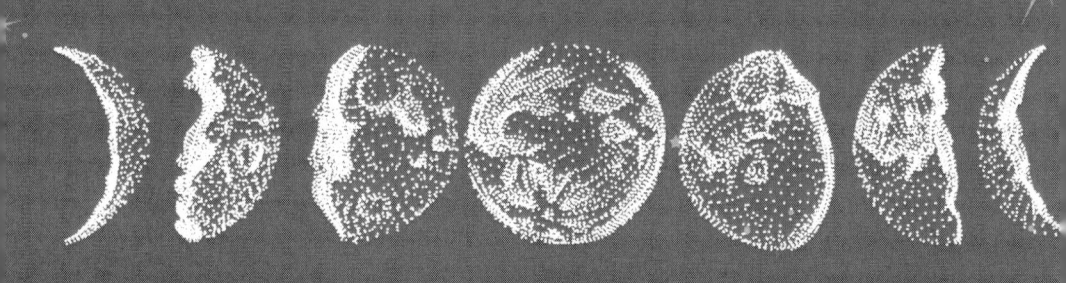

Hastings

OFFICER

CHAPTER FORTY TWO

I wrenched with all my might, my hands slipping over folds of skin, Plunger howling excitedly while the doors rattled wildly under the assault of whatever the fuck was beyond them.

I cried out as I fell backwards, Plunger's weight crashing down on top of me as he was finally wrenched free of the shackles which had held him to the table. But my screams were smothered as he fell on me, his ass slamming down on my face, my nose delving between his oil-slicked cheeks, his balls slapping the back of my throat as they fell between my parted lips.

Plunger toppled aside, rolling across the tiled floor with a whoop of triumph, leaving me retching and sobbing in his wake.

Horror enveloped me as the reality of what I'd endured spilled through all the dark pieces of my soul, tainting everything they touched and staining them with this memory.

I would never be the same again.

I'd seen things now. Lived through horrors untold. Smelled the worst life had to offer. *Tasted* things.

I heaved again, vomiting all over the floor then lunging away as Plunger patted me on the head like I was a good dog.

"There now," he crooned. "I knew you'd do me nicely."

"Argh!" I hoisted myself to my feet, stumbling away from him through a patch of my own vomit, my eyes watering as the oil from his flesh dripped into them.

"You still hankering after the Incubus?" Plunger asked, shifting back into his Fae form, though I wasn't certain which was worse as his little cock bobbed while he bounced on his heels.

"Yes," I choked out, looking away, glancing at the door which had finally fallen still.

Silence reigned beyond it. Had the thing which had been so desperate to gain entrance to this place gone or was it out there still?

"This way, sir," Plunger called, beckoning me after him as he scampered across the room, drawing open a door I hadn't even noticed beyond the cabinets that lined the back wall.

Plunger dove through it and I was left with no choice but to follow him.

We stepped out into a brightly lit corridor where numbers lined a row of doors, though they ran in no sequence I could discern.

Plunger seemed to know precisely where he was headed though, scurrying along, the slap, slap, slap of his bouncing cock punctuating his steps.

I gagged again, pressing the back of my hand to my lips to stifle the noise as I followed as close to him as I could bear to place myself.

Plunger hurried all the way to the end of the corridor then pointed at a door marked with a number twelve which seemed oddly fitting after all that we had suffered to get here.

I rallied my strength, casting a blade of ice in my hands before nodding at Plunger to get him to open the door.

I bellowed a battle cry as I charged into the room, the sight of Sin and his brother on two tables there only causing me to pause for half a second.

There were Fae in medical scrubs surrounding them, bloody blades poised over chests which were being cut open right before me.

Vard cried out, lunging at me, a jar clutched in his arms which sparkled with golden light. He threw a fist at me but the sound of Sin bellowing my name, the sight of his open chest and the group of Fae content to go along with this horror show consumed me just as the memory of Plunger's balls tickling the back of my throat rose its head once more and I vomited straight into his face.

Vard yelled out, throwing himself backwards while Plunger tackled the closest nurse, taking him to the ground.

"Come here, puppy dog!" Sin called, a big smile aimed my way despite the clamps currently holding his chest cavity open. I latched onto that smile, that one point of brightness in this sea of sick depravity.

I swung my arm back then hurled the ice blade at him as hard as I could, my years of training on the Pitball pitch serving me well as my aim stayed true. The blade severed the leather strap securing Sin's wrist and the Incubus called my name to the heavens in praise.

"Hasslings, you're a miracle man!" he yelled and okay, he'd gotten my name a little wrong, but I'd done it! I'd found him and freed him and followed the destiny which Rosalie had set out for me and-

I barely registered the man who ran at me from the corner of the room, only realising he was at my back as a fist coated in stone collided with my skull. And everything fell into darkness.

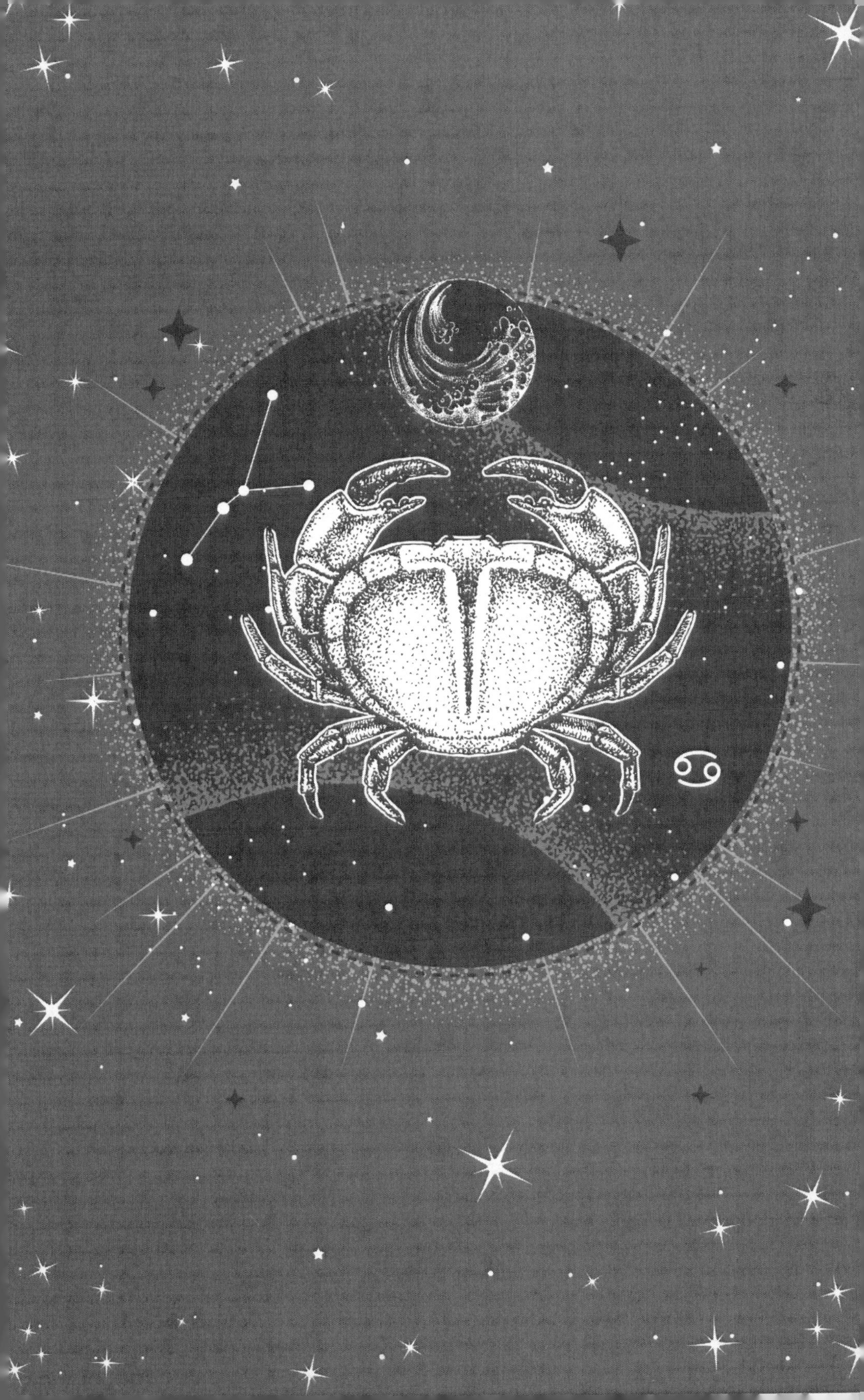

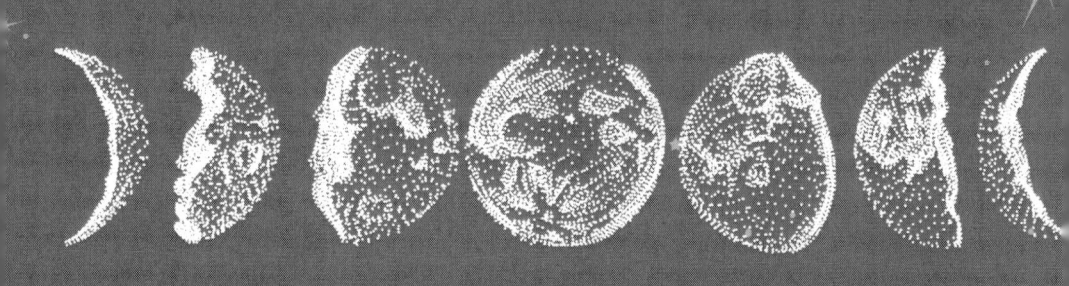

ETHAN

PRISONER #1

CHAPTER FORTY THREE

I was battered, exhausted but still full of all the wrath of battle. This beast wouldn't get the best of me. I was a Shadowbrook and Gustard was nothing but a ghost in the shell of a monster.

He swung at me with bloody claws and I ducked back, missing the attack by mere inches, but despite losing a hand, he had still landed plenty of blows. I was torn between healing myself just enough to continue the fight and not burning myself out of magic before the moon could restore it. I ran as often as I could, letting the light of the moon seep into my skin and recharge me, but there wasn't time to run enough. Gustard kept coming, throwing his weight at me and trying to get me off my feet. I never stopped moving, side stepping and blasting him with shards of ice.

His skin was torn from my attacks but still, he didn't slow. His body was a machine built for war, and I was the sole soldier in his sights.

He swung for me again and I cast a shield of ice against my arm a beat before his claws impacted. The shield shattered, taking the worst of the hit, but Gustard's hand closed around my arm and he swung me at the wall of the tower.

I slammed into it, my head cracking against the stone and blood wetting my mouth as I slumped into the snow at its base.

Fuck.

Get up.

Come on, get up.

My limbs were leaden, the world spinning too fast for me to see straight. The hulking shape of Gustard closed in on me and my hands wouldn't react as I willed them to move. For magic to rush into my fingertips and blast an attack at this monster who had dared laid hands on my mate. He'd had his vile gang beat her in Darkmore, had left her bloody and bruised, and would have done far worse to her had he gotten the chance.

The thought of it alone set my blood boiling, my heart rioting with the need to protect her from Gustard once and for all. To seek vengeance on him for all he'd done to her, all he'd ever thought to do to her.

The crushing blow of his claws slammed against my head and I was knocked sideways, tossed like a ragdoll onto the ground while my vision swum even more. The hot, wet drip of blood slid down my neck and I knew what this came down to. A second, nothing more. That was how long I had left to act or death would come for me as swiftly as the wings of a nightingale and steal me away into the nevermore.

I didn't belong there. Not yet. Not while my Rosa still breathed. I would remain at her side, I would be her protector, her mate, her warrior.

A spear of ice formed in my grip and I rolled as Gustard leaned over me, preparing to finish me. One more swipe of those claws was all it would take.

A howl of pure love left me as I thrust the spear at his chest and stuck him under the ribs, my blade driving in deeper and deeper.

A screech tore from Gustard's throat as I pushed that spear in as hard as I could, using the full force of the strength I possessed. It sliced through him like a hot knife through butter, punching out of the other side of his body and ending him with a finality that made me release a heavy breath.

Gustard's screeches were silenced and I shoved him backwards with a grunt of effort, rising to my full height as I did so and gazing down at the dead monster at my feet.

I pressed a hand to my chest through a tear in my shirt, sending healing magic into my veins while I caught my breath. The numbing air was stealing away the bite of pain in my injuries, but it was a relief all the same as they finally knitted over.

My gaze shifted to the open doorway and I stalked inside, ready to help track down Sin, Max and the Lion Order that had been stolen from my brother.

I gazed at the stairs and started up them, the wail of dying Fae carrying like birdsong all throughout the tower. And I knew that my pack mate had to be close.

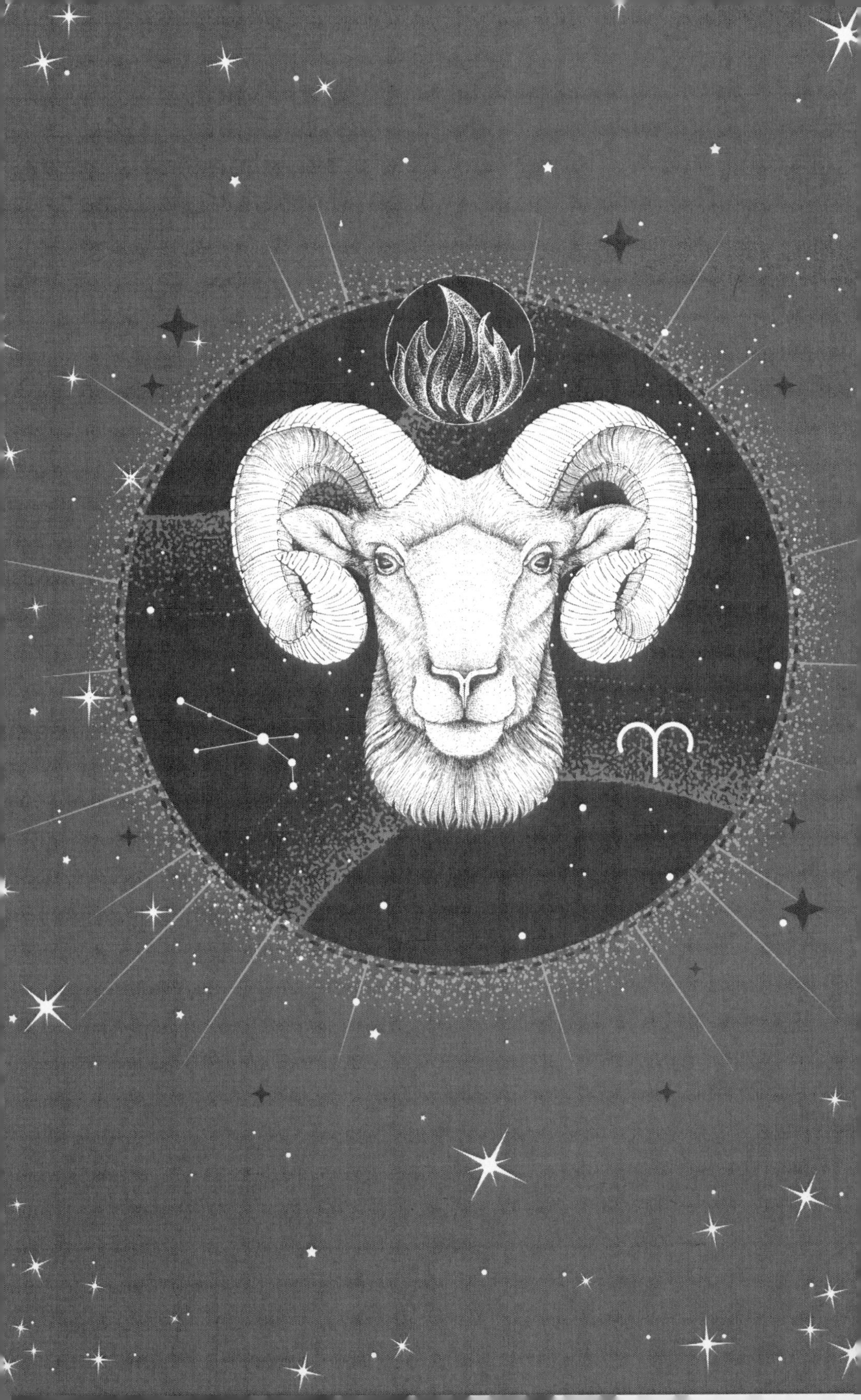

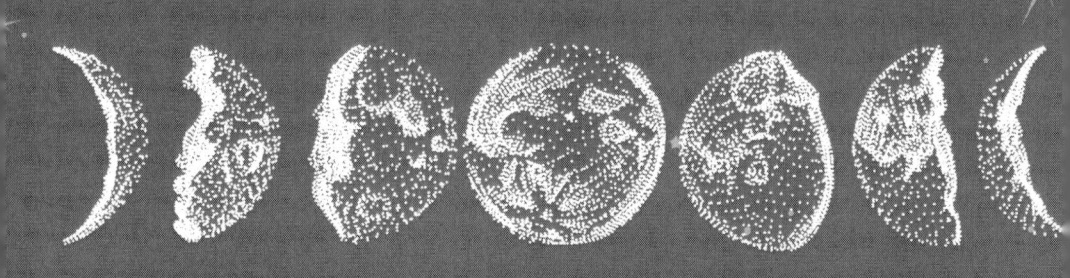

CAIN
COMMANDING OFFICER

CHAPTER FORTY FOUR

Benjamin's beastly form swept overhead and I swung a flail of flames at his underbelly with a growl spilling from my lips. It crashed into his scales and threw him off course, his wings beating to try and counter the strike, but Rosalie sent chains of metal out to capture them, binding them to his sides and bringing him to the snowy ground in a collision that rocked the earth.

He struggled to get free, his immense bulk shattering one of the chains and I knew my time was almost up.

"Kill him!" Rosalie cried, running around to Benjamin's jaws, trying to strap his mouth shut with her chains. The red glow of the fire in his throat shone through his scales and I saw the blast coming as Rosalie's binds snapped and his mouth flew open.

"No!" I bellowed, shooting forward with a burst of speed and shoving her out of the way as the fire blasted from his jaws.

It slammed into me and I was thrown onto the ground from the force of the flames, engulfed as they burned into my chest. The snow melted around me in a pool as Benjamin towered over me and blood bubbled at my lips. His gaze turned to Rosalie as she stood to face him once again, but a snarl left me at him looking at her with a promise of death in those murderous eyes.

Rosalie cast a dagger in her grip, hurling it at him, aiming between his eyes but it deflected off of his scales, slamming down into the earth beside me.

The scent of burnt skin and the bloody hollow in my chest made it hard to move, my fingers flexing with the need to heal myself, but I was almost tapped out. Benjamin was about to blast hellfire at her once more and with just a scrap of magic left to me, I took the fallen dagger into my grip and swore on the moon that this woman would not die at the jaws of my oppressor.

Within a whip of fire that could have cracked the sky in two, I sent the dagger flying towards his open jaws, every ounce of power I had left going into the cast. It slammed into the back of his throat and drove upwards at the will of my fire, slicing in with a certainty that could only equal death.

Benjamin roared, his legs shuddering, eyes wheeling from Rosalie to me as horrified realisation found him. Then he came crashing to the earth, his life leaving him in a rush, finally releasing me from the chains of my past.

A heavy breath left me and it was laced with all the what ifs I had hoped to claim in this life. Rosalie was crying my name. I swear I heard the moon whisper to me that I had done well and then the world was too dark and death was tearing me away from the sole Fae who owned me to my core.

Death stole all chance for goodbyes, the sureness of it closing in around me and guiding me from Rosalie Oscura. She was the last thing I saw, haloed by moonlight with my name on her lips. And peace found me through the love burning in her eyes. Because if there was one thing in this world that had been worth giving everything for, it had been her. Forever her.

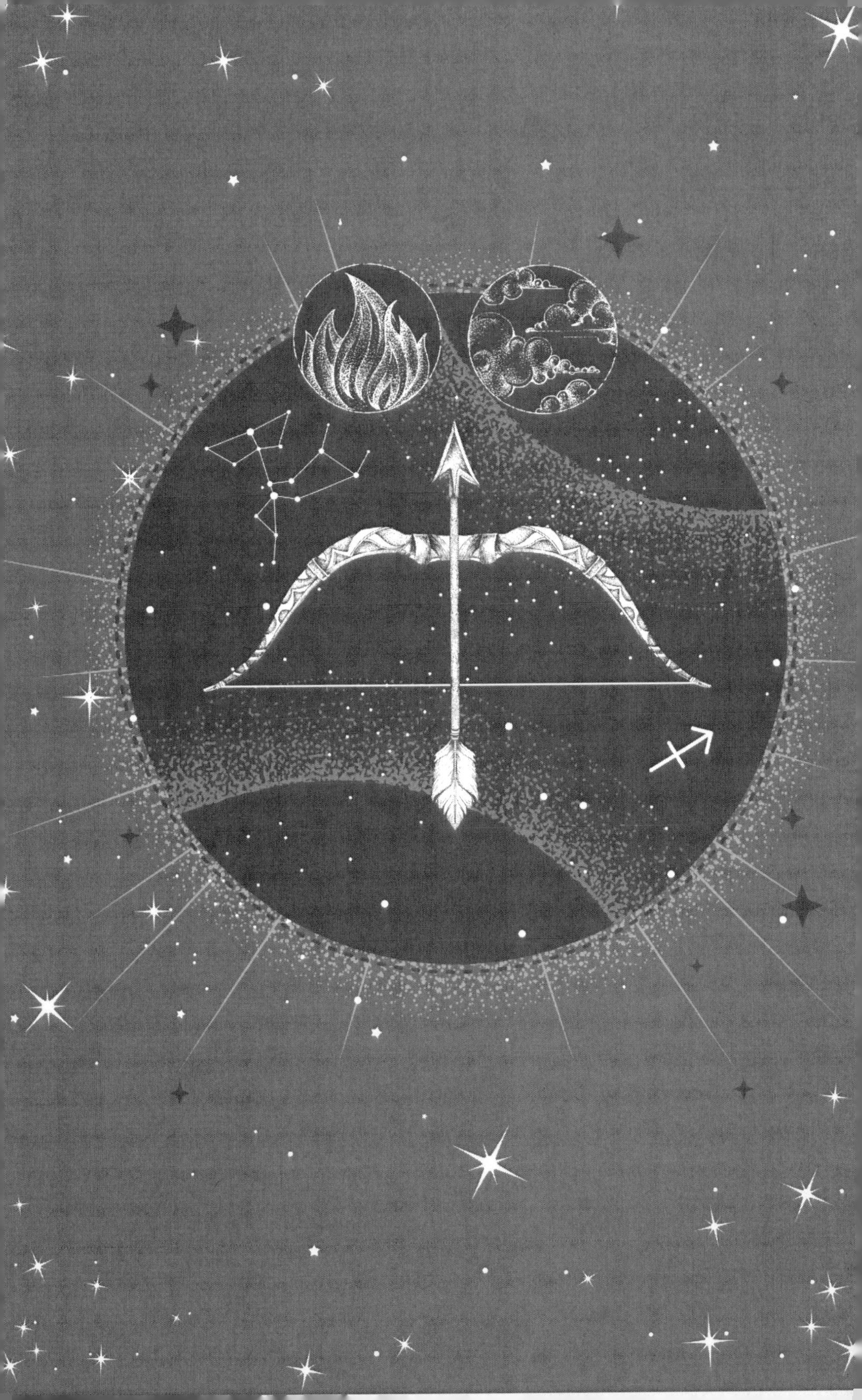

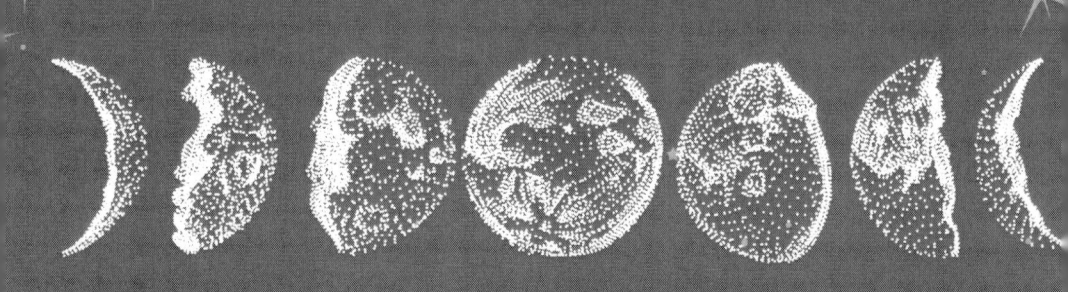

SIN

PRISONER #88

CHAPTER FORTY FIVE

With my chest agape and bloody, I'd torn the key to my magical cuffs from the pocket of a weaselly looking nurse then bit his ear off for good measure before releasing myself along with my magic. Now I was thick in the fray, bringing down a world of carnage upon the unfortunate souls who were close enough to taste my wrath. But they had caused this, they were sinners of the stars, their essences nothing but soot and cinders. I'd reduce them to less than that when I was done here.

Casting a chain of fire, I swung it around my head like a lasso and caught a fleeing little nursey around the shoulders. A sharp tug of my magic sent him skidding across the room to land at my feet. And what a place to be when your death was written in the sky.

"Time to go to sleep," I growled, casting more lashes of fire around his limbs, ripping him apart with them until his screams stopped screaming.

Two more nursesy-pies came at me at once, magic and fury crashing against my air shield, but I was not just any Fae. I couldn't be caught by the weak and these two looked as fragile as toothpicks. My air magic dealt with the first, bursting his lungs with a pop and a hiss, the next went out more spectacularly. Blood splashed and screams painted the inside of my skull as I took his head from his shoulders in a way that could only be described as extravagant. But that was me. No one could make a disco out of death like I could.

"Sin!" Max yelled for the hundredth time, and I finally turned from my blood bath, the nurse's severed head swinging from my fist as I gave my brother the attention he desired.

"Yes, ma boy?" I called, tossing the head away and watching the arc of blood paint the walls in a red, red rainbow.

"The cuff key," he demanded and I threw him the slippery thing, ripping his restraints off of him too before turning to hunt down my next victim.

Vard had scarpered from the room already, Lion jar in tow most-likely, but he wouldn't get far before I caught up with him. However, the time for chasing Rolands into the night hadn't yet come, because I wouldn't be leaving until I was done making a pretty mess of this room. As I grabbed a scalpel from a nurse's hand and stuck it in her eye, I set her hair ablaze and whirled around, seeking out the one I needed to kill most of all.

Jerome was by the door, stepping over Hastings who was slumped on the floor looking as sad as a sack of lemons and making a bid for escape, tossing a fearful glance over his shoulder at me. I grinned, my teeth still tasting of blood since my ear-ripping escapade and the sight of that got Jeromeo looking all kinds of terrified.

"This is what you wanted, brother!" I hollered as he sprinted out into the hall. "Deep down, you knew what would happen if you crossed me!"

Max sat up as he got his magical-blocking cuffs off, healing himself and aiming his hands at a male nurse, taking the asshole to the ground with a blast of water.

I gave him nod, leaving him to finish off the last of the minions and prowling after Jerome. The time had come for vengeance. The slow kind. The take-my-time over it kind. It was a show, this was, the warm-up act had finished and now it was time for the main event. The crowd were holding their breath in anticipation, the curtain was rising and the one they had all come to see perform stood centre stage in his costume of destruction.

I felt Max being pulled after me by the spell our father had cast on us and the fight followed him into the hall at my back.

Jerome raced down the corridor, tossing a wall of earth out behind him to slow my pursuit. I punched a hole in it with air, barely missing a step as I continued after him, a predator in the night, taking my sweet, sweet time.

Jerome met a dead end, raising his hands to blast a hole into the wall that blocked his exit, but I whipped out a finger and barred his way with a powerful air shield.

I boxed him in, enclosing him in a cube of air and watching as he struggled within it, trying to break out like a fly caught in a greenhouse.

He turned to me, his eyes frantic, that usual coolness about him lost to terror. I had that effect on people. Maybe it was the way I did my hair, or how I dressed. Something about me unsettled folk for sure, but I'd never thought I'd see the day when I unsettled Jerome.

I cocked my head to one side, regarding him with a sharp tug in my heart, like a small duck was living in there, pecking at the insides. Glenda, I'd call it. Or perhaps its cousin was Glenda and mine was called Eduardo. Either way, my heart duck was unhappy and it had everything to do with the man in my box.

"Jeromeo," I sighed. "Why?"

Such a simple little question, but oh how many sorrows it held.

He shook his head, a little breathless as he searched around him for a way out, but his gaze only landed on me again. His throat bobbed then he hitched on a smile, one that made me frown and think. I couldn't place the emotion, it was eluding me, just a mosquito dancing in the air, buzzing around my ears, but I missed every time I swatted at it.

"Sin," he laughed, though it sounded a little tight. "You won the game!"

"The game?" My frown grew frownier.

"This. All of it. It was a game, just like you said. I wanted to see how far

I could take it. Hasn't it been fun?" He laughed again, though it was thick, shaky.

"It has been fun," I admitted. "Those chains holding me down tickled a bit. That was good. And the bit where I killed all those screamers, I liked that."

"Yes," he said keenly. "I knew you wanted them all dead. I led you right here to them. It was all part of the plan. For you. I did it for *you*. My brother."

"Brother," I exhaled, a smile to my voice, but my frown inched in again. Something wasn't adding up. Two plus two equalled five, everyone knew that. But this? I wasn't coming out with the right answer. Like all the numbers were jumbled, giggling as they pranced out of reach. "You did this…for me?"

"Yes, Sin. Of course I did," he said fervently, moving to the edge of my air box and pressing a hand to it. "Now come on, let's get out of here. We'll go together. We'll never look back. We can start afresh, it'll be just like before. We can head to the woods, we'll find Mrs Piggles."

I liked that thought. Me, him and Mrs Piggles. But it was missing some people now. I needed more than my brother and a pig in a nice scarf to keep me happy, and that was telling of how much I'd grown. "What about Rosalie? And Roary, and Ethan, and Cain, and our pet Hasslington?"

"They can all come too. But we'll go together now and find them later."

"Maximus can't stay here alone." I looked back over my shoulder where my brother was still thick in the fight, the screams pitching through the air and splash of blood telling me he was doing a fine, fine job of murdering our foes. We really were of the same blood. And I wasn't going to abandon him here.

"Well he…he's too wrapped up with the law. You can see him another time. He'll be fine here, he's the strongest Siren in the kingdom, Sin. But you and me, we gotta get out of here before the FIB show up."

He offered me his hand and I reached for it, dropping my air shield and taking hold of his palm. His fingers tightened on mine and he tugged to draw me closer, but I resisted, the creases on my brow getting deeper.

"I was on that table with my chest open…"

Jerome's throat bobbed.

"They were about to extract my Incubus. Take it out and not give it back. Was that part of the game?"

"Course not," he blurted. "I was about to step in."

My fingers locked tighter around his, crushing them in my grip. "The numbers in my head are balancing on top of each other, and they're giving me an answer I don't want to see, but I think I can't unsee it. It's looking me right in the eye."

"What are you talking about?" Jerome tried to pull his hand from mine, but I didn't let go.

"They're stacked up and chirruping the truth at me, Jeromeo. Why'd you do this? Why?"

He snatched his hand away, a blade appearing in it as he used his earth power and with a swipe of his arm he stabbed it right in my neck.

The betrayal stung me like a wasp, the truth a monster that had been there all along, living in his eyes, always staring out at me. I'd been used. Used like an old rag to scrub a filthy window. And Jerome knew how I felt about being used. He knew I hated being the Incubus everyone needed, everyone except myself. And all along, he'd been the worst of all.

I ripped the knife from my neck and he backed away, preparing to cast again, but I was upon him like a wraith, latching his limbs to his sides with air while driving his own knife into his chest.

We hit the ground and his pleas and cries for help punctuated every stab of the blade into his body, his death a cruel thing layered in pain. I dragged it on for as long as I could before silencing him with a final swipe across his throat. A ragged noise of pain left me as I leaned down and kissed his forehead, hating him, loving him, my brain just a casket full of lamenting souls, all wailing their grief and bidding Jerome goodbye.

I was confused as I sat beside him, his body twitching and blood bubbling at his lips, his death coming slow but with a certainty there was no avoiding.

I tossed the blade beside him, a traitor's weapon ensuring a traitor's grave. "That's how the cookie crumbles, I suppose. You betray and lie, then you get what's coming in the end. Either that or the bad guy wins, and I don't let them do that, Jerome. You became bad to the bone, and I put Fae like you in deserving graves. It's what I'm best at, what the stars made me for, I think. It's why I'm cracked, because only someone shattered inside could do the things I have to do. But so long as I'm still here walking this earth, I'll keep putting them in the ground, planting them like daisies. It keeps worse from happening. Kiddies shaking in their beds at night, worrying when the mean man will come home to hurt them. I make sure they don't come home, and if the world fears me for delivering justice to monsters, so be it."

A hand pressed to my shoulder and healing magic flowed through me, stealing away the sharp pain in my neck. Looking up, I found Maximus there, taking in the tears on my cheeks and the hurt in my eyes.

"He got what he deserved," Max said darkly. "True brothers don't use each other. They don't sell each other out."

"Even if their brother is death in Fae form?" I rasped.

Max took my hand, drawing me to my feet and cupping my cheek in his hand. "Even then. I think I'm starting to understand why you do the things you do, Sin. I see why they want you locked up, and I see exactly why you shouldn't be."

I leaned into him and his arms came around me, his embrace firm and bracing. Trust was a little bird placed in the hands of a goliath, and when that trust was broken, I need only remember I had the wings to fly away.

A clash of fighting rang out further down the corridor and we took off towards it, a whoop leaving me as I found Ethan there. Of course he'd come. And that meant Rosalie and the rest of her pack were here too.

Ethan was fighting with a group of guards, their numbers forcing him backwards. We raced in to join the fight at his side, his eyes brightening at the sight of us. The guards were fierce, driving us back and back until we were forced to blast a wall apart and retreat outside into the snow.

A bellow made my heart skip and leap, and from the depths of the shadows from whence we'd come, a beastie or five came racing into the battle, some of Vard's twisted creations with all their teeth and claws and ugly glory. The true fight was just beginning, it seemed, and I was alive with the promise of death upon the air.

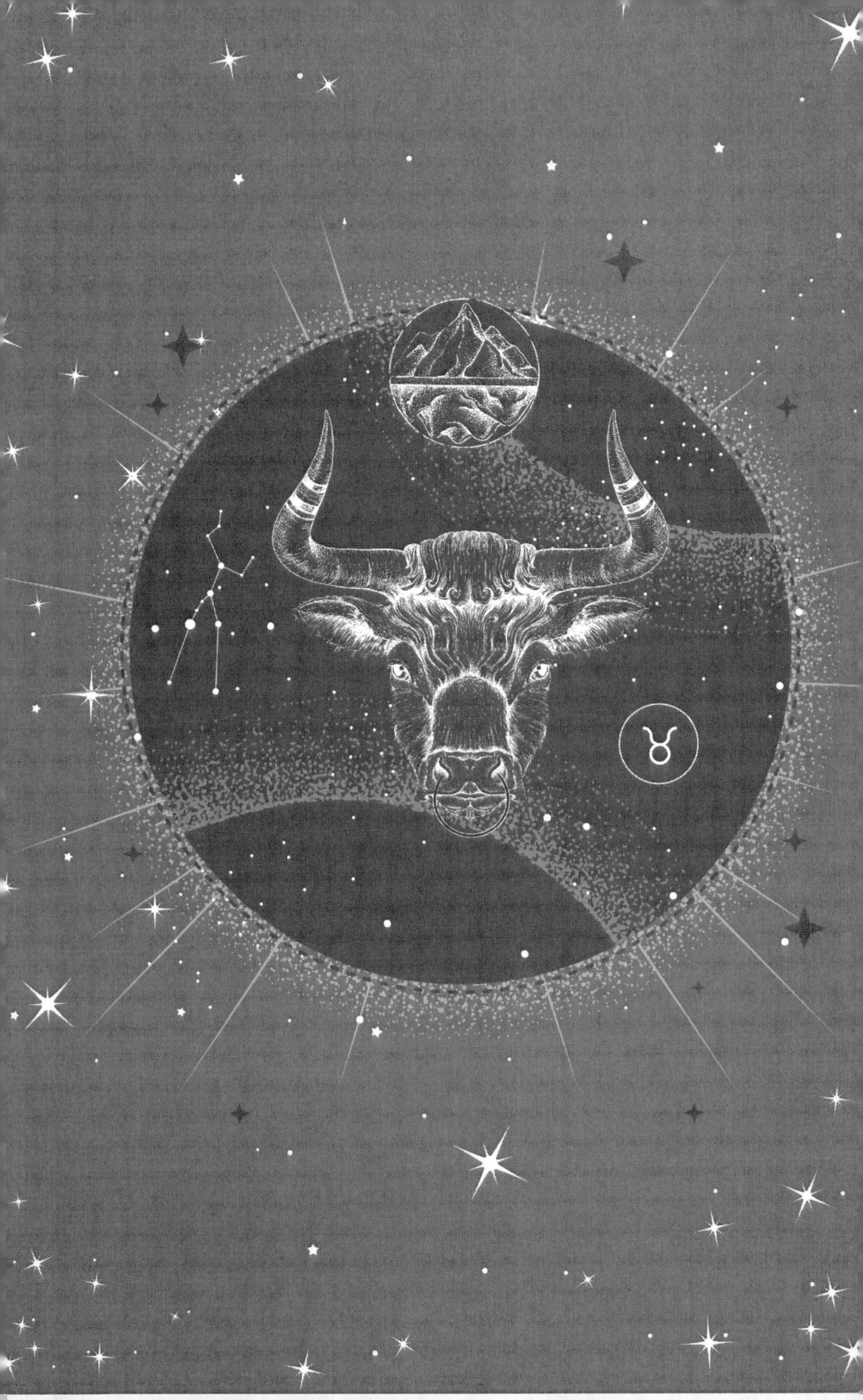

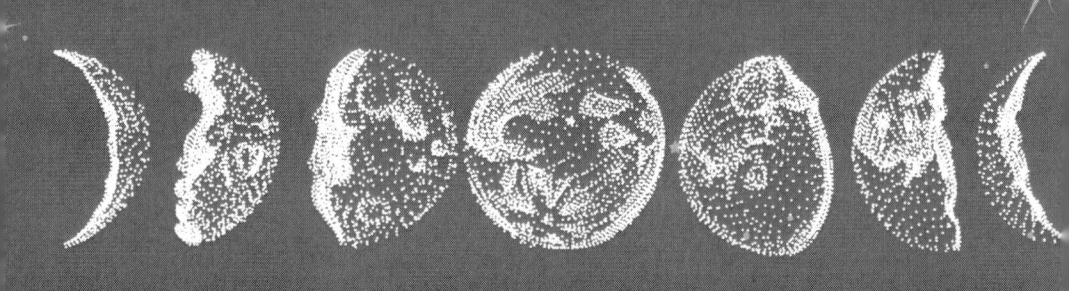

Rosalie

PRISONER #12

CHAPTER FORTY SIX

"**M**ason," I gasped, scrambling across the ice and dirt which separated me from him, the blood of the Dragon he'd killed in his final moments staining the ground all around us.

Benjamin hadn't shifted back into his Fae form upon his death the way most Fae did and the hulking mass of his dead body shadowed the fallen form of Cain before him.

I dropped to my knees at his side, taking his hand and gripping it fiercely, tears burning the backs of my eyes as his fingers failed to curl around mine.

"You can't leave me," I told him, a snarl riding up my throat with the words, my skin tingling with power as I called on everything I was, trying to force healing magic into his flesh.

But I couldn't find the thread of his magic to bind mine to. Couldn't find that intrinsic piece of him which defined the place his soul and his power mixed, creating an alleyway for my own magic to tether to his.

My view of his features shimmered and blurred, tears marring the bloodstained skin, making it harder for me to look at him.

His shirt had been burned from his flesh in several large patches, the curse which I had given him standing out starkly even through the blood and gore that stained him. It had spread. Further and further it had spread until it coated him like he was a canvas constructed for its art.

I shook my head, my insides twisting into a sharp-edged knife as I looked at the stain on his flesh and felt the weight of their burden. The moon had cursed him for my sake and now I felt the heavy shackles of responsibility weighing down on me too. I'd done this. I was the one who had spoken the words. His fate might have been different without this tarnishing his destiny.

"I won't accept this fate," I growled, my gaze lifting from Cain's too-still features and finding the sky above where clouds shrouded the celestial being who was bound to me as surely as I was bound to it. "I won't."

My skin tingled as power grew within me, the cool light of the moon shimmering to the surface of my flesh and lighting me up from the inside out.

The clouds themselves seemed to pay attention as more light spilled from me, coating me in armour and calling out to the moon to face me and they parted to make way for her to see me.

Moonlight puddled over us, dripping from the sky, soaking us in its light as surely as if we had been doused in water.

I clung to Cain harder, my eyes burning with the brightness of the moonlight as I glared up at the sky and bared my teeth.

"He paid with his life for mine," I spat. "He gave everything so that I might survive. But what is my survival worth if I can find no joy in it? Every moment of my life has been tarnished by the pain I have suffered in one form or another. At the hands of my papa, in the brutality of war, from the loss of the man I loved to that underground hell and now this? How much more will you watch me suffer?"

The moonlight continued to spill from the sky, falling over us in sparkling lumps which appeared like snowflakes. They tumbled past me, all of them moving with purpose, directing themselves onto Cain, touching down on his skin and melting into his flesh in every place where the curse had stained it.

I sucked in a sharp breath and held it, my tears spilling down my cheeks then falling still as I watched in amazement while the moon washed him free of the curse, every piece of it fading away until nothing at all was left.

But as I tightened my hold on his hand, expecting his lids to flutter, his grip to close around mine, his lips to part on a ragged breath, instead I was gifted nothing but that stillness.

I shook my head, refusing to believe that the moon would abandon me now, when I needed her more than ever, when I was so close to shattering without her.

Because she had heeded my call to break the curse.

But that wasn't enough to return Cain from the claws of death.

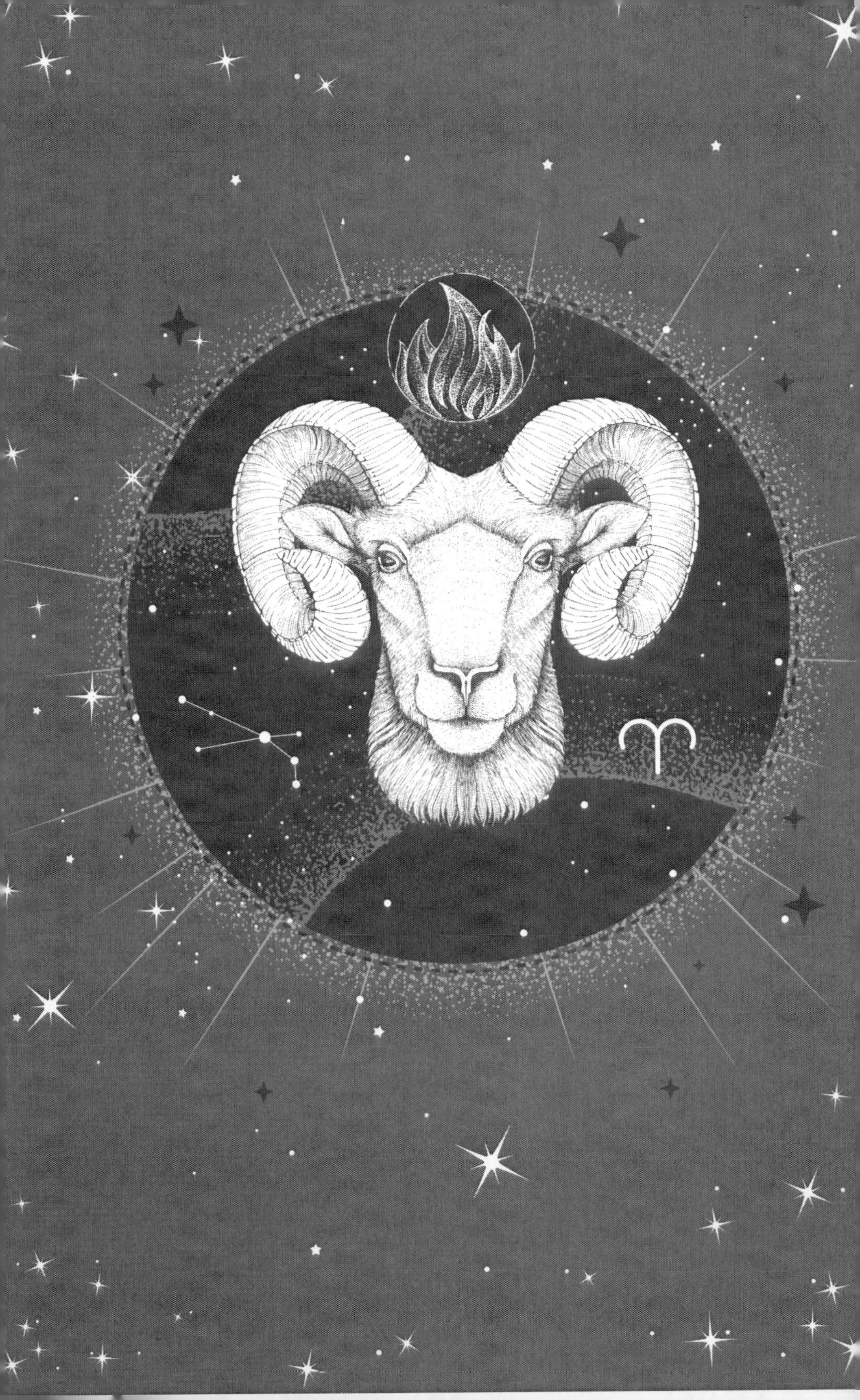

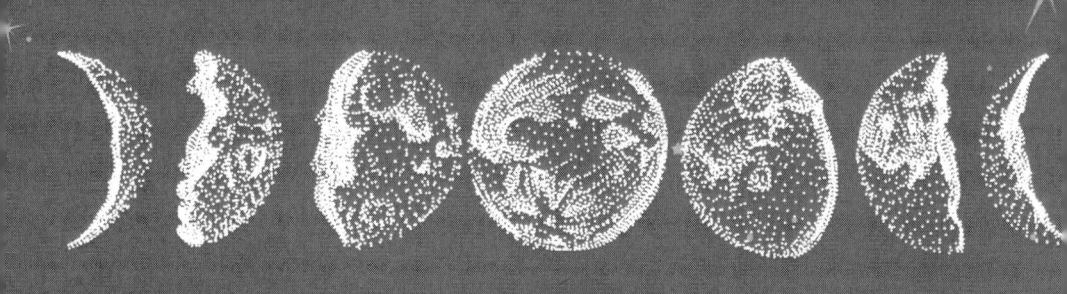

CAIN
COMMANDING OFFICER

CHAPTER FORTY SEVEN

"Mason?"

The voice was familiar, haunting in ways, but so damn comforting too. I looked up, finding myself kneeling on a riverbank where a golden mist hung in the air. Across the eerily still water was a boy with warm eyes and a bright smile. Merrick looked just as he had the day he'd died, youthful, full of life, but there was an ethereal quality to him here in this strange place.

"I'm sorry," the words I'd wanted to say to him all these years spilled out and his form burned a little brighter.

"It wasn't your fault," he called and the weight I'd been carrying since his death finally eased enough that I could breathe. So simple were those words that it was hard to believe the impact they had. "Benjamin's soul has been delivered to the Harrowed Gate where all the damned ones go. Come see." He held out a hand in an offering and the river seemed to shrink, like he was suddenly nearer.

The slap of a paddle hitting the water made me turn my head and a hooded figure came drifting down the water. That heavy gold mist descended and I lost sight of Merrick as the figure approached.

"Mason Cain," he spoke in a withered voice, my name like a summoning that drew me to him. "It is time to cross into the after. Your soul is perched here because you are clinging to something that no longer belongs to you. Let it go and board my ferry."

I turned my head, sensing that very thing I was leaving behind, my thoughts latching onto Rosalie. It felt as though she was just there in the heavy mist that had descended at my back, like if I strode into it, I might find her there in the hanging fog.

"It is a blessing to be missed and to miss in return, it means you have lived well," the Ferryman said. "Now come. It is time."

His hand reached out from within his cloak, a gnarled, skeletal thing that curled around my arm. My skin lit at his touch as if with moonlight, a glow igniting along my flesh and making the Ferryman snatch his hand back.

"You are Moon Touched," he gasped. "It has been many, many a century since I have witnessed the power of She."

I looked down at my hands, the glow in them rushing across me until my soul shimmered like liquid silver. I couldn't feel my pulse but I could hear it, the drum of my own heart, so close, so near.

I turned and realised it wasn't my own heart at all but that of the Fae I had fallen so irreversibly in love with that nothing called to me louder than the song of her lifeforce.

"I'm here!" I called, standing abruptly, seeking her out in the mist, somehow sure that she was seeking me in return.

"I cannot take you," the Ferryman whispered, his voice akin to spitting fire. "The moon demands another fate."

"Rosalie!" I cried, stepping into the mist, reaching, running, hunting. "I'm here!"

Hands found me, wrapping around mine and pulling, her fingers ignited in moonlight just as mine were. I felt a force at my back, pushing me toward her and was sure the moon herself was guiding my soul away from this hallowed place.

I didn't look back, certain that if I did, death would find me once again. My gaze was set on the mist as those hands pulled and pulled, leading me back from this realm until a blackness swallowed me up that was impenetrable. The atmosphere was thick and putrid. My lungs hurt, everything hurt and by the stars it felt good because this was life. In all its pain and rawness, this was *living*.

I heaved in a lungful of air, my eyes flying open as I found myself on my back beneath Rosalie, her skin still shining with all the glittering beauty of the moon. Her tears were silver, crashing onto my skin and healing every wound on my flesh. I gazed at the miracle of her, then to the healed skin of my chest and finally to the bareness of the places the curse mark had once laid.

"Rosa," I gasped and her eyes flew open, her fear and grief sliced apart by joy.

"*Mason*," she groaned then her lips were upon mine and I tangled my hand in her hair, feeling the weight of her and knowing that there was nothing in this world that would ever take me from her again. In life, I would follow her, and in death I would find her.

A rush of power flooded my veins and as Rosalie drew back, we both looked to the waning moon marks that had ignited on each of us right over our hearts, like a symbol of the life she had just restored to me.

"You denied death my soul," I breathed.

"It wasn't death's to take," she said, her lips finding mine again. "You are my mate."

Those words stirred a world of desire in me, but as I drew her flush to my body, I remembered there was still much to be done.

"It's time to finish this," I said heavily and she nodded, rising to her feet and drawing me after her, our fingers intertwined and my need for her painfully sharp. When this was over, I'd never part from her again.

I took in Benjamin's fallen body, turning from him and knowing I wouldn't need to look back upon the past anymore. The future where all my focus lay,

My gaze settled on the entrance to the tower where a furious fight had spilled out onto the snow, guards and monstrous beasts battling with Sin, Ethan and Max, all of them closing in around us.

I felt a protectiveness wash over me that extended beyond Rosalie out to the men she had claimed as her mates and knew I couldn't see them fall this day.

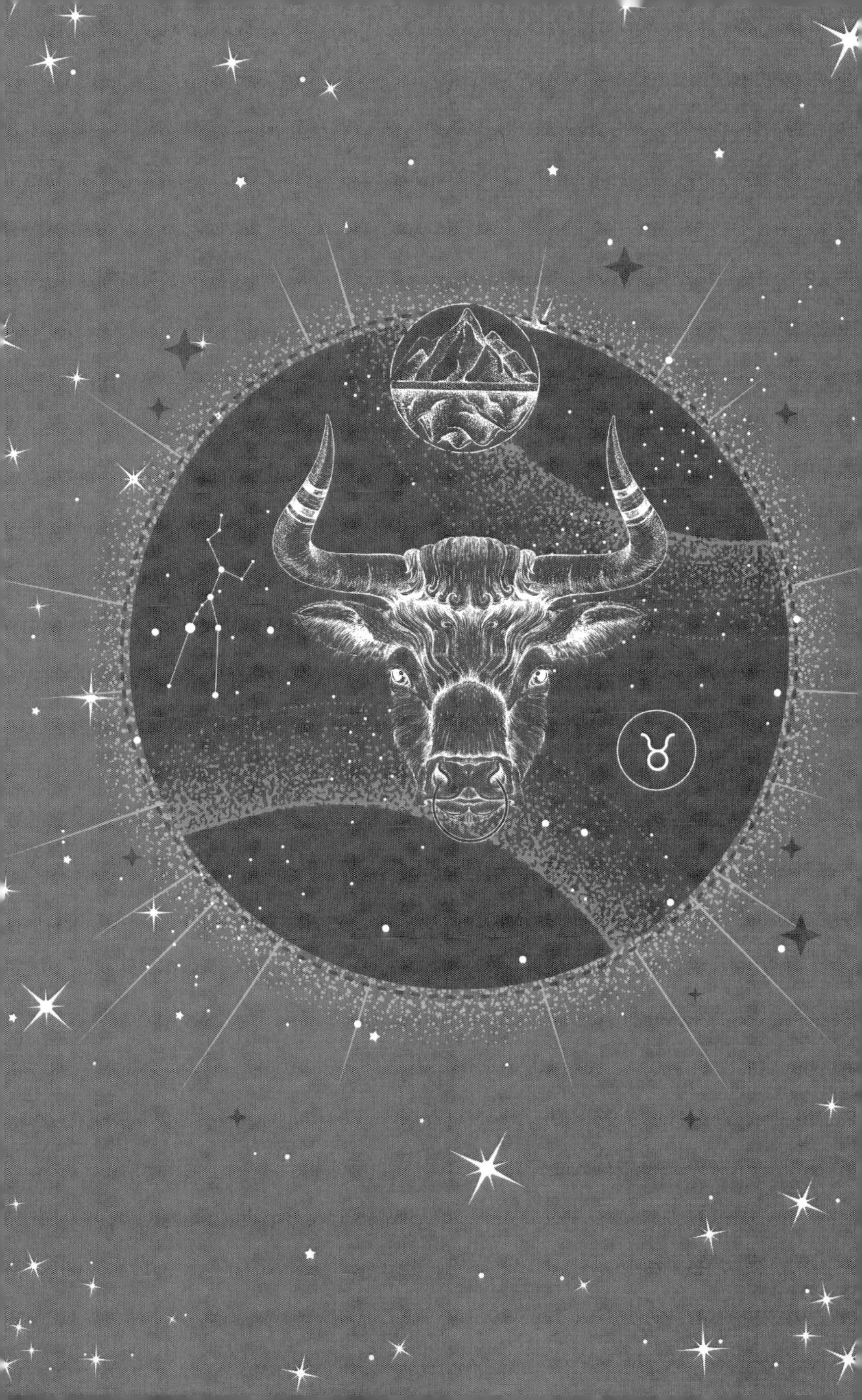

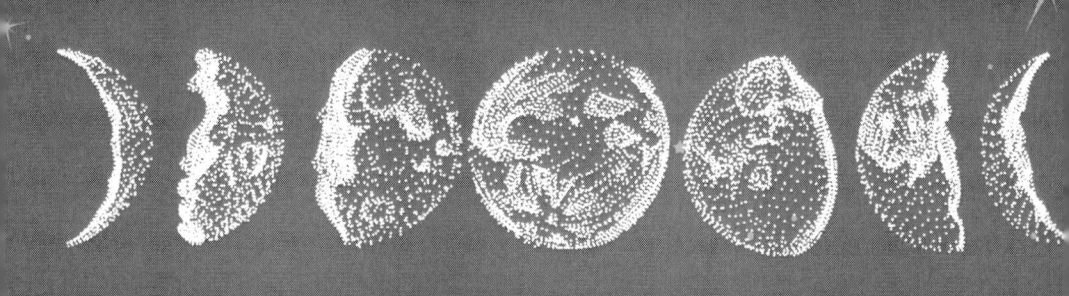

ROSALIE

PRISONER #12

CHAPTER FORTY EIGHT

I turned from Cain, my flesh still buzzing with the magic of what had just happened between us and my heart thrashing with adrenaline. It was a pure force of will not to tear the clothes from his flesh and claim him entirely right there in the middle of the chaos with the moonlight pouring down on us and blood staining my flesh.

But I couldn't give in to that urge just yet. Because a flash of movement had just caught my eye and I spotted Vard racing away towards the snow-covered mountains, his form already shrinking in the distance as he sped from the melee of battle.

"*Go*," Cain barked, his eyes following mine to the monster who was so deserving of the death I had in mind for him. "I'll clear you a path."

The guards and remaining monstrous creations were putting up a ferocious battle all around us; Ethan, Sin and Max all caught up in the fight with them and more still racing for me and Cain.

I looked around for Roary but couldn't spot him anywhere, my gut twisting with concern. But I knew what my mate would want me to do. He wouldn't want me hunting for him; he'd want me to chase after his Lion. So that was what I would do.

I gave Cain a sharp nod and he shot from me, ripping into the guards who had gotten closest to us and hurling a fireball into the face of a winged beast which dove from the sky in my direction.

Its shrieks of pain and fury filled the air, and I ripped my coat off as I broke into a run, hurling the fabric aside before wrenching my shirt over my head and tossing that away too.

I howled loudly, Ethan echoing the call from somewhere at my back as I unbuckled my pants and shoved them down.

I leapt into the shift, the last of my clothes falling from my body or tearing right off of it as I burst into my Wolf form and howled again, moonlight gilding my silver fur so that I shone far brighter than the snowy landscape.

The scent of terror filled my nostrils as I locked my gaze onto Vard and with a snarl that curled my lips back from my teeth, I raced after him into the wilds.

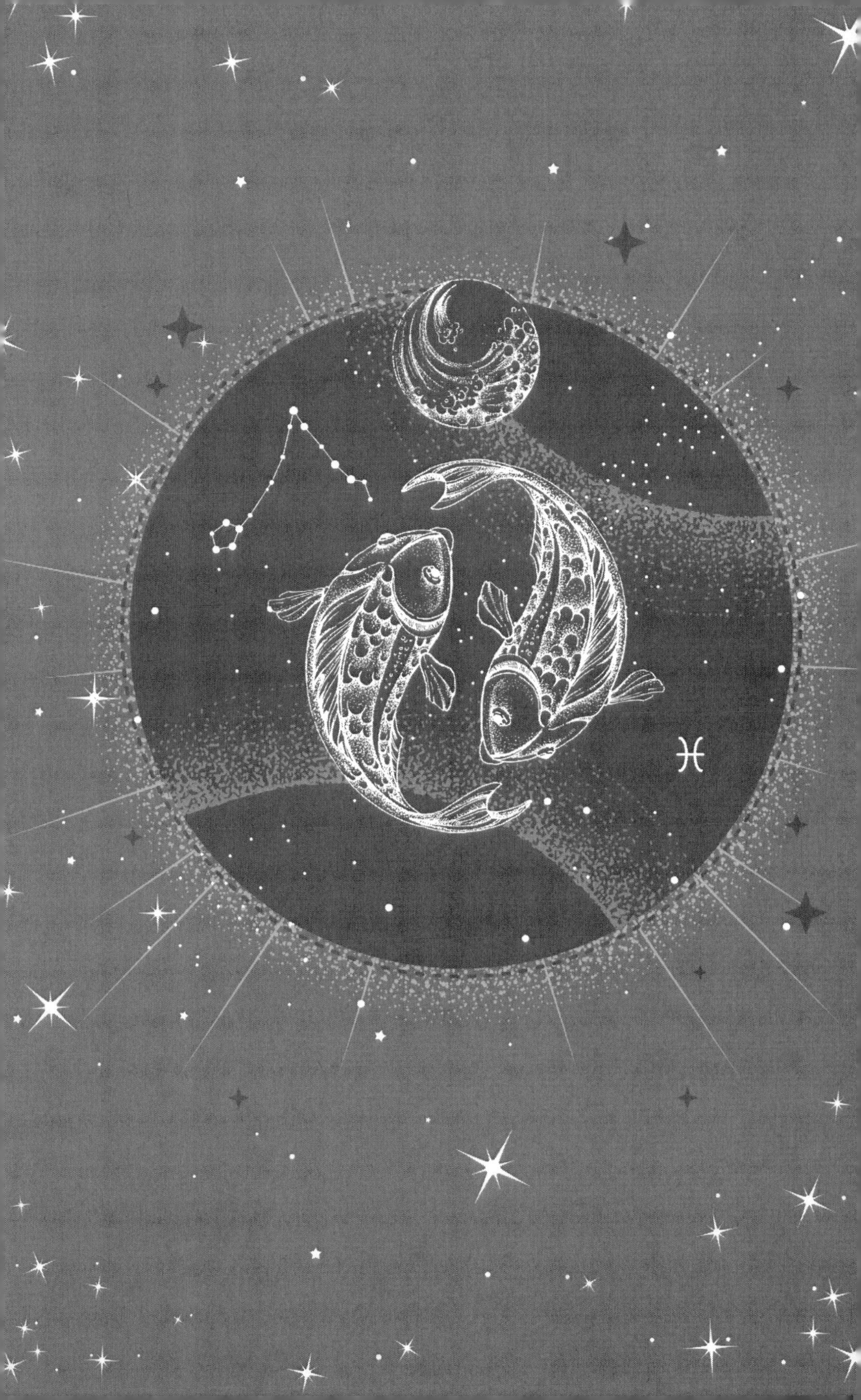

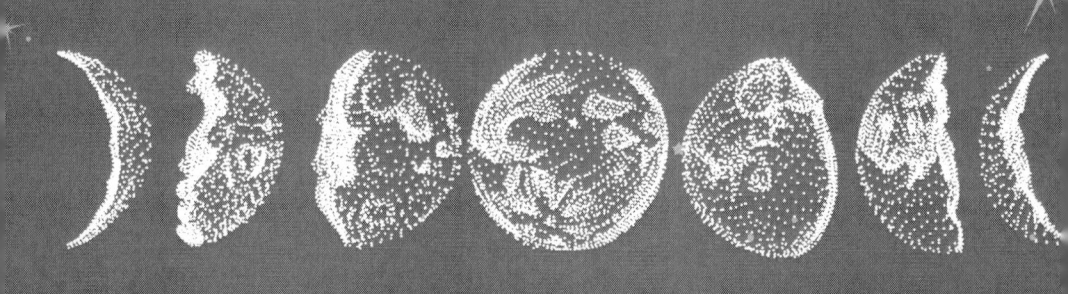

ROARY

PRISONER #69

CHAPTER FORTY NINE

I flung open the door to the room at the very top of the tower, expecting a fight to ensue as I finally tracked down Sin and Max along with Vard and my Lion. But the room was just a long storage space with a window at the far end giving a view back down to the snowy plain beyond. I'd fought tooth and nail to get up here, killed guards and monsters alike to make it here and *this* was all there was to be found?

I cursed, running to the window and flinging it wide, hearing the sounds of battle carrying from below before my gaze locked on the clash of Fae.

I could see Cain among them, Ethan and Sin too along with Max Rigel, but my heart didn't rest until I locked sights on Rosalie's silver Wolf form racing out towards the horizon. I frowned, my gaze narrowing in on the dark figure she was chasing into the snowdrifts and my heightened eyesight picked out Vard's face as he threw a frightened look over his shoulder. Locked under his arm was the glimmering golden form of my Lion, contained in a jar like it was nothing more than a trapped butterfly.

A growl ripped from my throat and I swung myself out the window, casting a sheet of water ahead of me and turning it to ice at once. The platform sloped down right to the ground and I didn't hesitate as I started running down it, sprinting at full pelt and fixing my focus on Rosalie and Vard.

With my Vampire speed, it wasn't long before I was catching up, the icy wind whipping around me and setting the hairs rising along my arms. I didn't slow as I passed Rosalie, my fangs bared and my bloodlust rising before I leapt at Vard and brought him crashing down to the snow.

My hand locked around the jar, saving it from the impact of the collision as we rolled and Vard screamed. Rosalie ripped Vard from my grip, tossing him in the snow beneath her and slamming a paw down on his chest, her teeth bared as he whimpered in terror.

I shoved to my feet, carrying the jar toward him. "Tell me how to return it to my body."

"You cannot undo what has been done!" Vard cried. "My work will outlast me, even if I die this day."

"Liar. Tell me how to reverse it," I snarled and Rosalie's claws dug into his chest, making Vard wail in pain.

"There is no reversal," he spat. "You are my Nightroary and you always will be."

"I am not your anything!" I boomed and he flinched.

"If I am to die, then my legacy will live on through you," he hissed, his fingers twitching.

I lunged, trying to douse the flame he cast, but I missed and it came speeding towards me. No, not me. *The jar.*

The fire slammed into it, shattering the glass and my Lion spilled out of it, the ghostly form of it like smoke pouring across the snow, still glowing that golden glow. But it was fading. Already dimmer, losing light by the second.

"No!" I roared, dropping to my knees, trying to gather it in my hands, bringing it to my chest and feeling its essence swirling around in my palms.

Rosalie howled in grief over my loss, running to me and abandoning Vard.

The Seer shoved to his feet, tearing away across the snow and I barked at Rosa, "Don't let him go!"

She turned from me reluctantly, a mournful howl leaving her as she raced after Vard, the monster who had stolen my Lion from me.

I knelt in the snow, trying to gather the shadow of my former self against my body, desperate to keep hold of it.

"Please stay. Don't go. Don't leave me," I pleaded, cupping the shimmering smoke in my hands and watching the life fade out of it. A vital part of me would die with it and I would never be whole again. "I can't let you go."

My Lion glimmered, its glow growing fainter and fainter until it was nothing but smoke, evaporating into the freezing air. My hands shook as I tried to grasp at the emptiness in its wake, but there was nothing there.

It was gone.

The absence of it was terrifying, its loss a pain I couldn't bear to accept.

My fingers flexed, each of them tingling, slowly drawing my attention to them as that sensation grew.

A shimmer of silver light made me turn my arm over, finding my mate mark gleaming on my wrist. A ragged breath left me as I touched it, the silver glow turning molten gold, flaring to life and making my heart thunder in my chest. That flood of light washed along my skin, dousing me in its beauty and making me gasp in confusion as it sank into my blood. The light of the moon slid into my chest and I could have sworn it was stitching the pieces of my broken soul back together, weaving something utterly beautiful into my being. With a feel of rippling, heated liquid, something settled inside me and I shivered at the sensation of my Lion reuniting with my body, the power tumbling through me, giving me a head rush.

I glanced up at the moon in shock, sensing her watching me and a thanks parted my lips in a heady groan. She had done this, granted me this gift and allowed my Lion to return to me. I could feel how easy it would be to shift, to return to that incredible, natural form of mine and let it free at long last.

I was made anew, reborn as a beast that was built from the man I had once been as well as the man I had become. A man who belonged to that stunning creature out there in the snow from now until eternity.

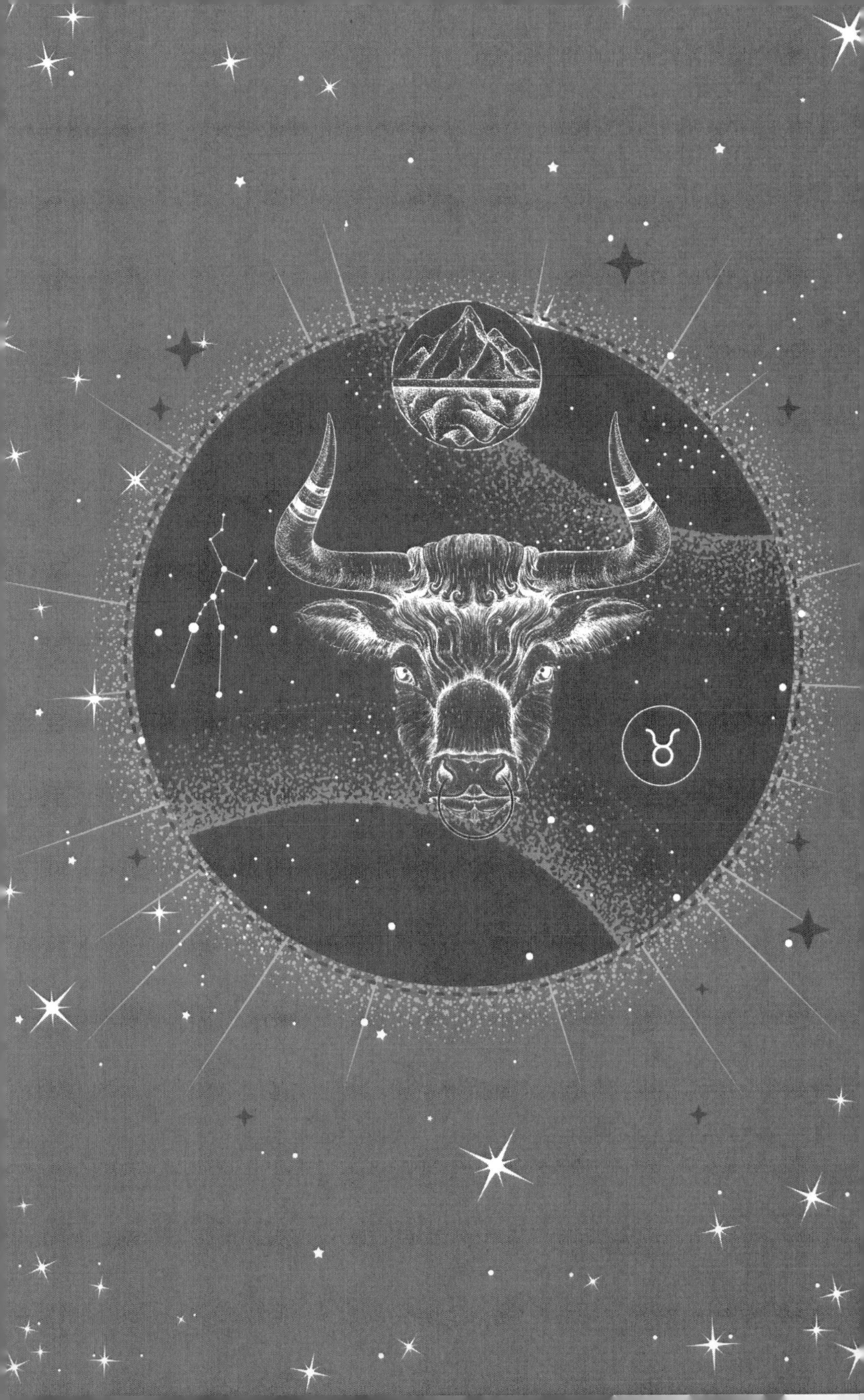

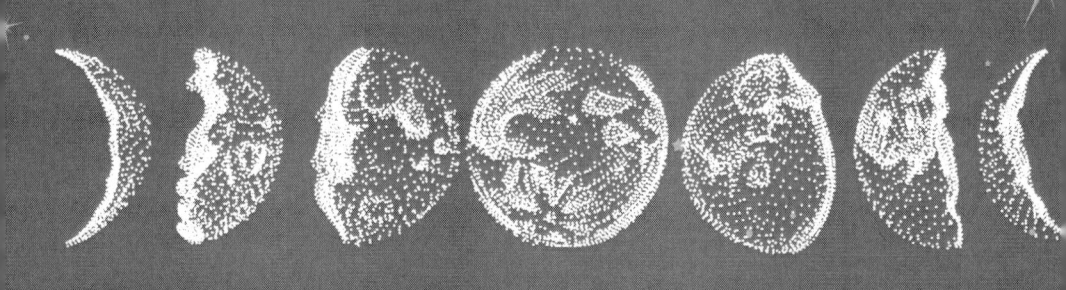

ROSALIE

PRISONER #12

CHAPTER FIFTY

I couldn't bear to look back at the shattered glass, at Roary scrambling to capture what he had lost but as I closed in on Vard, my teeth bared and his death screaming through my ears, a sound akin to the singing of the stars themselves tore through me and hope simmered within my soul.

I pounced, slamming into Vard and flattening him beneath me, his screams drowning out all but that most beautiful of sounds.

My teeth sank deep into his shoulder and I whirled around, hurling him from me, the roar of a Lion echoing through my blood as my eyes fell on my mate in his shifted form.

Roary roared again, shaking his mane of stunning, dark hair before breaking into a run, his eyes locked on the screaming, crying Vard who was trying to crawl away through the snow.

I sucked in a sharp breath as Roary shot into motion, his powerful body moving so fast that it became a blur. Both Lion and Vampire at once, two Orders housed in one Fae.

He leapt at Vard, his teeth sinking through flesh and bone, the screams of the bastardo who had caused him so much pain and suffering falling to silence at last as his head was torn free of his body and hurled away into the heaped snow beside us.

I paced forward, my eyes wide as I stared at the miracle who was my mate, my kindred spirit, the man I had loved since I was too young to even fully understand the meaning of the word. My Lion. My Roary. My mate.

I nuzzled against him and he leaned into me, the wonder in his eyes sparkling in the moonlight before he released a powerful roar which the others echoed in cries of triumph over the bodies of the beasts they had vanquished in their own battles.

And as the snow tumbled from the sky in clumps lit with moonlight, a howl broke from my lips to join with theirs and I knew in my heart that our pack was whole at last.

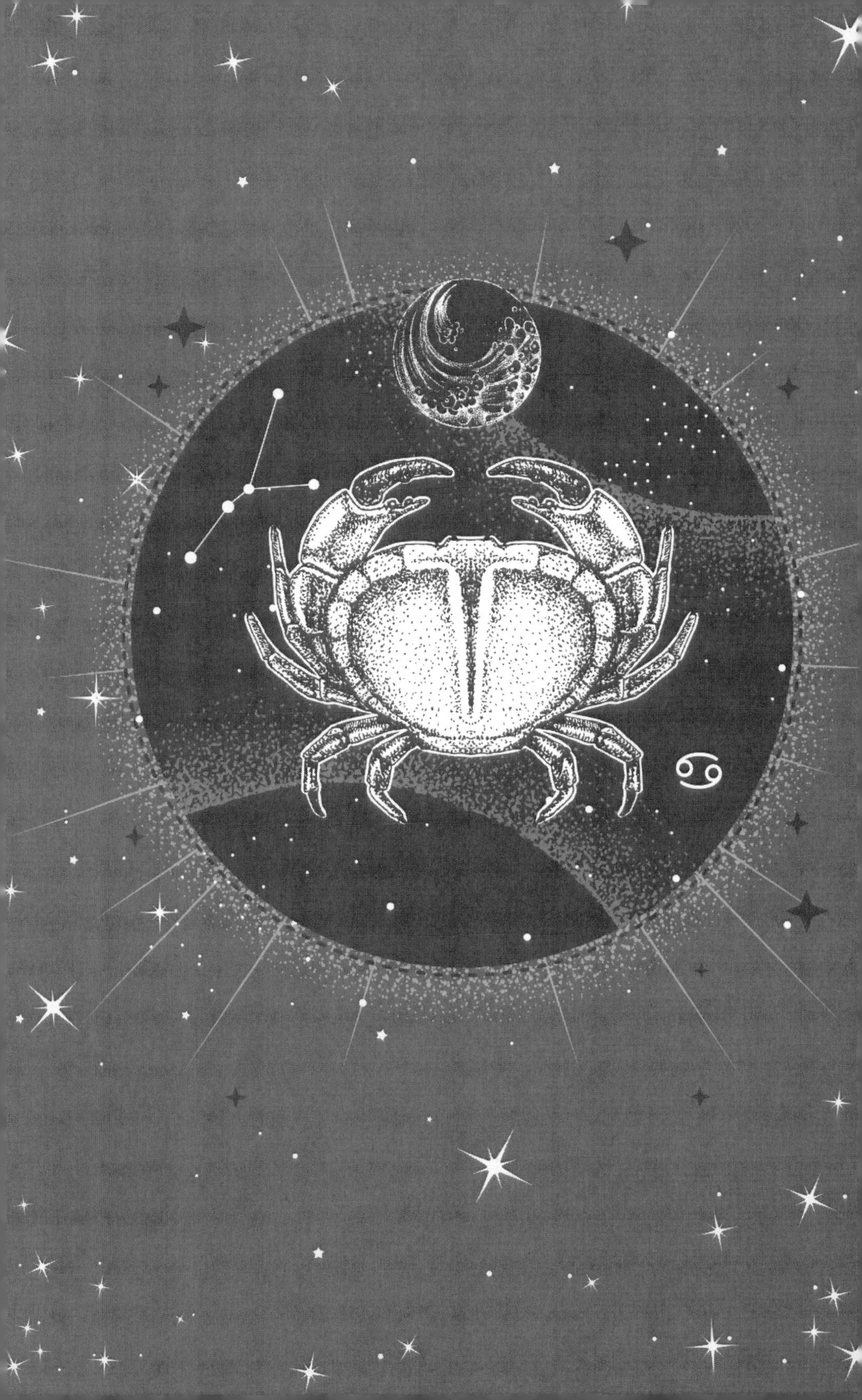

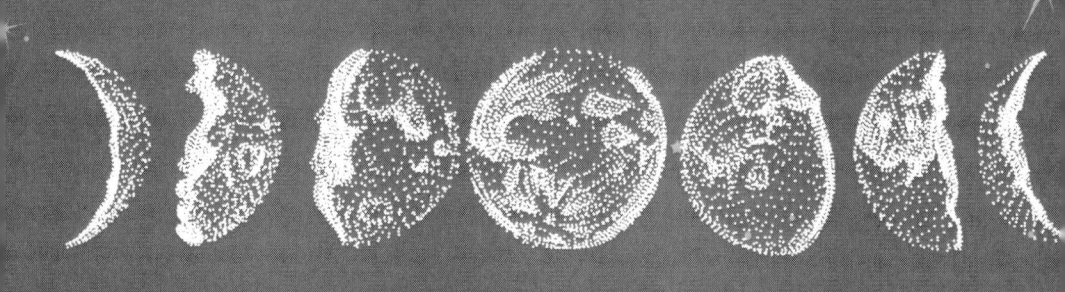

HASTINGS

OFFICER

CHAPTER FIFTY ONE

I coughed as the scent of smoke filled my lungs, my chest heaving as I inhaled and a clump of hair lodged itself in my nostril, causing me to choke and panic as I flailed for air.

My arms collided with folds of flesh, my forehead slamming into something which slapped loudly against my skin before crashing into my nose and mouth, making me cry out in alarm as I found myself pinned down by a weight poised just over my head.

"Arghhh!" I cried, flapping and flailing, tears leaking from my eyes as I begged for death because surely the embrace of that couldn't be so cruel as this truth which was life.

"I got ya, lad," Plunger crooned, standing at his full height and finally releasing me from the smothering weight of his body.

"Why?" I gasped while desperately trying to force the hair from my nostril.

"I was protecting you, see?" Plunger said. "This whole place is going up in a flame and a flam with us in the depth of its bowels.

"Then we need to get out of here!" I gasped, pushing myself upright and fighting back a retch as I looked at him in his shifted form.

"Yes siree," he agreed then dove headfirst into the tiles at our feet as if they were water, his claws flipping them aside and hurling dirt in every direction as a huge tunnel opened up at incredible speed in his wake.

I hesitate, loathe to follow him into the dark but as I looked to the exit, all I could see were flames licking up the walls, the smoke billowing into the room and oppressive heat only confirming his claims. The tower was burning and we would too if we didn't leave.

I muttered a prayer to the stars, begging them to deliver me from this place then dropped into the hole.

It was dank and cold beneath the ground, the Faelight I tossed up illuminating the tunnel ahead of me where I could make out Plunger whacking his ass against the walls while singing about his method to himself.

I scrambled after him, still blowing loose hairs out of my nose and mouth, cringing to myself and swearing on all the stars that I would bathe for a month long if I only made it out of here.

A great rumbling started up behind us, the tower itself cracking apart and I cried out as I broke into a run, tripping and falling against the loose folds of Plungers skin just as he turned upwards, heading for the sky.

My cheek slid down the folds of his ass, a cry of horror tearing from me once more which was drowned out by a tremendous boom as the tower collapsed in full.

I directed water beneath my feet, launching myself up and out of the tunnel as a cloud of dust and debris roared through it and I was launch fifty feet into the air above the snow-covered plains beyond.

I fell on my back amid a group of six Fae who all stared down at me in alarm, Rosalie's face shining out at me amid Wilder, his brother, Shadowbrook and Cain.

"Hi," I wheezed, waving up at them.

"Ah shit. I knew I was forgetting something," Sin said, glancing at the rubble of the tower which he had clearly taken part in destroying with his fire.

Rosalie smacked him on the bicep. "For fuck's sake," she hissed.

"Didn't hear you mentioning it, love," Ethan muttered.

"That's because…" she faltered, looking at me with an apologetic expression on her face. "I'm a total stronzo apparently. Sorry, Hastings. But I knew you were too tough to be taken out by a little tower tumbling down."

She offered me a hand and I let her pull me to my feet and heal me, not really taking in her words as I blinked at the destruction of the tower, trying to figure out what had happened.

"We couldn't have done it without you," Rosalie said, patting me on the shoulder.

"Yeah," Cain agreed, looking uncomfortable as he gripped my arm. "You practically took down this whole criminal organisation."

"Even the Dragon?" I muttered, looking at the huge dead body which lay sprawled beyond the ruins of the tower.

"Oh yeah," Sin said enthusiastically. "You took that Dragon down good, right before finishing the rest of 'em off and stuffing Roary's Lion back up his butt where it belongs. You're a damn hero, Hasslings. A fucking legend."

"Shit, I must have hit my head harder than I thought to have forgotten all that," I said, confusion clouding my thoughts.

"Is that…Plunger?" Roary asked with a grimace, pointing to the mole shifter who was stuck in a snow drift, only his ass on show.

"Yeah," I said slowly, all too much of time with the mole shifter still ripe in my mind. "I saved him right before I cut Sin loose and then-"

"Then you saved the world," Sin said dramatically and though the rest of the group exchanged several unreadable looks, they all quickly agreed.

"To the unforgettable Hastings!' Rosalie said loudly, lifting my arm into the air. "May his heroics go down in history."

"Aside from the fact that none of us can ever speak of this to anyone again," Roary murmured.

"Yeah," Rosalie agreed. "Aside from that."

I grinned at them as I looked out at the devastation I had caused, nodding seriously because I knew I wouldn't be able to tell anyone what I'd done here and the evil son-of-a-guns we'd brought down, but it turned out I was a hero. And I could live with that.

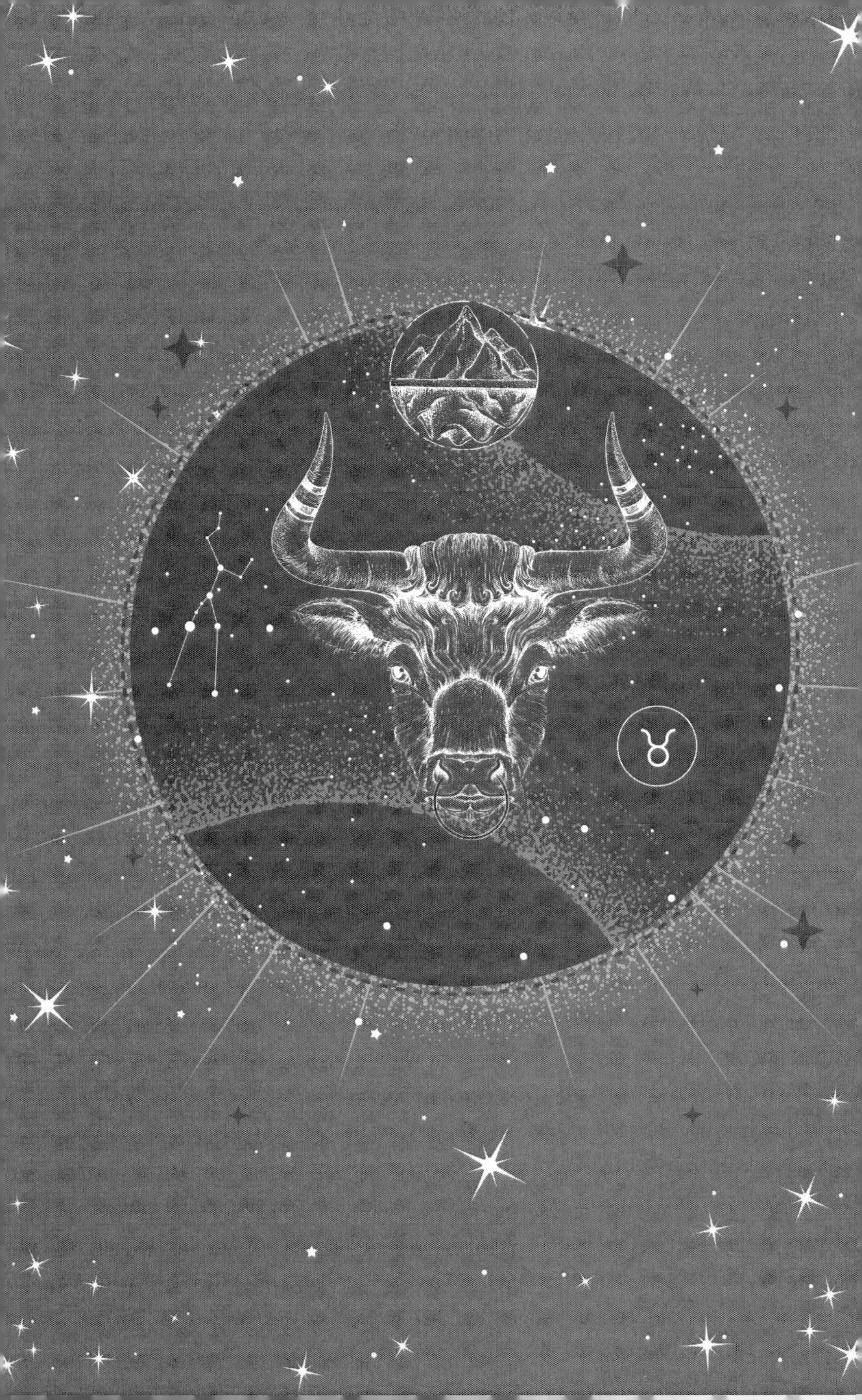

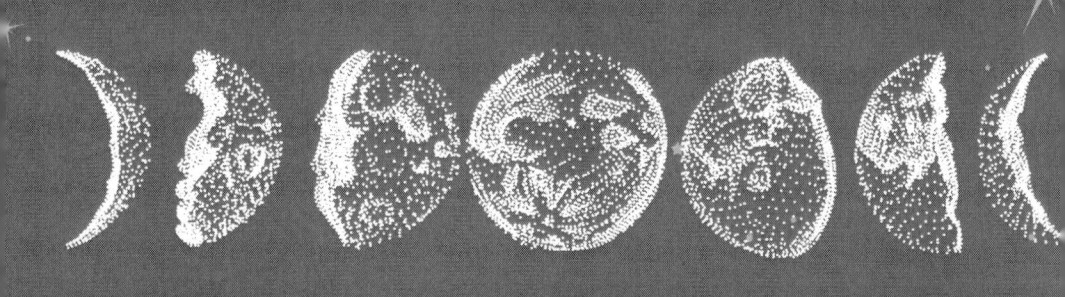

ROSALIE

PRISONER #12

CHAPTER FIFTY TWO
ONE WEEK LATER

The week since we had brought down Vard's criminal organisation had passed in a flurry of chaos that I was still struggling to take in. Max had been good to his word, not only helping us cover every scrap of evidence about the grotesque science Vard had practiced, but also in solving the issue of our criminality. Tiberius had also decided to trust Sin based on his other son's word and had released them from the bond which kept them together at all times.

It turned out that helping save the kingdom from one of the most wanted war criminals to have escaped the justice of the reigning monarchy came with a bag full of pardons, albeit that they were somewhat hushed up.

Officially, Roary couldn't be pardoned because of the death bond he had struck all those years ago, but every record of his crimes including any photographic ID of him had been mysteriously deleted from all of the FIB databases.

Cain and Hastings had been 'rescued' and retired from their posts as guards at Darkmore without any further investigation, while the years added to Ethan's after the mishap in Darkmore had been removed, meaning he was a free man.

For me and Sin, it was slightly different, both of us having been given a complete pardon under the claims that both of us had been secretly working for the FIB up to and including our incarceration at Darkmore. Every murder Sin had committed had indeed been carried out against Fae well deserving of their fates and my crimes weren't all that easy to pin down in the first place.

All in all, we were free in the truest and fullest sense of the word and it was a fact that was only just beginning to sink in. Plunger had headed off, disappearing down a Mole hole one night without a goodbye. Soon after, I'd received a postcard with a Bear paw print on it and a photo of the mountains with the message 'Your tunneller discovered his calling in our caves, hound. Sending well wishes.' If Pudding could tolerate Plunger's company then that was up to him, but I hoped to never to see his bare ass while he dug his way into a hole again.

I stepped into my bedroom in the Oscura stronghold, pausing on the threshold as I found all four of my men awaiting me there, their heads turning to me the moment I had appeared.

"What is it?" I asked, tension coiling through my limbs at the fierce looks I was receiving, my hackles raising in anticipation of some threat I was yet to comprehend. But that made no real sense. All threats against us had finally been vanquished and we were beyond the point of needing to jump at shadows.

"We've been having a little chat, wild girl," Sin said in a low voice, moving away from his position beside the window, tugging his shirt off and tossing it aside as he prowled towards my bed where Ethan already perched.

"About?" I asked, my eyes slipping from him to Roary who was smirking at me from where he leaned against my wardrobe, to Cain who stood with his arms folded close to the place where Sin had been standing before he'd moved.

"Well, the way I see it, we have a problem," Sin said, kicking his boots and socks off before jumping onto my bed and reclining against the pillow.

"Oh?" I stepped fully into the room, closing the door at my back and locking it for good measure because in this house there was always some nosey stronzo lurking close by.

"Yeah," Sin sighed. "We've been back from saving the world a full week and each of us boys have only had our pocket sticks rocked two times each."

"Pocket sticks?" I questioned and Roary snorted.

"Four times," Cain said in a low tone which made Sin frown sharply, his arm swinging out to point at my Vampire in accusation.

"How did I miss that?" he barked.

"You were sleeping once and the other time I think you'd gone to pick grapes with the pups," Cain shrugged, a cocky look on his face which was well enough deserved in light of the orgasms he'd gifted me during those stolen moments in his arms.

"Yeah, well, this is exactly the shit I'm referencing," Sin said, his gaze flicking back to me. "There's too much one cock action taking place for a pack this full of man meat."

"Is that right?" I asked, a breath of laughter escaping me.

"It is. Which is why I'm gonna have to take the reins and start organising us as a unit. First things first – we gotta get our group antics in order. Which is why I want you on your knees in front of me wild girl, taking a cock in the ass and another in the cunt. I'll look you in the eyes while you come all over them then we'll see where to go from there until all the ingredients in this room are fully satisfied with the proceedings."

"Is that so?" I purred, moving further into the room, my eyes slipping from Roary to Ethan, to Cain and then back to Sin. "And what if I have another idea in mind?"

Sin's smile widened and he waved a hand at me in deference.

"Then by all means, proceed," he said.

I grinned as I considered my options then strode for Ethan who still sat perched on the end of my bed, tugging my shirt over my head as I approached him.

Ethan grinned cockily, removing his own shirt before I could reach him and I removed my pants, socks and shoes before moving to straddle him in my underwear.

I kissed him deeply as his hands closed around my waist, a moan sliding from me as I languished in the taste of his tongue against mine.

His hands skimmed up my back, finding the clasp to my bra and undoing it with a flick of his thumb.

I rolled my hips, feeling the solid press of his cock through the fabric of his sweatpants and riding my clit over it as my arousal rose with every second.

I raised a hand, beckoning for Cain and my Vampire shot to me, moving to stand at my back, his fingers teasing my hair over one shoulder before his mouth moved to my neck.

"That's it, big boy," Sin purred as he watched us. "I know you've been desperate to work your way into one of these sandwiches, haven't you?"

"Fuck off, Wilder," Cain grunted, his hands sliding over my shoulders, taking hold of the straps of my bra and tugging them down my arms.

I rolled my shoulders to let him remove it, the small piece of fabric landing alongside all of Cain's clothes as he took them off in a flash of movement.

He moved closer to me, the heat of his rigid cock driving against my spine and I bit down on Ethan's lip as anticipation coiled through me.

I turned my head to take a kiss from Cain's lips, Ethan's mouth falling to my breast and sucking my nipple between his teeth.

I beckoned Roary closer to us as I leaned back, exposing more of my skin for him to claim and he shot to me too, his clothes left behind with the motion before he dropped to his knees beside me and sucked my other nipple into his mouth.

I moaned loudly as his fangs sank into the firm flesh of my breast, and Ethan pushed his hand into my panties, caressing my clit.

Cain kissed me harder then abandoned my lips, driving his fangs into my throat and taking more blood from me so that I grew lightheaded between the two of them.

I smirked at my Incubus who sat watching us with a predatory need in his dark eyes and finally beckoned him to us too.

Sin crawled across the bed to me, pressing up close behind Ethan and pushing onto his knees so that he could take a kiss from my swollen lips.

"You taste like the perfect sin, wild girl," he murmured into my mouth.

"I think that title is yours," I teased, feeling him smile against my lips.

I shifted my weight forward, driving Ethan down onto the bed beneath me and pushing Sin back until he knelt just beyond my Wolf's head, his lips never once leaving mine.

I took hold of Cain's hand and guided it to the side of my panties, encouraging him to tug them off and moaning as Ethan coupled the motion with the press of his fingers inside me.

Roary moved onto the bed at my side as I caught Ethan's sweatpants, helping me to tug them off of him and releasing the solid length of his shaft beneath me.

I caught Ethan's cock in my fist, knocked his hand aside then took him into me with a ragged moan which sin devoured as he kissed me harder.

Cain moved away from us in a flash but returned within moments, slicking his cock with lube and driving it between my ass cheeks with a strained curse.

I gasped as Ethan thrust into me harder, my spine arching as my hands fell to my Wolf's chest and I broke my kiss with Sin.

Ethan stole my mouth for his own and Cain filled my ass with a long, slow thrust which had me gasping his name as every muscle in my body flexed and writhed at the promise of pleasure.

Cain started moving inside me and Ethan matched his rhythm while Roary caught hold of my chin and tugged to turn my mouth to him instead.

He kissed me deeply and I reached for him, taking his solid cock into my fist and working the bead of precum from his tip over the head of it before pumping him in time with the thrusts of Cain and Ethan's dicks inside me.

Sin grunted with frustration, fisting my hair in his big fingers and tilting my head up so that I was looking at him where he knelt above Ethan.

I licked my lips as I dropped my eyes to his cock, knowing what he needed and smiling prettily for him as he shifted forward and pressed it to my lips.

I parted for him, Cain thrusting into me so hard that I was forced forward, a moan stifled by the thick shaft of Sin's cock as I took him right to the back of my throat.

"That's it," Sin growled, his grip on my hair taking control of my motion. "Now we can stop going easy on her."

I sucked in a breath as my four ruinous souls chuckled around me, hands gripping my flesh tighter, bodies moving closer and as one our movements became more rampant, almost violent.

They drove themselves into me with brutal need and I cried out as I came with a rush of bliss that didn't come close to finishing them with me.

They fucked me harder, praising my name as I took them all at once, Roary's mouth dropping to my throat, his fangs piercing my flesh again.

Cain cursed as he drove his cock into me harder, a flash of his speed vibrating through me as he closed in on his climax, the force of it driving my clit down against Ethan so hard that when he came, I went with him.

Sin laughed darkly, fucking my mouth while I sucked and flicked him with my tongue until with a ragged gasp, he came down my throat, the salty taste of his lust filling my mouth.

Ethan rolled us over as Sin withdrew, a dark chuckle escaping him as he took advantage of the lust haze I'd fallen into and bent me over the bed the way he so loved to do.

He slapped my ass as he drove me face-first into the sheets and I could only pant curses at him as he fucked me hard and deep until I was coming again, my pussy squeezing his cock tightly, forcing him to give in and finally fall with me.

We collapsed into a heap of sweaty, tangled limbs on the bed and Sin toyed with my hair while Cain knotted his fingers with mine.

"Not bad for a first rodeo," Sin murmured thoughtfully. "Let's give it a ten minute recovery period and then I'll give you my notes for round two."

I laughed, shaking my head in disbelief as my racing heart fought to settle and my pleasure-washed limbs fell entirely out of use, but if the press of hard bodies and harder cocks surrounding me were anything to go by, I knew that our night of debauchery had only just begun.

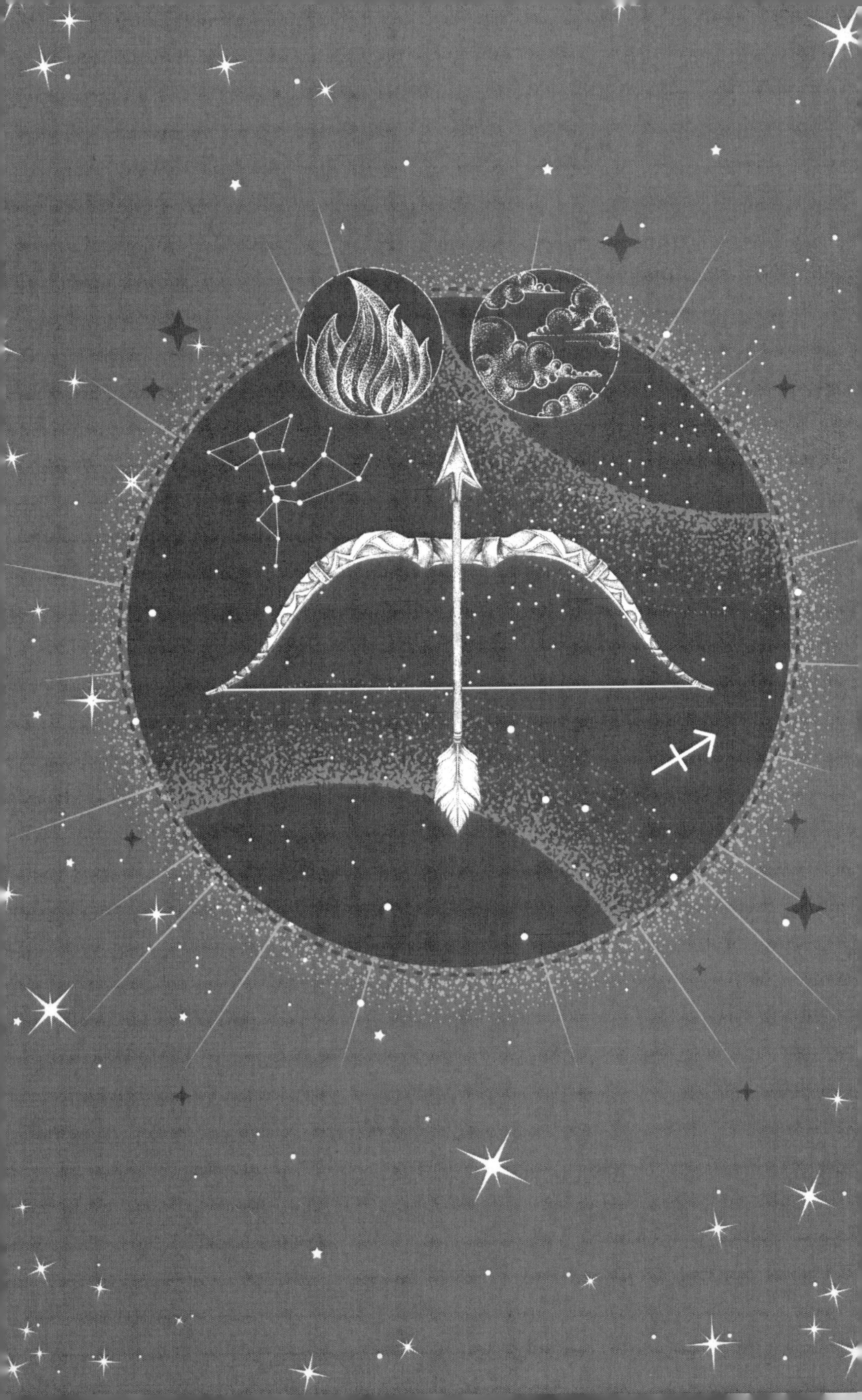

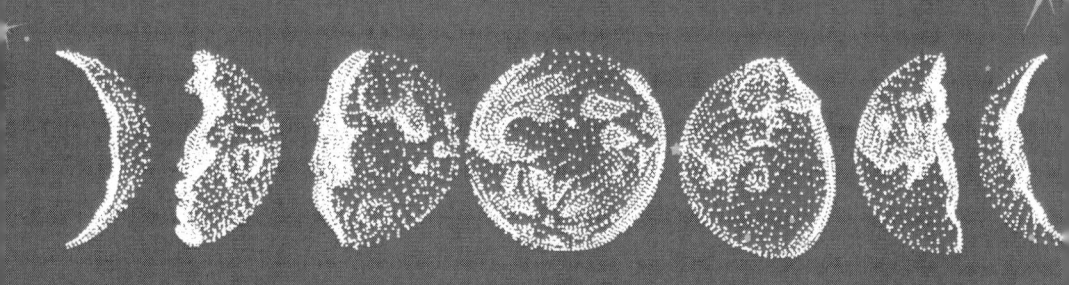

SIN
PRISONER #88

CHAPTER FIFTY THREE
A FEW WEEKS AFTER THAT

I'd spent a whole weekend with my dad and Maximus, off on a camping trip where we'd sat around a campfire. I'd sung songs and burned shit, which was just my kind of fun. Dad seemed to have enjoyed putting out my fires and he'd asked me a bazillion questions about my life while I'd asked a bazillion questions in return. We were becoming something real special, something I'd never had before. He'd even asked to see me weekly, wanting to ensure we forged a proper bond and I was all giddy inside about that as I skipped up the driveway to the Oscura household.

Rosalie was out on the porch with Hastings, Cain and a few of the pups, playing a game of snap that was causing the youngens to roar with laughter. As I got closer, I realised Rosalie was making the deck fly out of reach as a snap came up and the pups all leapt up to try and grab it from the vine she'd cast.

I used air to capture it for myself, clapping my hand against the deck. "Snap!"

"Sin!" a cry of elation went up from the pups and they all ran at me, the little ones climbing my legs while others prodded and pulled at me. I gave them all kisses and hugs then ran up the porch steps and snared my wild girl in a kiss that made Hastings blush.

Our little pet guard cleared his throat and Cain rolled his eyes when I let our girl go.

"Did you have fun?" Rosalie asked as I swung my pack down onto the boards and the pups descended on it, seeking out gifts. And there were plenty of them in there. Pretty rocks and shiny leaves I'd collected on our trail walks, plus a bunch of fancy twigs.

"It was the best, sugar lips," I purred. "But nothing beats coming home."

"I don't think we can keep calling this home much longer," Cain said. "Bianca has made plenty of unsubtle comments about us getting our own place."

"That's because she's tired of the pups asking why there's a ghoul living in Rosa's room that starts wailing in the night." I smirked and Rosalie elbowed me.

"She has a point. Much as I love it here, I think we could use our own space," she said.

"It would be nice to have my own bedroom," Hastings commented and Rosalie gave him the side-eye.

"We can get you your own water bowl with your name on it," I said brightly.

"Well, er, I could just use a glass," Hastings hedged.

"Er, Jack…" Cain started.

"Jack Hastings!" a woman shrieked, and we turned to find a blonde lady stalking up the drive with Aunt Bianca bustling along beside her.

"Oh my stars," Hastings whispered, pulling his fringe down over his eyes. "That's my mom."

"You have been missing for weeks!" his mom yelled. "Not a call. Not a message. Nothing! And now I track you down and you're here loitering around on somebody else's porch with a smile on your face. Well you are in *big* trouble."

"I belong here, Mom. I'm one of them now," Hastings insisted, lifting his chin.

"Oh are you?" she snapped, shoving up her sleeves as she made it to the porch and Hastings side-stepped behind Cain. His mom yanked him out by the ear and slapped him around the head for good measure. "You've had me worried sick. And your father has been wilting with concern. You will come home this instant!"

"But *Mom*," he hissed, his ears turning beetroot, and I sniggered.

"No buts," she growled, showing her inner beast. "Home. Now." She pointed back down the drive.

"Do forgive me, Mrs Hastings," Bianca said earnestly. "If I'd have known he belonged elsewhere, I would have sent him your way sooner."

"Oh good stars, it's not your fault," Hastings' mom gushed, then turned her sharp eyes on her son again. "*Go*."

Hastings bowed his head, muttering a goodbye to us and stomped off down the driveway with his mom berating him all the way.

"So much for him being the dark in the dead of the night," Cain said with a low laugh.

"He'll come visit though, right?" I asked hopefully. I liked having him around. Crow-thing liked him too, although my bird liked everyone here. He was always busy flying around with the pups, even chasing Dante into the sky in his Dragon form like a fearless little Crow-thing.

"Anyway, I've got a date with a danger noodle. See ya in a bit." I kissed Rosalie on the cheek, then lunged at Cain to kiss his cheek too, but he swerved me, knocking me stumbling toward the front door.

"Danger noodle?" Cain muttered, and my smile widened as I headed inside to meet with one of the Oscuras who was good at inking skin. I was officially going to become one of them and I'd decided to get my mark somewhere that wasn't my ass cheek or the middle of my forehead. It was a surprise for Rosa, proof that I was part of her family and that I would never be leaving, because no way was I bitter that I was the only one without a mate mark. Not at all. I wasn't doing this just to make my own mark. Absolutely not. Except maybe a bit. Just a little. A smidge.

"This is too cute, Sin," Rosalie purred as she arrived in the garden where I'd laid out some blankets and pillows for us under the stars. Ethan had headed off to visit his family and Roary and Cain were having their Vampy alone time. They liked to sit in a quiet room together and just…chill. Seemed like bore-town to me but they got their kicks out of it. Me? I liked being around the hustle of the house, playing hide and seek or tag with the Wolf pups.

A few of them were peeking at us through the vines at the end of the lawn and I shooed them away with a grin.

"Do you want some of those?" I asked as I took Rosalie's hand and led her onto the blankets, puffing up a pillow for her head as we lay down.

"What, grapes?"

"Pups," I said as the kids went tearing off through the vineyard with howls of excitement.

She fell very quiet and I frowned, unsure if I'd said the wrong thing. Sometimes I did that. Saying things that sounded right in my head but came out all spikey and twisted. I was getting better every day at reading my honey pie's frown lines.

"Maybe," she said at last. "Not yet. And I'm not sure what way I want that all to look. But maybe."

"I like maybes. They taste like change and change is always exciting."

"Some would say terrifying," she countered, and I barked a laugh.

"Not me."

"No, not you, Wilder." She leaned in and kissed the corner of my mouth, the gesture sweet like candy.

"I did something." I pulled up my shirt and showed her the Oscura Wolf mark curling up and around my hip bone.

"Sin," she breathed, touching it and sending a bolt of electricity through me. "It's perfect."

"And I had a moon inked on this side too. Just for you. For my wild, wild Moon Wolf." I pointed to my other hip bone where a gibbous moon was freshly tatted.

She leaned in to kiss it and I growled with desire as her warm lips left heat dripping through my skin. She gasped and as she lifted her head, my brows dragged together at the sight I found waiting for me. My inked moon was glowing silver, as bright as a shimmering coin. The moonlight was pouring over us from above and as I looked up at the celestial being who had so many secrets hidden in her hat, the truth of what she had just offered us became starkly clear. My tattoo was changing, and Rosalie tugged up her shirt, revealing the very same mark curling around her hip bone.

We came together in a hungry kiss, my hands in her hair and her fingers digging into my shoulders. It was pure and subtle and perfect. My Order was so tangled up with desire and sex that the moon had mated us as simply as this, between the sweetness of our lips.

I was hers and she was mine. We wanted nothing more than each other, just as we were. Brain full of bees and all.

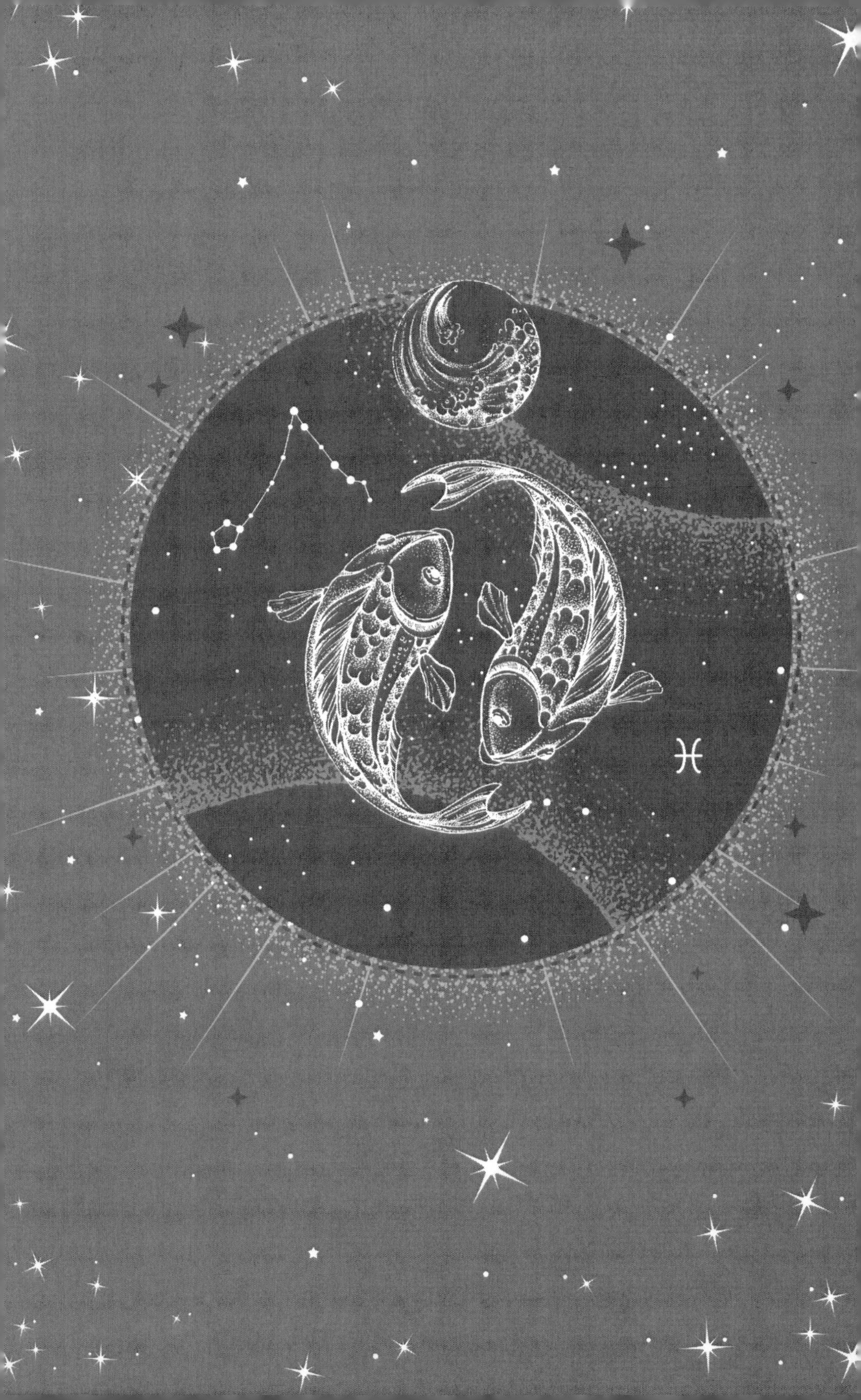

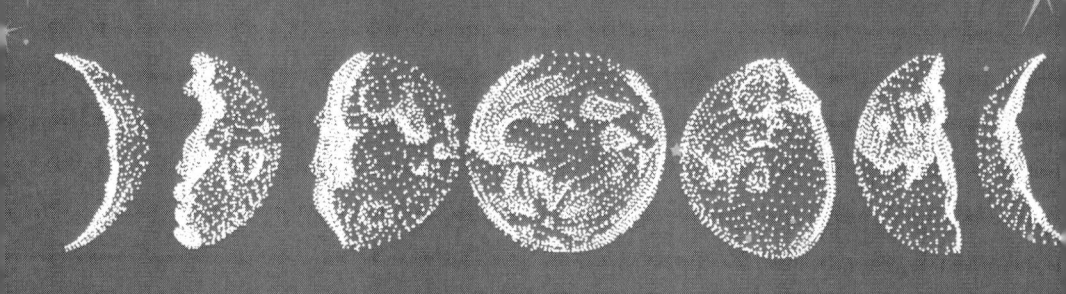

Roary

PRISONER #69

CHAPTER FIFTY FOUR

A FEW MONTHS AFTER THAT...

"You don't have to do this, you know? You don't owe him anything," Rosa murmured to me, her fingers winding around mine and squeezing.

"I know. But my mothers want this and after seeing them, I guess…I dunno, I can feel the rift in the family. I want to make it right if I can. At least to a point where we can be civil."

"I'm not one for giving second chances, but it's on you," Cain said from my other side.

"You gave Rosa plenty of chances," I said, cocking an eyebrow at him.

"That's different. It's the dick-whipped rule. Once your dick's been whipped, all rules are meaningless. Murdering, pillaging, thieving, it's free game now and the law can't do anything about it so long as it's in the name of love," Sin chimed in, glancing back from the window by the front door, the curtain pulled aside where he'd been peeking out at our driveway. Our house was on the Oscura estate – technically. I mean, it was a few miles from there and we had acres of land and forest around the villa-style house that was full of brightness and sunshine, so we certainly had our privacy. But we could visit the Oscura stronghold whenever we liked, and Bianca was always excited to have us back.

"That's highly inaccurate," Cain drawled, but his mouth lifted slightly in amusement.

"I think it's a good thing," Ethan said from Rosa's other side. "Family is everything. It's not like you have to forgive everything he did, but maybe something can be reconciled between you."

"Maybe," I muttered, the sound of a car engine drawing my attention.

"They're here!" Sin squealed, half hiding behind the curtain as he stared down the drive, shimmying in and out of sight, then pressing his full face to the window.

"Real subtle," Rosa laughed.

"I'm not going for subtle, I'm going for unnerving," Sin said, flapping the curtain like the wing of a bird. "I'll keep your Pops on his toes."

I smiled, happy to find out how unsettled Sin could make my father.

A bright pink Porsche pulled up on the drive followed by a sleek black Faezerati. Leon stepped out of the first car with two of our moms, Safira with her flowing blonde mane and Marie with her soft dark curls, while my father exited the second car with my mom Latisha on his heels, her short black hair and dark features as striking as always. My father was an imposing man with a golden mane that fell about his broad shoulders in a waterfall of waves; my mothers were slight in comparison to him, but they were powerful Lionesses in their own right. The sunlight caught in my father's mane as he tossed his head and his hair rippled and shimmered. He looked older than the last time I'd seen him, though not a single silver hair had found its way into his mane yet, everything about him speaking of pride.

My hair had grown out a little since it had been cut, and it was pushed back stylishly. I'd expected seeing him in all his Lionhood would have stirred up shame in me, but I found I didn't care anymore. I was who I was because of all I'd been through and if my father couldn't accept me as I was now, then he didn't need to be a part of my life. I was prepared for this to be the last time I saw him.

Rosa's fingers tightened on mine as Sin flung the door open and went sprinting out to hug Leon, the two of them spinning around together with whoops of delight.

Despite Sin's more sadistic tendencies, him and Leon seemed to be on a wavelength that made me realise they were pretty similar people. The chaos they caused when they were together was unmatched, and Aunt Bianca had yelled at them more than once at the Oscura household for riling up the pups or causing general carnage. She'd caught them making a hot air balloon out of a large tarp and a wicker basket once, sending a pup up in it with a combination of fire and air magic. It had made it a foot off the ground before Bianca had come out swinging a frying pan at their heads and scolding them colourfully in Faetalian. They were now to be supervised any time they wanted to do 'craft activities' with the kids.

My mothers came running inside, colliding with me, kissing my cheeks and cooing over what a big strong Lion I was. I hadn't yet told them I was a Vampire too, but today was that day and I wasn't going to shy away from the truth of all that had happened to me.

Leon stepped inside carrying Sin on his back, my brother running forward to hug me while Sin cried 'yee-hah!', and Rosalie released my hand with a laugh.

"He's waiting for you, bro," Leon said. "Best you go see him one on one, I reckon." He clapped me bracingly on the shoulder. "Good luck."

I headed outside, the sun beating down on us and the scent of dust filling the atmosphere. My father straightened when he saw me, his eyes falling to my short hair and his jaw pulsing in response.

"Leon forewarned me but I... didn't realise the extent of it. Are you well, my boy?"

I blew out a dismissive breath at that comment, folding my arms and leaning back against the porch post, letting him come to me if he wanted, but I wasn't going to close the distance between us. "Do you think I'm some fragile thing now, Father? A broken puzzle with the edges cut off?"

"No," he said firmly, taking a step closer and then hesitating again. He bowed his head, running a hand over the back of his neck through his silken mane. "In fact, I think quite the opposite. You did the impossible, pulled off the greatest prison escape the kingdom has ever seen."

"So I've regained your pride while spending ten years without it," I scoffed. "I'm not sure what I was thinking in asking you to come here. Now that I see you, I don't think I want to look at your face."

He gave me a sheepish look then stepped closer and closer, moving faster until he was right before me. He was a large man; he had always seemed like a giant when I was a cub, but now I stood eye to eye with him and I didn't feel small at all. It seemed he was the small one actually.

"I'm so sorry for my behaviour," he blurted. "I've been such a prideful fool. I'm ashamed of myself for how I acted, how I cut you off. It was the way of my father and my father's father. I should have known better than to follow in their ruthless footsteps. You're my boy. My cub. I raised you and loved you and that's all that matters in the end. I've wasted so much time being a damn fool, is there anything I can do that'll earn your forgiveness?"

I deliberated as he reached for my hand, his eyes full of desperation. My jaw was hard and a large part of me wanted to turn my back on him for what he'd done to me all those years ago.

"There's no action you can take that'll undo your rejection. And if you're coming to me now because I'm hailed as some hero among the Nights, then I don't want you on my doorstep. This here is my home. My pride. You're not a part of that unless you're here for better or worse."

"I understand," he breathed, his eyes dropping to his shoes. "If you give me one more chance, son, I swear, I surely swear I won't let you down again." He held out his hand, clearly offering me a star vow on the fact but I shook my head at the offering.

"I don't need the threat of the stars keeping you coming back. You do it on your own or not all."

"Then I'll do it, Roary," he swore. "Your mothers told me all along to show you grace and mercy. They're better than I'll ever be, but I'm here now and if you'll have me, I'll stay. I'll be the father I should have been."

The words were tempting, tugging on the strings of my heart and reminding me of my childhood. This man had carried me on his shoulders and swung me in his arms. He'd played with me, loved me fiercely and shown me loyalty like family should. But then he hadn't. And that betrayal left scars on me that were never going to heal. But perhaps they might fade, in time.

"One chance," I grunted. "That's all. Turn your back on me again and I'll never speak your name in this life another time. Any future cubs I might bear will never know of you. It will be as if you never existed."

His throat bobbed as he nodded. "I won't let that happen."

I released a heavy breath then pushed away from the porch post, sliding an arm around his shoulders. He grabbed me tight, crushing me in his grip and nuzzling me as a purr rattled through his chest. And I knew, at long last, all was right with the world once more.

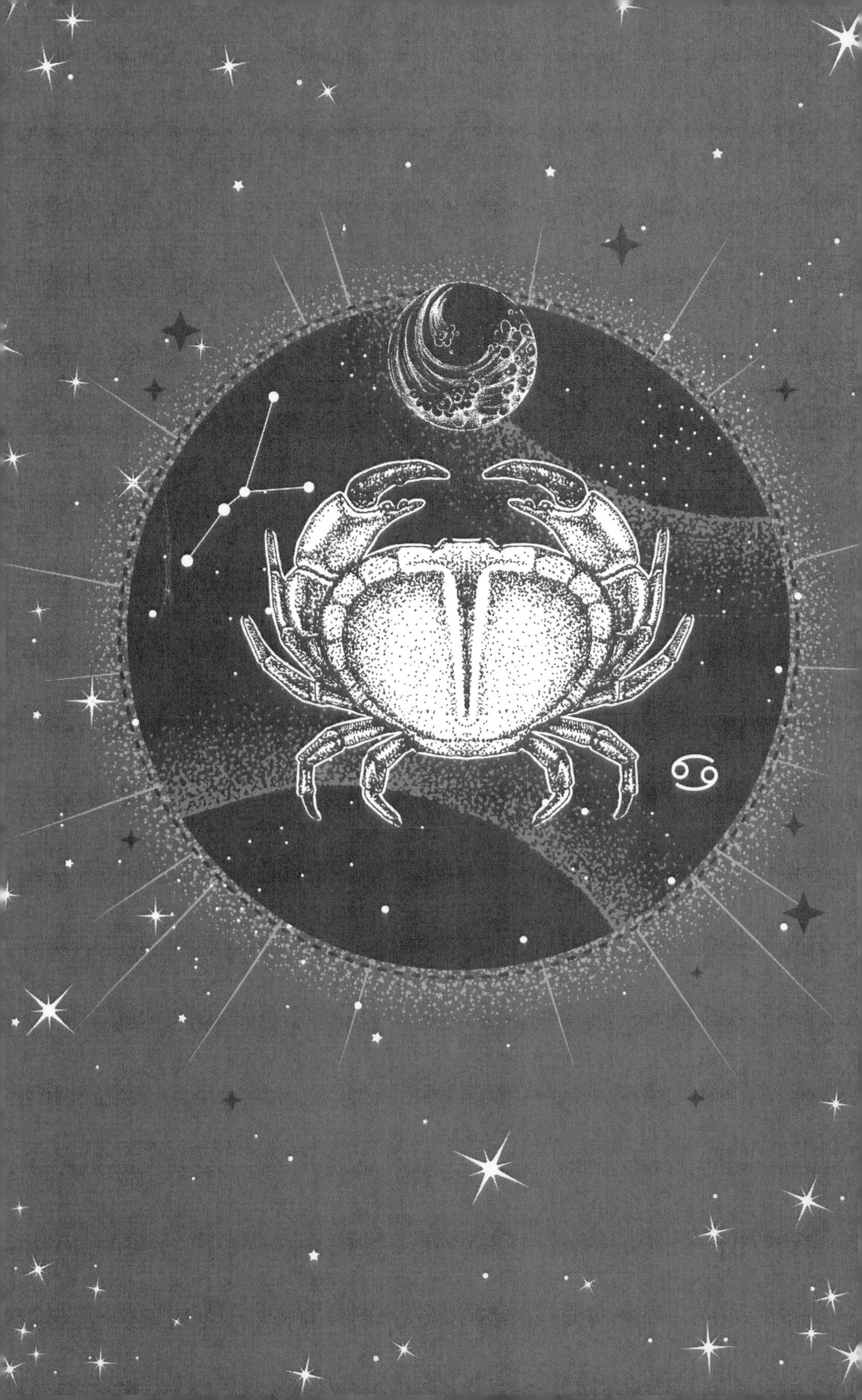

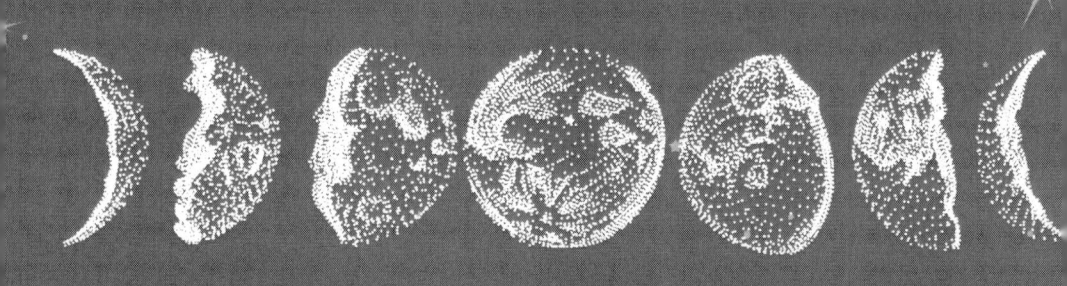

ETHAN

PRISONER #1

CHAPTER FIFTY FIVE

TEN YEARS LATER

"Don Julio stop hanging your little sister out the window," I clipped, and the long-haired ten-year-old sheepishly pulled Mimi back inside by the strap of her playsuit. Our six-year-old redhead slapped him around the ear, stomped on his foot and shouted, "Stronzo!"

"Language!" I called after her as she sped off down the hallway, and all I got in response was a manic laugh. Wildlings, the lot of them.

I guided Don Julio into the lounge where Mason was sitting on the crescent moon couch with our four-year-old, Gianna, on one knee, and our five-year-old, Marco, on the other. He was somehow balancing them there while reading a book to them.

Sin was sitting on the sun-shaped footstool, shuffling in closer and keenly listening to the story, and I realised they were reading The Fae Who Flew to Flamoo. It had been one of my favourite childhood stories and it had gone down a hit in this house. Over the past years, we'd taken in any lost child we'd come across in Alestria, adopting them from bad situations and giving them the life every child deserved. Our family had grown to include seven kids at this point and none of us seemed inclined to slow down in adopting more.

I rested my shoulder to the doorway, encouraging Don Julio to go join them, but he just mimicked me instead on the other side of the door, gazing at them with love just as I was doing. His blonde hair was growing into something of a mane, and I got the feeling he was mimicking his Papa Roary who had regrown his over time. It was longer and shinier than it had been before and I swear the amount of hair products he used in it was bordering on insanity, but damn did it pay off. I might have borrowed a few of them from time to time.

"-oh I wish I could fly, the Fae did cry," Mason read, putting on a little voice for the Fae girl who was the main character in the story. "And down from the sky, with a swoop and a swish, came a beautiful Harpy with scales like a fish. "I can help, oh you'll see. I'll take you as far as the billabean tree. So on hopped the Fae to his new friend's back, and they took off with a-"

"Whoosh!" Sin cried along with Gianna and Marco, knowing it by heart. "Then a flap and a CRACK!"

"Oh no, the Fae cried!" Mason took back over. "We've hit a big beast. He has scales of pure red and he came from the east."

Sin snatched the book, gazing at the words hungrily and my smile lifted as he started reading it. He had been learning along with the kids these past years and I was kinda proud of him.

He put on a deep, booming voice. "I'm not just any beast, I'm a hoarder of gold. And I'm the most fearsome creature in the land, I've been told."

The kids shrieked their delight, urging Sin on and he sprang up onto the footstool, arching his spine and using air to make two pillows flap like wings beside his back.

"Noooo, do real one!" Marco demanded.

"Not inside, you'll break the chandelier," I laughed, and they all looked around, finding me and Don Julio watching.

"Dad! Tell Papa Sin to go outside," Gianna begged like I held all the power in the room.

I smirked, nodding to Sin. "You heard them."

"*Yes*," Don Julio said excitedly and Cain stood up, keeping Gianna hugged to his side while Marco went racing to the large doors across the room, throwing them wide and beckoning us after him.

"Mama!" Marco called. "Come see, come see!"

I picked up Don Julio, racing outside as Sin went barrelling out the door and Cain boomed a laugh as he followed with Gianna. I wondered if Hastings had arrived yet; he was due to join us for a barbeque this afternoon with his two pups Nala and Kado, both of them born to Rosalie's cousin Maria who Hastings had married within six months after the events at the Polar Capital. He was the kind of father that wore socks with his sandals and carried kids supplies around in a pink backpack that was covered in glittery moons. He was the most sensible Fae in the world, yet still insisted he had a twisted soul and wouldn't speak of his 'dark past' in front of his kids. I was pretty sure Sin had filled them in anyway in a much more colourful way than Hastings probably would have liked.

Rosalie was out on the lawn in a pair of denim shorts and a white t-shirt, looking like my favourite view in the world. I tucked Don Julio under my arm and he wriggled wildly as I sprinted down the grass and tugged my beautiful mate into a hug that Don Julio was trapped inside. He wriggled until he didn't, his laughter rising as we both tickled and nibbled at him.

"Stop – stop," he said through his laughter. "Papa Sin is about to do the thing!"

"What thing would that be? He does a lot of things," Rosalie mused as Don Julio got down and went running back up the lawn to where Sin was pulling off his shirt and readying to shift.

Beyond Rosa, the play area was busy with our other four children where Roary was running around with them. Rosalie's dirty knees and hands said she'd been scrambling around on the dusty wooden obstacle course herself only a few moments ago and the look was edible on her.

Mimi was swinging from the bridge with our other five-year-old, the blonde-haired Eloin, and they were shouting taunts at Roary who was pretending to be an FIB agent out to catch them. Our eight and nine-year-old boys Tusca and Harvin were hiding behind him in the tunnel, stifling their laughter as they stuck sticky leaves to his jeans.

"Papa Sin has a surprise," I called to them, and the kids squealed, abandoning the game at once. Mimi threw herself off the bridge, putting blind trust in Roary to catch her, and he shot forward with a burst of Vampire speed to do so, cursing her before breaking out a grin. He had to keep that particular skill secret, his second Order something we all worked to hide. He, Cain and Rosalie would semi-regularly sneak off to the Hellion Hunt to let Roary enjoy a bit of freedom, and here on our estate he was able to bite our beautiful Moon Wolf and express himself fully.

It was strange how the two Orders had found a balance inside him. Sometimes he needed space, while other times he couldn't get enough of nuzzling all of us, and I swear to the stars, his Charisma made me want to offer up blood to him. I sometimes found myself rousing in the night to slide my wrist under his mouth only to snatch it back and growl when I realised what he was up to. He rarely bit anyone but Rosa though, his desire for her far outweighing any call for blood he might have for the rest of us. But he'd drank from each of us on occasion, calling my blood 'serene', while Cain's was 'volatile', and Sin's was 'volcanic'.

My gaze trailed over Mimi as she whooped and hugged Roary. She might just have been the wildest of them all, but it was a pretty close call. I'd caught Harvin climbing the roof just yesterday and Tusca was always looking to do everything his brother did.

Though none of us were family by blood, there were no greater bonds than the ones we'd found together. This group of misfits who had built a pack as one and found more love between us than I could ever have imagined. If I'd thought my own past dreams of family life had been good, it was nothing to the reality. This was happiness brought to life, and every new lost soul we added to our family only brought more joy, more wholeness to us all.

Rosalie had her Aunt Bianca's open heart, extending her love and affection to every Fae who needed her and who she needed in return. Every one of our children placed a glimmer of starlight in her eyes and I was all for adding more, because I felt that very same glow in my heart and wanted her to feel it tenfold.

Sin shifted into the huge green Dragon form that was a mimicry of Lionel Acrux's Order – though thankfully he didn't shift his cock the way the original fantasy had directed. A bellow rolled from his open jaws that sent bubbles spilling across the grass and up into the sky. The kids whooped excitedly, racing to pop them and Don Julio shifted into his grey Wolf pup form, snapping his teeth to burst them. Our little lioness Mimi shifted too, her golden fur shimmering in the sunlight as she raced to pop as many bubbles as she could.

"No fair!" Eloin shouted, having no Order of her own yet, but Don Julio swept himself under her so she was riding his back, making her squeal in delight.

Tusca had surprised us all last month when he'd Emerged as a Pegasus and he shifted now, revealing his sunshine yellow pelt as he raised his head and popped the bubbles with his horn.

I pulled off my shirt and Rosalie bit her lower lip as she took in my bare chest, leaning in to kiss me, and I felt her grin staining my mouth with a smile of my own. "Let's play, love."

She nodded, pulling her shirt off and racing away from me as she dropped her shorts and shifted into her large silver Wolf form while I followed, chasing her down as a black Wolf.

I swiped at bubbles as Sin let out another stream of them and he beat his wings, ready to take flight. Cain leapt onto his back with Gianna locked tight against his side and Eloin ran to climb up with them, snuggling close to the once-grumpy Vampire who rarely looked unhappy these days.

Sin took flight with another roar that let a cloud of bubbles spill into the air. Rosalie released a howl that we all echoed, that sound like the song of our family, our love. And I knew, no matter where any of my pack went in this world, if they were ever lost, they could always hear the howl of the Oscura Wolves and find their way back home.

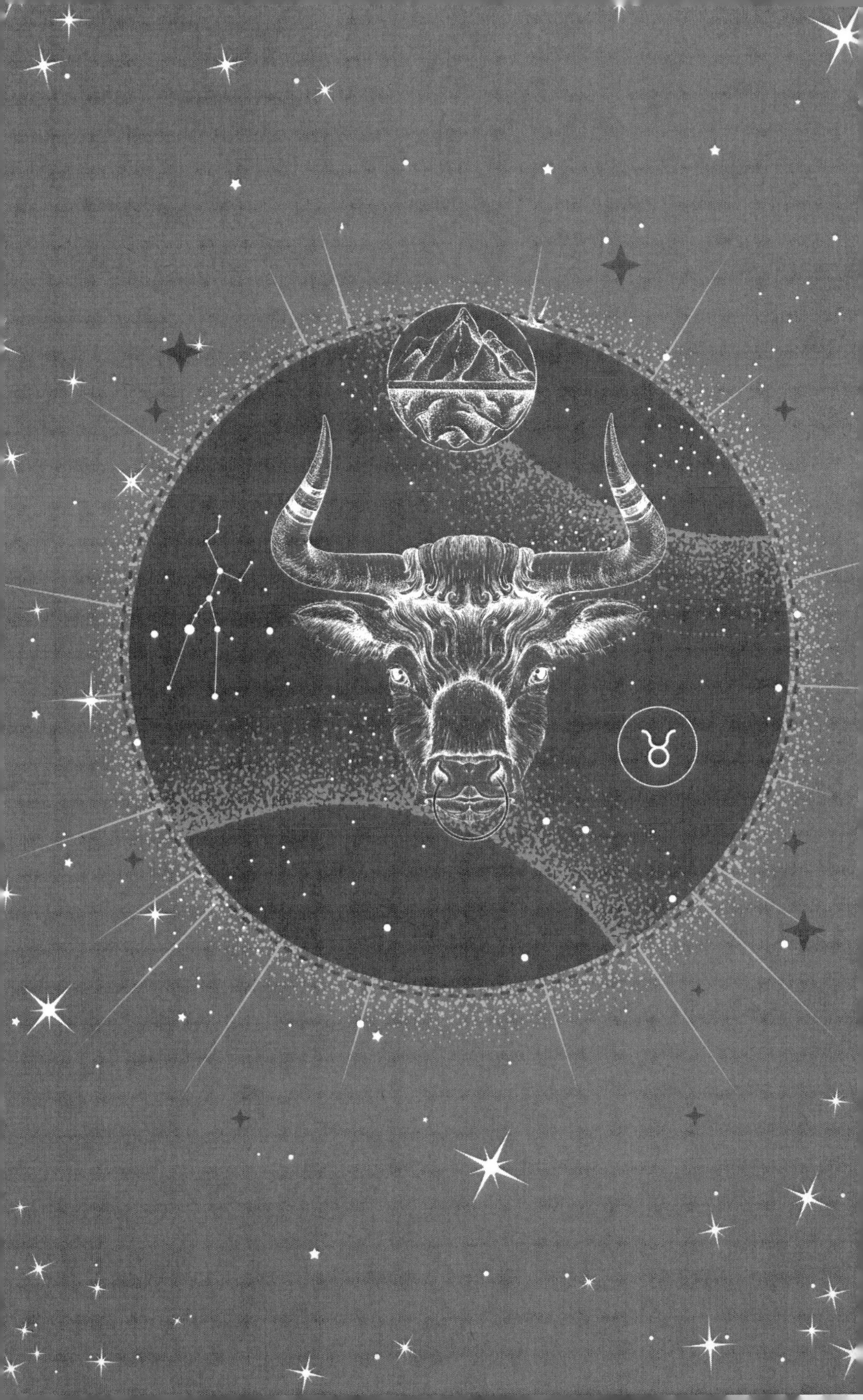

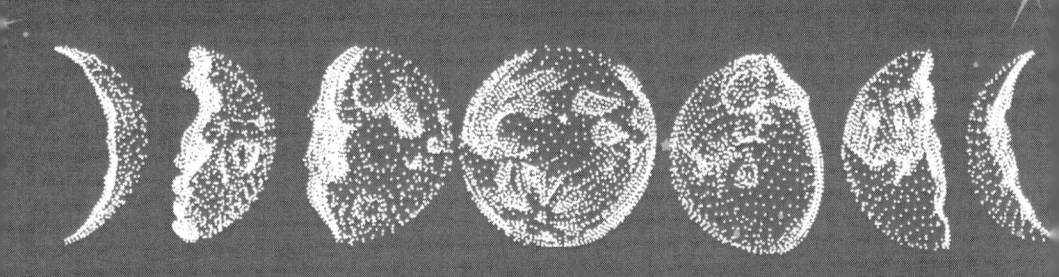

Rosalie

PRISONER #12

CHAPTER FIFTY SIX

TWO YEARS AFTER THAT

I laughed wildly as I ran through the vineyard, ducking between the rows of grape vines, hunting my prey. They were out here. All seven of them and likely their papas too were lurking in the greenery, no doubt scoffing grapes while they tried to out-run their mother.

I crept as silently as a ghost through the rows of vines, my senses alert for the sound of soft giggles – probably from Sin – or perhaps little footfalls.

"They're behind that row," Taya drawled, and I looked around, finding her standing at the end of the line of vines I was creeping down, her arms folded and face set in a mask of utter boredom which only a thirteen-year-old could manage. She was the newest member of our found family, a girl I'd run into on a job downtown, skulking behind the trailer of a nasty bastardo who had owed the Oscuras money. Her dark hair hung forward, shadowing the features of her angular face, those unusually silver pupils.

I'd recognised the haunted look in her eyes the moment I'd first looked at her, felt a stab of pain in my heart as I found a reflection of the girl, I'd once been staring out at me in fierce defiance of her lot in life.

I'd offered her bastardo papa a trade – the end of his debt for her – and of course he had given her up in a heartbeat. Then I'd given her the real choice – asked if she had anywhere she wanted to go or anyone who she wanted to be with, the answer to which was a sharp no. Then I'd asked whether she wanted to join my famiglia or fall upon the mercy of the state where I could at least bring her to a decent group home. Thankfully, after a long and shrewd assessment in which she insulted my clothes, my hair and told me I was in need of a manicure, she'd decided to give life with us a shot.

It had been a long six months since she'd joined us and she was still finding her feet in many ways but that scowl, the edge of a smile on her lips and the fact that she was opening up to me about the things she'd survived in her short life told me that she'd always been destined to find us, and us her in return.

"Spoil-sport!" Mimi yelled and I snorted in amusement.

"Run off and I'll come find you again," I offered, the giggles of my little pack of hellions confirming that they'd taken the deal.

"You could join us," I offered and I could tell she was tempted, that the pup she'd been had longed for carefree days playing in the sunshine and that all of her chances for that had been stolen and sullied by the rough lot life had handed her. "Come on," I urged. "You can help me hunt?"

Taya's lips twitched into the closest thing I'd seen to a smile from her and she nodded once, though I could almost see the shutters drawing down within her eyes at the same time, the concern that if she let herself embrace this life then it would only end up snatched away from her again.

"Come on, mia bambina," I purred, a smile spreading across my face. "We'll make it a competition to see which one of us catches the most of them."

Taya's smirk deepened and she turned from me, breaking into a run and cupping her hands around her mouth as she released a long howl to the moon, warning the rest of the pups that she was coming for them.

My heart swelled at the sound, tears pricking in the backs of my eyes as

I felt her giving in to the call of the pack we had built, letting herself believe that this could truly be her famiglia too.

Sin's wild cackles echoed across the valley as he broke from cover and ran from Taya at full speed. Ethan howled as he raced away too in his Wolf form, Gianna and Marco screeching with laughter from his back.

Cain shot into the distant trees carrying Eloin with him and I barely even flinched as Roary collided with me, winding his arms around my waist and pressing his lips to my neck as he kissed me.

"What's that beautiful smile for, love of mine?" he murmured, and I looped my arms over him, holding him close and smiling even more broadly as I leaned into his embrace.

"I was just thinking," I said softly, watching as Taya sprinted at full speed down the hill, determined to catch her prey, relishing in the freedom and joy of a family the way I had learned to do so long ago. "That life turned out pretty okay for us, didn't it?"

"That's an understatement if ever I heard one," Roary said, kissing me again.

"A morte e ritorno," I said because it felt like we really had gone to death and back to claim this sanctuary and I was determined to relish every moment of life we had claimed for our own.

"A morte e ritorno," Roary echoed before wrenching me off of my feet and hoisting me into his arms. "Now let's go catch some pups."

My laughter carried away over the hills and beyond as he shot after them, the wind whipping the sound up into the sky, staining the clouds with it and marking this land with the happiness we had claimed. And there was nothing in this world or any other that I could have asked for beyond that.

AUTHOR NOTE

Ah the sweet relief of the happy ever after. And for us the conclusion of this story really is an ending because not only has it marked the final book in the Darkmore series but also the final book we currently have planned for the kingdom of Solaria. (I meannnn, never say never because we have Tharix, RJ, Taya, the spares, the future Heirs and plenty of other lil' Fae babies whispering ideas in our ears but for now, we are done!)

So this is it! The last in a collection of 23 books and novellas which we have currently written spanning 15 years of Solarian stories – and if you haven't read the others then of course this is your sign to read about Dante and his dark origins in Dark Fae plus find out the details of the war and much more besides in Zodiac Academy.

For those of you who have been there with us throughout all of these books, I'm sure you will feel the same sense of mourning which we do in finally saying goodbye to these characters and this kingdom and it truly feels like the end of an era to be writing this note now.

But they do live on, between these pages and in the hearts of those who fell in love with them, forever awaiting the moment when you choose to flip open a book and visit them again.

We want to thank you for reading this series and for supporting us in this utterly insane journey we have been on. This is far from the end though and we are so excited to be bringing you <u>Never Keep</u> next – set in the same world as Solaria but on a separate continent divided by war, filled with lust, betrayal and enemies to lovers which will make your heart pound, break and shatter in all the best ways.

We love you all so much and are so excited to continue this journey with you,

Susanne and Caroline xxx

DISCOVER MORE FROM CAROLINE PECKHAM & SUSANNE VALENTI

To find out more, grab yourself some freebies, merchandise, and special signed editions or to join their reader group, scan the QR code below.

Made in United States
Cleveland, OH
18 May 2025